THE
INVESTIGATOR

Book **Two** of the
Munro Family Series

CHRIS TAYLOR

LCT Productions Pty Ltd
18364 Kamilaroi Highway, Narrabri NSW 2390

ISBN. 978-1-925119-05-3 (Print)

The Investigator is a work of fiction. Names, characters, places, brands, media and incidents either are the product of the author's imagination or are used fictitiously. Any resemblance to actual persons, living or dead, events, or locales, is entirely coincidental.

Published in the United States of America

DEDICATION

This book is dedicated to my amazing grandmother, Ivy Kosseris, who continues to inspire me, even at the age of ninety-six and as always, to my husband Linden, who is my very own strong and sexy hero.

ACKNOWLEDGEMENTS

As usual, no book comes into being without a lot of help and support by my friends and family. A world of thanks must go to my friend and fellow author Angela Bissell, critique partner extraordinaire, and a girl who loves the Munro family as much as I do.

To my editor, Pat Thomas, thank you for being the best editor in the world. To Alisha for my fantastic cover. My sister, Nicole Guihot, for her excellent editorial comments and suggestions. Nic, I hope you like the final result.

To Amy Atwell and her incredibly capable staff at Author EMS. Thank you for your expertise and your sense of humor. Book formatting doesn't cover even half of what you do.

To the fantastic writer organizations such as Romance Writers of Australia, Romance Writers of America and Romance Writers of New Zealand for all the help, support and encouragement they offer new and aspiring writers, including me.

To my readers, thank you for your support and love for the Munro family. Your encouragement and enjoyment make this journey all worthwhile.

And lastly, to my friends and family, especially my husband and children. Thank you for putting up with late dinners and even later conversations as I've emerged day after day from the sometimes scary but always enthralling world I've created on my computer.

A woman who thought she could run away from her past...

At fourteen, Kate Collins ran away from home. Ten years later, her mother has disappeared without a trace. Faced with no other choice, she returns home. Kate's convinced her stepfather's responsible, but he's a highly decorated police officer. Who will take her accusations seriously?

Banished to a small country town after reporting his city superiors for corruption, Detective Riley Munro is never going to accuse the town's recently retired Police Commander of murder. But Kate's fear and distress seem genuine and her mother does seem to have disappeared. With reluctance, he agrees to investigate.

After making rudimentary enquires, he's told Kate's mother is on a cruise. The information pans out. On the verge of closing the case, Riley is taken by surprise when he receives a subtle threat from his boss, the new Police Commander, to leave Kate's stepfather alone.

Why would the new Commander feel the need to warn him off? With his instincts on alert, Riley digs deeper and discovers not only is Kate's mother in a wheelchair, she also hates the water.

Is Kate telling the truth? Is her stepfather, the former Police Commander, guilty of murder? Or is Riley allowing the sad vulnerability in Kate's beautiful eyes to cloud his judgement?

THE
INVESTIGATOR

PROLOGUE

Watervale, New South Wales

Kate Collins crept through the darkened house. Her heart hammered. Fear clogged her throat. Her jaw was clenched and her lips were so taut, she could barely breathe.

She cracked open the back door. Its slight groan of protest sounded loud in the utter stillness. She froze, straining to hear the slightest noise, knowing he was a light sleeper.

Nothing.

She released what little breath she had in a rush. The house offered silent encouragement.

Careful to avoid the loose floorboard, she opened the door wider and made her way down the back stairs, her tattered sneakers noiseless on the scuffed concrete steps.

The grass, white with frost, crunched beneath her feet. She crept across the backyard, her muscles sluggish with cold and tension.

The shadows in the yard reached for her. She gritted her teeth against the rising panic and fisted her hands. Telling herself they were only trees, she forced her way past them in the pre-dawn light. In a couple of hours, he would know she was gone. By then, she'd be miles away.

The back fence loomed close in the dimness, sagging under the weight of an overgrown potato vine. Keeping a tight rein on her relief lest it be short-lived, she tossed her solitary bag to the other side and hoisted herself over the rusted barbed wire, careful not to catch her jeans on the vicious, tetanus-ridden points.

She landed on the other side and retrieved her backpack from the frozen ground, her numb fingers fumbling with the straps. She shrugged it onto her shoulders then jiggled it to distribute the weight of her meager belongings. She tucked her ponytail into her knitted beanie and tightened the sash of her old woolen coat. Her eyes closed on a brief prayer, seeking courage and a bus that was running on time.

She filled her lungs until they hurt, then started down the still-dark laneway, each step taking her farther away from the only home she could remember.

She didn't look back.

CHAPTER 1

Ten years later

Detective Riley Munro leaned backwards in his regulation black vinyl chair. Dropping his heavy boot-clad feet onto his desk, he stacked his hands behind his head and sighed. In just over an hour, his shift would be over and the weekend would be his.

A long hot shower and some fresh clothes were first on his list, followed immediately by an ice-cold beer. He'd just returned from Jack Sampson's dairy farm where he'd paddled around in mud and cow shit while old man Sampson badgered him with infinitesimal details of the farmer's stolen prize-winning Jersey.

Riley had actually been paying attention until Sampson took him into the milking shed and he'd made the mistake of standing too close to the golden beasts. Their glossy, caramel-colored hides and black, soulful eyes were deceiving. Unaware of the perils of coming into close contact with confined cows, he'd been taken by surprise when a sluice of sloppy shit disgorged from the nether regions of one of the beasts and drenched him from hip to ankle. Sampson had laughed his head off. Riley failed to see the joke.

Grimacing at the memory, he closed his eyes and sighed again. Thank God it was Friday. His mind drifted to the possibilities a couple of days off would afford. The very delectable Lucy would be more than willing to take his call. They'd only just met, but there was promise in her coquettish, green-eyed gaze and the sultry tilt of her chin. Besides, it was past time he forgot about Iris. It had been six months since she'd walked out on him, spouting excuses about why she didn't love him anymore and all the while, she already had her next lover lined up and ready to go.

Six months. More than enough time for him to get over her, even if it did sometimes feel like it only happened yesterday.

Anger and residual hurt seared through him. He ground his teeth and fought off the memories. It was bullshit. He was a decent guy, one who deserved better than the Irises of the world.

He shook his head in an effort to clear it of his dark thoughts. Maybe he'd go down to The Bullet and swap shoptalk with the boys, have a game or two of pool and listen to a few tunes on the jukebox. Now that they'd kicked the smokers out, he didn't have to struggle against the persistent urge to light up. The bar would provide a modicum of relief from the boredom he'd felt since his arrival in Watervale almost three months earlier.

He tamped down his irritation. It was his own fault he'd ended up in this backwater, after all. If he'd had the brains to shut his mouth and look the other way like all the others had, he would still be enjoying the action-packed, shit-hot lifestyle of a city detective.

Instead, he'd gotten all moralistic. Taken the high road. And look where it got him. Doomed to shuffling paper in some forgotten country town.

The shrill ringing of the telephone on his desk interrupted his musings. Dropping his feet to the floor, he leaned over and picked up the receiver.

"Watervale Police."

He was greeted with silence and cleared his throat.

"It's Detective Munro. Can I help you?"

More seconds ticked by. With a muffled curse, he went to

hang up. And then he heard a sharp intake of breath. The faint sound gave him pause. He tried again.

"Hello? Is anybody there?"

"My mother's missing. I think my stepfather's murdered her."

His gut tightened, both at her words and her tone. The husky voice brought to mind images of cigar smoke, whiskey and Demi Moore. But the accent was wrong. He struggled to place it.

"Excuse me? I'm not sure if I heard you right?"

"You heard me right."

The voice was firmer now, bristling with quiet efficiency.

"My mother's been missing for at least a month, maybe longer," the woman continued. "I'm sure that bastard's done something to her."

Riley straightened in his chair. The profanity coming from that voice was all wrong. Cradling the phone between his ear and his shoulder, he reached for the notepad and pen on his desk and scribbled notes.

"Look, Miss...?"

"Collins," she eventually supplied. "Kate Collins."

"Okay, Miss Collins. You'll have to come into the station and make a statement. I'll need a full description of your mother—a recent photo would be good—and anything that makes you think she's met with foul play."

Another pause, and then, "I'm only in Watervale for the next fortnight. I need you to move on this right away. I'll be there in ten minutes."

The line went dead.

Riley stared at the phone in his hand and shook his head as his plans for the evening slipped away.

The door opened. His partner entered on a gust of wintery air. The ancient heating downstairs didn't have the strength to reach the cold concrete of the stairwell. Detective Chase Barrington sauntered toward him and then pulled up short. His hand waved back and forth in front of his face.

"Phew, Munro, you stink like shit. Where the hell have you been? You'd better go and find a shower, mate. In less than an hour, we'll be out of here. The ladies won't want to come within a mile of you smelling like that."

Riley grinned back at him. "I'm trying out a new blend of designer cologne—*eau de cow crap*. What do you reckon?"

Chase didn't miss a beat. "I reckon you're full of shit."

Riley laughed out loud. Chase grinned back at him and then raised a questioning brow. "So, who are we going to line up for you tonight? Sonia? Or maybe Sally will be there? Hang on, there was a new one last week. What was her name again? Lorraine? Lavinia?" He snapped his fingers, his face alight. "No, that's right. Lucy! She was all over you, mate. I'll bet if you give her a little more encouragement tonight, you'll be in."

Riley ducked his head and looked away. "Back off, Barrington," he muttered. "Who says I'm looking to get laid, anyway?"

"Are you kidding? I'm worried about you, Munro. You've been here nearly three months and I haven't seen you take home a single piece of ass yet." Chase strolled over and propped his hip against Riley's desk, one leg swinging loosely like a pendulum as he eyed him somberly. "You do like *girls*, don't you?"

Heat flared in Riley's eyes and crept across his cheeks.

"Of course I do. It's just that... I'm just not..." He blew out his breath and looked away. "I've just come out of a relationship. It ended pretty badly. I'm happy to be going solo right now."

Chase winked at him. "Hey, nothing wrong with that. I love playing the field. Easy come, easy go. That's my motto." He leaned in close, his voice dropping lower. "I've lined up buxom Belinda tonight. The good news is, she's got this cousin who's also built in all the right places, if you know what I mean. She'd be happy to give her a call."

"Thanks, mate. But you go ahead. I just took a call from some lady who wants to report her mother missing. She's on her way in to make a statement," Riley replied, grateful for the excuse.

"Want me to sit in?"

"Nah, I wouldn't bother. Probably nothing to it. Besides, one of us might as well get a head start on our Friday night."

Chase hefted himself off Riley's desk, sending a pile of paperwork precariously close to the edge.

"All right, then, Munro. Suit yourself. Don't say I didn't offer." He headed toward the door and then turned briefly to throw over his shoulder, "See you Monday."

Kate turned the rental car into the graveled parking lot beside the Watervale Police Station and cut the ignition. Night was closing in and the air had a sharp bite to it. Darkness fell so much earlier in the winter. She'd almost forgotten how cold it could be here this time of year.

She shivered and couldn't say if it was from the cold or the tension that still knotted her belly. Surely, making the phone call had been the hardest part? Now all she had to do was enter the building. Push the memories away and walk inside.

Easy.

Drawing crisp air deep into her lungs, she released it one molecule at a time in an effort to still her insistent pulse. *Think of your mother, Kate. She's never gone this long without contacting you. Something's not right. That's why you've finally found the courage to return. You've flown halfway around the world. Just get it over with.*

The pep talk seemed to work. Guilt replaced some of her fear. She'd left her beloved mother in the care of a husband who was more monster than man and now it seemed she'd disappeared.

Tears burned behind Kate's eyes. She blinked them away, refusing to give herself the luxury of crying. Her mother was missing. It was Kate's fault and it was her responsibility to fix it. It was as simple as that.

She took a calmer breath and stepped out of the car.

Tugging her coat around her, she locked the vehicle and tossed the keys into her handbag before squaring her shoulders and heading toward the illuminated doorway of the police station.

Kate glanced around her. The place was just as she remembered. The stringent smell of ammonia irritated her nostrils. Scored vinyl floor tiles that had weathered to dirty beige mocked her memory. She pushed the image aside and focused on the row of thin steel bars that guarded the opening above the reception desk.

She turned at a noise behind her. A strange smell seemed to emanate from the man who closed the distance between them, but it was his smile that captured her attention. Well-formed, masculine lips stretched open to reveal startlingly white, even teeth. Her gaze locked on his. She'd never seen eyes so dark—such a deep brown they were almost black—like his closely cropped hair. His eyes seemed to see straight through her. Her belly clenched with nerves.

"Miss Collins, I presume? I'm Detective Munro. We spoke on the phone."

His voice slid over her like warm toffee. His rich, latte-colored skin and the broadness of his nose hinted at aboriginal ancestry, but his accent bespoke a private school education. He wasn't in uniform, but he exuded the same air of deceptively casual authority she'd grown up with. Instinctively, she took a step back.

A slight frown marred his otherwise smooth forehead. Mistaking her reticence, he said, "I'm sorry, I'm afraid I don't smell the best. I had a run in with a dairy cow. I was on my way home to shower and change when you called. Hopefully, we can get this over with quickly."

Without waiting for her reply, the detective turned and headed toward a stairwell at one end of the reception area.

Kate scanned the waiting area. It was after five-thirty. Keyboards had stilled. The ringing of phones was only sporadic. She'd deliberately chosen this time to minimize the likelihood of running into someone familiar.

She looked over toward the stairwell where the officer had disappeared. With a sigh of resignation, she walked toward it and started the ascent. She'd come this far. She might as well do what had to be done to finish it.

Riley Munro's thoughts centered on the woman who climbed the stairs behind him. Christ, she was a looker. More Gwyneth Paltrow than Demi Moore, but still beyond adequate compensation for the delay of his Friday night revelry.

She was younger than he'd pictured. Despite the blond hair pulled back into a tight, uncompromising bun, her face was clear and unlined. An expensive-looking black coat covered a pair of tailored charcoal-gray, woolen pants and concealed much of her tiny frame, but nothing could hide the ocean-deep blueness of her wide, wary eyes. Nor the full softness of her mouth that had fallen slightly open in surprise when he'd met her in reception. He was sure her reaction hadn't entirely been a consequence of his drenching in the dairy.

He was used to confusion and surprise from newcomers— as if banishment to the small country town perched in a far outpost of northern New South Wales wasn't punishment enough. When he'd shown up for his first shift in Watervale, it became clear he was the only aboriginal detective in town. During the ensuing months, he'd come to expect curious stares.

Slanting a look behind him, Riley watched as the woman reached the top of the stairs.

"Over here," he said, striding toward the nearest interview room.

She took a cautious step forward and then hesitated. Her gaze darted around the squad room, glancing off the jumble of vacant desks.

"It's change over," he said by way of explanation. "Most of the day shift's gone home. Night shift's doing a hand-over in the tearoom."

Her gaze clashed with his. The wariness in her eyes had intensified to something that looked akin to fear. He wondered at her curious reaction, unable to ascertain what might have caused it.

"I-I'm... I'm s-sorry," she stuttered, her gaze skittering away from his. "Maybe there's someone else who could do this? You're on your way out. I don't want to keep you..."

The voice was as he remembered: low, husky and now a little uncertain.

She was right. His shift had ended. It was time to go home and shower and prepare for some R & R at The Bullet.

"No, it's fine. I didn't have any plans. Just another Friday night." The words were out of his mouth before he realized it.

She eyed him steadily, as if she could smell his lie. *Don't be stupid, Munro.* It was probably the smell of cow shit that was turning up her nose, not some supersonic ability to detect falsehoods.

Breaking the eye contact, he opened the door to the nearest interview room and moved into the small, windowless space. Pulling out a chair, he indicated the one opposite.

"Take a seat and we'll get started."

A frown creased her forehead. She hesitated before reluctantly lowering herself into the other chair. Riley understood her reticence. Most people felt off balance in the stark, sterile environs of a police interview room, especially if it was their first time.

In an effort to put her at ease, he offered her a reassuring smile and reached for the notepad that had been left on the desk by a previous occupant. Pulling a pen from his pocket, he scrawled the time and the date at the top of a clean page.

"Right, then. Let's make a start." He cleared his throat. "We'll begin with your full name and address."

Her gaze lowered to her hands which now lay twisted in

her lap. Her mouth tightened and her flawless skin suddenly seemed leached of color.

Curiosity tingled his nerve endings. First the odd reaction in the squad room, now this. Even for a first timer, her reaction seemed a bit over dramatic. He watched her closely and waited her out in silence.

She finally spoke, as he knew she would. Her words were halting; her voice laced with an accent he had yet to identify.

"My name is Kate—sorry, Kathryn Jane Collins. Most people call me Kate. I live at apartment 5B, 17921 Kensington Court, London."

Riley started in surprise. "London? As in the UK?"

"Yes. I flew into Sydney late last night and caught a connection to Grafton this morning. I hired a car and arrived in Watervale a few hours ago." Her voice hitched. "I'm here to find my mother."

Her gaze glanced off his and then returned to her lap. "As I told you earlier, I can only spare a fortnight at the most. I have a business in London that needs attention."

Riley angled his head and continued to write. "That explains the accent. What line of work are you in?"

Her lips relaxed. "I'm an art dealer. I have my own small but exclusive gallery in London. I have a major exhibition opening in three weeks."

"Where are you staying?"

She hesitated. "I've checked into a motel on Byrnes Street—The Jackeroo, I think it's called. You can leave a message at reception if you need to reach me."

"No cell?"

Another pause. Her lips compressed. With reluctance, she provided her number.

Riley took down the details, then sat back in his chair and looked at her. Her hands were still fidgeting in her lap and her gaze darted away from his each time their eyes connected. His cop instincts went on alert. Something wasn't right, but he couldn't quite put his finger on what was askew.

Tossing his pen down, he leaned back in his chair.
"So, tell me about your mother."

Kate felt his unswerving gaze and struggled to keep her mask of control in place. Her chest felt like it was being slowly squeezed in a vice and panic threatened at the edge of her consciousness. On top of her fears for her mother, she'd been forced to return to Watervale. And not only to Watervale, but to the police station.

She took a surreptitious breath and eased it out on a silent sigh. It wouldn't do to let him know how much she hated her stepfather. If this man was like all the other officers she'd encountered in her youth, he'd never think badly of one of "their own." She'd slipped up when she lost her temper during the phone call. She couldn't afford to do it again. She steeled herself to look up at him.

"My mother is Rosemary Watson. She married Darryl Watson when I was four."

"Darryl Watson? That sounds familiar. Why would I know that name?"

Her smile was humorless. "You obviously haven't been in town very long, Detective Munro."

"You're right. I rolled into Watervale three months ago. Relocated north from Sydney." He shrugged. "Had to get out of the big smoke. Too much noise, too many bad guys. I didn't have time to scratch myself." He flashed a smile that didn't reach his eyes, once again displaying those perfect teeth.

She ignored the tiny flutter low in her belly. "Three months? I guess that explains it, although, I would have thought three months was enough for anyone to have heard about the legendary Darryl Watson."

The lazy smile stayed in place. "Enlighten me."

"Darryl Arthur Watson, pillar of Watervale society, Local Area Commander for twenty-five years. The mayor even gave him the keys to the town."

A single dark eyebrow lifted. "Commander Watson, of course. No wonder the name sounded familiar. I walk by his photograph in the foyer every day."

"The wall of honor." Kate bit down on her rancor. She really had to be more careful.

The detective seemed not to notice. He stretched his body out in the chair, lifted his arms above his head and opened his mouth wide on a cavernous yawn. "When did he retire?"

She shrugged, irritated. "I couldn't tell you. Sometime during the last ten years, I guess. He was still well and truly ensconced here when I left."

"You've been gone that long? Ten years?"

She offered a tight nod.

"Never been back?" Curiosity was plain on his handsome face.

Kate remained silent. Let him draw his own conclusions. She couldn't care less what he thought. All she cared about was finding her mother.

A pang went through her. Fear and stress and the fact she was still jet lagged sharpened her tongue. "Is any of this relevant, Detective? I fail to see how my absence from Watervale or the date my stepfather retired could possibly have anything to do with my mother's disappearance."

He stared back at her, his face now impassive.

Impatience surged through her. She glared at him, anger and frustration and the ever-present fear swirling to the surface. "I'm sorry, but it seems I've had the grave misfortune of approaching the laziest officer on the Watervale Police Force. An officer who would prefer to waste my time on nonsensical trivialities rather than actually doing something about finding my mother."

She stood and leaned over the desk, the slight height advantage her movements gave her steeling her spine. Her eyes burned with desperation.

"Look, Detective. I've already told you she's been missing

for at least a month. I know something's happened to her. I just *know*."

To her horror, hot tears welled up in her eyes. A flush of embarrassment glazed the officer's cheeks and he looked away.

His discomfiture enraged her. "Would you at least have the courtesy of looking at me and *pretending* you give a damn?"

CHAPTER 2

Riley stared back at her, his initial discomfort over her emotional outburst fading. He watched as she pulled a tissue out of a black leather handbag that looked like it cost more than he made in a month.

Deciding to give her a few moments to compose herself, he stood. "I'm going to grab a cup of coffee from the machine. Can I get you something?"

The woman sniffed and swiped the back of her hand under her nose. The unconscious action made her seem even younger. Blue eyes met his for a brief instant before falling away.

"Coffee, please," she murmured.

"How do you like it?"

"Black."

Riley bit back the instinctive quip her answer provoked and refrained from commenting. He headed to the tearoom and returned a few minutes later armed with two black coffees.

She'd resumed her seat and now sat calm and composed, like a CNN newsreader, the tears completely evaporated.

Surprise shot through him. It hadn't taken her long to get a grip on herself. He'd have to remember that. Maybe she was one of those women who could turn it on and off as they pleased, whenever circumstances dictated?

As much as the thought irritated him, he couldn't help but

feel a surge of admiration. Regaining composure so quickly was a talent he'd like to have.

He sat the Styrofoam cup in front of her. She glanced up and murmured her thanks. Returning to his seat, he took a sip of his coffee and sighed.

"It appears we have gotten off to a rocky start, Miss Collins. How about we try again? I'm Riley Munro, one of the detectives here. I'm sorry if I offended you with my manner. I didn't mean to. It's just that..." He shrugged. "It's been a pretty slow week—hell, what am I saying? It's been a pretty slow *month*."

He offered her another grin, hoping to put her at ease. "This afternoon, I got called out to investigate a stolen cow. No one told me there are certain places you should never stand when you're in a dairy shed during milking." He sniffed with great exaggeration at his clothes. "But hell, I can't complain. It's the most excitement I've had since I arrived here."

She gave him a slight grin that changed everything about her. His gut caught on her cool beauty and the sad vulnerability in her eyes. He wondered if there was a man in her life.

The thought was intrusive and as irritating as it was unwelcome. Clearing his throat, he pulled the notepad toward him and got busy finding his pen.

"All right, let's keep going. How old are you?"

"I'm twenty-four. Born June eighth, in Sydney.

"Ah, so you've spent time in the big smoke, too?"

Her face gave nothing away. "I was born there. We moved to Watervale when I was four."

"We? As in, you and your mother?"

She nodded.

Riley looked down at his notepad. "You said your mother married Commander Watson when you were four. I take it they'd known each other from before?"

"No, she met him not long after we moved here. They'd only known each other a few months when they married."

Her voice was distant and controlled—as if she was

talking about strangers. It was in stark contrast to her earlier emotional outburst.

"Okay. Let's talk about your mother." He looked up from his notes and eyeballed her. "What makes you think she's missing?"

Her gaze held his for a millisecond before skittering away. He again waited her out in silence. She drew in a deep breath. Her fingers stilled in her lap, seemingly by conscious effort.

"I've been living in London for the last three years. My mother calls me every week, without fail and we email each other all the time—at least once or twice a day." She caught his gaze. "It's been over a month since I heard from her. Heard *anything*." Her gaze slid away. "It's not like her."

Riley studied her closely. Her hands once again moved restlessly in her lap. And what was with the eye contact thing? *What was she hiding?*

"All right, so you haven't had any contact for a few weeks." He shrugged. "Maybe she went on a holiday? Have you called Commander Watson?"

Fury erupted behind her eyes in the seconds before they skirted away from his. Her voice was colder than a winter evening in the Snowy Mountains. "She would have told me—and yes, I called but he didn't answer."

She was lying. He was sure of it. Riley stared at her, trying to work it out—trying to work *her* out.

He kept his tone light. "You live ten thousand miles away. Why would she tell you if she's going on a holiday? Maybe they've gone away together? That would explain why the commander didn't answer."

Her jaw tensed. A pulse played a rapid staccato beneath the pale skin of her neck. When she spoke again, her voice vibrated with anger.

"She has *not* gone away on a holiday."

Riley held her gaze, unperturbed, probing with his eyes. "How can you be so sure? Maybe she's gone skiing? I've heard they've had record snow falls down at Thredbo."

The woman leaped up, knocking her chair over. Her hands had tightened into fists. She paced, her steps jerky—anger and frustration radiating from her tense form. When she turned to face him, her eyes blazed.

"You're not *listening*. I already *told* you. She has *not* gone on a holiday. And definitely not snow skiing. For God's sake, she's in a *wheelchair*."

———————

Kate felt a moment's satisfaction when the detective's mouth fell open. It gaped for a few moments before realization took hold and he snapped it closed. The look on his face was almost comical. Almost. If things had been different, she might even have laughed.

But they weren't. Her mother was missing and the more she thought about it, the heavier the fear that resided deep down inside her grew. Something was wrong. Dreadfully wrong. It wasn't like her mother to stop contacting her. And then there was that last email…

Before the guilt of it overwhelmed her, Kate forced her attention back to the detective. With a steadying breath, she leveled him with a look, pleased when her voice came out close to normal.

"So, Detective. Are you prepared to sit there and hear me out or do I have to go and get completely riled up all over again?"

A dark stain inched up his neck.

"I'm sorry, Miss Collins, truly, I am. You might have made mention of the fact your mother was in a wheelchair a little earlier."

It was the second time he'd apologized in almost as many minutes. More than he was likely used to. She should probably go a little easier on him. After all, she could have offered the information about her mother's incapacity at the outset. Besides, she needed his help.

"You're right. I'm sorry, too. I—I'm upset and worried

and...right now, all I want you to do is listen to me and then tell me what you're going to do about finding her. Deal?"

She held out her hand, concentrating with fierce determination to keep it steady. The piercing look he shot her was disconcerting. It was the same look he'd given her when they'd met. It took all her willpower not to look away. Again. She almost collapsed in relief when he shook the proffered hand.

"Deal. Provided you agree not to withhold any further information I might consider important."

His hand was warm and strong, engulfing hers. Nerves jangled in her stomach, like the fluttering of a thousand butterflies—nerves that had nothing to do with her being inside the belly of the police station.

Seemingly undisturbed, he dropped his gaze to the notepad in front of him. She picked up the overturned chair and sat back down.

"My mother was diagnosed with multiple sclerosis when she was twenty-eight," she informed him. "Four years later, she was confined to a wheelchair."

He looked up in surprise. "She was in a wheelchair when she met the commander?"

"Yes. She was thirty-six when we moved to Watervale. She wanted to get out of the city, away from the memories of my father." Kate looked away. Her voice lowered. "Or so she said. I was only a child."

"How did she meet the commander?"

Keeping her gaze fixed on his notepad, she answered with a shrug. "I don't know. No one ever told me and I never asked. All I remember is, it seemed like only a short time between living in the rented house on Sunnyside Lane and moving into *his* house on Baxter Road."

The detective drilled her with his stare. Kate's breath caught and she wondered if he'd picked up something in her tone. After a few moments of silent scrutiny, he looked down again at his notes and she swallowed a silent sigh of relief.

"What kind of a relationship does your mother have

with the commander? Twenty years is a long time. They've obviously made it work."

A barrage of words fought for airtime. Kate gritted her teeth and strove for casual nonchalance. "I really don't know what kind of relationship they have. As I said, I was only four when they married and I left Watervale ten years ago."

"Come on, Miss Collins. You must have some idea. I assume you lived with them until you were fourteen or so? Even a self-absorbed teenager notices something about the way her parents interact."

"Don't call him that. He's never been *my* parent."

The words were out before she could stop them. Curiosity lit the dark depths of his eyes. She concentrated with fierce determination on the gray and pale blue geometrical pattern woven into the navy carpet and did her best to ignore the weight of his gaze.

"What kind of relationship do *you* have with the commander?"

Her head snapped up. The question was even deadlier for its gentle delivery. She met his unwavering stare.

"I fail to see how the question has any relevance whatsoever to your investigation, Detective. It's *their* relationship you ought to be examining. I've already told you what I think." She shook her head, feigning disinterest. "Really, didn't they teach you *anything* in detective school? It's quite obvious you never learned to *listen*."

His eyes glittered with anger and Kate wondered if she'd gone too far. He leaned forward, his bearing now intimidating.

"Oh, I've listened plenty, Miss Collins and all I'm hearing is a load of bullshit about a mother who supposedly hasn't bothered to contact you in the last little while and a transparent bid—for reasons I've yet to determine—to implicate one of the town's finest in some unthinkable act. You're not a very good liar, Blondie. I damn well know you haven't bothered to call your stepfather."

She tensed and her fingernails bit into the softness of her palms. *How had she given herself away?*

"What did he do to you?" he sneered. "Grounded you once too often? Cut off your allowance?" His gaze raked over her. "I can just imagine what a handful you would have been. Is that why you're here to accuse him of homicide?"

The detective pushed back his chair and stood, towering above her. He bent over the desk, his face inches from hers.

His voice lowered. "That *is* what you're trying to tell me, isn't it? That Darryl Watson, Watervale's longest-serving Police Commander, has murdered your mother?"

Kate held his stare, refusing to be intimidated. She'd come this far. She'd be damned if she'd let some macho, misogynist detective deter her now. If he wouldn't help her, she'd find someone who would.

Cold steel lined her backbone and roughened her voice. "If that's the way you really feel, Detective Munro, then I suggest we end this interview right now. I need to find someone who's prepared to listen to what I have to say. *I'm* not the perpetrator here. Apparently you don't believe that."

The legs of her chair slid easily along the industrial carpet as she pushed away from the desk. She collected her handbag and pulled her coat tighter around her.

He watched her without comment, his face implacable. Debilitating despair weighed heavily in her limbs. She couldn't believe it had all been for nothing. She hid her shaking hands in the pockets of her coat, unwilling to let him witness another instant of her distress. With her shoulders taut and head held high, she walked toward the door without a backward glance.

His voice reached her halfway across the room. "I'll track down Commander Watson in the morning. I'm sure he'll be able to sort this out."

She barely broke stride. With her lips compressed against the pain, she left the room and made her way to the top of the staircase and started down.

Riley stared after her, frowning. Damned if he knew what was going on, but she was definitely hiding something. He hadn't been a cop for nearly a decade without picking up a few tips, despite what the woman thought. She was a bundle of inconsistencies. And it was obvious she knew far more than she wanted him to believe.

By her own admission, she'd lived with the Watsons for ten years and had kept in regular contact with her mother after she left. He didn't buy for a second that she wouldn't know how it had been between the two of them. Especially being a woman.

Having two sisters, Riley knew firsthand how intuitive women could be. He'd never been able to keep anything secret from either of them. Except the one he'd been carrying around for the last three months. The one he'd managed to hide from everyone—even his twin. As far as his family knew, he'd been the one to request the transfer.

Familiar feelings of anger and disappointment permeated his bloodstream. Riley scrunched his eyes up in an effort to ward them off and focused instead on the woman who'd just left. The woman who looked like a million dollars, but every now and then let her guard down and spoke like a tramp. The woman who obviously had secrets of her own.

She had all the trappings of a well-educated, successful, intelligent woman, yet she hadn't called the commander. He'd bet his house on it. There was something about the way she'd stared at him when she'd answered, as if willing him to believe her. It might have worked on a rookie, or someone less observant, but not on him.

And her story just didn't make sense. No one went to the police before they'd done the most basic of enquires. Calling her stepfather, the person in the best position to know her mother's whereabouts, was a no-brainer.

It's what he would do. It's what anyone would do. Pick up the phone and call. But she hadn't. She'd flown halfway across the world and still hadn't contacted her stepfather.

His frown deepened. He doodled on his notepad, giving his thoughts freedom to roam. What was it with her and Darryl Watson? Riley hadn't been in town long enough to meet the retired officer, but you didn't get to be the Local Area Commander—or the LAC as they were known—for a quarter of a century and have your picture hung from an impressive gold frame smack bang in the middle of the main wall of the reception area if you weren't looked upon well.

Maybe she was jealous? It wasn't unusual for kids to feel like the spare wheel when a parent remarried. Perhaps she'd spent her childhood feeling left out and harbored some sort of grievance against him? Maybe she'd left home in a fit of teenage rebellion over some slight—real or imagined—and it had never been resolved? She'd admitted she hadn't been back to Watervale since she'd left.

If she'd run away at fourteen, there was every possibility there'd been some kind of falling out. It didn't necessarily indicate fault on the part of her parents. Teenagers ran away from home all the time. Most stayed away for only a week or two, but not all of them.

CHAPTER 3

Kate pulled the pins out of her hair and tugged at the elastic. The tight bun was released and she sighed. Her hair fell in a cascade across her shoulders. Tossing the accessories onto the top of the cracked Formica vanity, she braced her arms on either side of the stained sink and stared at her reflection in the mirror.

Tired, pallid skin shone sickly under the cheap fluorescent light. Dark smudges bruised the delicate skin under her eyes, emphasizing her fatigue. She hadn't slept properly since the last email she'd received from her mother.

At the thought of her mother, she squeezed her eyes shut. Despite the physical distance between them, over the years since she'd left, they'd renewed and strengthened the bond that had always been there between them. It may have been weakened during the last decade her mother had lived with Darryl, but even he hadn't been able to sever it.

Whilst Kate had never found the nerve to tell her mother the truth about her abrupt departure, Rosemary had finally accepted her explanation and, over the ensuing years, they'd formed a closeness once again.

Kate hadn't been lying when she told the detective she communicated with her mother on a daily basis. Living so far away, and knowing what her mother's husband was capable of, Kate had felt an even greater need to stay in contact. To check on her.

Not that the man's evilness had ever extended toward

her mother. At least, not that Kate was aware, but it hadn't completely alleviated the guilt that had surrounded her every time she thought of leaving her mother behind.

Rosemary had suffered one blow after another. Kate's father had died not long after she'd been born, leaving her mother alone and almost penniless. The multiple sclerosis had struck her down in her prime, robbing her of her youth. Then, Darryl had appeared on the scene.

To Kate's mother, he'd been a knight in shining armor, rescuing her from the harsh knocks life had dealt her. She'd found someone who loved her, cherished her and wanted to protect her from the challenges that had been thrown her way. Outwardly, he'd even loved her daughter.

Kate's heart thumped hard at the memory. Familiar fear coiled deep inside her, ready to strike the moment she paid it heed. She didn't blame her mother for not knowing the truth. Rosemary's handicap forced her to live downstairs. She was clueless to what went on above her after dark and Kate had loved her too much to share her pain.

Scrubbing at her eyes in an effort to banish the images that lurked behind them, Kate turned on the faucets and splashed water over her face. Blinking droplets from her eyes, she pressed a towel against her skin and breathed in its clean, lemony smell. In contrast to the overall dinginess of the motel room, the blindingly white bath towel was soft and luxurious.

Her thoughts returned to the detective. Anger reignited inside her. He was no better than the rest of them. He'd treated her with barely disguised disdain. The wall of blue—solid, impenetrable, impassable.

Bastard.

She thought he'd be different. The sound of his honeyed tones on the end of the phone had lulled her into believing it was possible and when she'd seen him, the genuine warmth in his eyes had given her hope. He'd looked open, friendly, willing to listen—nothing like the policemen she'd grown up around.

But then he'd started the interview and the illusion had

disintegrated to ashes. He was exactly like all the rest. Despite his pretty boy looks and his killer smile, he'd paid her lip service and had done squat. And then he'd taken the insult even further—he hadn't even pretended to believe her.

Her shoulders slumped in defeat. She padded out of the tiny bathroom and sat on the edge of the bed. It squeaked in protest, but she lay down anyway, too tired to care. At least the heating worked. The room was pleasantly warm, cozy even. Clad only in her underwear, she curled up in a ball and replayed the afternoon's events.

He'd known she lied about calling Darryl. She'd seen it in his eyes and in the subtle turning down of his mouth. It wasn't like she hadn't tried to build up the courage. She just hadn't been able to bring herself to do it. Each time she picked up her phone to dial Darryl's number, panic had stiffened her fingers and nausea had choked her throat.

Even now, congealed fear moved in the pit of her stomach, sliding with insidious intent through her veins. For almost a decade and a half, it had been ever present inside her, but from the moment she realized she'd have to return to Watervale, it had intensified into cold, stark terror.

Rage exploded inside her, white-hot and searing. She hated the power he still held over her. She thrashed against the feelings of helplessness and panic, rolling across the bed with her arms locked hard around her waist. She wasn't a child anymore. She wouldn't let him best her. Not again.

Never again.

Fierce determination surged through her. Pushing herself upright, she reached for her phone before her courage withered. Her heart hammered against her chest. She could almost smell her fear.

She'd do it. For her mother's sake, she had to. It was obvious the police weren't going to help her. Just as she'd always known, she was on her own. She dialed his number with fingers that trembled.

Riley strode through the doorway of Watervale's local drinking establishment and waved to Sonia from across the room. Although there was a golf club on the hill that catered to a more upmarket clientele, he preferred the dimness and casual camaraderie of The Bullet. Besides, he could always catch up with Sonia here. She worked the bar four nights a week. Her friendly brown eyes lit up as he approached.

"Hey, there," she greeted him. "How was your day? It looks like you could do with a beer."

He smiled his thanks and pulled out a stool, resting his elbows on the bar. "You know me so well."

"Not as well as I'd like to." She winked and her gaze lingered on the open expanse of skin at the base of his neck and then moved lower. "I'm always happy to extend our acquaintance."

He grinned and returned her once-over. The low-cut black top she wore was covered in sequins that sparkled under the overhead lights, drawing attention to her generous cleavage, as it was no doubt meant to. A short black skirt molded to a sweet ass and was complemented by a pair of black fishnet stockings.

They'd first swapped stories over the scarred wooden bar on his second night in Watervale and Riley couldn't deny he'd felt a spark of interest. It had been months since he'd parted ways with Iris. His ego might have taken a bruising, but he was still a man with physical needs that he'd ignored for far too long.

Sonia's cute button nose and spontaneous smile was just the medicine he needed after the uptight austerity of his ex. Iris had even controlled their most intimate moments, directing the how and where and when until most of the fun and all the impulsiveness had been taken out of it. Looking back, he couldn't believe he'd put so much time and effort into the relationship. He almost felt sorry for the man she'd left him for.

Pushing the memories aside, he picked up his glass and took a healthy swallow. The beer was cold and refreshing and slid easily down his throat—a welcome feeling after the day he'd had.

Images of Kate Collins immediately clamored for attention. She was beautiful, in a cool ice-blonde untouchable way. But then she'd gotten angry and her controlled facade had cracked. Passion, albeit anger, had flamed in her eyes—eyes so wide and blue he'd felt lost in them. Even now, the thought of her made his pulse race. His response to her hadn't helped his objectivity and that had irritated him all evening.

"I see you made it out of there, after all. You certainly smell a lot fresher."

Riley glanced up as Chase pulled out the empty stool next to him and ordered a beer.

"Yeah, it didn't take as long as I thought."

"So, what was the story? They found the old girl wandering down the road, right?"

Picking up his glass, Riley took another swallow. "Nope, nothing like that. The daughter took offence to my manner and stormed out of the office before I could do more than cover the basics."

"Sounds like you're losing your city-boy charm. Maybe the women of Watervale have started to catch on?"

Riley ignored Chase's jest. "For your information, she's not a local, although she did spend most of her childhood in town."

Chase looked curious. "Really? I've lived here all my life. Who is it? I might be able to shed some light on her."

"Kathryn Collins. Goes by Kate."

Chase frowned. "Kate Collins. Can't say I remember her. How old is she?"

"She's a couple of years younger than you, but she says she left town ten years ago. Her mother's married to Commander Watson."

Chase's eyes widened. "Kate Watson? Christ, is she back in town? I wonder how she turned out? I had a hard-on for her all through high school. She was a real looker!"

Riley bit back an instinctive protest. "Yeah, well nothing much has changed. She's a looker all right."

Sonia placed a schooner of beer in front of Chase and

hovered close, making no attempt to disguise her interest in their conversation.

Picking up the glass, Chase nodded his thanks and took a sip before turning back to Riley. "So, Kate came in to report her mother missing?"

"Yeah, but she went further than that. She thinks the commander's murdered her." Riley shook his head. "Can you believe it?"

"She always was a bit of a drama queen," Chase replied. "I was a couple of grades ahead of her at school, but I remember her having a reputation for being a bit of a troublemaker. She was always getting into strife with the principal, Mr Savage. Not that it mattered to me. With looks like hers, she could get away with anything. Besides, old man Savage was a bit of a jerk."

Chase nodded toward Sonia. "You remember Kate Watson, don't you? You were in the same class. What do you think she was like?"

Glad for the invitation to participate in their conversation, Sonia leaned across the bar. Her breasts in full view, pressed provocatively against the wood.

"Kate Watson. Yeah, I remember her. She took off halfway through the eighth grade. Never saw her after that. It was right before the athletics carnival. Most of us were glad. It meant at least some of us had a chance at winning a ribbon or two."

"She was an athlete," Riley stated, raising his eyes from Sonia's chest.

She shrugged. The movement sent her cleavage wobbling. Riley braced himself, half-expecting the bountiful flesh to spill out onto the bar.

"I guess so. She wasn't competitive or anything. You never saw her training. But she was fast. She used to win all the sprints."

"What was she like in school? Did she have many friends?" Riley asked.

Sonia looked thoughtful. "I don't know. I guess she did. Like Chase said, she was really pretty. A lot of the girls didn't like her. Mainly because of that, I think—jealous, most of them. She was always popular with the boys." She gave Chase a pointed look. "Not that she paid them any attention. She kept to herself a lot of the time. You'd best talk to Cally Savage. She knew her better than anyone."

Riley turned to Chase with a raised eyebrow. "Any relation to the principal?"

Chase nodded slowly. "Yeah, his daughter. I remember Kate used to hang around Cally a bit. Before Kate took off."

"Where can I find Cally?" Riley asked. "Is she still in town?"

"No, she fell pregnant at sixteen," Chase replied. "Not a good look for the principal of Watervale High who was forever preaching morals and the art of restraint. So, he threw her out. She lives in Armidale, now. As far as I know, she's attending university over there. Or maybe she's finished..." Chase shook his head. "Hell, I can't remember, but her father's still in town. He might even still be the principal. Her mother died a few years back. Cancer, I think."

"Where does he live? I'll give him a call. It might help if I can talk to his daughter. It would be interesting to know what made Kate Watson leave town and when she changed her name to Collins."

Chase drank the rest of his beer and set the glass back down on the bar. "Yeah, sure. The Savages live over on the eastern side, on Jackson Avenue. They live in the nicer part of town, not far from Commander Watson. Wait until you get a look at some of the homes over there."

Sonia scoffed. "Homes? That's like calling the White House a bungalow."

Riley frowned, barely listening. "I'm not sure what's going on with little Miss Collins, but I got the impression something's not quite right. I'm going to get to the bottom of it, whether the blond ice queen likes it or not."

Surprise lit up Chase's features. "Ice queen? You can't be talking about the same Kate Watson? That girl was pure fire."

30

Kate gripped the phone until her knuckles turned white. The call connected and her stomach catapulted downward.

"Yes?"

His voice was exactly as she remembered. Bile rose in her throat. She bit her lip and tasted blood.

"Who is it?" he growled.

She barely heard him over the rushing sound in her ears. Memories overwhelmed her as he had years earlier. But he wouldn't this time. Not again. She wouldn't let him. Her voice was ragged when she finally got it to work.

"Where is my mother?"

"Well, well, well. The prodigal child has returned."

The sly malice in his tone hit her like a physical blow. Fury flooded her veins.

"Don't go quoting biblical bullshit to me, you sanctimonious bastard."

"*Tsk, tsk, tsk.* That's no way to speak to your father."

She was on fire. Her forehead. Her ears. Her cheeks. Her throat. She was going to combust from the heat of her anger. "You've never been a father to me."

"Maybe not, but I'm the only one you've known and surely better than the useless hobo that fathered you." Unlike hers, his voice remained calm, unruffled, as if they were discussing last week's weather.

The derogatory reference to her father scorched her heart. She bit down hard on the moan of despair that ripped through her. She wouldn't give him the satisfaction of knowing he'd wounded her.

Her fingernails bit into her palm. Her breath came fast. She dug deep to find the strength to fight him.

"Tell me what you've done to my mother, or I swear to God, I'll kill you."

Derisive laughter grated against her ear. "My dear, dear Kathryn, you of all people should know there is no God."

CHAPTER 4

Riley traced yet another blue, felt-tipped circle around the name he'd written on his blank, yellow legal pad. *Darryl Watson.*

Despite his best efforts over the weekend to forget about the woman who'd attended upon him at the station late Friday afternoon, he'd spent the nights since tossing and turning while a kaleidoscope of images had tumbled through his mind. Even a Sunday spent browsing the paintings on exhibition at the local art gallery hadn't been sufficient to remove her from his thoughts.

If anything, gazing at the myriad of colorful artworks had only served to heighten her presence in his mind. She'd told him she was a successful art dealer. He wondered how a girl who had run away from home at fourteen had managed such a feat.

It was mid-morning, but the station was quiet, as usual. Crime in the picture-perfect town of Watervale ran from the non-existent to the merely mundane: the occasional domestic disturbance, the odd drunk driving charge and now and then a break and enter. No one could remember the last murder, or if there had ever been one.

The letters on the page mocked him in their blue-biro boldness. He should call Watson and get it over with. It wasn't like Riley was going to make any accusations against the former commander. He wasn't stupid. He'd learned something from the fiasco in Sydney.

The easiest way to sort things out was to speak with the man in the best position to know. He still couldn't work out why Kate hadn't done that. It's exactly what anyone else with nothing to hide would have done.

With an impatient shake of his head, he pushed aside a couple of files on his desk and reached over to pick up the phone. After punching in numbers, he listened as it dialed out. It was answered on the third ring.

"Yes?"

The voice was deep and well-modulated and brought to mind expensive cigars and single malt whisky. *Power.* Sudden nerves tickled the back of Riley's throat. He coughed to clear it. The situation was delicate. The man on the other end of the phone was a decorated police officer. Riley was the new kid in town and still reeling from a run-in with his former superiors.

"Commander Watson?" Riley used the former title out of respect.

"Yes."

"It's Detective Munro from the Watervale Police. I'm sorry to call you, sir, but I've had a report that your wife might be missing. I was wondering if you could bring her to the phone."

The man chuckled on the other end of the line. "I can't rightly do that, sonny. I'm afraid she's not here."

Riley bit his lip, but continued. "Okay. When do you expect her home?"

"Well," the amiable voice replied, "you might try calling back again in about three months."

"Three months?"

"Yeah, she's gone on a holiday." Watson chuckled again. "Not any too soon, either. She sure did need a rest."

Riley scribbled notes. "I see. Can you tell me where she's gone? I understand she's in a wheelchair."

The amiability cooled slightly. "Who did you say you were again? Munro, was it? I don't think I know you."

"I arrived after you retired. I've been in town three months."

"I see. A whippersnapper straight out of the Academy, I'll bet. I've lost count of the number of fresh recruits that were sent out here for me to straighten out."

Riley tensed at the insult. "I've been an officer for nearly a decade."

"*Hmph.*" Watson dismissed Riley's experience with a derisive grunt.

Refusing to allow the man to bait him further, Riley continued with his line of questioning.

"Your wife is unable to walk around unassisted, isn't that the case?"

"Yes, Rosemary's in a wheelchair. It doesn't mean she's housebound. She's gone on a cruise. One of those round-the-world trips. It takes about four months. She left early in July."

Riley's eyebrows lifted in surprise. "Really? She was happy to go alone in a wheelchair?"

"The cruise line was very accommodating. They have special suites for disabled passengers. They couldn't do enough for her."

"Which cruise line is she traveling with?"

"Princess Cruises. 'A Princess Cruise for a princess,' that's what I told her."

Riley grimaced at the cliché, but forged on. "Did you use a travel agent?"

"Yes, we did. Rosemary wanted to book online—she's a whiz on the Internet, but I don't trust it. There's no way I'm going to put my credit card details into a computer for who knows who to get hold of.

"I went to the local travel agency—the Thames. I booked the holiday for her myself. Rosemary thought it was good karma when she saw the name. It reminded her of Kathryn, her daughter. The girl lives in London, you know."

"Yes, Kath—Kate told me that."

"Kate now, is it? So, you've been talking to her? I guessed as much. Well, if you're talking to her again, you must tell her I said hello and that I miss her. I haven't seen her for years. I guess she thinks she's too good for the likes of Watervale now that she's a hotshot art dealer. It's just like her to cause a stir the minute she arrives back in town."

Riley ignored the comment. "She's worried about her mother. She hasn't heard from her for a month. I take it your wife has been in contact with you since she left?"

"Well, you see, it's like this," Watson explained. "The cell phone reception's not real good on the ship and it's hellishly expensive. Rosemary decided to leave her phone at home and take her laptop. The plan was that she'd Skype me, but the silly woman left it behind. It was on the kitchen counter when I returned from Sydney.

"I couldn't believe it when I saw it sitting there. That thing's practically an extension of her arm. But later on, when I was thinking about it, I figured she must have left it behind on purpose. She probably wanted to get away from it all. Enjoy the scenery in peace and quiet... You know what I mean?"

Riley stared thoughtfully at the notepad in front of him; he was perplexed. It sounded a little strange that a woman not only in a wheelchair, but traveling alone, would choose to leave without any means of communication, especially in this day and age, but maybe Darryl was right? Maybe his wife wanted to get away from it all? Maybe that's why Kate hadn't heard from her?

"Does that mean, you haven't heard from her at all since she left?" he asked, wanting to be sure.

"That's right, Detective. I haven't. But I'm not worried about her. The girls at the travel agency assured me she'd be given the five-star treatment. I'm sure she's having the time of her life. She always said she wanted to travel."

"Where did she embark?"

"Sydney. I drove her down there myself. Took me most of the day and just as long to get back, but I didn't mind. It's the first real holiday she's had in a long time."

"Why didn't you go with her?"

The question sat quietly between them. Riley waited for Watson to reply.

"It's like this, sonny. I get seasick even thinking about

boating. I've always been that way. But Rosemary, well, it's about the only thing she really wanted to do. Go on a cruise. She'd heard from some of her friends that all they did was sit around and eat and take in the scenery and that suited her just fine."

Still harboring a vague disquiet, but unable to think of anything else to say, Riley ended the call by asking Watson to let him know if his wife made contact and then he slowly replaced the receiver in its port.

Well, that was that. Rosemary Watson was on a holiday. A cruise. A four-month, round-the-world cruise, no less. Odd, but not totally out of the question. There was only one way to know for sure.

He picked up the phone again and asked directory assistance for the number of the Thames Travel Agency. Within moments, his call was connected. After assuring her of his identity, the woman who called herself Elaine Spencer confirmed they had a booking in the name of Rosemary Watson for a cruise that had departed just over a month earlier.

Riley hung up the phone, more than a little relieved. Watson had been telling the truth. His wife was exactly where he said she was—enjoying a holiday away from everyone and everything.

Riley couldn't imagine how tough it would be to spend every day in a wheelchair and Rosemary Watson had been doing it for more than twenty years. No wonder the woman needed a break.

The timing fit in with Kate's story, too. The only thing that didn't fit was Kate's insistence her mother had met with foul play—and that her stepfather was responsible.

Why would she jump to such a wild conclusion? By all accounts, Darryl Watson was a well-respected member of Watervale society. He may have had a fair dose of arrogance, but Riley had yet to meet a man who'd risen to one of the highest ranks of his profession who hadn't picked up a little attitude along the way.

It was Kate's motivation that stumped him. It was obvious

she disliked the man, but what did she have to gain by blackening her stepfather's name? What had happened in her past to make her so damned vindictive?

Riley frowned, not at all sure he wanted to know. After the debacle in Sydney, he was more than reticent to throw around accusations about high-ranking police commanders, even former ones.

His shoulders slumped on a heavy sigh. He hoped it wouldn't come to that.

Kate paced the small confines of her motel room dressed in her favorite pale blue angora sweater and the woolen pants she'd worn a couple of days before. The feel of the whisper-soft fibers against her skin soothed her, as they usually did, and helped to remind her of her successful life in London and the courage she'd employed to attain it.

She was well-respected in the international art world and clients traveled across continents to purchase pieces from her collection. In three weeks, she was holding a major exhibition of artworks so rare invitations to the event had been offered to only the most wealthy of her clients.

Despite the fact she employed two trusted assistants, it was imperative she return to London in time for that show. Her clients expected her to be there. *She* needed to be there.

There was just enough room between the cheap double bed and the wall to make her pacing worthwhile. Usually when she traveled, she went for something far grander, but in Watervale the three-star motel was the best the town had to offer. Besides, she didn't intend to stay long. As soon as her mother was found, she'd hop the next plane to London, this time with Rosemary in tow. There was no way she'd leave her with Darryl another minute. The problem was, she didn't know how to go about finding her and while she prayed desperately it wasn't true, she still couldn't shake the feeling her stepfather had removed her mother permanently.

After stocking up on supplies over the weekend at the local supermarket, she'd finished her usual breakfast of fresh fruit and coffee a couple of hours earlier and had spent the time since wracking her brain to come up with a plan. She couldn't just confront Darryl, or go to the house—even if she found the courage to face him. He'd been a serving police officer for most of his adult life. He'd never be foolish enough to leave incriminating evidence lying around—he was way too smart to be careless.

Besides, who was she kidding? She'd barely managed to hold it all together when she'd telephoned him. She'd never be able to set foot in his house. Not again. Never again.

But Detective Munro could.

The thought took hold and grew fragile roots. Her pacing slowed. He hadn't taken her seriously the first time, but today might be different. No doubt by now he'd called Darryl. Maybe her stepfather's explanation, or lack of one, had ignited his curiosity… She could only hope it would be so.

But what if it didn't?

Panic gripped her heart at the thought the detective might accept whatever excuse Darryl offered. Agitation rose inside her. She had to make the detective believe her. Or another detective. There had to be someone who would listen, someone untainted by Darryl Watson's glory.

Every minute counted. The longer her mother was gone, the quicker any evidence of her departure deteriorated, until eventually there would be nothing. It would disappear. Just like, deep down, she believed her mother had.

Chase called out from the stairwell, "Hey, Munro! There's someone downstairs to see you."

Riley stood and wove his way through the clutter of desks and cardboard boxes that bulged with old files and police briefs and caught up with his partner at the top of the stairs. "Who is it?"

"Don't know. One of the uniforms called out to me on the way up."

Riley slipped past him and jogged the rest of the way down. Striding into the foyer, he pulled up short. His gut clenched like he'd been kicked by a bull and suddenly nerves jammed his throat.

Kate Collins stood off to one side, staring out the small window beside the doorway. Her mouth was taut. Her arms were folded across her chest.

Even the glamor of her outfit—a pale blue turtleneck made of some kind of soft, fluffy wool and the same pair of charcoal-gray pants she'd worn when they'd first met— couldn't disguise the tension in her body.

He stepped forward and held out his hand. "Miss Collins. We meet again."

She hesitated, and he noticed an infinitesimal clouding of her eyes. His heart skipped a beat and then her hand, warm and fragile, was in his. He tried not to notice how good it felt.

"Detective Munro, thank you for seeing me."

The control was back. Her voice was firm, cool, polite. She gave him a smile that didn't reach her eyes and abruptly released his hand.

"What can I do for you, Miss Collins?"

She looked around at the assortment of people who crowded the waiting room. A constable stood behind the reception desk, attending to enquiries. Her gaze returned to Riley's.

"Is there somewhere a little more private we can talk?"

"Of course, come upstairs."

He indicated for her to precede him. The heavy winter coat she'd worn when he'd last seen her was absent and as she began to climb the stairs ahead of him, his gaze came to rest on her nicely rounded butt.

The faint scent of her perfume wafted down to him, rich and exotic, like a bowl of crushed frangipani flowers and cinnamon. He shook his head. What the hell was he doing, thinking such ridiculous thoughts? It was bullshit. She was a client, a member of the public who had come to him for help. He'd best remember that.

She hesitated at the top of the stairs.

"Go straight ahead, first room on the right. Same place where we talked on Friday afternoon. It should be vacant."

Riley bounded up the last remaining stairs and entered the interview room a few seconds behind her. She stood staring at the blank white walls, her arms once again crossed in front of her.

"Take a seat," he said. "Can I get you anything? A cup of coffee? A can of Coke?"

She gave a slight shake of her head and sat down gingerly on one of the gray, molded plastic chairs. She shifted as if to rest her elbows on the scarred wooden table, and then halted as her gaze absorbed its grimy surface.

Years of dirt, sweat, secrets and fear permeated the cheap wood. He didn't blame her for not wanting to make contact with it.

Taking a seat opposite, he tugged out the notebook and pen that habitually lived in the pocket of his shirt and scrawled the date and time on a fresh page and then braced himself for the impact of her eyes.

Throughout the long, night hours of his weekend, they'd burned themselves onto his retinas and he was leery of falling victim to their cobalt spell again. If he wanted to get to the bottom of it, he needed to keep his wits about him. She might be the most gorgeous woman he'd ever been this close to, but that didn't mean he'd let that attraction he felt interfere with his job.

He was a professional. He knew how to keep his distance—even if his cock didn't want to. The thought soured his mood and put him on the offensive.

"You lied to me, Blondie. "I've spoken to Darryl. You never called him and your mother's alive and well and enjoying a well-earned holiday. I've closed the file." His voice was harsher than he'd intended and he felt like shit when her eyes filled with desperation.

"No, no! You can't do that! I have to find her! I have to know where she is!"

With grim determination, he forged on. "I just told you where she is. I'm beginning to think your stepfather was right. Perhaps you do have a thing about stirring up trouble. I guess coming in here with your puppy-dog eyes and sad story was one way to do it, but it pisses me off to have my time wasted. There are a lot more important things I could be doing with it."

"What? Like trying to dodge cow shit? That *was* what you were doing before I turned up, wasn't it?"

Her sarcasm surprised him. His lips tugged upwards before he got a grip on himself. She didn't look the least bit contrite about her language. In fact, sparks now shot out of her eyes and twin spots of anger colored her cheeks.

He hadn't expected her to come out fighting. He'd just flayed her character like a cat o' nine tails and yet she was ready to stand up to him again. He tamped down the flash of admiration and continued. "Falsely reporting criminal activity is an offence, Miss Collins. I could have you arrested."

She held out her wrists, surprising him once again. Their eyes met and held for weightless seconds. His gut knotted from the impact. Blood flooded to his groin.

He pushed his chair back and it almost toppled over. "I'm going to get a drink," he managed to croak. Dragging his gaze away, he stumbled from the room, pulling the door closed behind him.

Riley leaned against the wall outside the interview room, his breath coming fast. *Christ, what the hell was wrong with him?* She was just a woman. A woman seeking help. He was there to "protect and serve." That's what he'd sworn to do. Yet all he'd done was argue and insult her and all because of his inability to control his body's response whenever he got anywhere near her.

Disgust flooded through him. It wasn't her fault he found her attractive. She'd done nothing to encourage his attention—at least *that* kind of attention.

So, she'd lied to him about calling Darryl. He wasn't entirely comfortable with Watson's story, either. Watson's wife, his *wheelchair-bound* wife hadn't been heard from for at least a month and her husband hadn't sounded the least bit concerned. The cost of the calls be damned, Riley didn't know any husband who would think zero communication for as much as four months was a good thing.

Not a husband who cared.

He pushed away from the wall and strode toward the vending machine nearby. He selected Coke twice and waited for them to tumble one at a time into the metal basket. From the look of Miss Collins, he suspected she drank Diet Coke, but he knew better than to hand her one of those. He had learned something from his sisters.

With his body now firmly under control, he squared his shoulders and headed back to the interview room.

———————

"So, let's go back to the start, shall we?" the detective said as he sauntered back into the room with two Cokes. Kate swallowed a sigh. She didn't know what game he was playing, but she was sick and tired of it. Every minute they wasted boded ill for her mother and Kate still didn't have a clue where the woman was. Was it possible her mother *had* gone on a holiday? She clung to the tiny flame of hope that flared to life inside her.

"You talked to Darryl," she said as calmly as she could manage.

His eyes probed hers. "Yes, I called him this morning."

So, he had believed some of her story. That was a start.

"What did he say about my mother?"

The detective returned to his chair and opened his can of Coke. The crack of the aluminium tab as the soda met the air was loud in the silent room. She waited him out, while he chugged down half of its contents. The Coke he'd pushed in her direction remained untouched between them on the table.

He set his drink back down. A strong, tanned hand reached up to wipe moisture from his mouth. Dark brown eyes, keen with intelligence, assessed her. She refused to squirm. She'd done nothing wrong. All she wanted was his help.

Snagging his notebook, he picked up his pen off the table. His gaze flicked to her. "I already told you. Darryl said she's gone on a holiday, just like I suggested to you on Friday. She's sailing around the world on a cruise ship."

Confusion filled her mind, followed quickly by denial. "A cruise? No way. He's lying. My mother hates the ocean. There's no way she'd go on a cruise. She can't even swim."

The detective shrugged. His voice remained mild and unperturbed. "Perhaps she changed her mind? After all, how well can you know her? It's been ten years since you lived with her." He leaned over and took another mouthful of Coke. "Maybe she took swimming lessons?"

Fury gushed through her arteries, setting her face on fire. Before that absurd comment, she'd fooled herself into thinking he was taking her seriously. She'd even allowed herself to hope he would believe her and want to help. His ridiculous remark about swimming lessons proved how wrong she'd been. Was he even aware of how utterly *ludicrous* it sounded?

He was laughing at her. The disappearance of her mother was a joke to him. Disappointment crushed her, weighing down her limbs, making it almost impossible for her to stand and make her escape.

She bent to retrieve her handbag. Tears blurred her vision. She bit her lip and tasted blood as painful and acrid as her failure to convince him.

Despair hovered over her, but she refused to pay it heed. If this good-for-nothing detective with the way-too-sexy eyes wouldn't help her, she'd find someone who would. She'd go through the whole squad. Hell, she'd go to the next town, if that's what it took to convince someone in law enforcement about the duplicity of one of their own.

All she wanted was a little help to find her mother.

Holding her body stiff, she averted her gaze and rose and made her way to the door. The smell of his fresh, woodsy cologne on the air was the final insult. It teased her nose, reminding her of fleeting moments of peace and freedom on long, lazy Sundays hiking in the forest with Cally

CHAPTER 5

Riley stared at the small pile of police statements on his desk and tried to find the enthusiasm to compile them into the lever arch folder that sat near his elbow.

Jack Sampson's prize-winning cow was still on the loose, but Riley had managed to interview some of the surrounding neighbors and a couple of old-timers who regularly propped up the far end of The Bullet's tired wooden bar. They'd offered their own opinion about the stolen beast and it wasn't one Sampson would be keen to hear.

After speaking with Sampson's cronies, Riley had done a criminal record check and had discovered Sampson had a previous brush with the law. Fifteen years earlier, Sampson had been convicted of insurance fraud. It was an interesting development. Riley wasn't foolish enough to believe leopards changed their spots.

"Oh, Detective Munro, I'm glad I caught you."

Riley looked up as Detective Sergeant Mike Hannaford lumbered toward him. Riley was sure the squad's recently appointed Local Area Commander meant for his smile to be friendly, but his smarminess only put Riley on edge. Hannaford had been in the job a week when Riley arrived and he'd heard nothing but grumblings about the man since.

After Riley's Sydney experience, nothing the upper echelon did could surprise him, but many in the squad were still adjusting to the idea of their former lackadaisical coworker being elevated to such a lofty position.

Riley tilted his chair on its back legs and folded his arms across his chest. "Is there something you need, sir?"

"No, no, no. I just thought I'd stop by and say hello." Hannaford spread his arms wide and then stepped closer, propping his hip against Riley's desk. "How're you going with Jack Sampson? Has that cow turned up yet?"

"Not yet, but I'm working on it."

"Good, good." Hannaford patted at the graying strands of hair that stretched precariously across his head from his razor-sharp side part.

Silence fell between them. Another minute passed. Riley scratched at his own dense crop with the end of his pen, knowing he should be trying to be more amendable toward his superior, but somehow unable to make the effort. "Was there anything else?"

A flush crept up Hannaford's thick neck. His fingers pulled at his tie. His gaze fixed onto something beyond Riley's shoulder.

"Yes, well, you haven't been working here very long and I wanted to stop by and let you know how it is. We're a tight group here; we look out for each other." His hand moved lower and he plucked at small pieces of lint that clung to his immaculate navy suit pants.

Riley froze. Images of his final meeting with Detective Inspector Shattler in Sydney flashed across his mind; the moments just before his career had gone to shit.

Someone had told Hannaford about the circumstances surrounding his transfer...

The LAC smiled again. "We always have each other's backs, Detective Munro. In fact, Commander Watson—do you know him? Anyway, Commander Watson and I still golf together twice a week; every Wednesday and Friday."

Riley's heart rate picked up its pace. Midnight-black eyes bored into his. The threat was unmistakable.

Relief surged through him. It had nothing to do with Sydney. This was about Watson and his wife—the woman who might or might not have gone missing.

Riley was filled with curiosity. *Why would Watson tell his golfing buddy about the phone call?*

His musings were interrupted when Hannaford glanced at the gold Rolex on his wrist. The oily smile returned.

"Look at the time. Where has the day gone? I have to be down at the mayor's office in half an hour. Thanks for the little chat, Detective. I've enjoyed it. I'll talk to you later." Spinning on the heel of one highly polished RM Williams boot, Hannaford turned his back on Riley, heaved his bulk across the squad room and disappeared down the stairs.

Riley straightened in his seat and pulled his chair in closer to his desk. Adrenaline buzzed through him. He'd doubted Kate's story from the start. Not the part about her mother's disappearance—her reaction to his indifference was too genuine for him not to believe she really thought the woman was missing—but he'd definitely harbored doubts about the whole my-stepfather-has-murdered-her thing. He'd been prepared to put it down to an overactive imagination and leave it at that.

But Watson had felt the need to relay Riley's call—or at least the gist of it—to Hannaford. Riley's boss. Watervale's newest commander.

Why would Watson do that? It didn't make sense. If his wife was truly on a holiday, why would he feel the need to inform Riley's superior of the call? And why would Hannaford feel the need to warn Riley away? The LAC might not have said that in so many words, but Riley was an expert at reading between the lines. He was convinced it's what the man had meant.

Determination flooded through his veins. He'd always loved a challenge. Just as quickly, he tamped it down. Hadn't he almost lost his career by interfering where he wasn't wanted? What would it take to get it through his head that for some people within the force, the normal rules simply didn't apply?

His misplaced idealism and finely honed sense of justice had seen him banished to the boondocks and he barely hung onto the threads of his career. Though thinking about the fiasco in the city still turned his stomach, he'd learned his lesson. If you were high enough up the ladder, there were certain things people would turn a blind eye to—would even condone and encourage and be part of.

He didn't need Hannaford to remind him of the way the men in blue stuck together. He'd experienced it firsthand and wasn't keen to be on the wrong side of that impenetrable wall of loyalty again.

Kate's fear-filled eyes swam before him. He ran an impatient hand through his hair and gritted his teeth, doing his best to ignore the prick of guilt from his conscience.

Why him? Of all the officers she could have contacted, why did it have to be him? He'd arrived in Watervale with only one goal: To lie low and keep his head down. To do his time and get out. Two years, Detective Inspector Shattler had told him. Two years of banishment to a dead end town like Watervale.

He'd already done three months. In a year and a half, he could apply for another transfer. Three months after that, he could leave Watervale, head back to the city and get his career and life back on track. He was still hopeful he'd be forgiven for his unwelcome breach of the unspoken code of loyalty.

Of course, he'd never work at his old station again, and he didn't want to, but surely there were other commands that hadn't been tainted by police corruption? Despite the way he'd been treated, he refused to believe the entire New South Wales Police Force was defiled.

Eighteen months. It was nothing in the scheme of things. He was barely thirty. There was still plenty of time to carve out a worthwhile career.

But now, because of a few unsettling questions from his conscience and a woman with a fiery spirit and a heart-wrenching cloak of vulnerability, there was yet another threat to his derailed career.

If he ignored Hannaford's warning and looked harder at Watson, he might as well hand in his resignation there and then and join the unemployment queue. What little he'd managed to salvage of his career after the debacle in Sydney would disappear like a fistful of ashes in a windstorm. Calls would be made, stories would be told and suddenly, no commander in the State would want him on their team.

Could he live with himself if he turned his back on Kate and her desperate plea for help? Could he ignore the persistent ache in his gut that told him things weren't quite right?

The endless sleepless nights since he'd left Sydney were proof that his conscience refused to rest easy, despite his reluctant acceptance of how things were. The fact that he'd kept the real reason for his departure from the city a secret from his family, even his twin, made him squirm with discomfort. All four of his brothers were in law enforcement—two were decorated State police officers and two were Federal Agents. How could he hope for them to understand why he'd kept his mouth shut and had looked the other way?

Just thinking about the smug smile on Detective Inspector Shattler's face as he'd laid out the facts of life in a police command had Riley burning at the injustice of it, but at the time, he'd felt he had no choice but to accept the man's decree. Shattler was a big player. He was on first name basis with the Premier of New South Wales. There had been talk he'd make Commissioner. The thought of fronting up to Internal Affairs and telling them their anointed one was corrupt had filled Riley with dread. He'd never have seen the inside of a squad room again.

Perhaps he was overreacting? Hannaford could have been merely looking out for an old mate. Maybe Riley was jumping to conclusions, thinking Watson had mentioned the phone call to Hannaford because the former commander had something to hide? After all, until Hannaford's approach, Riley had barely even considered the anomalies in Watson's story.

So, the former commander was an inattentive husband. There was no crime in that.

Riley scrubbed at his hair in indecision. If he could confirm Rosemary Watson was on the ship, everything would be sweet. His conscience would be clear and Hannaford need never know Riley had made the call.

With a sigh of relief that he'd nearly resolved the dilemma, he reached for the phone on his desk and dialed once again the number of the Thames Travel Agency.

The afternoon light waned and the temperature gauge on the dashboard of Kate's rental car showed the air outside had cooled. Her breath came in short harsh pants, despite the pep talk she'd given herself before she left the motel.

She took another sip of the steaming black coffee she'd picked up at the McDonalds' drive-through. The caffeine probably wouldn't help slow the hammering of her heart, but drinking it gave her something to do and took her mind off the house that stood in benign solitude across the road.

She'd parked as far away from the property as she could while still keeping the house in sight. Her nondescript rental car was half hidden behind a thick stand of pine trees and her eyes were concealed behind a huge pair of designer sunglasses.

She was slumped low in the seat. With anxious fingers, she patted the pale pink scarf she'd tied Jackie O style around her hair. The fact that the single garage beside the house stood empty gave her a modicum of relief, but knowing her stepfather could arrive home at any minute kept her nerves on edge.

She'd already been there twenty minutes, trying to gather the courage to walk up the drive. It had been more than a decade since she'd been there, but from the look of the place, it could have been yesterday.

The front lawn, winter-yellow, was neatly mowed and the

low Murraya hedge running along two sides of the fence had been shaped with military precision. The spiky, skeletal arms of the thick stand of rose bushes that bordered the concrete driveway were bare, but had been closely pruned and sported fresh mulch. Her stepfather had always had a green thumb.

The house was much as she remembered it. The impressive, two-story red brick mansion had weathered the years well. That was more than she could say for herself.

Oh, she looked all right from the outside. Some of the men she'd met in Europe had even called her beautiful. But she knew what was hidden beneath the designer clothes and cultured English accent—in those hidden places where it really mattered, in the darkest hours of the night when the nightmares couldn't be banished with a pep talk, the soft glow from a lamp or a glass of chardonnay.

With a deep breath, she uncurled her fingers. Catching sight of her ragged nails, she silently farewelled her French manicure. She'd chewed them almost down to the quick. Just another thing the bastard had managed to destroy and she'd only just arrived back in town.

A car came over the rise behind her and bore down like an avenging angel—or was it the devil? The shiny, black pickup truck slowed momentarily and then roared on past her. With her heart in her mouth, she slid lower in her seat and pretended to be absorbed in the map she'd left on the seat on the passenger's side.

She peered above the folded paper and gulped when brake lights came on. The vehicle slowed and turned into her stepfather's driveway.

She sat immobilized. The fear she was well-accustomed to took over and liquefied her limbs. Darryl alighted from the car and sauntered toward the house.

Watching him, her blood turned to ice. She began to shake. Her fingers stuttered over the ignition key and she cursed with increasing desperation when it refused to turn. Nausea writhed in her stomach. She was going to be sick. Right there. In the rental car.

She looked around in increasing desperation for a plastic bag—something—anything.

She shouldn't have come. All the years she'd stayed away, all the years of healing had been swept away like sandcastles at high tide. She was fourteen again and running from a monster.

She bit back a sob, but another rose up behind it. With her fist in her mouth, she tried to hold them in, gasping and willing the memories away.

She wouldn't give in. She wouldn't let him defeat her again. She wasn't a helpless teenager anymore. She'd learned how to fight back.

But no matter what she told herself, the agony gripping her heart intensified until she could do nothing but give it release. With gulping breaths, the sobs she'd tried so hard to contain overwhelmed her.

She didn't know how long she sat there falling apart, but the sound of another vehicle approaching caused her to lift her head and peer through the late afternoon light.

She made out a late model iridescent-green sedan just in front of her. A Holden or a Ford—she'd never been good with cars—and it was dirty, like it had been driven through the mud. It slowed and turned, coming to a stop in the driveway behind her stepfather's black beast.

Scrabbling around in her handbag for some tissues, Kate wiped her eyes and blew her nose and looked up in time to see Detective Munro step from the sedan.

Her pulse leaped. He was tall. She hadn't really noticed that about him when she'd spoken with him. Probably because she'd been too caught up in her reasons for being at the police station—that, and the fact his liquid-chocolate eyes and gleaming smile had drawn most of her attention.

Her gaze took in the worn denims and pale blue chambray shirt he wore with casual grace. He pulled off a pair of aviator sunglasses and glanced around, as if sensing her watching him. Ducking reflexively, her knee connected with the bottom of the dashboard. She yelped and rubbed at the reddening mark. When she looked up again, he was gone.

CHAPTER 6

Riley's gaze skimmed over the small white sedan parked on the side of the road a short distance away and then came to rest on the impressive house in front of him. The double-story brick home was one of the largest he'd seen in Watervale. He looked around, canvasing the immaculately kept front yard for clues.

This didn't look like a house where evil lurked. Everything was tidy and in its place, from the pile of garden tools stacked neatly against the garage to the hose that lay looped in precise coils beneath the garden faucet. Even the trash bins stood discreetly to one side, unobtrusive and out of the way. He slipped off his Ray Bans and made his way up the concrete path to the extra-wide front door.

His knock was answered almost immediately, as if the owner had been watching his approach. A towering hulk of a man who appeared to be somewhere in his late fifties stood on the other side.

"Darryl Watson? I'm Detective Munro. We spoke on the phone."

"Where are your manners, sonny? It's Commander Watson to you."

Refusing to be intimidated, Riley eyeballed him. As far as he was concerned, Darryl Watson had lost his right to Riley's respect the minute the man had telephoned Hannaford.

"I'm sorry, Darryl. I was under the impression you retired a few months ago."

Riley's barb drew blood. Angry color crawled up Watson's neck until it suffused his cheeks. Riley cursed himself silently for his wayward tongue. The way he was going, Hannaford would have him out on his ear before he made it back to the station.

"What's this all about, Munro? I thought we straightened this out when you called yesterday?"

Riley made a show of taking out his notebook and pen and flipping to a page with writing scrawled all over it.

"Yeah, well... See, here's the thing, Darryl. Your travel agent helped me get in contact with the *Sun Princess*. I talked to the cruise ship's purser. He says your wife never boarded."

Surprise lit up Watson's face. Doubt nibbled at the edge of Riley's consciousness. Either Watson was an excellent actor, or he truly believed his wife was on the ship.

"What are you talking about? Of course she boarded."

"No, Darryl. She didn't."

"Listen, you young whippersnapper. I know you're just trying to do your job. Look at you—you're as eager as a new puppy—even with a decade of experience under your belt. I remember what it was like. When I was your age, I champed at the bit with every telephone call that came in. And you know what? I admire your enthusiasm. I really do. We need fellas like you protecting our town."

Watson gave Riley a hearty slap on the back. "The only thing you need to do is hone your radar. You've got it all wrong. I'll bet Rosemary's sunning herself on a deckchair even as we speak. Why don't you step inside and we'll have a beer? I'm sure we can sort this out in time for dinner."

Curious about what the man had to say, Riley followed him through the entryway and into a large, open-plan kitchen and living room. Expensive pieces of custom-made furniture were tastefully arranged around the room. Hundreds of Swarovski crystal figurines were displayed in a tall glass cabinet. Down lights had been installed to show them to their best advantage. Original Sir Arthur Streeton paintings hung on the walls of the living room.

A single plate and coffee mug sat in the kitchen sink. Watson looked at it, a half-embarrassed expression on his face. "The cleaning's slipped a bit since Rosemary left. Why don't you take a seat over there and I'll get us a beer."

Riley glanced over at the oversized white leather modular couch. Matching silk cushions in various hues of aqua and green graced the seats. A glass coffee table stood nearby, a small pile of home magazines artfully scattered across its top. The entire room looked like something he'd find inside one of their glossy covers.

He turned back to Darryl. "Thanks, but I'll pass on the beer. I'm still on duty."

"Ha, don't you worry about that, sonny. I'm not going to tell anyone." Watson winked and opened the fridge.

Riley gritted his teeth. "Thanks, Darryl, but a Coke will be fine."

The other man shot him an inscrutable look and then shrugged. "Suit yourself."

Riley caught the can of Coke one-handed and took a seat on the couch. It faced the biggest flat screen television he'd ever seen. A large window with late-afternoon sun seeping through the open blinds looked out onto the street. Darryl joined him a few moments later with a beer in his hand and sat down at the far end.

Mindful of its shaky journey, Riley opened the Coke with caution. Even still, the cold, dark liquid fizzed over his hand and dripped onto his jeans.

"Sorry about that, sonny. It must have gotten shaken up a bit."

Darryl didn't sound the least bit contrite. Anger flared in Riley's gut and his jaw clenched. He reached for the tissues on the coffee table and wiped the sticky mess off his fingers.

"So, Darryl, what's the story? And don't tell me your wife's cruising the high seas because we both know damned well she's not. I'm sure I don't have to tell you how much she hates the water."

Darryl's face didn't change, didn't move an inch. Riley felt another sliver of doubt. *Christ, it was happening again, just like in Sydney. But this time, maybe he'd called it wrong?*

Had the ship's purser been mistaken? Had Kate lied to him about her mother's water phobia? Was it possible Rosemary Watson really *was* on the ship?

Darryl shook his head, a smile of condescension turning up his lips. "Of course she's on that ship, sonny. I told you, I drove her there myself. Right down to the wharf at Circular Quay. I know Rosemary hates the water. She can't swim. I nearly busted my insides laughing when she told me she wanted to go on a cruise, but she insisted that's what she wanted to do."

Riley struggled to keep his tone even. "I know what you told me, Darryl. Now I want the truth. The thing is, like I told you, I called the ship." He leaned forward and set the Coke down on the coffee table. His gaze snagged on a glossy Princess Cruise Line tourist brochure that sat amongst the pile of magazines. Another round of doubts assailed him.

Darryl's eyes narrowed a fraction. He tilted his head back and chugged down another mouthful of beer. "I've told you everything I know, Munro. I don't know what else you want me to say."

Impatience surged through Riley. Once upon a time, before Sydney, he would have torn Watson's explanation and condescending attitude to shreds, but his confidence had been shaken. He was no longer sure of his footing when it came to knowing right from wrong—or more accurately, knowing when to take issue with the wrong.

His gut told him something was askew, but did he really want to put the final nail in his career coffin by accusing the former commander of something untoward?

He stood and prowled around the room, his footsteps muffled on the thick carpet. An antique oak desk was pushed up against the wall under the window. A Toshiba laptop sat on top of it. The power button glowed a lime-green color, but the lid was down.

He wandered closer. His gaze skittered over the neat pile of papers in one corner of the work surface. The document on the top caught his attention.

The Last Will and Testament of Rosemary Kathryn Watson.

With a casual flick of his wrist, he turned over the first page and skimmed the contents. It was dated July fourth. A little over a month ago.

Spinning on his heel, he lasered Darryl with his gaze. "What day did you take Rosemary to meet the ship?"

Darryl frowned. "I think it was the third or the fourth of last month. I can't remember exactly. I didn't know it was going to be important."

Anger tightened Riley's gut. "Let's cut the bullshit, Darryl." He picked up the will and waved it back and forth. "Your wife visited her lawyer to sign *this* on the fourth, so there's no way she was on the ship. You've already told me it took you most of the day to get there. I can't see you detouring to the lawyer's office on the way."

He moved closer and stood over Darryl where he sat on the couch, calmly drinking.

"Admit it, Darryl. Your wife didn't board. She's not on the fucking ship."

This time, he got a reaction. Within seconds, Watson had gained his full height. His mouth opened, spewing beer through the air. He choked and gasped and his cheeks turned crimson, but it was the ice that burned in his eyes that gave Riley pause.

"How *dare* you! How dare you come into my house and accuse me of—whatever it is you think I've done. You've made a couple of phone calls and glanced at a confidential document on my wife's desk. Big deal. All of a sudden, you think you know everything. Let me tell you, sonny. You know *shit*. And if you'd looked at that will a little closer, you'd have noticed I'm not mentioned in it."

Darryl continued to glare at him. "I'll tell you something else you may not know," he added. "I might have retired, but I still have friends in your office. Good friends. *Loyal* friends."

Riley's body stilled. He should simply shut his mouth and leave, while he still had the right to call himself detective. The thought raged through his mind and was overtaken by another one: He'd stayed silent once before and the shame of it still kept him sleepless.

Anger sprang to life inside him and found its voice, low and guttural. "Are you threatening me?"

Watson shrugged, now completely composed. "Take it how you like." He moved closer. They were almost eyeball-to-eyeball, although Watson outweighed him by at least thirty pounds. Riley refused to look away, even when Watson's voice lowered to a menacing growl.

"Listen and listen well. I'm going to say this one more time. I drove my wife to Circular Quay. That ship was berthed right alongside the wharf. If you say she didn't board, then she didn't board. I'm through arguing with you. She must have changed her mind, gone somewhere else. Women have been known to do that, you know."

His gaze raked Riley's face. "Or maybe you don't." His lips turned up in a sneer. "There probably aren't many pretty white girls that would want to go near a mixed breed like you. Not for more than a night or two, anyway. Even then, it would only be to satisfy their curiosity."

Riley's blood boiled. His hands clenched into fists. In less than a second, his barely leashed control snapped. He closed the distance between them and grabbed Watson by the shirt.

Watson's gaze burned into his, full of defiant contempt. That look was the sluice of cold reality Riley needed to bring his fury under control. Watson wanted him to lose it, was urging him to lose it and if he did, that would be the end of Riley and his career. Watson knew it as well as Riley did.

Sucking in a ragged breath through his tightly clenched teeth, Riley released him and stepped away.

Darryl made a show of shaking his shirt free. With his hands fisted at his sides, Riley drew in gulps of air. If he cared for his career at all, regardless of his suspicions, he had to leave. *Now.*

He turned toward the entryway. Unable to resist a parting shot, he swung back and narrowed his gaze on Darryl's. "Don't go leaving town."

Watson smiled complacently. "Don't worry, Munro. I'm not the one going anywhere. Oh, and by the way, you were right. I remember now. The ship departed on July tenth."

With his anger simmering just below the surface, Riley turned and strode to the door. The flawless front yard confronted him again and he smiled without humor. Now he saw it was all an elaborate facade. He didn't know what other secrets Watson was hiding beneath his veneer of polish, but Riley sure as hell aimed to find out.

Darryl watched from the front window as the unmarked police car reversed out of his driveway and headed in the direction of town. He still seethed at the audacity of the young detective who had invaded his home.

Who the fuck did the prick think he was, marching into Darryl's house and poking his nose into Darryl's business? And not only interfering where he was clearly not wanted, but the bastard had the gall to accuse him of doing away with Rosemary. He may not have said it in so many words, but neither of them had been in any doubt about what he'd meant.

Where did the asshole get off? Didn't he know who Darryl was? The prick said he'd been in town a few months. Surely, word had filtered down to him about the importance of staying on the good side of the former commander?

Darryl's eyes narrowed in disgust. Either the police grapevine had failed to do its job, or his influence in the force had diminished.

He refused to believe the latter. It wasn't possible. Watervale's police force was still comprised of many of his friends—friends who had benefited greatly, both professionally and financially, from Darryl's influence. There was no way they would turn their backs on him. They owed him too much.

All it would take was a quiet word in the ear of someone

who mattered and their lives would be destroyed. He hadn't spent the better part of three decades in the police force without acquiring a considerable number of favors...

His thoughts returned to the young detective and another wave of anger surged through him. It was just his luck that his slut of a stepdaughter had filed the missing person's report with a newcomer. Almost every other copper in the station would have nodded and patted her hand and offered all of the expected platitudes and then would have promptly filed the report in the trash.

But she'd been interviewed by the new prick and he'd lived right and royally up to his name. When he'd called Darryl and questioned him about Rosemary's whereabouts, it had become obvious the newcomer hadn't been initiated into the way things worked in Watervale. If he had, the call to Darryl would never have happened.

Darryl was secretly relieved to have been given advance notice that he would have to work a little harder to maintain his deception. He'd formulated a plan and when the young detective had come calling, as Darryl knew he would, he'd been ready for him, right down to the travel brochure he'd oh-so-casually laid out across the coffee table. Everything had been going dandy until the prick had spied the will.

Darryl cursed, part of his anger now directed toward himself. It had been a stupid mistake leaving the will on Rosemary's desk. He'd tossed it there in a fit of pique nearly a month ago and hadn't given it another thought. It had been careless and if there was one thing he prided himself on, it was knowing how to be careful.

Not that it mattered too much. What he'd told the detective was true. Rosemary owned shit. It was the fact that the bitch had cut him out—*him,* Local Area Police Commander, Darryl Watson—that had pissed him off.

A shaft of fire spiraled through his gut. Ever since he'd found out about the will and its contents, his ulcer had been playing up something fierce. His wife of twenty years had written him out of her will. As if he was nothing, a nobody. The humiliation of it.

What was worse, until he'd stumbled across it in the bottom drawer of her desk, he hadn't suspected a thing.

They'd both made wills not long after they'd married. Although Rosemary had come to him with little more than the clothes on her back and a cowardly daughter in tow, he'd thought it important to make her feel she was an equal partner in their marriage—and she had been—at least in the early days.

Despite her disability, Rosemary Collins had been beautiful. Her navy-blue eyes were both mysterious and intriguing and hinted at secrets he yearned to uncover. Her rich, golden hair had cascaded like a thick swathe of silk down her back. He couldn't wait to feel it spread across his bare skin. Though confined to a wheelchair, her figure had been enviably slim. In contrast, her breasts were full and round and bountiful, pressing teasingly against her shirtfront, pulling the fabric taut.

He hadn't been the only hot-blooded male in Watervale who'd lusted over the newly arrived widow. The fact that she'd had all of the single male population and even some of the married ones walking around town with hard-ons had only increased her desirability.

He had to have her. He had to have her, so no one else could. It was as simple as that.

When they'd married a scant few months after her arrival, he'd been the happiest man in the world. Despite the inconvenience of the child that came with her, he'd spent countless hours enjoying the bounty of Rosemary's body—a task made even more enjoyable knowing how many others wished they were in his place.

In the early days, he'd paraded her around town for everyone to see and lust after. He'd taken her to balls and dinners and other social outings, always insisting she dress provocatively. He loved to see the agony and the envy in the glazed eyes of his colleagues as they looked on and hankered.

But, like all new toys, after awhile, the novelty wore off. The thrill of twisting the men of Watervale into hard knots of unfulfilled desire eventually lost its shine. Over time, Rosemary's looks faded and he became less and less enamored of her charms. It was about that time he began to notice Kate.

The child had been little more than an inconvenience in the early days of his marriage. Right from the beginning, he'd made sure she was banished to live on her own upstairs, away from her mother and the constant bids the girl made for her mother's attention and he'd barely noticed the kid in his everyday comings and goings.

But, as the years passed and his desire for Rosemary waned, he noticed just how much the girl had grown—and how beautiful she'd become. She was the image of her mother. His interest in the girl became more focused. The more he studied her, the more he wanted her...

And now she'd returned.

Her arrival had taken him by surprise. He'd never expected her to come home, even when her mother stopped contacting her. It was the one thing he hadn't planned for. The fact that she had not only returned, but had gone to the police, created an added complication.

He'd had it all worked out. Over the preceding days, he'd carefully dropped subtle and not-so-subtle hints among his friends that things weren't so rosy at home. He'd cunningly let them know his wife's condition was deteriorating and his ability to care for her had become strained and even though he was loathe to do it, he couldn't help but contemplate the necessity of moving her into a nursing home.

His friends had responded exactly like he'd expected. They'd commiserated with his predicament and had congratulated him on his devotion to Rosemary for so many years. They knew it couldn't have been easy for him, caring for an invalid wife.

He'd made all the right noises and had accepted their murmured words of support with gratitude and humility. He'd thanked them for their concern.

His plan had been brilliant. He'd continued to foster the

impression that Rosemary's condition had worsened. And then, he'd made the announcement: He'd arranged for her to go on a holiday—a four-month cruise. It was probably the last holiday she'd have.

Despite recent setbacks, he was still confident the plan would work. The day after she was due to return to Watervale, he planned to make it known the holiday hadn't been able to slow the downward turn of her health and he'd had no choice but to settle her into a nursing home in Sydney. He'd make it clear it was what she wanted and that it was for the best.

No one would question his decision and if the truth were known, no one would even care. In recent years, Rosemary had kept more and more to herself. The few women she'd fostered friendships with had either faded away or had been the wives of his police colleagues. He was more than confident there would be no questions asked from that quarter.

Watervale would continue as normal. In time, Rosemary Watson would be forgotten. Eventually, it would almost be like she'd ceased to exist.

It was only with the return of her daughter that his plan had begun to fray at the edges.

Darryl drew in a deep breath and released it slowly, allowing the tension to ease from his shoulders. He was damned if he'd let his stepdaughter ruin everything. He would do whatever it took to see his plan through, including thwarting the overeager detective.

Pretending to get confused over his wife's departure date had been a stroke of genius. It was further proof he had nothing to hide. The detective would know an officer of Darryl's experience would make sure he had a watertight alibi, if it came to that.

It would stand to reason that if he had something to hide, he'd have the date of Rosemary's departure fixed firmly in his mind. Appearing confused about something so important as the date her cruise departed—in effect, the last time he'd seen her—was not an expected way to maintain his cover, if in fact, that was what the detective assumed Darryl had been doing.

Detective Munro.

Darryl frowned in thought. He'd discovered the man had transferred from a command in Sydney. That, in itself, was suspicious. The fact he had family in the nearby area didn't cut it. No one as young as Munro elected to be transferred to a backwater like Watervale without being prompted from someone higher up.

There was more to Munro's transfer than he was letting on. Darryl would bet on it and he never wagered on something he knew he wouldn't win.

It was just the way he was.

CHAPTER 7

Kate secured the sash of her thick terry housecoat around her waist and picked up the cup of hot soup. She sank into the motel room's solitary armchair and tried to focus on the evening news that blared from the television a few feet away.

She took a bite of her microwave dinner and sighed. Not exactly gourmet dining, but she hadn't felt like socializing and the room service menu had been unilaterally uninspiring. In a town the size of Watervale, word was probably already out that she'd returned. No doubt her disappearance a decade ago had conjured up wild stories and people would be keen to see her for themselves.

Not that she cared what anyone thought. All she wanted was to find her mother and return to her life in London. She might have told Detective Munro she suspected her mother had met with foul play, but for all of her suspicions, she hadn't given up hope Rosemary was still alive and that there was a reasonable explanation for her lack of communication.

A sharp rap at the door caught her attention. Her pulse jumped. The only person who knew where she was staying was the detective. Unless he'd told someone—someone like Darryl.

Fear clawed at her throat. Darryl knew she was in town and he knew why. He also knew she'd gone to the police. Anger lit up inside her: The detective had ratted her out.

Stupid, so stupid for her to have thought she could trust him. He was a cop. They were all the same. Part of an impenetrable boys' club. She knew that. She'd always known it. She'd fallen for his knock-out smile and the understanding she thought she'd glimpsed in the dark depths of his sparkling brown eyes.

The knock came again, this time more insistent. Adrenaline surged through her. She refused to be a victim again. Hunting around for a weapon, she came up with nothing but a four-inch stiletto. It would have to do. She'd aim it straight for Darryl's eyes.

Plastering herself against the wall nearest the door, she moved the curtain an inch and peeked out through the dirty window. The dim fluorescent light outside her door barely breached the inky blackness. She caught a glimpse of worn jeans and a blue chambray shirt and the air left her body in a rush.

It was him. Poster-boy.

And then her insides knotted up for an entirely different reason.

———————

Riley knew she was in there. He'd seen the slight movement by the window right after he'd knocked. Besides, the room was lit up, the TV was on and a small white rental car was parked right outside the room. If she'd wanted to pretend she wasn't in, she'd have to make a better effort than that.

"Miss Collins, it's Riley Munro. I know you're in there. Please open the door. We need to talk."

A moment later, the wooden panel eased open and Kate stared back at him, motionless. Her eyes were huge in her pale face. Within seconds, he'd taken in her shower-damp hair and housecoat.

Housecoat? Christ, it was only a little after six. Who went to bed at that hour?

She lifted her chin and crossed her arms in front of her. The defensive movement lifted her breasts, deepening the shadow between them. Riley's body tightened and he fought to maintain his neutral expression.

"What are you doing here?"

Her words sounded brave, but he caught the tremor in her voice. The light glanced off a shiny black sandal in her hand. It had a vicious-looking heel. He frowned.

"Who were you expecting?"

Her hand fell to her side, but she didn't release her grip on the shoe. He lifted his hands in surrender. "I come in peace, I swear."

Mistrust darkened her eyes. She bit her lip and indecision colored her cheeks. He snatched a breath, her easy beauty suddenly confining his oxygen.

Then she turned abruptly and took a seat in an armchair that had seen better days. In fact, the whole room had seen better days. Riley's gaze wandered over the cracked paintwork and faded carpet. She seemed so out of place, surrounded by its dinginess. Like a rare orchid in a bed of geraniums.

He closed the door and sat on the edge of the only bed. It was still made up, although the cushions had been pushed to the floor. *At least he hadn't pulled her out of bed.*

The thought dropped a tumbler-full of erotic images into his mind. Long, sleek limbs...full, soft breasts and those luscious lips. His cock stirred. He clenched his jaw on a groan.

"What are you doing here, Detective?"

Her voice had gained strength, dragging him from his lurid thoughts. He scrubbed his fingers through his hair and then sighed and dropped his hand to his side. "I stopped by your stepfather's house this afternoon."

"I know."

"Of course you do. You were there." It was only when he'd spied the rental car outside her room that he'd realized it was the car he'd seen outside Watson's.

She held his gaze for a moment and then turned her face away. "You saw me."

"Yes, though you managed to surprise me. I thought you hated the man."

She turned back to face him. "You misunderstood me, Detective. I don't just hate him; I *despise* him."

The venom in her voice was palpable. After his run-in with Watson, he could almost understand her animosity. Still, she'd left home ten years ago. Surely that was long enough to get over some silly teenage disagreement?

"Did you speak with him?" he asked.

A shudder ran through her body. Her arms came around once again to tighten across her chest. Riley kept his gaze studiously averted from her breasts.

"No. I stayed in the car."

He cleared his throat. "I talked to Darryl. Nice house. Someone has a fine eye for detail. The place looks like something out of *House and Garden*." He eyeballed her. "I'm curious; what was it like growing up there?"

Her expression closed. He could almost see her shutting down. Her eyes lost their sparkle, lips compressed and color fled from her cheeks. He was left facing an emotionless mask. Something indefinable tugged at his gut. Bracing himself, he waited for her to answer.

She stared blindly at the television. When she finally spoke, her voice was raw. "I ran away when I was fourteen. How do you think it was?"

He studied the pain on her face, wanting to look away, but needing to gauge its legitimacy. Watson was a selfish, egotistical pig, but that didn't make him a murderer. And yet, that was exactly what Kate wanted Riley to believe. He needed to find out why.

"I've been meaning to ask you about that," he replied.

She swung around to face him and her eyes flashed fire. "My leaving has nothing to do with it. My mother knew Darryl and I didn't get on. I called her from a payphone a couple of weeks after I left. I told her I had to get away. She was upset, but she understood. That was it. I got on with my life and we stayed in regular contact. Her disappearance has nothing to do with me. I don't know how many times I have to tell you: It's Darryl you ought to be looking at."

"That's part of the problem, Blondie. You keep insisting he's responsible and yet there's not a shred of evidence that points to him. In fact, there's not a shred of evidence your mother's met with foul play."

She opened her mouth to protest, but he cut her off. "I saw a brochure on the coffee table at Darryl's house. Princess Cruises. The same cruise line your mother booked with. I rang the travel agency. They confirmed the booking. The only thing that's out of order is the fact that the ship's purser told me she didn't board."

Kate gasped. "Sh-she's not on the ship? Is that what you're saying?"

Riley nodded. "Apparently not. Darryl says he drove her down to Sydney to embark. Took her right to the wharf, or so he says, but I had the purser check the manifests. Twice. Your mother didn't board."

"What if Darryl's lying? What if he didn't take her down there at all? What if he's lying about the whole thing?"

"Okay, but he's gone to a lot of trouble. The brochure in the house, the travel agent. They both support his story."

Kate's eyes narrowed. "You don't know him like I do. He's cunning. He's sly. He knows how to cover his tracks."

"Why would he do that? What reason would he have to do away with your mother? They've been together for twenty years. Why now?"

She turned away from him, veiling her eyes behind a thick blanket of lashes. Her arms once again were folded across her chest.

He stood and crowded her with his body, refusing to allow her to withdraw from him again. He needed to know what she was hiding.

"Talk to me, Kate."

She moved away from him and backed up against the door. Her eyes were frantic. "I don't know! I don't know! I don't know why he'd hurt her. All I know is that he *has*! H-he must have! She would have called me, emailed me—done *something!* There's only one reason why she wouldn't—and that's if she *couldn't.* Either he has her locked up somewhere or—or worse and she can't get to a phone or her computer. It's the only thing that makes *sense.*"

Tears spilled onto her cheeks and she brushed them away, her movements jerky. He steeled himself against the desperation in her voice and pressed on.

"Give me a name. Tell me who else I can talk to. I need to talk to someone who knows them, both of them, as well as you do."

"You still don't believe me, do you?" Her voice rang with accusation. He looked away.

"I don't know what to believe, but you're not exactly what I'd call an impartial witness. You've already admitted you have issues with Darryl. You won't tell me what they are; you won't tell me why you left; and you won't tell me why the hell you think Darryl has hurt your mother."

He made an effort to slow his breathing down. "Look at it from my point of view. You turn up after a ten-year absence and start pointing fingers at one of our finest law enforcement officers. An officer who has been married to the same woman for twenty years. An officer with a perfectly unblemished record, not even so much as a parking ticket and certainly no evidence of any domestic violence."

He shook his head. "There's nothing to indicate anything's out of the ordinary in your mother's life except *your* say so...and the basis for your accusations is so flimsy it's almost laughable. She stopped contacting you. So what? It's not a crime to want some time away, time to yourself. If I'd spent more than half of my life in a wheelchair, I'd probably want to get away from everything, too."

Seeing the tension in her body and the mutinous expression on her face, Riley sighed and tiredly ran a hand through his hair. "Look, believe it or not, I'm trying to help you. I know I'm not saying the things you want to hear, but that's my job. I investigate facts, not fantasy. For some reason, you have a beef against your stepfather. Fine. You wouldn't be the first. Shit happens. I've met the man and he's not exactly overflowing with goodness and virtue. But that just makes him a lousy person. It doesn't make him a kill—"

"My mother had a housekeeper," she interrupted. "Mrs Fitzgerald. I'm sure you understand, there are a lot of things that are impossible to do when you can't walk."

She spoke slowly, tiredly. Her shoulders slumped forward. Riley could barely look at the bleak despair that clouded her eyes.

"Okay. That's good." He reached for his notepad and pen. "Let's hope she's still working for them. She could shed some light on your mother's whereabouts. Do you know where she lives?"

"She used to live on Carol Avenue. I'm not sure if she's still there."

He took down the details. "It's a starting point, anyway. I'll chase it up tomorrow."

Tucking the notepad and pen back into his shirt pocket, his gaze drifted around the room and lit on an expensive-looking laptop. A colorful pattern of geometric shapes chased each other around the screen. He looked back at her.

"Darryl said your mother spent a lot of time on the Internet. There was a computer on the desk in the living room when I visited. Do you know what brand she had?"

Kate's eyes widened in confusion at the sudden change in topic, but she answered quickly. "Yes, I do. I bought her a Toshiba laptop a couple of years ago. I sent it to her from the UK."

"Darryl said she was going to take it with her to Skype him from the ship, but for some reason, she left it behind."

Kate paled. Riley stepped forward, alarmed. She stumbled back against the door, her hand up to her mouth, her eyes filled with horror.

"Oh, my God! Her laptop was there? She never goes anywhere without it. That computer is her life; it's her window to the world. Oh, my God! He's killed her! I told you! He's killed her! I know it! I just *know* it!"

Without warning, she turned and pummeled Riley's chest with her fists. He braced himself against the attack, holding his arms straight at his sides until she calmed enough that he could stop her without force.

His heart constricted at the sight of fresh tears welling up in her eyes. A shiny wisp of blond hair fell across her face. She scraped it away with impatient fingers. Finally, her tortured gaze found his.

"Why won't you *believe* me? How many times do I have to *tell* you? He's done something to her. You have to make him tell me where she is!" Her voice cracked. As if a torrent had been unleashed, she cried in heartbreaking sobs.

With fierce reluctance, his arms came up around her and he drew her in close against his chest. She cried against his shirt. He tried not to think how well her head fit the hollow of his shoulder.

Long moments later, she pulled away and stared up at him. Her face was red and blotchy. She sniffed and then looked away.

He pulled a clean handkerchief out of his pocket and handed it over to her. She took it in silence, her eyes conveying her thanks. He turned away and walked back to the bed.

What the hell was he doing? Another minute or two and he would have been crushing those oh-so-kissable lips against his and to hell with everything. He no longer doubted her mother was missing, but had she disappeared voluntarily or was there something more sinister at play? And, if so, who was responsible?

He'd formed his own opinion of Watson. The man was a right royal prick, but as Riley had told Kate, it didn't make him a murderer. And why would Watson have come up with such a far-fetched story to explain her absence? A wheel-chair bound woman who couldn't swim and hated the water had gone cruising on the high seas? It was totally and utterly unbelievable. He must have known people would be doubtful. A cop of Watson's caliber and experience would know that the implausibility of his story would be the first thing the police would seize upon. Of all the ways Riley could describe the former commander, stupid wasn't one of them.

Darryl had been married to Rosemary for two decades. Why would he suddenly decide she had to be done away with? If things had really gotten that rough, divorce was a hell of a lot less risky than murder, even for an ex-cop who knew the ropes.

And what about Kate? Beautiful, distant... He sensed she hid a lifetime of secrets. There was more to her fallout with Darryl than she was telling. Far more, if the bitterness in her eyes at every mention of his name was anything to go by.

It troubled him that her insistence on Darryl's guilt might have arisen from a different motive—something related to her volatile past—and have nothing to do with the woman who may or may not have come to a violent end.

He raised his gaze to hers and tried to ignore the vulnerability that stared back at him.

"Tell me about your mother's will."

Kate's breath caught in her throat. Her pulse rate skyrocketed. How the hell had he found out? No one knew about the will. No one but her and her mother and the lawyer who'd drafted it.

There was no way her mother would have told Darryl. She was the one who'd sworn Kate to secrecy—had made her swear it on her life.

She swallowed the lump of emotion that had lodged itself in her throat and steadied her gaze on Riley. She hadn't called him Riley—not to his face—but that was the way she'd begun to think of him. A strong and sexy name; it was perfect for him. Too bad he was one of *them*.

How much did he know? Maybe he was just fishing?

Maybe he didn't know anything about it at all. She decided to call his bluff.

"How would I know anything about my mother's will? I've been living in the UK for the last three years. Besides, it's none of my business. I've never even discussed it with her." The lie tasted bitter on her lips, but she held his gaze without flinching.

Which wasn't easy.

He seemed to see right through her, right into her soul, right into the place where her darkest secrets had been buried for more than ten years.

But that was impossible. He knew nothing about her. No one did. She'd told Cally about it once, but they'd both been children and her secret had been way beyond what either of them knew how to deal with. After that, she'd given up.

Well, if you called running away giving up. She called it survival.

Kate felt the heat of his gaze on her face and swallowed. His voice was soft in the tense silence.

"Why are you lying to me?"

Her gaze skittered away. Guilt burned up her neck, scorching her with its relentless heat. "I-I'm not."

"Bullshit." The same mild tone was now laced with steel.

She gritted her teeth and thought fast. She couldn't tell him the truth. *Could* she?

His gaze felt as heavy as her secrets. Coolly assessing, waiting, watching, probing for a chink in her armor.

He moved closer, looming over her.

"Your mother made a will right about the time *you* said she went missing. I only have your word that you don't know you're the sole beneficiary." His eyes hardened. "And right now, Blondie, your word's worth squat."

CHAPTER 8

Riley frowned unseeingly at the paperwork that lay on the desk in front of him and thought about last night. Kate had appeared surprised when he'd dropped his bombshell about her mother's will, but what did he really know about her? She could be an award-winning actress, for all he knew.

He hadn't forgotten how quickly she'd composed herself after her loss of control during their first interview. She'd told him she was an art dealer, but he hadn't even bothered to check her story. She'd told him Darryl was a murderer. She'd told him a lot of things.

If she'd known about the will beforehand, it gave her a strong motive to make her mother disappear—except that under New South Wales law, they had to find a body before she could make a claim. Maybe she didn't know that? Or, maybe she was just biding her time, waiting for the right moment? Building suspicion against her stepfather slowly but surely so that when a suitable amount of time had elapsed, she could "discover" the body and watch Darryl hang for it.

Was she really that vindictive? That cold? That calculating?

He shook his head to stem the jumble of thoughts. Until now, he prided himself on being an astute judge of character. Had his hormones gotten his head totally confused? Was he looking past the obvious because he wanted her? Or, perversely, was that the reason he kept trying to find excuses for her guilt?

Had his self-esteem been damaged more than he wanted to admit when Iris left him for another man? He could now see he'd had a lucky escape, but at the time, he'd been devastated. Was there some kind of residual hurt he'd refused to recognize, or did he subconsciously feel the need to jeopardize his next relationship?

What the hell was he talking about? A relationship? He and Kate weren't in a *relationship*, or anything like it, for Christ's sake.

He glanced up and caught sight of his boss strolling into the squad room. He stifled a groan.

Great. Just what he needed.

He reached across his desk and made a grab for his morning coffee. He was going to need a caffeine hit to get through this one.

"Good morning, Detective Munro. How are things?" The suit was flashy, the comb-over still wet.

Riley smiled through gritted teeth. "Fine thanks, sir."

"You found that cow yet?"

Riley shook his head and filled his mouth with coffee so he didn't say something he'd regret.

"I spoke to Commander Watson last night. He was a bit upset after your visit." Hannaford's tone was still light but the black eyes that pinned Riley had a feral gleam.

"I thought I told you to stay away from him? You're not trying to cause trouble are you, Munro? Perhaps I should call your old commander—Detective Inspector Shattler, wasn't it? I'm sure Commander Watson knows him. They've both been in the force for decades."

Riley eyeballed his superior, refusing to back down. "I was merely following up on a missing person's report that was made last week."

"You were enquiring as to the whereabouts of Commander Watson's wife. I believe he told you she was holidaying." Hannaford's eyes narrowed. "Need I remind you, Munro, that Commander Watson is a pillar of Watervale society? He has had to put up with a lot in his life. He gave everything he had to this town, kept it in good shape for more than twenty-five years and in his down time, he cared for his disabled wife and her child. The man's a saint.

"That stepdaughter of his was nothing but trouble, right from the start. She had a penchant for telling lies. She used to give Darryl grief like you've never seen. Most of the town breathed a sigh of relief when she up and left."

"That's not the way she tells it."

Hannaford shook his head and looked down at Riley with growing anger. "You're not listening to me, Munro. The girl was trouble. Hell, she wouldn't know the truth if it came knocking on her door. Between her and that little Savage slut she used to hang around, I don't know how Darryl put up with it."

Riley frowned at the mention of the name Savage. Sonia had mentioned it on Friday night, at the bar. Cally Savage had been Kate's school friend. He'd meant to look up her father.

He made a note on the pad in front of him, catching Hannaford's frown out of the corner of his eye.

"Are you listening to me, Munro? Let me make myself clear: I don't want Commander Watson being annoyed again. If you want to know anything about his family, you come to me. Got it?"

Riley didn't bother to conceal his surprise. "I didn't realize you knew them so well."

Hannaford's face became shuttered. "Let's just say, I'm a good friend of the family." He turned and heaved his bulk toward his office before Riley had the chance to question him further.

With the late afternoon sun glinting off the aluminium window frames of the Watervale Police Station, Riley dialed the number Cally Savage's father had given him. The man had been oddly curious about why Riley needed to contact his daughter, but Riley resisted the man's pointed questions and had politely left his house.

The phone rang out for what seemed forever. He was about to hang up when it was answered.

"Cally Savage."

"Oh, hello. It's Detective Munro from the Watervale Police Station. I was wondering if I could talk to you about Kate Col—I mean, Kate Watson?"

"Kate Watson? You mean the Kate Watson whose stepfather's the Police Commander?"

"Yes, although Darryl's no longer the commander. He retired a few months ago. I understand you knew Kate from school?"

"Yes, we were friends when we were kids. She's all right, isn't she? I mean, you're not calling because something's happened to her, are you?"

He noted the concern in her voice and hastened to reassure her. "No, nothing like that. She's fine. In fact, she looks great. She goes by the name of Collins now."

There was silence on the other end of the line. Riley heard the sound of a child calling out in the background. When Cally spoke again, her voice was rough with emotion.

"Collins. That's her father's name. Her *real* father. I'm not surprised she ditched Watson. She couldn't stand that man."

Riley sat up straighter, flicking the lid off his pen and drawing his notepad closer. "Really? Even back then?"

"Yes, Detective. Even back then. *Especially* back then. Darryl Watson used to make my skin crawl. He was one of those guys you didn't want to be around. The few times I did visit Kate at her place, I made sure I was never alone with him."

A slow, hard thud started in Riley's chest. He stared blindly at the blank page in front of him. "Did she ever say anything to you about Watson hurting her?"

Cally's voice lowered, becoming harder to hear over the noise in the background. He strained to hear her words over the phone.

"I don't think I should say anything more, Detective. Not before I talk to Kate."

Stifling his disappointment, Riley thanked her for her help. "I'll give you my number. Who knows? You might remember something you think I should know."

After giving her his contact details, he ended the call. Images swirled around in his head as he tried to make sense of what she'd told him—or, more to the point, what she hadn't.

Could Darryl Watson have abused his stepdaughter? Was that the reason for her sudden flight and continued animosity more than a decade later? Was this her way of evening up the score? Or was it just another example of the Kate Watson described by others—the trouble-seeking teenager, teller of tall tales?

He dragged air deep into his lungs and held it there until his pulse slowed. If Kate had been abused, as abhorrent as the thought was, it gave her a strong motive for wanting to see her abuser suffer.

Setting her stepfather up for questioning about his wife's disappearance by repeatedly telling the police her mother had been murdered could lead to charges being laid against the former commander, if someone bothered enough to investigate—someone like him. Someone new to town, someone who didn't have an emotional connection to the man who'd been given the keys to Watervale.

Especially if the missing woman didn't materialize. Maybe it was all part of Kate's charade? To make him think she relied upon him; to act like she needed him.

Had she set out to bamboozle him with her beauty and vulnerability so he would eat up her story and set about destroying the man who'd destroyed her?

Unless the abuse theory was utter bullshit. Then his prognosis went down the toilet about as fast as bad seafood and he was back where he'd started.

But the thought persisted. Did Kate really believe her mother had been murdered, or was it all just an elaborate ploy?

Revenge was a dish best served cold. Or so they said.

Riley shook his head in disbelief. Cold...? More like frozen. And if he really believed Kate had been abused, what did he intend to do about it?

The ringing of the phone on the bedside table in Kate's room at The Jackeroo pierced the silence. She tensed. She'd been in town nearly a week and it hadn't rung the entire time. Her thoughts skittered around who it might be. None of them were comforting.

The plaintive noise continued and she shook her head with impatience. For God's sake, is this what her life had come to? Jittery over answering a damned phone?

She strode over and picked it up. "Kate Collins."

There was a slight hesitation and then she heard a voice from her past that sent relief flooding through her limbs.

"Hello, Kate. It's Cally."

"Cally? Cally *Savage*? I don't believe it! How on earth did you know I was here? How are you? *Where* are you?"

Cally's laughter sounded just as it had when they were teenagers. It was almost as if the years hadn't moved forward at all.

"Whoa, Kate! One question at a time. You certainly haven't changed. I never could get a word in edgewise."

Kate drew in a breath and tried to control the leap of gladness in her heart. It had been too long since she'd shared a conversation with a friend. A real friend. Over the years since she'd left, she hadn't felt comfortable letting her guard down and had formed only passing acquaintances with the people she'd come into contact with. Even her assistants didn't know much more about her other than she'd moved to London from Australia.

"Cally, it's so great to hear from you. Tell me everything."

There was silence on the other end of the phone. Kate wondered at it, her curiosity piqued. She hadn't spoken to

Cally in more than ten years. She had no idea what twists and turns her friend had traveled in her life since then.

"Cally, are you all right?"

"Yes, I'm fine," came the soft reply. "I guess you haven't heard?"

Kate was gripped with foreboding. "Heard what?"

"I'm living in Armidale with my aunt. I-I have a son. Jack. He's eight."

Kate did the quick calculation in her head. "Eight? Cally, you must have been—?"

"Yes. I was sixteen. I dated Lachlan Brady in high school. I-I got pregnant."

"Wow," Kate murmured, trying to process the news that her best friend had a child by a member of one of Watervale's most prominent families. "Wow, you and Lachlan Brady. I can't believe it. How is he?"

"W-we're not together anymore. In fact, we haven't been together since before Jack was born."

"Oh, I see." Kate couldn't think of anything else to say.

"Enough about me, I'm dying to know what happened to you. It was almost as if you'd disappeared into thin air. You'd talked about leaving, of course, but I had no idea you meant it. When your mom told me you'd been in contact..."

Kate heaved a sigh. It would be a relief to talk to someone about it, someone who knew her from way back when.

"I know. It wasn't exactly planned. One night I just made up my mind to leave. I packed a bag and hopped a bus to Sydney. I'm sorry I didn't call you. Mom told me she'd let you know."

"I can't believe how brave you were. You make it sound so simple and I'm sure it was anything but. I don't know if I'd have had the courage to do it back then."

Kate brushed aside the admiration in Cally's voice. "It's amazing what you can do when you don't have a choice."

"Don't I know it," Cally murmured, her voice rough with emotion.

Tears pricked Kate's eyes. She couldn't begin to imagine

Cally's life, raising a child alone, and yet her friend didn't sound unhappy. Kate had never allowed herself to imagine a family of her own. A family meant letting someone get close and that wasn't something she was prepared to do.

But listening to Cally speak about her son, she felt a yearning that was completely foreign. When at last the feeling subsided, she felt emptier than she had for a long time.

Tucking her emotions firmly back into the box where she'd locked them for so many years, she cleared her throat and spoke again. "How did you find me?"

"I had a call from a police officer from Watervale—a Detective Munro. He was asking questions about you and Darryl."

Kate's stomach dropped like she'd just stepped into a free-falling elevator. A buzzing sound filled her ears and she had to strain to hear Cally.

"I didn't tell him much. I wanted to talk to you first."

Kate found her voice at last. "I'm glad you did."

"I realized if the police from Watervale were calling to ask about you, there was a fair chance you'd returned home. I rang all five motels in town. The Jackeroo confirmed you were a guest and put me through to your room. I hope you don't mind. I really wanted to talk to you. Not just about that, but...everything." Cally's voice faded into a murmur of hesitation and uncertainty.

"Of course, Cally. Of course I don't mind," Kate hastened to reassure her. "It's great to hear from you. I only wish you were still here, so we could meet in person. I could do with a hug right about now."

"I'm hearing you, Kate. It's been a long time for me, too."

A moment passed. Cally broke the silence. "What brings you back to Watervale? And please tell me why the police are asking questions about you."

Kate sucked in a breath and held it for as long as she could. In silence, she willed the heavy knot of dread that lay deep inside her to ease. "My mother's missing."

"Oh, Kate! That's awful!"

"Yes." It was all she could manage.

"Do the police have any idea where she might be?"

She cleared her throat again. "No, not at this stage. Darryl told them she'd gone on a cruise, but the police have since discovered she didn't board the ship. Right now, no one knows what's happened to her."

"Oh, Kate, that's terrible. They're not suspecting foul play, are they?"

Kate bit her lip, fighting the despair that threatened to overwhelm her. "I-I don't know what they think," she whispered.

"I don't know what to say, Kate. I wish I was there to give you a hug."

"Me, too."

Images of Riley bombarded Kate's thoughts and her stomach clenched in response. Those eyes, that smile, the utter confidence he exuded—like nothing and no one could stand in his way.

As if reading her mind, Cally chuckled in her ear. "I'm not sure what he looks like, but that detective sure sounded yummy on the phone."

Kate's pulse quickened. An awkward laugh escaped. "Yeah, he's pretty easy on the eye."

"I *knew* it. I bet he's got a body to die for."

"*Mm*, yeah, he's got it all happening there, too."

"Oh, Kate," Cally squealed, reminding her of when they were teenagers. "It sounds like you know him pretty well."

Kate's cheeks went hot. "He's a police officer, Cally. You, of all people, know how I feel about them. And anyway, my life's in England, now. Watervale holds nothing but bad memories."

"You and I have a lot in common. I haven't been home since before Jack was born," Cally admitted quietly.

Kate felt a burst of surprise. "What about your mom and dad? Don't they still live here?"

"Mom died a few years ago. As far as I know, Dad's still there."

"I'm sorry, Cally. You and your mom were pretty close."

"Not as close as I thought."

Kate took a moment to process Cally's words. She wondered what had happened to change things.

Cally sighed. "It's a long story and one best not told over the phone. We should make plans to meet up somewhere."

A tiny smile tugged at Kate's lips. "I'd like that."

Listen, I'm going to have to go. Jack's calling out for me. Is there anything I can do to help find your mother?"

Unwilling to worry Cally with her fears, she hastened to reassure her. "No, no. It will be fine. I'm sure she'll turn up somewhere."

"Well, if you're sure there's nothing I can do—?"

"I'm sure. But thanks for offering. And it's been great to hear from you."

After exchanging contact details and promises to speak again soon, Kate ended the call and slumped down on the bed.

Memories of her stunted youth crowded her head and along with them, the fear. The only bright points of her entire childhood had been the stolen hours she'd spent alone with her mother and the times when she'd been able to escape with Cally, running through the mist-laden forest on the edge of town. Dense with undergrowth, the smell of damp soil had filled her nostrils. Running through the forest as fast as she could had helped to keep the fear away, at least for a little while.

But that was years ago. She was an adult now and she couldn't keep running away, no matter how much she wished differently.

CHAPTER 9

Riley parked his iridescent green police vehicle outside the offices of Cole & Westport. It was almost a week since he'd taken the initial report from Kate and he was no closer to discovering the truth. His call to the Watson's housekeeper had gone unanswered, so he'd turned his attention to the next person on his list: Rosemary Watson's lawyer. He'd spied the firm's logo on the cover page of her will. A call to directory assistance had done the rest.

The law firm was one of four that serviced the town and its surrounds and was known for its representation of blue-collar clients. Not the sort of firm he'd expect Watson to patronize, but maybe that was the reason his wife had chosen it.

The old weather-board house which served as office premises had been freshly painted and looked smart, but not intimidating. Twin borders of dwarf agapanthus lined the concrete walkway which led to the front door, providing the only visible greenery in the winter-bare garden.

As he entered the house, the heavy scent of roses assailed his nostrils. His gaze was drawn to the reception desk, where a huge bouquet of blood-red flowers had been arranged in a crystal vase. The middle-aged woman sitting behind the counter caught him looking at the display and smiled a little self-consciously.

"They're from my husband. It's our anniversary. Twenty-seven years today. He really shouldn't have. They must have cost a fortune this time of year." The smile softened. "But roses are my favorite."

The look on her face made something grip Riley's heart tightly. He wondered what it would be like to love someone so long and so well. He fought to keep his expression neutral.

With a slight shake of her head, she offered a rueful smile. "I'm sorry, I shouldn't be rabbiting on like that. What can I do for you?"

"I'm Detective Riley Munro. I called earlier. I'm here to see Ronald Westport."

"Of course, Detective. Just take a seat. I'll let him know you're here."

Riley headed for one of the vacant chairs that lined the walls of the sparsely furnished waiting area. Only one other client sat in the room. The man's grizzled cheeks and red-rimmed eyes suggested he'd survived a hard night—or maybe three.

Riley reached for a fishing magazine from the pile on a low pine table in the middle of the room. Settling back against his chair, he flicked through it, barely registering the pictures that filled its glossy pages.

Tossing the magazine back onto the pile, he sat forward and thrummed his fingers against his knees. Patience had never been one of his virtues.

An occasional whiff of stale tobacco wafted toward him from the man in the corner. Riley's heart rate spiked and he bit down on the almost primeval surge of need. What he'd give for a satisfying drag of poisonous chemicals deep into his lungs. He'd quit over a year ago, but he still craved nicotine like a newborn baby craves milk. It was stupid and it was deadly, but it wasn't called an addiction for nothing.

"Detective Munro? Mr Westport will see you now."

Riley bit back on a sigh of relief and stood. The door near the receptionist's desk opened and an elderly gentleman with a full head of snowy white hair stepped into the waiting room and held out his hand.

"Detective Munro, I'm Ronald Westport. Please, come through."

They walked past partitioned walls that dulled the sound of keyboards and murmured conversations and turned into a well-appointed, corner office. The bright, mid-morning sunshine filtered through the oversized windows and bounced off an impressive array of framed certificates, gilding the room with light. A huge oak desk dominated the room, almost bowing under the weight of a paper stack of other peoples' problems.

"Take a seat," the lawyer offered, squeezing his sparse frame between the desk and his faux-leather chair and the boxes of files piled high on the floor behind him.

"So, Detective, what can I do for you?"

Riley sat forward, reassured by the keen light of intelligence leveled at him from the other man's eyes. "I'm here about Rosemary Watson."

Something flared in the blue orbs that studied him. "Ah, Rosemary Watson." His voice held an air of finality. "I wondered if the police would be stopping by."

———————

She could do it.

She knew she could. For her mother's sake, she could do this.

Kate's heart thudded against her ribcage. She stared at the nondescript building which housed the local constabulary. The ordinariness of its facade mocked her. A building as plain and common as it was shouldn't have had the power to instill the bone-numbing fear she felt at the thought of stepping inside it. Again.

Of course, it wasn't the building. It was what it represented that terrified her: The Police brotherhood: All for one and one for all. Too bad she was completely out of options.

She had to see Riley again. It was imperative to know whether he'd discovered anything about the whereabouts of her mother. She straightened her spine and told herself that walking into the Watervale Police Station was a world easier than it would be to walk into No.16 Baxter Road.

Kate blotted at the film of perspiration that had gathered on her upper lip, despite the crispness of the wintery day. Scrabbling around in her handbag for a tube of lip gloss, she swiped a generous amount across her parched lips. Patting a non-existent stray strand of hair against the tight confines of her bun, she squared her shoulders and opened the car door.

Her confident stride across the asphalt and up the front stairs of the station belied the tangle of nerves and nausea that jostled for position inside her. The mantra repeated itself in her head: *I can do this*. After all, she was good at facades. Her whole life had been an illusion.

Riley stared back in confusion at the unflinching gaze of Ronald Westport. The lawyer's words hit the back of Riley's skull and bounced forward. "I'm afraid I don't understand."

Westport's narrow face grew somber. Splicing his fingers together, he rested his chin on the makeshift platform and placed his elbows among the mess of papers on his desk.

"Mrs Watson came to see me about five weeks ago. I was surprised to see her. I've known her husband, Darryl, of course, for years in his role as the Local Area Commander and even before then, but I've never done any work for either of them. Darryl favored one of my opposition up on Main Street."

"What did she come to see you about?"

The lawyer's mouth tightened. "Is she dead, Detective Munro? Is that why you're here?"

"No, no, nothing like that," Riley hastened to reassure him and prayed silently that was true.

"Then I'm afraid I can't tell you. I'm sure you've heard of client confidentiality and legal professional privilege."

"Of course, it's just that when you said you'd been

expecting the police, I assumed Mrs Watson had told you something that would lead you to make such a statement. You must agree, it's a fairly odd thing to say."

Westport's eye contact didn't falter. "Mrs Watson asked me to draft her a new will. I assume you already know that, or you wouldn't be here. Apart from that, I can't tell you, other than to say she left with me a sealed envelope that was to be opened in the event of her death."

Riley went to speak, but Westport cut him off. "Before you ask, I don't know the contents of the envelope, Detective. She gave it to me already sealed. I witnessed her signature across the seal and locked it in my safe." His eyes filled with challenge. "And there it will stay until you furnish me with a Death Certificate."

Riley sat back against the hard wood of his chair. "You're right," he replied, his tone affable. "I saw your logo on the bottom of Rosemary's will." His gaze drilled into the lawyer's. "I also know what's in it."

Westport refused to be intimidated, shrugging as he began to shuffle files around his desk. "So, you read the will. What more can I tell you?"

"Did she come in alone?"

Furrows dug deep across the mottled forehead. "Yes, she did. I can't say if someone dropped her off here or if she caught a cab, but she did ask my receptionist to call the disabled taxi when it was time for her to leave."

"How did she appear?"

The lawyer frowned again. "What's this all about, Detective? I might be old, but I'm not stupid. If Rosemary Watson's not dead, then something else is going on."

"You're right. Again. There is something going on. I'm just not sure what it is, yet."

"Have you spoken to her husband?"

"Yes, of course. He told me she'd gone on a holiday. Did Rosemary say anything to you about going away?"

"No, she didn't mention anything like that. She wanted to have the will prepared and finalized as quickly as possible, but she said nothing about leaving town."

"How quickly?"

"Normally, I take instructions at the first appointment and then get the client to come back in a couple of weeks later to approve the draft. Once that's done, the will is finalized and executed before the requisite witnesses.

"Mrs Watson didn't want to do that. She waited outside in reception until I'd prepared a will based on her instructions and she signed it the same day."

"How long did she wait?"

"I guess it must have been at least a couple of hours."

Riley sat forward again. "That's a little odd, don't you think? Especially given that she lives in town. Did she say anything about why she was in such a hurry?"

Westport shook his head. "No, the only thing she did say was that she didn't want to have to make another trip downtown to see me. Something about the cost of the disabled taxi, if I recall."

Riley pulled out his notebook and scribbled in it.

Westport frowned. "This is all off the record, Detective. I probably shouldn't be saying anything at all."

"Mr Westport, Rosemary Watson is missing. No one's seen or heard from her for over a month. Not even her daughter."

The lawyer's face paled. "Not even Kate? Rosemary would never cut off contact with Kate. Not after what happened." His eyes narrowed. "You do know about...?"

Riley offered a tight nod. "I know Kate ran away from home at fourteen."

Westport nodded. "Rosemary told me about it when she attended upon my office. I'd heard the rumors, of course. Watervale's a small town and we were talking about the daughter of the Local Area Commander."

"Stepdaughter," Riley said.

Westport shrugged. "Stepdaughter, whatever. I understood from Rosemary she married Darryl when Kate was a small child?"

Riley opened his mouth to answer, but the lawyer cut him off with a shake of his head. "It doesn't matter. Rosemary said she was devastated when Kate left. I can't believe she'd cease to have contact with her. If what you say is true, there must be something terribly wrong."

Dread slowly uncoiled in Riley's gut. Was Kate right? Maybe Darryl *had* done something to her mother? But, if so, what was in it for him? Rosemary's will had left everything to her daughter.

Another thought occurred to him. "Did Rosemary tell Kate about the contents of her new will?"

"Without Rosemary's consent, I'd rather not say any more."

Riley gritted his teeth. "Mr Westport, I'm investigating Mrs Watson's disappearance. It's possible the woman's been murdered. I understand your obligation to your client, but in the circumstances, surely you can see how your information might assist me." Riley fought to keep his voice even. "I'd like to ask you again: Did Rosemary Watson tell you she'd spoken to Kate about it?"

The lawyer closed his eyes. His shoulders slumped. When he opened them again, the expression in them was one of sadness and finality. "Yes, she did."

Thoughts ricocheted through Riley's head.

Kate had lied to him.

She'd told him she'd never discussed the will with her mother. Why had she lied? He was on her side. *Wasn't* he?

The truth of it was, he didn't know what to believe. Kate's distress over her missing mother seemed genuine, but she appeared to have a lot of reasons for wanting to make Darryl's life difficult—including her as yet untold reasons for running away. He still hadn't gotten to the bottom of that, but his suspicions were more than a little disquieting.

Kate had made no effort to hide how she felt about Darryl: She despised him. She'd used that very word. Was she capable of framing him for something he didn't do? Like *murder*?

Riley frowned and looked across at the lawyer. "What about Darryl? Did he know about it?"

"I don't know. When Rosemary asked for him to be written

out of her will, I advised her on the rights of a spouse, in particular their right to challenge a will."

"What did she say?"

Westport's lips compressed and his gaze turned somber. "She told me that challenging the will would be the last thing on Darryl's mind."

CHAPTER 10

Kate pushed open the glass door that led into the waiting room of the Watervale Police Station. Her earlier panic had made her short of breath, but she'd managed to quell the nausea and now just wanted to get it over with.

"Can I help you?"

She walked closer to the high counter and tried to smile at the young officer who stood behind it. His cheeks were as shiny as his hair. He looked fresh out of the Academy.

"Yes, I'm Kate Collins. I was wondering if Detective Munro's available?"

"I'll phone upstairs and find out for you. Won't be a minute."

Kate turned away from the boy's appreciative gaze and willed her apprehension to settle. Minutes later, footsteps sounded in the stairwell. Bracing herself for his assault upon her senses, she turned to face Riley.

It wasn't him.

Disappointment flooded through her. An unfamiliar, plainclothes officer strode forward, his arm extended.

"Miss Collins? I'm Detective Chase Barrington."

Kate shook the proffered hand and tried to reorientate her thoughts. She gave him a quick once-over. Dark curly hair grew thickly over a broad, unlined forehead, the riotous waves in keeping with the mischievous glint in his emerald-green eyes. Something tugged at her memory, but she couldn't place him.

"I'm sorry," she murmured. "I was looking for Detective Munro."

"Yeah, so Marty said. Riley's out on a job at the moment. I work with him. I thought I'd come down and see if there was anything I could do to help?"

Kate shook her head and tried again to stem the disappointment. He wasn't there. She'd psyched herself up for nothing.

"You can come upstairs and wait for him, if you like. I'll call him on his cell and let him know you're here."

She shook her head again, more vehemently this time. "Oh, no. Um, I mean, that's fine. I can come back another time."

"He's been gone all morning. He'll probably be back any minute." He extended his arm toward the staircase.

Feeling like she had no choice, Kate reluctantly gave in to the detective's silent encouragement and headed in the direction he indicated. She'd made it this far; she might as well keep going.

Chase's deep drawl followed her up the staircase. "You probably don't remember me, but I used to go to Watervale High. I was a couple of years ahead of you."

Kate wracked her memory, but still came up blank. Irritation surged through her. Any ordinary teenage girl would have branded such a good-looking face into her mind forever and yet, she couldn't place him. It just went to show how screwed up her childhood had been. Looking at boys was the last thing she'd wanted to do.

A flush crept up her neck. Chase drew even with her at the top of the stairs and she turned her face away.

"Hey, don't feel too bad. People are always telling me I have a common face." His grin told her he was joking. Of course he was. He wasn't blind to his attractiveness. And he was very attractive, yet when she stood next to this officer, her heart rate remained steady. Not at all like it was when Riley was around.

As her thoughts returned to the absent detective, she wondered again if she was doing the right thing by waiting for him. The more time she spent in the place, the tenser she became. She hated the station. It had always been Darryl's domain. She'd lost count of the number of times he'd threatened to lock her in the cells if she dared to breathe a word. At the time, she'd had no reason to believe he wouldn't carry out the threat.

"Can I get you a cup of coffee? A can of Coke, maybe?"

Kate stepped into the bustle of the squad room and her feet slowed. She glanced up at Chase and tried to remember what he'd just said. Something about a drink. She shook her head. "I'm fine, thanks."

"No worries," he grinned affably. "I'll go and call Riley and let him know you're here. Why don't you take a seat at his desk? It's right over there."

Kate turned to follow the direction he'd indicated. A cluttered desk, identical to the other half dozen desks that crowded the room, stood about thirty feet away. She drew in a breath and made her way over to it. She'd wait for Chase to call Riley, but if he couldn't reach him, she'd leave.

"Well, well, well. If it isn't little Miss Kathryn."

Kate tensed as an unfamiliar voice came from behind her. Hesitantly, she turned in her chair and took in the portly build and thinning gray hair of the man who had spoken. He was smiling at her with a smugness she found disconcerting.

Did she know him?

He thrust out a fleshy hand and she took it with reluctance. Uneasiness settled like quicksand in her belly.

"Detective Sergeant Mike Hannaford, Local Area Commander," he announced, as if it would jog her memory.

Kate stared at him. "I'm sorry, do I know you?"

Hannaford rocked back on his heels. "Of course you do. I've known you since you were knee high to a grasshopper." His gaze slid over her. "Although I must say, you're not so little anymore. I'm surprised you don't remember me. Your father and I have been friends for years."

Her uneasiness instantly morphed into fear. A pulse

hammered in the side of her neck and her hands grew slick with sweat. A friend of Darryl's was no friend of hers. She rose from the chair and backed away from him, her gaze darting around the room as she searched for Chase.

"Kathryn, are you all right? You're looking faint." His greasy voice glided over her, searching for cracks.

"I'm sorry; I have to go. Tell Detective Munro I'll catch up with him later." She turned and stumbled toward the stairs, biting her tongue to keep the panic at bay. She fled down the steps to the waiting room, almost falling through the glass doors as they opened and released her onto the street below.

Riley glanced at his watch. He hadn't meant to spend so long with the lawyer, but the information he'd discovered had been worth it. His stomach grumbled loudly, reminding him it was going on for lunchtime. His usual chicken and mayo roll and carton of chocolate milk was sitting in the fridge in the tearoom at the station. He'd expected to be back by now.

The phone in his shirt pocket vibrated. He tugged it out and answered the call.

"Chase. What's happening?"

"Yeah, Riley. Kate Watson was just at the station. She wanted to see you."

Riley's pulse leaped. "Was? Where did she go?"

"I don't know. I sat her at your desk and went to take a leak. Next thing I know, she was hurtling out the door." He paused. "I think Hannaford spoke to her."

"That would make anyone head for the door."

Chase laughed. "You've got that right."

"Did she say what she wanted?"

"No, mate. She told Marty she needed to speak to you. I only took her upstairs. I will say one thing, though. She's still a looker."

Riley tried to stem his annoyance. "Did she recognize you?"

"No, I don't think so. She gave me one of those brief, polite-stranger smiles when I introduced myself."

Riley's annoyance was replaced by a surge of satisfaction. "I can see you made a lasting impression in high school."

"Jealousy's a curse, mate."

"As if. It's me she asked for."

"Yeah, yeah, yeah. Tell someone who cares, Munro."

Riley changed the subject. "Did Hannaford say anything to you?"

"Only that Kate said she had to go."

Riley sighed. In a way, he was relieved she'd left. He didn't know whether he was ready to see her again. He hadn't had enough time to process the information Westport had given him and he had yet to talk to Margaret Fitzgerald, the Watsons' housekeeper. After the information he'd received from the lawyer, he was keen to speak to the elusive woman who was a part of the Watsons' daily lives— or at least had been a decade ago.

"Listen, I'm going to be out of the office a bit longer. There's someone else I need to talk to."

"Is this about Kate's mother?"

"Yeah. But keep it to yourself, all right? I want to see if I can work out what's going on. A few things aren't adding up."

"Anything you want me to do?"

"Nah. It'll be fine. It's all hypothetical at this stage. I might catch you for a drink later at The Bullet."

As he ended the call, Riley's thoughts returned to the woman who'd been stealing his sleep. He liked her. He really liked her. And he really wanted to believe her.

He just didn't know if he could...or should.

———————

Much to Riley's relief, when he knocked on the door of

the house owned by Margaret Fitzgerald, it was opened almost immediately.

"Mrs Fitzgerald?"

Inquisitive brown eyes set amongst a lifetime of wrinkles studied him through large tortoise-shell glasses. "Who wants to know?"

"I'm Detective Riley Munro from the Watervale Police Station. I'd like to ask you a few questions about Rosemary Watson."

The elderly woman stared at him. After a moment, she nodded and invited him to follow her inside. After hastily putting together a pot of tea, she ushered him into a sitting room.

"Do you take milk, Detective?" The housekeeper's cloud of gray-blue hair wafted above her ears and across her forehead like cotton candy. Riley was amazed her slight frame had the strength to drag around a dusting cloth, let alone a vacuum cleaner.

"No, thanks Mrs Fitzgerald. Black's fine."

"Call me Maggie, please." The old lady poured tea into matching china teacups and handed one to him. Taking the other cup and saucer, she sat back against the chintz-covered armchair opposite and sighed. "You remind me of my Laurie."

Riley took a cautious sip of tea, mindful not to burn his lips. "Is he your husband?"

Her eyes lost some of their sparkle. "Was. He died over twenty years ago. Cancer." She nodded sagely over the rim of her teacup. "His whole family died from it."

Riley remained silent, not at all sure there was anything he could say. The woman across from him set down her teacup and shrugged.

"Anyway, that's life, as they say. I managed to pick my sorry butt up off the ground and started a life without him. That's when I met the Watsons. I answered an advertisement for a housekeeper in the local paper."

"Tell me about Rosemary."

Maggie's expression softened. "A kinder soul you

wouldn't meet, Detective. It's a dreadful disease, you know. Just dreadful. Some days she can barely hold up her head. And now, as if that poor woman hasn't suffered enough, her eyes are throwing it in."

Riley sat forward. "What do you mean?"

Thin fingers fluttered around her face. "She doesn't want anyone to know, especially not Darryl." Concern clouded her time-worn features. "You won't tell him, will you?"

Riley dodged the answer with another question. "What's their relationship like? I understand you've worked for them almost from the time they were married."

She nodded. "They'd been married just over a month when I started working there. With Rosemary confined to a wheelchair, it was obvious why I was needed. Darryl's house hadn't been built with a disabled person in mind and he seemed more willing to pay me to do everything for her than to have the place adapted."

Riley pulled out his notebook. "It's a two-story place. I take it Rosemary lives downstairs?"

"Yes, she does. One thing Darryl had done was to install a bathroom on the ground floor. That and the double front doors were his only concessions to her disability."

Riley thought of Kate and frowned. "What about Rosemary's daughter? She was only young when you started working there."

Wrinkles deepened into folds across the woman's face. Her mouth tightened and a heavy sadness seemed to weigh down her slight shoulders. "Katie. Yes, she was four. That poor little girl."

Riley's hand stilled. "Why do you say that, Maggie?"

Disapproval backlit the brown depths of her eyes. "She was little more than a baby. They made her sleep upstairs, all alone. Her mother couldn't even come to her if she needed comfort in the dead of the night." She shook her head. "It wasn't right, if you ask me."

"Did you ever speak to them about it?"

Some of the anger eased out of her. "I talked to Rosemary about it once, not long after I started working there. She said it was what Darryl wanted. He wasn't used to a child in the house. I think it irritated him to have her underfoot so much. She had her toys, her books, her dolls—everything was upstairs, out of the way."

Riley pictured the loneliness of a little girl who wouldn't have had a clue why she'd been banished upstairs, away from the rest of the family. His heart clenched with sadness for the lost, little child and for the woman she was now, living with the memories.

"I guess as a new wife, Rosemary was keen to keep her husband happy."

Maggie pursed her lips. "I guess so. On laundry days, Katie and I would hang out the washing together. She was such a beautiful little girl. Always so anxious to please, but a bit of a loner. I used to worry she didn't have any friends."

Riley picked up his teacup and took a swallow. It was cool enough now to drink without pause.

"What about later? When she started school? Surely there were friends around then?"

Maggie shrugged, the slightest lift of one thin shoulder.

"I guess so. Once she started school, I wasn't around so much in the afternoons. Most days, I leave after Rosemary finishes lunch. Occasionally I stay later, if she asks me to. Sometimes, I think she just wants the company." Her gaze found his. "I can't imagine what it must be like to go through life like that, so dependent upon other people. It would just about drive me straight-through crazy."

Maggie looked away and stared out the window. Her voice lowered to a scratchy whisper. "I'm so glad my Laurie didn't suffer like that."

The old woman's gaze turned distant as she battled with her memories. Riley waited in silence. A few moments later, Maggie turned back to him, her face now drawn and despondent.

"It's a terrible thing, Detective, growing old. Don't ever let anyone tell you different."

Her comment hung between them, amongst the leftover tea things on the low coffee table.

Riley cleared his throat and changed the subject.

"Tell me about Darryl and Rosemary. Do they have a good relationship?"

"I guess so. What's a good relationship? We all have our ups and downs. They aren't going to win any awards for 'couple of the year,' but they seem to make it work. They've been together for over twenty years. That has to count for something."

Riley's gaze narrowed on her face. This woman knew the Watsons better than anyone. There had to be more she wasn't saying.

"Why doesn't Rosemary want Darryl to know about the problem with her vision?"

Maggie's shoulders slumped on a sigh. "You have to understand, Detective. Rosemary feels like she's been a burden to Darryl their entire married life."

"What do you mean? Has Darryl complained about her being a burden?"

"Not in so many words, but he sure lets her know as often as he can how much she owes him for marrying her. Sometimes, he can get quite nasty about it. That's why she wants to keep the deterioration of her eyesight from him as long as she can. She doesn't want to give him more ammunition."

So, Rosemary had secrets of her own. He shelved the thought away for further contemplation.

"How does she get on with Kate? Does her daughter know about her vision problem?"

Maggie shook her head. A small smile, laced with sadness and pride tugged at her lips. "That Katie is really something. I mean, she ran away from home with nothing but the clothes on her back and now she owns an internationally recognized art gallery—that girl's got some real grit."

Riley frowned, recalling Kate mentioned she was an art dealer. "How did she manage it?"

"I'm not really sure. Katie's leaving wasn't up for discussion. Rosemary was beside herself with worry when Katie first left. No one knew where she was. I think more than a fortnight passed before Katie contacted her. I was at the house the day Rosemary took that call. She nearly fell out of her chair when she realized it was her daughter."

Riley leaned forward, his tea now forgotten. "Tell me about it."

Maggie mirrored his forward movement and dropped her voice to a conspiratorial whisper. He didn't know why she was whispering. As far as he knew, they were alone in the house.

"I only heard Rosemary's side of it, of course, but I managed to get the drift." She lifted a thin weathered hand to her mouth and whispered through her fingers. "They'd had a falling out."

"Darryl and Kate, you mean?"

"Yes, of course, Darryl and Katie. I never did find out why. I just thought it was one of those things—you know, teenagers and their parents. She wouldn't have been the first one to run away."

"No, that's right. But it's a little unusual she stayed away for so long."

Maggie shrugged in reply. "I'm sure she has her reasons."

"Do you know what they are?"

Her only response was a non-committal shake of her head. Riley swallowed his impatience and tried another tack.

"When was the last time you were at the Watsons'?"

"A bit over a month ago. Early July. Darryl phoned me and suggested I take a break for a while. He said he was aware it was getting difficult for me to get up and down the stairs and to lug the vacuum cleaner around that big house."

She shrugged. "Not that I did much cleaning upstairs. With Katie gone, no one uses those rooms anymore. Still, I'm kind of pleased, as it turns out. I could do with a bit of a rest. My arthritis has been playing up lately."

"How much time are you having off?"

"I'm not sure. Darryl wasn't specific. He just thought I might need a break."

"Has he ever been that thoughtful to you in the past?"

Maggie looked toward the window and then down at her hands where they lay twisted in her lap. Her voice lowered. "No, I can't say that he has. I've been there twenty years with no more than a day or two off, here and there in all that time. Apart from paying my wages every week, I usually see very little of him."

"Did he tell you Rosemary was going away for four months?"

Maggie sat back against the armchair, her expression filling with surprise.

"No, he didn't. When is she going?"

"She's already left—about a month ago. Probably around the same time Darryl gave you the time off. She's sailing around the world on a cruise ship."

Great guffaws of laughter shook the slight frame. Riley's mouth dropped open in disbelief.

"Oh, Detective!" She clapped her hands. "What a wonderful story! I haven't laughed so hard in years. Where would you ever come up with something like that?"

"Why do you find it so funny, Maggie?"

Laughter still sparkled in the old, brown eyes. "Rosemary hates the water. She can't swim and it terrifies her. It's always been a struggle to get her into the shower and she'd never, ever take a bath. It's ludicrous to even imagine her on a cruise ship, stuck out in the middle of the ocean."

"Maybe she decided it was time to conquer her fears?"

Maggie's eyes closed and she drew in a deep, chest-expanding breath. When she opened them again, her gaze burned into his.

"When Rosemary was three years old, she nearly drowned. She fell into a dam on her parents' farm. She was under the water for more than a minute. It was only luck her father saw her go under and dove in to rescue her. Even now, years later, she told me she could still recall the way it felt in the cold, dark, watery silence of the dam, fighting for breath and knowing she was going to die. It was a feeling she never forgot."

Maggie's gaze seared him. "She was going blind, Detective. Even her doctor couldn't tell her how long her remaining sight would last. She's been dependent on Darryl for over two decades. She's barely stepped foot out of the house in all those years. She's not a brave woman." Her eyes narrowed on his face. "Can you honestly see Rosemary doing something like that?"

Disquiet seeped into Riley's veins and his heart started a slow, heavy thud. "Tell me, Maggie. When was the last time you saw her?"

CHAPTER 11

Kate squared her shoulders, drew in a steadying breath and pushed open the heavy barn-style doors of The Bullet. The dim lighting momentarily stole her vision and she waited in the entryway until her eyes adjusted to the darkness.

She looked about her, curiosity taking over the jumble of nerves, on this, her first visit. She'd heard all about The Bullet. It was almost as old as the town itself. Some of the older boys in high school had bragged about peeking between its wooden slats to catch a glimpse of the action inside. The girls had giggled and whispered about it behind their hands, secretly admiring the boys who were brave enough to get so close.

She'd been way below the legal drinking age when she'd left Watervale, and giggling over the antics of boys had never interested her, but curiosity about the place, and an increasing reluctance to spend any more time alone at the motel, had forced her through the doorway. Besides, she was all out of supplies and both of Watervale's supermarkets were closed.

As her eyes adjusted, she made out the dark, bulky shapes of bench tables and rustic wooden seats. A decent Saturday night crowd made up mostly of men, lounged in conversation against the bar and around the pool tables, a glass of beer within easy reach.

It was two days since she'd been to the police station.

Riley had left a message on her voicemail, but she hadn't returned it. It seemed all her courage had gone into her second attendance there and right now she was low on reserves. Besides, she couldn't bear to have him questioning her story all over again and she was sure if he had anything important to tell her, he would have found his way to her door.

Shifting her handbag more comfortably across her shoulder, Kate walked over to the bar and waited for the solitary barmaid to notice her. A few moments later, a buxom brunette with friendly brown eyes sauntered over, a smile of welcome on her brightly painted lips.

"Hey, if it isn't Kate Watson. I heard you were back in town. How have you been? You look like—wow! You look fantastic!"

Kate shuffled through her dusty collection of high school memories and tried to put a name to the face.

"It's Sonia Sevil. We were in the same year."

Kate shook the woman's outstretched hand and returned her smile hesitantly.

"Not that I'm surprised," Sonia continued. "You always were a stunner. I was so jealous of all that long blond hair."

"Really? I had no idea," Kate murmured, already regretting her decision to come here.

Sonia grimaced. "Yeah, that was the problem. You were always so freaking nice about everything, we couldn't hate you even when we wanted to."

"Why would you want to hate me?" Kate asked, genuinely surprised.

"Because you had it all—looks, brains, boys galore drooling after you; hell, you were even captain of the athletics team. There wasn't anything you didn't excel at." She leaned across the bar and smiled. "So, tell me, did you really kiss Justin Cooper behind the girls' toilets?"

"*What?* Justin *Cooper?* No way!"

Sonia's eyes gleamed. "I *knew* it. Even way back in high school that son of a bitch couldn't lie straight in bed."

Kate shook her head, nonplussed. "Why would Justin Cooper tell you he'd kissed me?"

"I guess he was trying to make me jealous. I had a thing for him back then, but there was no way I was going to let him know it. I think it was his awkward, screwed-up way of letting me know he liked me." Sonia rolled her eyes. "Men! You know how they are."

Kate answered with a mini-smile. She wasn't used to making girl talk, but she found she was enjoying the growing feeling of camaraderie between them.

Sonia smiled back. "What can I get you to drink?"

"Um, a glass of white wine would be great."

"House wine, all right?"

"That would be lovely."

Sonia winked at her. "Coming right up."

Within moments, a glass of chardonnay was placed in front of her. Kate picked it up and took a sip. The ice-cold wine slid down her throat. She breathed in the fruity smell and waited for the tingling feeling to glide through her veins. She'd never been a big drinker and alcohol of any kind always had that effect on her.

"What brings you back to town?" Sonia didn't try to hide her curiosity.

Kate couldn't blame the woman. Her departure a decade ago had been rather dramatic. She could only imagine the rumors that had passed from one teenage mouth to another.

But that was a lifetime ago. Her past had been buried so deep not even Sherlock Holmes would find it. And that's the way she wanted it. As long as she could find her mother, alive and well, and take her back to the UK with her, things would go on as normal. She'd return to London, settle her mother into a flat nearby and then pick up the threads of her successful life. She'd continue forward as if Watervale and her past no longer existed.

Aware that Sonia was still waiting for an answer, Kate settled on the truth.

"I've come to visit my mother. She used to email me all

the time, but a little over a month ago, she stopped. Not even a phone call. I just want to make sure she's all right."

A frown creased Sonia's forehead. "Actually, come to think about it, I haven't seen her around lately. Not that she's ever been one to get out and about much, but I usually see her sitting in her front garden every now and then. I drive right by your folks' house on my way home."

Kate's heart skipped a beat. "Really? Do you remember the last time you saw her?"

Sonia looked thoughtful. "Yeah, it must have been at least a month ago, come to think about it. That big old oak tree right near the driveway was still as bare as a slab of concrete. Your mom was sitting in her wheelchair with a laptop balanced on her knees. I remember thinking what a with-it kind of woman she was. My mother wouldn't even know how to switch a computer on."

"Was anyone with her?"

"No, I don't think so, but I was driving. I only saw her for a moment."

Kate's mind whirled. Her mother hadn't exactly sounded unhappy in her last few emails, but it was what she hadn't said that had led Kate to conclude her mother's relationship with Darryl had become strained.

Previous emails had often mentioned Darryl and what the two of them had been up to, but the later ones, the emails she'd received right before they'd ceased altogether, hadn't referred to him a single time. That was odd—as odd as her abrupt disappearance.

Despair settled on Kate's shoulders and she sighed under its weight. She wished she had someone to turn to, someone who would listen—*really* listen—and take her side, just once.

The familiar, tantalizing, masculine smell of expensive cologne teased her nostrils and accelerated her pulse. Then she noticed the change of expression on Sonia's face—as if a lamp had been switched on behind her pupils. The barmaid's teeth shone in the dimness and she turned away for a second or two of covert primping in the mirrored glass behind the bar.

Kate looked sideways. Riley pulled up the stool beside hers and lowered himself onto it with effortless athletic grace. His sleeve brushed hers and her insides clenched on a flutter of nerves.

He turned and smiled at her. A slow, sexy, thoughtful smile that darkened his eyes to the color of Old Gold Chocolate.

She averted her gaze, fighting the pull she felt when she looked into his eyes. A ball of heat unfurled low inside her.

"What's a gorgeous-as-all-get-out girl like you doing in a place like this?"

She rolled her eyes at his awful Bogart imitation. Despite her best intentions, a giggle spilled out. Then another. She lifted her gaze to his. She couldn't help it. Her lips widened on a smile.

He was funny and enthralling and sexy in his dark, French-barista kind of way. And he was genuine. She could see real caring in his eyes. In the way they darkened when he looked at her, and the tenderness in his smile. Her belly fluttered again and she was suddenly lost for words.

He spared her from having to formulate a reply by ordering a beer from Sonia, who hovered nearby.

"Crown Lager, right?" Sonia replied. "Big and busty and full of flavor, just how you like it." The barmaid winked and ran the tip of her tongue over the glossy fullness of her bottom lip.

Kate lowered her gaze and fumbled for some money in her handbag. The kernel of desire she'd felt moments before died a quick, merciful death. Embarrassment burned her skin. *Oh, God, Sonia had something going on with him.* She should have guessed. If the woman leaned any closer to Riley, her breasts would fall right out onto the bar.

Seizing a ten-dollar bill, she plunked it down in front of her and scrambled off the stool.

"Look, I have to get going," she mumbled, turning away.

"Hey, don't go rushing off." Riley stood, towering over her, the strength and breadth of his body at once both reassuring and intimidating.

Her gaze darted around the room and bounced

between patrons, pool tables, the jukebox, the heavy wooden entrance door—searching for an escape.

His hand was warm and firm on her arm. "Stay. Please, Kate." His eyes probed hers, seeking, searching, as if delving for secrets she could never divulge.

She shook her head, panic close to the surface. "No, um... Please, I have to go." The words came out in a rush. She couldn't meet his eyes.

"How about a bite to eat?" He squeezed her upper arm with his long fingers. "You feel way too scrawny."

Heat from his touch burned through her. He flashed his killer smile again and her knees almost buckled. He must have sensed her near-capitulation and coaxed her with another grin. "They do a great steak here."

"I'm not hungry," she protested and was immediately mortified when her stomach betrayed her with a loud rumble.

He chuckled. "See, I told you. Listen to your body. It knows what's best for you."

Fire spread across her face, even worse than before. She glanced back to Sonia who stood listening to the exchange, her petulant expression leaving Kate in little doubt about the woman's feelings.

Riley caught the exchange and his face filled with comprehension. "Hey," he said softly. "Why don't you find us an empty table? I'll bring the drinks."

Without giving her time to respond, he turned back to the bar. Kate veered away from the bar and headed toward the tables. She slid into an empty booth near a window.

Riley was right. She was starving. Peering through the window, she noticed the night had drawn in and only occasional lights from a passing car penetrated the inky blackness.

"Are you ready to order?"

She turned around. Riley placed a fresh beer and another glass of wine on the table, his smile back in place. She risked a glance in Sonia's direction, but the barmaid was occupied with a couple of young men who had just walked in.

Kate murmured her thanks and picked up the wine. She took a sip before setting the glass back down. "I hope I didn't mess things up for you with Sonia."

His eyes widened and he shook his head. "I've only been in town three months. I barely know her."

"That's not how it seemed to me." The words were out of her mouth before she could stop them. Flames licked at her cheeks and she closed her eyes. Why did she have to say something like that? She sounded like a jealous girlfriend. When she found the courage to sneak a peek at him, he looked flushed.

"We've shared a few conversations over a drink or two. I guess she must have gotten the wrong idea," he mumbled.

The heat in Kate's cheeks eased. She felt better, knowing he was just as uncomfortable as she was. He hadn't been obliged to give her an explanation. After all, she had no claim on him. But he had clarified things, and his explanation made her feel warm inside. She liked knowing what she thought mattered to him.

She looked at him again. Feeling shy and uncertain, she gave him a small smile.

His face stilled. His eyes darkened to black. He reached over and picked up her hand. Turning it palm-up, he rubbed a long, cold finger across the contours of her skin.

She stared at their hands, mesmerized at the contrasting contact. Heat. Ice. Light. Dark.

As if becoming aware of her scrutiny, he dropped her hand and pushed himself back against the wooden spine of the bench seat. His breath whistled through clenched lips. The same hand she'd been fixated on moments before scratched roughly at his closely cropped hair.

"I'm sorry. I shouldn't have done that. I don't know what I was thinking." He looked up, his dark eyes burning into hers. "You're involved in my investigation. We probably shouldn't even be eating together."

She held his gaze, wondering about his change of heart. "It didn't seem a problem a few moments ago."

He looked away, his eyes fixed on the old-fashioned

jukebox on the far side of the room. Alan Jackson was singing about the place he called home.

Riley's gaze tangled with hers again and her breath caught for the second time. In some sane, detached part of her mind, it annoyed her that he was able to elicit such a response from her with nothing more than a look. She barely knew him and she had every reason not to become involved with him...or any other man.

But it didn't seem to matter. Her belly twisted into nervous knots each time he looked at her and she tingled with awareness every time he smiled.

"What's the matter?" she asked, her voice low. "It's not like I'm a suspect."

He looked away again, but not before she caught the flash of uncertainty in his eyes. She shook her head, heat of a different kind igniting in her veins.

"Don't tell me you think *I* did it? You can't possibly think I'd harm my own mother?"

He squirmed and filled his mouth with beer, still avoiding her gaze.

Full-blown anger coursed through her. "Oh my God, you *do*! You saunter in here and corner me on the pretense of some friendly little tête-à-tête and all the time you suspect I'm involved in my mother's disappearance?"

She grabbed her handbag and slid across the wooden bench seat. He stood and she brushed past him in her haste to get out of the booth.

"No."

His quiet, monosyllabic answer reverberated in her ears, through the low murmur of conversation around them, over the sound of Alan Jackson crooning on the jukebox.

He held his arms out in a sign of surrender. "Kate, I didn't mean to imply you were a suspect. I know how you feel about your mother. You wouldn't be here, in Watervale, otherwise." His eyes burned into hers. "I know you didn't have anything to do with your mother's disappearance. What I don't know is why the hell you keep lying to me?"

His barb found its mark. He could tell from the slight flaring of her delicate nostrils, the sharp intake of breath. He waited for her to deny it.

Her shoulders slumped on a rush of air and her gaze lost its intensity. Her lips compressed and she gave a single, tiny nod.

Of acceptance? Defeat? He couldn't tell.

She reluctantly resumed her seat, the tension still apparent in her body. "You're talking about Mom's will."

He nodded and sat back down opposite her. "I went to see her lawyer."

"Harold Westport."

"He told me about it."

Her eyes flashed. "He had no right to talk to you. As far as he knows, my mother's still alive. I'll sue him for every penny he has for breach of confidentiality."

"First of all, the confidentiality belongs to your mother, not to you. If anyone's going to sue, it will be her. And if she's in a position to instigate a lawsuit, my work will be done."

Kate remained silent, tracing a finger up and down the frosted condensation on her glass. Riley watched and waited.

Finally, she dragged her gaze up to his. Her eyes were troubled. He held his breath, not sure he was ready to hear what she had to say. Her voice, when she spoke, was so low he had to lean forward and strain against the noise of the bar to hear.

"You're right. I did know. Mom told me a little over a month ago she was changing her will. She told me she intended to cut Darryl out."

A level of anger surged through him. He reined it in with a sheer act of will.

"Why did you lie to me?" he managed.

She offered him a half-hearted shrug and said nothing. Her insouciance infuriated him.

"That's it? That's all I get?" His fists clenched. He deserved better. He'd been busting his gut trying to get to the bottom of her mother's disappearance—trying to help.

Her gaze stayed fixed on the glass in front of her. "I don't know what you want me to say."

He sucked in his breath and tried to control his anger. Was she going out of her *way* to upset him? He was on her side. Didn't she know that?

With a gargantuan effort, he stifled his frustration and tried again, his tone as even as he could manage.

"I'm on your side. I'm trying to help you. Don't you *see* that?"

Her cobalt eyes stripped him of any pretense. "Are you? Are you *really*? Or is it because you don't even think a crime's been committed that you feel at liberty to butter me up?" Her voice turned sarcastic and her eyes regained their fire.

"What about my stepfather, Detective? The glorious, heroic, leader of the people? Where does he fit into all of this? I know you boys stick together. It's never been any different, but if *I* didn't do it, who did?"

Riley didn't flinch. "I'm reserving my opinion on Darryl. He's a selfish prick, but until I know for sure a crime's been committed, what do you want me to do?"

"I want you to take my *word* for it. I want you to *believe* me when I tell you my mother's missing. I want you to say, 'okay, we'll go and arrest him,' when I tell you my stepfather's responsible."

Tears glittered in the cobalt depths of her eyes. Riley shook his head and looked away.

Shit. If there was one thing he couldn't deal with, it was tears. They sucked him in every time. He couldn't afford to lose his edge. She, of all people, should know how things worked. He drew in a deep breath and prayed for patience—and for her understanding.

"You know it's not possible," he said. "If I had even one scrap of evidence there had been a crime, I'd be the first person to make an arrest."

Her expression remained angry, mutinous. Frustration arced through him.

"Look at it from my point of view. On one hand, I have Darryl Watson's estranged stepdaughter claiming he's committed some dastardly act upon her mother. Everyone in town knows the girl left on bad terms with him and there are others who remember her as a troublemaker.

"On the other hand, I have one of Watervale's most upstanding citizens telling me his wife has gone away on a holiday. I've seen glossy tour brochures strewn over his coffee table. The travel agency confirms the booking."

He ignored the voice in his head that reminded him there was no record that she boarded the ship and forged on.

"I've spoken to the lawyer who confirms the woman changed her will, leaving everything to her daughter."

His eyes drilled into hers for long, hard seconds. "No crime in that. People do it all the time, especially if they're planning to travel for an extended period of time. *You're* the only one who insists she wasn't going away."

And the housekeeper. He thrust aside the stab of guilt the unwelcome thought caused.

Kate's gaze remained defiant. "You think you're so clever. What about this scenario, hotshot? Mom had nothing to leave. Her estate was worthless. Nothing more than a small collection of jewelry and a few items that had sentimental value only. She owned nothing of any real value. Certainly nothing worth murdering her over. She changed her will as an act of defiance, to shove it up Darryl's ass, if you like. Things hadn't been so good between them. It was one way she could thumb her nose at him."

Riley drilled her with his eyes. "She told you this?"

"Yes. She emailed me about it not long before she made the appointment. She told me what she intended to do."

Anger narrowed his eyes. "And you're only *now* sharing this with me? Why didn't you say anything earlier, when I first asked you about the will?"

She shrugged and looked away. "You seemed hell-bent and determined to pin my mother's disappearance on me.

When you asked me about the will, I didn't know you'd already seen it. I knew what conclusion you'd draw when you discovered I was the sole beneficiary." She glared at him. "And you did."

Riley tugged at the short whorls of his hair and gritted his teeth. He drew in a breath and did his best to remain calm.

"Okay, so now we know the terms of the will had nothing to do with it. Whether Darryl was included or not and whether he knew about it before your mother's disappearance are moot. A worthless estate is a worthless estate, no matter how you look at it. No wonder he barely reacted when I read it."

Kate's lips twisted into a sneer. "He probably left it there on purpose, to throw you off track. It proved the will gave him zero financial motivation to get rid of her."

Riley nodded. Kate's observation made sense and it also explained Darryl's reaction, or lack thereof, to Riley's discovery.

His shoulders slumped on a sigh. He was going around in circles. Round and round and round and getting nowhere.

Lifting his beer, he took a sip and then set the glass back down on the table. "Okay, let's concentrate on what we do know: Rosemary wrote Darryl out of her will; their relationship had deteriorated to the point she didn't want to leave him anything; and we know that what she had didn't amount to much. At this stage, we don't know the reasons for the marriage breakdown." He cocked an eyebrow. "At least, I don't think we do?"

Kate shook head. "Mom never gave me any specifics— just that things between her and Darryl were tense. They'd had their ups and downs over the years. It was only when she told me she was leaving Darryl out of her will that I realized things had gotten a little more serious."

Riley nodded. "Their housekeeper told me much the same thing."

Kate's face softened. "You spoke to Mrs Fitzgerald?"

"Not about the will, but she did say your mother felt indebted to Darryl—for marrying her with the disability, for taking care of her, paying her medical bills. I can see how it could happen."

"I bet he took every opportunity to remind her, too," Kate shot back, anger re-igniting in her eyes.

Riley shrugged. "Maybe he did. Maybe your mother got tired of being made to feel like such a burden. Maybe they argued once too often and she decided to write him out of her will. Who knows? It doesn't turn him into a murderer."

Kate opened her mouth, her eyes shooting fire. He silenced her with a look.

"I'm not condoning his actions, but marriage breakdown is not a crime and divorce is a hell of a lot safer way to get out of a marriage than murder. I just don't buy your theory.

"Besides, under your mother's new will, Darryl wasn't set to inherit anything and even if he didn't know she'd changed it, a criminal can't benefit from their own crime. If, as you insist, Darryl has murdered your mother and he was convicted of her murder, he'd get nothing, regardless of the contents of her will. Your stepfather was a police officer for more than thirty years. There's no way he wouldn't know that." He held her angry stare. "Another reason why your arguments won't hold up. No motive."

Kate's chin jutted out at an obstinate angle.

"You're assuming he thought he was going to get caught," she fired back. "As you've so rightly pointed out, he's a long-serving police officer. He knows better than anyone how to get away with it. That's probably the reason why he came up with such a ridiculous story. He knew everyone would think he was way too smart to say she was off sailing around the world when she hated water, unless it was true. And you've fallen for it, Detective. Hook, line and sinker."

Riley ground his teeth until his jaw ached.

"Kate, you're not *listening* to me. Where's his motive? He had nothing to gain from her death. In fact, the only one with something to gain was *you*."

"You're wrong."

She spoke so quietly, he thought he'd imagined it.

"I'm sorry?"

Her chest expanded on a long breath of air. She lifted her head and the pain in her gaze branded itself on his heart.

"I said, you're wrong."

Chapter 12

Kate thumped the lumpy motel pillow and turned over in the bed for the hundredth time. The illuminated numbers on the clock told her it was after two. About six minutes since she'd last looked.

She'd left Riley at The Bullet demanding an explanation she was unwilling to give. She shouldn't have said anything. It was stupid and had only created more questions. If she hadn't gotten the hell out of there when she did, she'd eventually have given him the answers. And boy, would that have been a mistake.

Riley.

Though she knew there was no fairy-tale happiness in her future, there was something about him she found beyond attractive. Just the thought of him made her yearn that things were different. She ached to unload on him as he'd invited her to. And every time she was with him she longed to lean into the muscular warmth of his chest and let him ease the burden she'd carried for so long...to rely on his strength, his calmness, his logic.

But it was his logic that was the problem. His contrary arguments against her insistence Darryl was at the heart of her mother's disappearance made sense if he didn't know the truth, like she did. It wasn't his fault there were things he didn't know. Would never know—if she had any say.

She sighed and thumped the pillow again, her body prickly with restlessness. Fatigue lashed at her eyelids, but the turmoil of her thoughts refused to give her peace.

She looked awful. She hadn't slept properly since she'd arrived and even before then, her slumber had been anything but restful. The dark circles under her eyes looked almost comical and even makeup hadn't been able to completely conceal the paleness of her cheeks.

She didn't blame Riley for his interest in Sonia. The fresh-faced country girl was the epitome of health and her more than generous double-D cup size only increased her desirability.

Kate cupped her breasts, loose and unfettered beneath her silk nightgown. They barely filled her hands. Unless she counted the TV dinners, she hadn't eaten a proper meal since her arrival. She hadn't wanted to venture into any of Watervale's restaurants. There weren't too many to choose from and she couldn't bear the thought of fielding glances, or worse—questions—from curious locals. There was also the chance she could run into Darryl. He'd always been fond of eating out—at least, he had a decade ago, and she was disinclined to take her chances on discovering whether this was still the case.

So, she'd relied upon the kind of store-bought food she could obtain quickly and with the minimum of fuss. The only drawback was her forays into the supermarket had been limited to what she could prepare in her motel room. Even now, her stomach growled in noisy yearning at the thought of real food.

Tonight, she'd gone to The Bullet for dinner, counting on the fact that, in the past, Darryl had much preferred to drink at the up-market golf club rather than The Bullet. She'd also conceded she needed to force herself out of her room and into the bar in an effort to mingle with society again before she completely forgot how.

Then Riley had appeared and that had been the end of it. Even though a part of her had been eager to accept his dinner invitation, the sensible part of her brain had been grateful when his behavior had provided her with an excuse to leave—empty stomach, and all.

She'd fled back to the motel and after spending an hour pacing back and forth across the worn carpet, arguing for and against the reasons for coming clean with him, she'd sunk, exhausted, onto the tattered armchair, where her gaze had landed on her unappetizing microwave meal.

After a few desultory attempts to eat, she'd showered and changed for bed, but sleep had eluded her.

Her mother. Her stepfather. Riley. They'd swirled in a mishmash of images, one superimposed upon the other until her head spun like she'd just climbed off a ride at the local fair.

She'd crawled off the sagging bed and dug in her handbag for some aspirin, swallowing three straight from the packet. Then she'd sprawled back upon the bed, clutching one of the spongy pillows to her chest.

The illuminated face of the clock taunted her as another minute crawled past. The night was still and quiet. Her room faced onto the main highway that ran through the town, but even that appeared to be deserted.

Flopping onto her belly, she tried to banish every thought from her mind with a deep-breathing exercise. It was a technique she'd perfected years ago, when she'd had even more reasons to block out every scrap of feeling she had.

For a while, it took her mind off things, but all too soon, her thoughts returned to the present. The pervasive feeling of dread expanded in the darkness. She had to do something. She had to find her mother's body and bring her killer to justice.

And there it was.

At last, in the dead of night, she'd found the courage to confront the truth: Her mother was likely dead.

With the memory of Rosmary's last email imprinted on her brain, the truth couldn't be ignored. The tone of that last email had been one of desperation, the words of a woman who had run out of options. So desperate, Kate could have believed her mother had run away— would have believed it, if Darryl hadn't been the one who'd insisted that was exactly what had happened.

Kate ached with guilt and sadness. For ten years, she'd stayed away. For ten years, her relationship with her mother had been maintained from a distance via emails and telephone calls. She hadn't been there for her mother's birthdays, for the times when she'd been sick, the times when she'd been lonely.

Kate didn't kid herself. She'd been under no illusion her mother's life had been perfect. Rosemary may not have realized the full extent of her husband's evil, but from her shared confidences via email, it was clear he'd shown the nasty side of himself to her on more than one occasion and those occasions had become more and more frequent. Kate could only guess that his escalating maliciousness had been the reason for her mother's increasingly negative outlook in the weeks before she'd disappeared without a trace.

Chase strode into the squad room on Monday morning, shaking his head from side to side. "Munro, Munro, Munro."

Riley glanced up from his desk. "What did I do now?"

"*Tsk, tsk, tsk.* What the hell's gotten into you, mate? I took buxom Belinda home on Saturday night and all she went on about was how upset Sonia was that you dumped her." He rounded on Riley and waggled a finger in his face. "You cost me a night of passion, Munro, and for that, I'll never forgive you."

"What the hell are you talking about? How could I have dumped Sonia? We weren't even going out, as I recall."

"That might be so, but this is Watervale, city boy. You shared at least a couple of drinks and some pretty in-depth conversation, according to Belinda. That, my friend, almost constitutes a marriage proposal in these parts."

Riley groaned and shook his head. "Is she really that upset? 'Cause I talked to her at The Bullet on Saturday night.

I thought I'd straightened things out and, you know, explained how my interest lay elsewhere."

Chase's eyebrows disappeared into the thick curls that dangled across his forehead.

"Really? And who is this fair maiden? Do tell. No, let me guess. Your sudden change of heart wouldn't have anything to do with the appearance of Kate Watson, would it?"

Heat seared Riley's neck and Chase grinned.

"Don't try to deny it, mate. The answer's written all over your face."

Riley looked down at the paperwork spread out before him. "Yeah, well not that it'll do me any good," he muttered.

"I take it the fair Kate doesn't return your interest?"

Riley gave an impatient shake of his head. "It's not that. It's just that I'm investigating the disappearance of her mother. The case might turn into something more, yet. Kate might be involved."

Chase propped a hip against Riley's desk, his face turning grave. "Ah, now I get it. Awkward."

They sat in silence. Chase offered a sly smile and a single rogue eyebrow arched upwards. "Sonia's a whole lot less complicated. And according to Belinda, I think you might even get a second chance—with some serious sucking up and perhaps a dinner or two at one of Watervale's finer restaurants."

Riley pursed his lips. "Forget it, mate. I'm not interested."

Surprise lit the depths of Chase's eyes. "Well, well, well. This sounds serious."

Riley groaned and picked up his pen, pretending to read through the statement in front of him. Chase continued to sit there, grinning.

"Don't you have work to do?" Riley growled.

"Yep." Chase didn't move.

After reading the same sentence three times, Riley looked up again. "Well, are you going to go and do it?"

"Yep." Still, Chase didn't move until a grin split his mouth wide. "I'm merely enjoying the moment. You've been in Watervale a little over three months and have managed to ignore every one of the female hearts you've set aflutter and now, all of a sudden, one pint-sized female with a posh English accent has you all in a lather."

His eyes gleamed. "The best part is, you don't have a single clue what to do about it. And not just because she's involved in your case," he added when Riley tried to interrupt. "But because probably, for the first time in your life, you like a girl—*really* like her—and you're not sure if she likes you back." He gave Riley a look of pure innocence. "Did I miss anything?"

Riley's mood darkened. "It's not like that at all. You forget, I've had relationships before. I know what it feels like to *really* like someone. Hell, I know what it feels like to *love* someone. Now, get your ass off my desk and get back to work. Why am I always the only one who does anything around here?"

Chase unfolded his body, a knowing glint in his eye. "We'll see," he murmured, sauntering off in the direction of the tearoom.

Riley watched him go and grimaced. *The gall of the man!* Where did he get off speaking to him like that?

So what if he found Kate attractive? It wasn't like he'd fallen in love with her. The fact she was beautiful enough to have modeled for a fashion magazine meant squat. He'd never been the kind of guy to fall for someone because of their looks. Iris had been testament to that.

Granted, Iris had been attractive, in a classical kind of way, but it was her sharp mind and quick wit that had drawn him. It was only later he'd discovered she had no softness to her at all. To Iris, it was all about winning—at what, it didn't matter—and any means justified the end, no matter who got hurt along the way.

In the end, she'd just plain worn him out. He couldn't keep up with the frenetic pace such an attitude demanded. And he hadn't wanted to.

His laid-back outlook on life had driven her mad. It had been one of the reasons they'd split. At least, that's what she'd yelled at him as she'd stormed around their apartment packing her belongings. It was only later that he discovered she'd already lined up his replacement.

The thought no longer wounded him like it used to. He could only imagine it was the entry into his life of a certain exotic-looking art dealer who had made the difference.

Kate.

It was as if she'd invaded every corner of his life. As much as he wanted to deny it, he thought about her all the time and not just in the context of her mother's disappearance. If only things weren't so complicated. If only he knew how she felt. If only he had the confidence to find out. *If only…*

Riley swallowed a groan. Leaning forward with his elbows on his desk, he ran his fingers through his hair and wished he could scrub away the alluring images of Kate just as easily. He could still recall the moment in her motel room when her body had melted against him. It had felt like his soul had melded with hers; that if he'd had the courage to tilt her chin upward and kiss her like he'd wanted to, the world would have disappeared. Changed forever…

Which was plain stupid, really. His sisters teased him mercilessly about his romantic streak and he'd always denied it. Real men didn't wax lyrical about their love life. He'd be howled out of town if any of the boys got wind of it.

But he'd meant it when he'd told Kate he believed she wasn't involved in the disappearance of her mother. The more he got to know her, the more impossible it became to think of her as a cold-blooded murderer and as much as he'd argued Darryl didn't have a motive, Kate didn't have one, either.

So far, the only asset he'd found in Rosemary's name was a bank account into which her disability pension was paid every fortnight, with a grand balance of two thousand, four hundred and thirty-nine dollars. Not exactly a sum worth killing for.

So, what had happened to Kate's mother?

The last person to have seen her was her husband, when he dropped her off at the wharf at Circular Quay. Or so he said.

Riley picked up his pen and notebook from his desk and

slipped them into his shirt pocket. He stood and walked over to Hannaford's office. "I'm heading out for an hour or so," he called through the open doorway. "Got a few leads to chase up."

Hannaford squinted at him. "This about that missing cow of Sampson's?"

Riley averted his eyes. "Um, yeah. I have a couple of more people to talk to." Without giving him a chance to reply, Riley turned and strode toward the stairwell.

"Elaine Spencer, is it? I think we spoke on the phone last week. I'm Detective Munro." Riley extended his hand to the woman behind the counter of the Thames Travel Agency. She smiled and shook his hand with fingers that were considerably lengthened by bright red nails. Her jet-black hair and well-preserved features were in stark contrast to the wrinkles that criss-crossed her neck and the deep lines embedded around her mouth.

"Yes, Detective. I believe we did. You were calling about Rosemary Watson?"

Riley nodded and surveyed the small but tidy booking office. Glossy posters picturing exuberant holidaymakers in exotic locations lined three of the beige-colored walls. The fourth one was comprised of floor-to-ceiling glass and contained the double electronic sliding doors he'd entered through.

An office junior sat to one side at a crowded desk, pamphlets and tour brochures piled high near her elbow. She spoke softly into a phone and took notes on a yellow legal pad.

"So, Detective, what can I do for you?"

Riley returned his attention to the woman in front of him and flashed her a smile, keeping his voice casual. "I'm making a few enquiries about Mrs Watson. A member of her family is trying to contact her. She was meant to embark on a cruise about five weeks ago, departing from Sydney. Her husband told me he dropped her off at the wharf on the day of her scheduled departure, but she never boarded. He hasn't heard from her since. Some family members are becoming concerned."

The woman frowned. "Oh, I see. That sounds a bit strange. Just give me a moment and I'll pull up her booking for you. It ought to give us a little more information."

Elaine moved to the desktop computer and began tapping keys. A few moments later, she spoke again. "Yes, here we go. Rosemary Watson. She was booked on the *Sun Princess*. An around-the-world tour." She scrolled down the page. "It departed on July tenth."

"I know when it departed, but the thing is, Mrs Watson didn't board the ship. I spoke to the ship's purser. She's not on the cruise."

"Oh, yes, that's right. Now I remember. I gave you the phone number." A frown added years to her face as creases found their grooves and deepened. "So, she's not on the ship? That's odd. I wonder where she is?"

"Exactly. That's why I'm here. I was hoping you could tell me more about the booking—when it was made, who made it...that sort of thing."

"Of course, Detective. I'm sure Mr Watson wouldn't mind. He must be crazy with worry. It's very strange, isn't it? Very strange."

Riley chose not to comment. The man he'd met last week had appeared far from overwrought. That was one of the things that disquieted Riley most. He waited as Elaine pulled up the information he'd requested.

"Ah, here it is." Her gaze drifted over the entries on the computer screen. "It looks like it was paid in full by way of check on July eighth, a couple of days after the booking was made. Take a look."

She swung the monitor toward him. Riley leaned across the counter and skimmed over the data. "Do you keep a record of whose check it is?"

"No, but the receipt is generally made out to the drawer

of the check unless there is a specific request otherwise."

She opened a drawer and riffled through it, pulling out an old-fashioned receipt book. Flipping it open, she ran her finger down the various entries for July.

Riley stepped away and gazed around the office. The young girl was now off the phone and tapping on her keyboard, her honey-blond ponytail bobbing every time she turned her head.

"Ah, here it is. It's made out to Darryl Watson." Her finger traced down to the signature at the bottom of the receipt and tapped it with one of her elongated nails. "That's Isobel's signature. She might be able to tell you a bit more about it."

Riley returned to the counter and looked at the page Elaine indicated. The girl with the ponytail swung around on her chair, her eyes bright with curiosity.

"Is something the matter, Mrs Spencer?"

"Isobel, this is Detective Munro. He's here about Rosemary Watson. She was booked to go on the *Sun Princess*, but apparently, she didn't show. No one's seen or heard from her for a while. Her family's getting worried."

Clear blue eyes clouded with concern. "Rosemary Watson. She's the lady in the wheelchair, isn't she?"

"Yes, she is," Riley said. He turned and walked closer to the girl. "So, you remember her?"

She scrunched up her nose and crinkled her forehead in the way young women do who haven't yet learned to worry about wrinkles. "Not her; I never met her, but I remember her husband."

A tingle of premonition—the kind he often got just before a case broke—skipped down his spine. "Really? What do you remember about him?"

Isobel's lips widened into a smile, showing a neat set of colored braces. A blush stained her cheeks. She turned her gaze up to his. "He was just so romantic. Planning a secret holiday getaway for his wife. It cost him a fortune, but he said she hadn't been on a real holiday for years and that she was worth every penny. He couldn't wait to surprise her with it."

Riley frowned, recalling Watson's explanation about why Rosemary hadn't taken her cell phone. The cost of those calls seemed miniscule when compared to what he'd already spent.

Riley tugged out his notebook and pen and addressed Isobel again. "When did you first meet Mr Watson?"

The girl repeated the scrunched-up-face look and bit her lip. "*Mm*, I'm guessing it was July sixth. I'm sure he came in a couple of days before he paid. He came in to enquire about our holiday packages, when the next one was available—that sort of thing."

"Did he tell you she was in a wheelchair?"

A dreamy expression crossed the young girl's face. "Yes," she smiled. "That's what made it even more romantic. He paid for the very best stateroom on the ship. It cost a fortune, but it was the one most able to accommodate her disability." Her eyes widened in delight. "Isn't that about the most romantic thing you've ever heard?"

Riley stayed quiet. The young girl's impressions of Watson were about as far south of his own as was possible, but he duly recorded them in his notebook. "Did he say why he wasn't traveling with her?"

Another frown. Then a shake of the head. "No, I don't think so. It was all about his wife. How difficult things had been for her lately. How much she deserved some time away. How much she meant to him."

"So, he actually talked about that kind of stuff?"

"Yes, he did. I still remember him saying how she'd come into his life and had made it so wonderful. They'd had more than twenty years together and yet he loved her as much as he had the day they'd married." She sighed. "Oh, Detective, it was so romantic."

"Yeah, it sure sounds like it." He was having trouble reconciling the obnoxious, arrogant pig he'd encountered with the thoughtful, loving husband Isobel described.

He closed his notebook and slipped it back inside his shirt pocket, along with his pen. "Okay, well I guess that's about it for now. I appreciate your time." Nodding to both of them, he walked toward the electronic doors. They slid open almost soundlessly and a wall of cold air gusted inside. He pulled his jacket close and buttoned it up as he made his way out to the squad car, still no closer to solving the puzzle.

———————

Even the late afternoon sunlight that filtered through the window of Kate's rental car couldn't warm her. She forced air between her clenched teeth and did her best to ignore the anxiety that clawed at her insides.

She was clinging to her courage with her fingernails— what was left of them. Any second, she expected to lose her grip and it terrified her to think what might happen if she did.

She peered through the windscreen. Her gaze darted around like a startled bird, refusing to linger in one place for more than a second or two.

The garden was as tidy as always. The heavy scent of wattle filled the air and settled around her, bringing with it memories of her childhood. Memories she'd buried, along with all the other bleak moments of her youth.

The red and pink geraniums growing alongside the roses that lined the path that led to the front door were incongruously bright against the dullness of the grass. The sun was descending fast. It wouldn't be long and another night would be upon her: Yet another night of angry, restless questions buzzing inside her head, stealing her sleep and her sanity.

But right here, right now, none of it mattered. She was outside the house of her nightmares—outside the house her mother thought would be a haven for them both.

Kate took another breath and counted to ten. Releasing it on a sigh, she opened the car door, squared her shoulders and headed up the driveway. She could do this. She could. For her mother.

The front door opened long before she reached it. She shivered. He must have been watching. Nausea swirled in her stomach. Darryl strode down the path toward her, his lips turned up into a sneer.

"If it isn't our high-flying daughter finally come home to rest. And here I was thinking not so long ago we'd never see you again."

Kate came to a stop and braced herself against his taunts. His long-sleeved white linen shirt fit snugly around a still-muscular chest and was tucked neatly into the waistband of a pair of denim jeans that encircled a waist that had only marginally softened.

She was filled with jarring disappointment. She'd hoped his outward appearance had finally begun to reflect the degradation of his soul, but someone with far more influence than her over these things hadn't seen it that way.

She glared at him from behind her designer sunglasses, glad she'd taken the time to dress in her best. Let him scoff all he liked; he couldn't touch her now. Bravado surged through her.

"Shut the fuck up, Darryl."

His eyes narrowed in surprise. He nodded, almost approvingly. "Well, well, well. Our little girl's gone and got herself all grown up and she's grown a bit of a mouth along the way."

His gaze raked over her with slow insolence. Kate forced herself to remain still. Even covered from head to toe in her expensive winter woolens, she felt naked and unclean beneath his close scrutiny. She resisted the urge to protect herself with her arms and seared him from behind her lenses. He seemed impervious to the heat in her eyes.

"Not bad, not bad at all." His gaze slithered over her again. "A bit on the scrawny side, but I can see what all the boys at the station are in a lather about."

The insult drew blood. Anger clogged her windpipe. She sputtered and wheezed and tried to draw air into her suddenly depleted lungs.

"Cat got your tongue, Kathryn? It's not like you to be short of words. At least, you never used to be."

Nausea swirled once again in her stomach, depleting her

short lived courage. She couldn't go through with it. She had to get away. She turned to leave and then stopped.

White-hot rage boiled up inside her to the point where she could almost taste it. She spun on her heel and whipped off her glasses, her gaze intent on his face.

"I want the laptop." Low and guttural, she could barely believe the voice was hers.

Surprise momentarily slackened Darryl's features. He belched and she was almost overcome by the smell of alcohol. She stepped backward.

"Give me the laptop, Darryl. I know it's here. Riley told me."

A knowing grin split his features. He nodded and chuckled. "Ah, I see. Now it all makes sense. I knew there had to be a reason he came sniffing around here last week. You're fucking the young detective." He took a step toward her. Kate gasped, her tiny reservoir of bravery almost exhausted.

"Tell me, Kathryn. What's it like to suck black cock?"

Bile rose in her throat, harsh and acidic. She turned away, fighting the sudden urge to vomit.

Darryl laughed. The pungent smell of alcohol reached her seconds before he grabbed her by the hair and wrenched her head around. Tears of humiliation burned behind her eyes.

The man she hated most in the world narrowed his eyes menacingly, his face only inches from hers. His voice, in stark contrast to the expression on his face, was soft and soothing, almost as if he was crooning a lullaby.

"Kathryn, Kathryn, Kathryn. You were always so feisty, always ready to argue." He chuckled. "As if you could talk your way out of it." He shook his head. "You never learned. Right down to that last time, you never learned."

He leaned in even closer and pressed his mouth tightly against her ear. She shuddered and strained against his hold. Terror pumped through her veins.

"You do remember our last time, don't you?"

She cried out in agony and would have fallen if his hold

on her hair hadn't tightened. She was going to be sick. Right there, on his perfect lawn.

Defeat settled inside her, heavy and hard and cold. She'd failed. Her mother was gone and she'd never find her.

Darryl's voice, now strangely disembodied, floated into her ear.

"I remember that last time. It was such a special time. Just the three of us. My friend was so disappointed when you refused to let him play. Now I understand why. You should have told me you preferred black cock."

Pent-up sobs seized her chest in a vicelike grip. Her lungs refused to function. Lights spun behind her eyes, like sparklers that had been lit and left to their own devices. She was going to die. Right there. In Darryl's picture-perfect front garden.

A mighty thump hit her between her shoulder blades. She choked and gasped for air.

"Breathe, you little slut. I don't want you dying in my yard." Darryl's hand came down hard once again and she gasped. The lights behind her eyes receded.

She dashed at the tears now coursing down her cheeks and stared into his face with all the hate and fury she could muster.

"I want my mother's laptop. I bought it. I want it back."

Darryl let go of her and took a step backward, shrugging as if what had just passed between them was of no consequence.

"Take it. Why would I want the fucking thing? Waste of time, if you ask me. Your mother was never off it. Why she found it so interesting, I'll never understand." He shook his head. "All this new-fangled technology. I say, bring back the old days, when you could get by with a visit to the library and a letter in the post."

He offered her a conspiratorial wink. Kate bit down on her disgust. A few more minutes and she'd be out of there. She'd have what she'd come for and could leave. *Just a few more minutes.*

"Why don't you come in—for old times' sake? You can wait inside while I pack it up."

She froze. Nothing would get her to step inside his house ever again. "I'll wait here." She eyeballed him and prayed he'd let it go. She needed the laptop. She was sure she'd find the key to her mother's disappearance hidden within its cyber walls.

Darryl gave her a long, hard stare. Kate's breath caught again. After an interminable moment, he gave a half shrug and turned to head back inside. "Suit yourself."

She rubbed her arms through her coat and waited. The night air was almost upon them, heavy and moist. She longed for a hot shower and the security and warmth of her cheap motel room. She longed for the nightmare to be over.

The light in the opened doorway was blocked momentarily as Darryl made his way back down the front steps, a black carry case in his hand.

"Here you go. See, it wasn't all that hard, was it? Asking me for something? If you'd learned to do it sooner, life might have turned out a whole lot differently for you."

He closed the distance between them and his jovial expression disappeared. "But you never asked, did you Kathryn? You were too proud and too stubborn to ask me for anything. I'd have given you anything you wanted."

She held his gaze and clung to the last vestige of her courage. She was so close, so close to getting what she'd come for. "Give me the laptop."

"Here. Take it."

She reached out and grasped the case in nerveless fingers. His hand, huge and hairy, covered hers and tightened. Her heart almost doubled in on itself in panic.

"All the boys at the station breathed a sigh of relief for me when you left. I used to tell them every opportunity I got how hard it was trying to raise another man's rebellious whelp. Some of them had teenagers of their own. They knew exactly what I was talking about."

He released her hand and gave her a shove. She

stumbled backward on the damp grass and struggled to maintain her balance. Clutching the laptop to her chest, she backed away and then turned and nearly ran toward her car.

His voice rang out in the crisp stillness. "They haven't forgotten, you know."

Kate willed her feet to slow. The last thing she wanted was to give him the satisfaction of watching her run away.

By the time she reached her car, she trembled like she had a fever. Sweat poured off her forehead and burned her eyes. She rested her cheek on the cold metal of the roof and dragged in mouthfuls of winter air.

The brick in her stomach moved and clenched and twisted. She spun away and bent over at the waist. Seconds later, she heaved and vomited all over the shadowy strip of asphalt beneath her six-hundred-dollar boots.

CHAPTER 13

Darryl stared after the fading tail lights of his stepdaughter's rental car and watched until they'd disappeared. He had to give it to the girl, she'd grown some courage along with her curves. She'd surprised him by showing up on his doorstep and that wasn't easy.

He turned and headed back inside, closing the door behind him. Tugging another beer out of his fridge, he swallowed half of it before returning to his spot on the couch.

He hadn't expected her to ask for the laptop. The Munro prick had obviously worded her up. Not that it mattered. Darryl might bemoan the complexities of modern technology to anyone who would listen, but he wasn't stupid.

Once he'd realized the detective had spotted the computer on his visit, Darryl had known what he had to do. He cracked Rosemary's password on his first attempt and had combed through everything she had on her hard drive.

Not that there had been much. It was obvious his dear wife had spent most of her time surfing the Internet. He'd found a handful of folders in her Word program that contained copies of various newsletter services she'd subscribed to and not much else.

When he turned his attention to her email, things had become much more interesting. Scrolling through her Inbox, he'd noted the emails from her daughter. He'd opened all of them and had smirked at the girl's increasingly concerned tone.

A series of emails received by someone by the name of Daisyblu had caused him a moment's consternation. After reading their contents, he'd wracked his brain for who it might be. At last, it had come to him and he'd smiled, knowing there would be no danger from that quarter.

After deleting everything in Rosemary's Inbox, he repeated the process with the Word files. When Kathryn had asked for the laptop, he'd offered token resistance, knowing there was nothing on the computer that could incriminate him.

He was disappointed though, when she hadn't taken him up on his invitation to come inside. It would have been just like old times. Well, not exactly. She was no longer a teenager bending to his will.

In fact, the more he thought about it, the more he realized it was probably for the best. It was the same instinctive feeling that had caused him not to insist on her accompanying him into the house.

There was something different about her—a toughness that hadn't been there before. Somehow, somewhere over the years, she'd found the courage to stand up for herself and the new steel in her spine left him feeling a little disconcerted.

He'd have to watch her closely, in case she got any wild ideas into her head. He hadn't lied when he told her he still had plenty of friends on the force, but it wouldn't do for his carefully laid plans to go askew this late in the game.

CHAPTER 14

Riley began the climb to Bill Cannington's dairy shed which was perched high on a hill above the winter-brown valley. His breath puffed out on mini clouds of condensation. The air was even chillier than it had been in town and it didn't take long for it to bite into his lungs.

As fit as Riley was, his body was still acclimatizing to the higher elevations of Watervale and he was only halfway up the steep path when he had to pause and catch his breath.

The farm's owner had called him at the station. Although reluctant to impart too much over the phone, Cannington had hinted he had information pertaining to the Sampson case.

With Hannaford still on Riley's back about finding the missing cow, he'd pulled on his heavy coat and had headed back out into the cold. Now he wished he'd waited until morning. In a couple of hours, night would set in and he had no desire to be out there when the temperature dropped below zero.

A tall man with stooped shoulders who looked like he was approaching sixty appeared in the doorway of the dairy, wearing dirty overalls and rubber boots. Recalling his last encounter with a milking shed, Riley vowed to steer clear of it.

"We might talk out here, if that's all right with you," he said as he closed the gap between them.

"Don't tell me you're afraid of a little cow shit?"

Cannington smirked and Riley ground his teeth, wondering if Sampson had shared details of his humiliation with the entire farming community.

"Let's just get this over with, shall we?" Riley tugged out his notebook and pen and flipped it open to a new page. "I take it you're Bill Cannington?"

The man nodded.

"So, what do you know about Jack Sampson's missing cow?"

Cannington kicked at a clod of dirt in front of him and took his time replying. "What do you know about dairy cows, Detective?"

Riley shrugged, unperturbed. "Not much. What do you know about policing?"

A faint tilt of Cannington's thick lips was the only indication he'd heard, but when he met Riley's hard gaze, there was a glint of respect in his deep-set eyes.

"Not much."

"I guess that makes us even then, doesn't it?"

Cannington scratched at the graying bristle on his chin with a dirty fingernail. "Guess it does."

"Right, then. Now we have that out of the way, what do you know about Sampson's missing cow?"

Hawking a glob of phlegm, Cannington spat in the dust at his feet. "That cow ain't missin'. She ain't even left the farm. Call up Jersey Australia and tell 'em to look up her registration number in the herd book and then go and check the livestock. You'll find her right where she's been all along—in Sampson's back paddock."

Riley's heart began a slow, hard thump against his ribcage. Suspicion took hold, but he needed to be sure. He eyed Cannington quizzically and kept his tone even.

"What are you trying to say, Mr Cannington?"

Cannington landed another globule of phlegm on the ground, this time only inches from Riley's polished boots.

"You city slickers are all the same. You wouldn't know your arm from your asshole. What the hell do you think I'm tryin' to say? That wily old coot has been doin' it for years.

He files a police report about a missin' cow, gets it investigated so it looks all legit and then he claims it on the insurance."

"If everyone knows about it, why hasn't someone put an end to it?"

Cannington laughed without humor. "You're kiddin' me, right? How long have you been in town, Detective? Obviously not long enough."

Riley didn't answer. Cannington shook his grizzled head. "The boys at the station are in on it. Watson used to decide which cow would be the next to go missin'. He didn't want no doublin' up. That wouldn't be good for business. He was gettin' a cut of the insurance money. I've heard he's passed the reins on to Hannaford, now."

Riley's mind whirled. He tried to stem the feeling of déjà vu that flooded his consciousness. *Not again.*

Surely, not here in Watervale? The Local Area Commander on the take?

The farmer eyed him curiously. "I can see you're lookin' skeptical." He shrugged and peered into the distance at the mountains now deep in shadows. "Hell, don't take my word for it. Ask anyone. They'll all tell ya the same. Those that ain't in on it, that is."

His gaze landed back on Riley's. "I'm surprised you were the one to catch the case, to tell ya the truth. It's usually Hannaford who follows up Sampson's complaints. I guess it's just his way of havin' a laugh at the expense of the new kid."

Riley's head felt as foggy as the mist that had rolled in over the hills. There was a whooshing sound in his ears and he closed his eyes against it. His blood continued to pound. Stumbling, he almost collided with one of the wooden corner posts that supported the milking shed.

"Easy, mate. I didn't mean to rattle ya cage." Cannington reached out a steadying hand.

Riley breathed deeply. With an effort, he composed himself and hoped *this* story wouldn't make the rounds. Just what he needed, more fodder against the rookie detective. The town would never take him seriously.

Cannington peered at him with concern. "You all right?"

Riley grimaced. "Yeah, I'm fine. I guess I've been a little ignorant about the caliber of the officers I work with. I had no idea."

"Don't go too hard on yourself. It's not all of 'em. Watson was the main offender. We all thought it would stop when he retired, but instead, he passed the baton onto Hannaford. Probably worth too much money to him."

Nausea swirled in Riley's stomach and he pushed it down with an act of will. How could he have thought police corruption would be limited to the city? Worse still, limited to his former command?

To be truly honest, he'd been beyond shocked when he'd discovered his former superior, Detective Inspector Shattler, and some of his cronies had been siphoning off cash found during drug raids. His disbelief had turned to crushing disappointment and disillusionment when he realized no one in the command wanted to know about it. Even those who weren't on the take hadn't wanted to get involved and thereby, had effectively condoned it with their silence.

Riley would never forget the day his former partner had come to him and told him to leave it be and forget what he saw and go about his business of locking up the bad guys—if one or two of their colleagues profited as a result, was that really so bad?

Stunned, Riley had been unable to respond. A few days later, Detective Inspector Shattler had called him into his office and had told him he was being transferred to Watervale.

"Why hasn't anyone done anything about it? Why hasn't someone reported it to the Ombudsman or Internal Affairs or the Police Integrity Commission?" Riley asked.

Cannington laughed, but the humor failed to reach his eyes. "You have to be kiddin'? We're talkin' about the Local Area Commander. Who's goin' to have the balls to put *his* name in? We have to live here. If ya don't have the local law enforcement on side, you're in a world of hurt. Even a few beers down at The Bullet on a Friday night might become a hassle."

Riley stared at him in confusion. Cannington shook his head, his lips turning down in disgust. "You city slickers have no idea. Do you know how many miles you traveled to get here? We're fifteen miles out of town. And there's plenty of blokes further out than us. How many of 'em do you think call up a cab to take 'em home after they've had a few too many?"

Comprehension dawned. Dread settled in the pit of his gut. His skin prickled and his feet felt weighed down by concrete. The cow scam was probably only the tip of the iceberg. The corruption could be rife throughout the entire force. And what did it say about Watson, who, until recently, had been at the helm? Could he really be so deceptive? So completely amoral? And if so, was Kate right? *Was* he behind the disappearance of her mother?

As if he could read Riley's mind, Cannington cleared his throat and spoke again. "I hear you've been talkin' to people about Rosemary Watson."

Riley shrugged and remained silent.

"Watervale's a small town, Detective. Word gets 'round."

Riley strove to keep his tone casual. "What have you heard?"

"This and that. I heard you paid Commander Watson a visit. Apparently, he was none too happy about it."

"His stepdaughter's reported her mother missing. I was merely making enquiries."

Cannington stepped closer and lowered his voice, although as far as Riley could tell, there was no one else around for miles.

"I've never liked that son of a bitch. Corruption aside, I just can't stand to see the way he treats that girl."

Riley stilled. "Kate?"

Cannington gave a brief shake of his head. "No, not Kate, although he didn't seem to have much time for her, either. It's Rosemary I'm talkin' about."

"What do you mean?"

Cannington's unshaven jaw tightened. "He treats her like shit. That's what I'm talkin' about. She's totally dependent upon him and he never lets her forget it. She ain't got much money of her own. She has to beg him for everythin' she needs. If he doesn't want to give it to her, she just doesn't get it and he's one helluva mean son of a bitch."

"You've known her a long time."

"Yeah, I have. I knew her before she was married." Cannington looked out across the valley. The sun had dropped behind the mountain, shrouding the land in shadows. His voice was soft when he spoke again. "I met her the first day she arrived in town. I'd never seen such a pretty girl. She took my breath away."

Rearing back in surprise, Riley worked fast to stem the frantic flow of his thoughts. "You dated her?"

A nostalgic smile tilted Cannington's lips. "Yeah, I dated her. For a few short weeks, we were almost inseparable. I'd even drawn up plans to modify the farmhouse to make allowances for her wheelchair."

Riley had to look away from the bleakness in the other man's eyes. Silence stretched between them. He hated to break it, but he needed to know. "What happened?"

"Watson's what happened." The words were spat on the ground, where they lay untouched in the dust.

Riley's head spun. *Cannington had been in love with Rosemary Watson.* Maybe still was. Did his accusations against the former commander stem from his obvious dislike of the man who'd stolen his girl? Could it be a simple case of jealousy? It wouldn't be the first time that happened.

Could he dismiss Cannington's revelations as the unsubstantiated ramblings of a man who'd lost the girl and was now hell bent on revenge? Or was there some truth to his allegations?

An icy wind snaked through the opening of Riley's jacket and slithered across his neck. Goose bumps broke out on his skin and he pulled his coat tighter around him. The day was closing in. Night came early to Watervale this time of year. Or maybe it was the thought of well-entrenched corruption permeating a Police Service he'd pledged to honor that had him feeling cold to the bone.

Whatever it was, it was time to make his escape. He needed to sort through the tumble-dryer chaos of his thoughts and approach them with a calm and logical eye. Better still, he needed someone else to analyze them. Someone removed from the situation and the beautiful girl with the touching air of vulnerability who'd come home and stirred up a hornet's nest.

Bidding Cannington a hasty farewell, Riley half walked, half jogged down the steep incline to where he'd left his vehicle. The thin mountain air seemed almost devoid of oxygen and he was grateful when he reached the comfort of his car. He climbed in and started the engine and turned up the heat before reversing out of Cannington's driveway.

Questions came at him from every direction and he shook his head in confusion, knowing he didn't have the answers. He gripped the steering wheel until his knuckles showed white in an effort to stem their trembling.

It was a delayed reaction to the shock he'd received up on the mountain. Breathing deeply, he tried to calm his racing heart.

The phone in his pocket vibrated. He tugged it out, ready to silence the call, but then saw it was Clayton. It was odd how his twin seemed to know when he needed to talk. He pressed the talk button and answered, striving for normal.

"Clayton, how's it going?"

"What's wrong, Riles? You sound kind of weird."

Riley sighed. *So much for normal.* "You're right, I've had a shit of a day."

"Tell me about it. It's so damned cold down here it would freeze the balls off a brass monkey."

Riley nodded in silent commiseration. Clayton lived in Canberra, the nation's capital. Hundreds of miles south of Watervale, the temperature in winter was more often below zero. The snowfields were an hour away.

"You're right," he agreed. I have nothing to complain about up here."

"So, what's wrong? It can't just be the weather."

"Hang on a minute." Riley put his foot on the brake and flicked on his indicator, easing the vehicle onto the shoulder of the road. He'd been in Watervale three months and they still hadn't managed to fit his squad car with a hands-free phone kit. It wouldn't do his standing in the community any good to be caught talking on the phone, especially while negotiating the tight bends between Cannington's farm and the station.

He pulled on the park brake and left the ignition running, pumping up the heat before he turned his attention back to their conversation.

"Actually, Clay, I'm glad you called. I've just been told the former LAC and his successor are up to their necks in shady dealings. My head's spinning. I'm feeling sideswiped."

A low whistle sounded in his ear. "Wow, you sure know how to give your day a lift."

"Yeah, you can say that again. Question is, what am I going to do about it?"

Clayton sighed into the phone. Riley let the silence stretch between them. It was a comfortable silence, one that didn't need to be filled with words.

A few moments later, Clayton spoke. "How reliable is your information? Has it come from someone you can trust?"

"That's the problem. I don't know. It just happens the source of the allegations is also in love with the old boss' wife and my informant didn't go to any trouble to hide the fact he's unhappy about the way she's been treated."

"I thought you were working on a missing person's case?"

"Yeah, I was. Still am. See, it gets better. The woman involved in the love triangle is the same one no one's heard from for the last month or so. How's that for giving my day a lift?"

Clayton chuckled. "You always did like a challenge, Riles. I'm sure you'll work it out."

"Gee, thanks, mate. I knew I could rely on you."

"No problem, big brother. I'm sure a man of your esteemed years will know what to do."

Riley choked. "Yeah right, like you can talk. I'm only the older by about two minutes."

"Three minutes and forty-five seconds, I think Mom said. Every minute counts, Riles. We both know that."

"Yeah, yeah, yeah. Whatever."

"So, what are you going to do?"

Riley tapped a finger to his lips, trying to sort out his scattered thoughts. "I don't know," he finally admitted. "I'm consumed by this missing person's case. I feel like I'm on overload. And now, to be tossed into what looks like a messy IA investigation—Christ, it's the last thing I need, especially after what happened in Sydney."

Riley clamped his mouth shut, but it was too late.

"What do you mean, after what happened in Sydney?"

"Um…yeah, forget about it, okay. It's nothing."

"You've never told me why you transferred to Watervale. Are you sure you don't want to talk about it?"

The care and concern in his twin's voice clutched at Riley's heart. For three months, he'd carried the burden alone. It would be good to share it. He prayed Clayton would understand.

"I took offence at what I considered systemic corruption within the ranks of my former command. When I raised my opinions with some of my colleagues, I was told to look the other way. The next day, the LAC told me I'd been transferred to Watervale."

"*Fuck!* You're kidding!"

The outrage in Clayton's voice went a long way to calming Riley's anxiety.

"Nope."

"Now it makes sense. I couldn't for the life of me work out why you'd give up a promising career in the DEA, headquartered in Sydney, for a job in a one-horse town in the boondocks. Why didn't you tell me earlier?"

Riley sighed. "I didn't know what to say. I was ashamed. I'd run away with my tail between my legs and hadn't even offered a whimper of protest. I should have gone to IA. I should have gone to the Police Integrity Commission—

something. Instead, I scurried off to the bush to hide. And they—they continue to get away with it."

"Jesus. You sure know how to complicate your life."

Riley thought of Kate and how much he liked her. "You don't know the half of it."

It was Clayton's turn to sigh. "I wish I knew what to say to you, Riles. I'm as outraged about it as you and I hate like hell thinking they might get away with it, but to tell you the truth, I'm not sure I would have done anything different. You were put in an unconscionable position: your career over your conscience. It couldn't have been easy."

"You have that right, bro. It's been keeping me sleepless since it happened. I keep going over and over the options in my head and every way I look at it, I always come out feeling I made the wrong decision."

"Don't beat yourself up about it, Riles. You're always able to make contact with IA, even this far down the track. I'm sure you won't be the first officer they've interviewed who has sat on something like this."

"Thanks, Clay. I appreciate your support. And you're right. It's never too late to do the right thing." Riley thought about Watson and Hannaford. A fierce surge of determination pumped through his veins. The debacle in Sydney wouldn't be the only thing he'd set right.

"Do what you have to do, Riley. You know I'll be here for you."

"Thanks, bro. It means a lot. How are Ellie and the kids?" he asked, referring to Clayton's family.

"They're fine. Mitchell turned one a couple of months back and babbles incessantly. Olivia spends most of the time on her iPad. I'm lucky I have Ellie to talk to."

Riley smiled a little wistfully. He wondered what it would be like to come home to someone you loved at the end of a long working day. An image of Kate filled his mind. The thought of the greeting he'd give her made him feel warm all over. Then he remembered how things actually were between them and forced all the cozy images from his mind.

Promising to keep in touch and thanking his brother once again for his support, Riley ended the call and pulled back onto the road.

Night had settled in around him. The shadows had melded together and were now indistinguishable against the tall stands of pine that stood back from the road.

He turned on his fog lights and used the wipers to swipe at the mist that had coated the windscreen. He still wasn't used to how quickly dark consumed the valley. It was like a switch had been flicked.

Mindful of kangaroos and the damage they could do, he eased his vehicle through the darkness, scanning the road ahead of him for animals. His mind continued to churn on the day's discoveries. Kate. Darryl. Hannaford...

The idea that even more senior police officers could be involved in corruption started a slow, cold burn of anger deep in his gut. It was selfish, dishonest men like these and the ones in his squad in Sydney, who forever tarnished the names of the thousands of loyal, honorable officers who served the State with truth and integrity.

It was bullshit and it wasn't right that a bunch of unscrupulous officers got away with it. Well, not this time. He wouldn't make the same mistake again.

CHAPTER 15

The lights of Watervale appeared below him and Riley sighed. It had been a long day and satisfactory answers had been few and far between. He headed for the office but looked forward to clocking off and heading home for a long hot shower, followed by a cold beer in front of the television.

Back at the station, he checked his email for messages. The third one was from Kate. She'd phoned a couple of hours ago.

Please call.

Two words typed by the office girl. No return number, but Kate knew he already had her cell. Fatigue weighted his shoulders. It was after seven. He didn't know if he had the energy to be clear headed enough to talk with her that evening. He read the words on the screen again.

Please call.

He sighed and pushed the pile of paperwork to one side of his desk and picked up the phone, refusing to acknowledge the way his pulse had picked up its pace. He dialed the first three numbers from memory and then hesitated.

Please call.

It sounded so like her. Short and to the point, but it also sounded lonely.

Knowing he shouldn't do anything this evening, but unable to stop himself, he replaced the receiver and pushed back his chair. Striding across the near-deserted squad room, he grabbed his coat from his locker and shrugged it on. Moments later, he headed for the stairwell.

Kate stared at her still-silent phone and willed it to ring. Where was the detective? And why hadn't he called? After finding the courage to call the police station, she'd been crushed with disappointment when the girl who'd answered told her Riley wasn't in.

Out on a job, apparently. Kate had tried his cell, but was told by the disembodied computer voice that it was either switched off or out of a cell phone service area.

She looked away and her gaze fell on her mother's laptop. She still hadn't scrounged up the courage to switch it on. The Toshiba sat where she'd left it on the counter, next to the television.

Her belly grumbled and she remembered she still hadn't eaten. After her run-in with Darryl, the last thing she'd felt like was food. She pulled open the door of the bar fridge and stared at the uninspiring contents: a couple of green apples and half a ham and cheese sandwich left over from lunch. The miniature bottles of liquor sat untouched in the door compartment.

Her stomach growled again and she sighed. She was going to have to go out foraging for something decent to eat. There was nothing else for it.

She collected her woolen cloak from the battered closet near the bathroom and pulled it on. She picked up her handbag and threw her phone inside. Catching a glimpse of herself in the mirror opposite the bed, she sighed and tossed the bag onto the table and began to riffle through it.

Her fingers finally closed around a tube of soft-pink lip gloss. Leaning toward the mirror, she swiped it over her mouth. Her skin still looked far too pale, but it would have to do. She wasn't in the mood for any more sprucing.

She found her room key beside the laptop. Her fingers trembled slightly as they hovered over the computer's shiny surface. Scrunching up her eyes, she promised herself she'd look at it after she'd eaten. She needed the time to fill her stomach with hot food and strong courage.

Tossing the key into her handbag, she removed the chain on the door and released the deadlock.

Pulling the door open, she gasped.

CHAPTER 16

"**O**h, my God!" Kate exclaimed. "I didn't hear you pull up. You scared me."

Riley lowered his fist and dropped it to his side, almost as surprised as she was. "I was about to knock."

She had a hand flattened against her chest. A pulse fluttered in the side of her neck. Her face was pale, except for her lips which sparkled in the overhead light with some kind of shiny, pink lipstick.

"I'm sorry. I didn't mean to startle you." He stepped back to give her some room and to allow his heart rate a chance to steady itself. His gaze swept over the golden sheen of her hair, pulled back in its customary tightly leashed bun. A few strands had mutinied and curled around her ears.

She smelled of cinnamon and crushed frangipani and warm, soft woman. He'd never been so acutely aware of her.

Boy, was he in trouble. He hid his feelings with a well-practised smile. "On your way out?"

She nodded.

"Dinner?"

"Yes." She gave a half-shrug. "I'm all out of supplies."

His gaze caught on the soft, peach-colored blouse that peeked out from her open coat, complementing another pair of woolen slacks, these ones black. Long boots of the same color encased her feet, their chunky, three-inch heels elevating her to just below his shoulder.

His gaze traveled upward again and landed on her lips. They were parted. She licked them nervously. Blood flowed to his groin. He tried counting by twos to change the direction of his thoughts and cleared his throat.

"I haven't eaten, either. Would you like to share a table at The Bullet? We could give it another go, if you like?"

She frowned and shook her head. Her mouth opened. He could tell she was going to turn him down. He sent her another smile, one even his mother found hard to resist.

"Please? It'll be my treat."

She bit her lip, indecision plain on her face. Slightly desperate, he played his final card.

"You wanted to talk to me, right? And you need to eat. If you come with me, you can do both." He offered another smile.

The tiniest grin tugged at her lips and the tension in her shoulders eased. "Okay, I guess. I do really need to talk to you."

Relief rushed through him and he grinned. "Good. Great. We can go in my car."

Another tiny frown appeared between her eyebrows, but she shrugged and pulled the door closed behind her. Riley walked toward his vehicle parked a short distance away and hurried to open her door. She squeezed past him, her coat sliding against his arm.

His breath caught.

Christ, what was going on? He wasn't some callow youth hoping to get to first base. What would she think of him, this woman with the movie-star looks who lived in London and had the posh accent to prove it? This woman with her ethereal beauty and air of worldly sophistication that was so at odds with the sad vulnerability he caught every now and then in her expressive eyes?

Watson's taunt rang in his ears, but he refused to dwell on it. Watson was an asshole and now had zero credibility. Riley wouldn't pay credence to anything that came out of the bastard's mouth. Besides, Riley was proud of his heritage and the fact that he was bi-racial. His parents had raised him to know the importance of love and of family. He'd learned through their example to discount the small minority of people who wanted to belittle him for who he was and what he stood for and he'd grown up determined not to give them any power over him.

His father was the first aboriginal to be appointed a judge in the New South Wales District Court...and he was Riley's inspiration. His father gave him the courage to stand tall and take charge of his own destiny. Who he became and what he made of his life had nothing to do with narrow-minded attitudes or the color of his skin.

Closing the passenger door, he moved to the driver's side and climbed in. Kate glanced across at him, a nervous half-smile hovering on her lips. Excitement and anticipation surged through him. He gave her his full-wattage grin before switching on the ignition and heading into the quiet night.

The Monday night crowd that mingled in the heated comfort of The Bullet was smaller than it had been on Kate's first visit. Another country tune played on the jukebox, its volume pitched low. She followed Riley as he wended his way through the mostly vacant tables until he found one tucked into a darkened corner at the back.

Sliding into the booth opposite him, she lowered her handbag to the floor and tried to stem the butterflies in her belly. He smiled across at her and her stomach flip-flopped, just like it had when he'd done it outside the motel.

He was so sexy he took her breath away. But it wasn't just that. She'd met scores of sexy men in Europe. None of them had made her heart palpitate this way. None of them had made her feel like she was the most beautiful woman in the world.

The attraction had as much to do with his old-fashioned manners and the depth of emotion and character she sometimes caught in his dark brown eyes; eyes that revealed a keen intelligence, kindness, concern, understanding, and something else. Something that made her feel that if he could see her deepest, darkest secrets, he'd still look at her and want her.

An almost unbearable urge to tell him the truth about everything surged through her: to tell him about her past; to tell him about Watson; to tell him about her mother. She opened her mouth to speak.

"Well, aren't you two looking cozy? What can I get for you? Wait a minute, a chardonnay and a beer, right?"

Kate closed her mouth so abruptly her teeth clicked together. She turned toward the barmaid and sent up a silent prayer of thanks for Sonia's timely interruption. *God, what had she been thinking?*

"Sounds good," Riley replied, flashing the girl a friendly smile. He turned to Kate. "Is that all right with you?"

She swallowed and managed, "Yes, a chardonnay would be fine. Thank you."

Sonia's gaze remained on Riley, her voice clipped, but polite. "Would you like to see the menu? Kitchen closes at eight."

"Yes, thanks."

Sonia walked away. Riley's heated gaze pinned Kate to her seat. "I'm starving," he murmured, his voice heavy with innuendo. "How about you?"

Long seconds passed. Breathing became optional. She dragged her gaze from Riley's and tried to still her racing heart. A minute later, Sonia returned with two menus.

"Here you go. The special tonight's lamb curry stew and fresh rolls."

Kate's mouth watered.

"Sounds great," Riley said, handing his menu back to Sonia without looking at it.

"Make that two," Kate added.

Sonia scribbled on her pad and then collected the other menu. "It shouldn't be long. Chef wants to make it home before the snow."

"Snow?" Riley raised an eyebrow. "I didn't realize snow fell this far north."

Sonia nodded, dark curls bouncing around her face. "Well, they're not making any promises—you know how these weathermen are—but there's talk we'll see the first fall tonight."

Kate tried to suppress the shudder that rippled through her. She'd always dreaded winter, the season when night arrived too early and stayed way too long. She'd learned the hard way that safety came only with the daylight.

Sonia wandered away. Riley frowned at her. "What's wrong?"

His expression was soft, caring, kind. Things she craved but couldn't have. Tears threatened at the back of her eyes. She bit her lip and willed them away.

Her fingers seized on the bright red napkin on the table in front of her. Without conscious thought, she folded and unfolded it over and over until Riley's warm, strong hand closed over hers.

"Kate, talk to me. Please."

There it was again. The tone, the gaze, the genuine interest and unexpected kindness. She weakened. Something tore loose from deep inside her and she shuddered again.

She took a ragged breath and eased it out, but her courage failed her. "I guess I just don't like snow," she whispered.

He said nothing, but his eyes darkened—impatience and disappointment evident in their depths. A deep weariness seeped into her bones. She was tired, so tired, of having to be strong, of having to hide her pain and her fear. The urge to confide in him, to share her burden, even for a short time, was overwhelming. The words spilled over.

"I-I didn't have the best of childhoods. In fact, there wasn't much of my childhood I didn't despise."

He didn't flinch. He didn't even move. Just his eyes—they flooded with compassion and understanding. She could drown in them.

"You're not alone there. I remember many a night crawling under my covers and crying myself to sleep."

His admission surprised her. She shook her head, confusion warring with warmth deep inside her as she absorbed what he'd said. What he'd shared.

"What were you crying about?"

Riley glanced away and she felt oddly bereft with the loss of eye contact. She willed him to look at her again, and when he did, she tensed at the hurt she saw.

He picked up her napkin and smoothed it out. "I was the only bi-racial student in school," he said finally, his voice low, as if the memories still had the power to affect him. "Actually, that's not entirely correct. I was the only one who looked different. I have several brothers and sisters, but they took after my white mother. I took after my father. He's a full-blooded aboriginal."

Kate shook her head, astonished by his admission. "But you're gorgeous," she blurted, unable to fathom how this good-looking man could ever have felt insecure. "You have amazing skin. And eyes. And your body..."

A flush stained his cheeks and he looked away. "Thanks, I'm glad you think so. My parents made sure we all grew up with a healthy self-esteem, but when you're eight and are the object of someone else's cruel prejudice, it takes a little effort to ignore."

"Your parents must be amazing people. I can't imagine what it must have been like to experience the bigotry of such narrow-minded individuals, but look at the man you've become?" she said, amazed at her boldness.

His flush deepened, but she was determined to continue. "You're a detective who's worked hard to get where he is. You haven't let life knock you back. You've met all the roadblocks head on and I bet you haven't once run away."

A shadow passed over his face but was quickly gone. His lips tugged upwards, an amused expression replacing the somber one of a moment before. "How can you say all that? You barely know me."

Kate stared at him. "I know it. From the moment I met

you, I knew you were the one who would help me—even when you pissed me off." She allowed a small smile. "I saw straight away you were bi-racial. I don't have to be Einstein to understand that you've probably felt you had to work at everything just that little bit harder to succeed. I don't mean to trivialize but it's probably like being a woman in some ways. I knew you were the one to do the job. You were exactly what I needed. Someone used to going the extra mile."

"You called me lazy." His eyes challenged her, the heat in them making her heart skip a beat.

"I was angry. I was desperate and I was beginning to think you wouldn't help me, despite my initial impressions."

He leaned forward, his elbows on the table. "I thought you were a stuck-up, spoiled brat."

He'd moved close. So close, she could smell the familiar fresh woodsy scent he exuded. Each time, it tantalized her and played havoc with her pulse. A thousand golden butterfly wings flapped against the wall of her belly.

"You used the past tense," she whispered.

His eyes flared in the dimness. "Yes."

Her eyes locked with his. Her heart broke away from its constraints and galloped against her chest. The heat from his chocolate brown eyes drew her in, closer and closer. Deeper and deeper.

"Here we go, two lamb stews, and rolls on the side. And here are your drinks."

Sonia set the food and drinks down in front of them. Kate's mind scrambled for purchase. The delicious aroma of meat and vegetables wafted toward her, making her stomach growl.

After the last few minutes with Riley, she hadn't thought she'd be able to swallow a bite, but the tempting smells of the dish proved hard to resist. Picking up her spoon, she sampled the stew and sighed in rapture.

"*Mm*, this is to die for, and I mean that in the best possible way."

Riley grinned. "Well, maybe not to die for, but it *is* pretty good."

Kate smiled around a mouthful of food. "Hey, if you'd been living on microwave dinners, this stew would have you ready to end it all."

He frowned. "Microwave dinners? You've been here over a week. Surely you've eaten something more substantial than that?"

She shook her head and took another mouthful.

"How come?"

She shrugged and kept her gaze fastened on her bowl. "I didn't feel like socializing."

He remained silent. After a few moments, she snuck a peek at him and saw understanding in his eyes.

She didn't need to say anything else. He got it. Mixing with the locals would mean she had to answer questions— questions with answers that had been buried years ago, along with her childhood.

"Now I feel bad for making you mad at me the last time we were here. I derailed your first decent meal in Watervale since your return."

She shrugged again, not wanting to dwell on the reasons they'd hadn't parted amicably. "Tell me about your family."

Riley swallowed a mouthful of food. Picking up his napkin, he wiped his mouth then scrunched the red cloth into a ball before dropping it back on the table.

"My family..." A wry smile tilted his lips. "Are you sure you want to hear this?"

Kate nodded and broke off a piece of still-warm roll. "Yes, I do."

Pushing away from the table, Riley leaned against the back of the wooden bench seat and laced his fingers across his stomach.

"My family. Well, as you already know, my father's aboriginal. The Honorable Duncan Munro was the first aboriginal judge appointed to the District Court in New South Wales."

Kate's eyebrows rose. "Wow!"

Pride glowed in his face. "Yeah, it is wow. He's still sitting on the bench at Grafton."

"Was that where you were born?"

"Yeah, all seven of us."

"*Seven*?"

Riley grinned. "Yeah, I have a lot of brothers and sisters."

"How many of each?"

"Two sisters and four brothers. One of my brothers is my twin."

She shook her head, her smile wide. "You have a twin? How fabulous."

"It would have been better if we'd been identical. We could really have had some fun."

"Are you close?" she asked.

"Yeah, we're close. We all are. I usually hear from some member of the family at least once or twice a week."

Yearning flooded her and thoughts of her own lonely childhood weighed heavily. "They sound wonderful," she murmured wistfully.

"You wouldn't say that if you knew them. Sometimes they're a right nuisance, a pain in the neck, especially when my sisters weigh into an argument. They're always so *right*."

Kate couldn't hold back her smile. "I can't speak for sisters, but as a woman—well, it's because we usually *are*."

Riley's eyes glinted teasingly. "You women, you're all the same."

"So, tell me about your sisters."

"Chanel's the baby of the family. She's seven years younger than me."

"So that makes her how old?"

Riley shifted in his seat. "Um, early twenties, I suppose."

Kate rolled her eyes. "Shy about your age, Detective?"

He raised a single eyebrow and something fluttered in her belly.

"You already know how old *I* am," she protested.

"Twenty-four. June eighth, right?"

She swallowed her surprise, secretly impressed. But then again, he was a detective. It was his job to remember details.

He leaned forward and lifted his half empty glass to his lips. Kate watched the play of muscle and sinew in his neck as he swallowed. God, she really had to stop ogling him like he was a jumbo-sized tub of her favorite caramel crunch ice cream.

Returning his glass to the table, Riley grinned. "Okay, I'll give it up. I had a birthday the month before last. June ninth. I'm thirty."

Her eyes widened and her lips followed suit. "Really? Wow, that's like—um—wow!"

"I hope it's a 'wow, our birthdays are so close' and not a—'you're thirty, that's seriously old,' wow."

A chuckle fell out of Kate's mouth. She couldn't help it. He was so goddamned gorgeous. She couldn't remember feeling so relaxed and comfortable in the presence of a man. Ever. "You were right the first time," she hastened to assure him. "Besides, thirty's not that old."

His answering smile curled her toes. Her hands clenched against the jolt of heat that seared low in her belly.

"I'm glad you think so." His voice glided over her like melted marshmallow. She dropped her gaze to her bowl and busied her fingers with the spoon, suddenly flustered. Filling her mouth with a piece of meat, she chewed the tender morsel until it had almost disintegrated.

His gaze remained warm on her skin. He waited in silence, as if he could see straight through her. The thought made her even more nervous. Another spoonful followed the first and then another. A wry grin tugged at his lips.

"Boy, you sure weren't kidding when you said you were hungry."

Kate eyed the nearly empty bowl and flushed. She kept her gaze fixed on the checked tablecloth and finished what remained of her stew with as much dignity as she could muster.

"Would you like some more?"

She choked, heat scorching her cheeks at the amusement in his eyes.

"No, thank you," she managed. "That was lovely and more than enough."

"You're sure? I wouldn't like to see you go hungry."

She shook her head. "No. Thanks. It was great. Just what I needed."

Riley leaned further back. "Well, I must say, it's nice to find a woman with a healthy appetite, although I'll be damned if I know where you put it."

His gaze raked over her, trailing heat in its path. The warmth slid over her and again, settled low in her belly. She squirmed on the hard bench seat and crossed her legs tighter.

A smile, soft and gently teasing, coupled with a knowing gaze, warm and full of promise, beckoned her closer. His hand reached across the table and picked up hers, encompassing it in his warmth. Her heart pounded. She tried to drag her gaze away from his but found she couldn't.

"I hardly know you and there are things you haven't told me. But I like you, Kate. I like you a lot."

The admission was delivered in a tone as gentle as the look in his eyes. Still, panic threatened to overwhelm her yearning to get to know him better. What she wouldn't give to put the horror of her past aside and give in to the feelings of safety and security this wonderful man projected. If only it were that easy.

Slowly, carefully, she disentangled her fingers from his and withdrew her hand. He stared at her, searching for answers. She looked away.

He sighed, a mere whisper of sound, then picked up his glass and drained it. Setting it back down, his gaze captured hers again. Disappointment shadowed his eyes.

"I wish you would trust me."

Her thoughts whirled. She wanted to trust him—she did. She'd give anything to be able to unload her troubles onto someone else's shoulders, particularly a pair of shoulders as broad and as strong as his.

She shook her head. "It's not a matter of trust."

"Then what is it?"

Kate closed her eyes. This wasn't the time or the place, no matter how much she wished otherwise. Finding her mother had to remain her one and only priority.

"I wanted to talk to you about Darryl. I think I may have something for you." She played with her napkin, nervously.

Riley's expression became shuttered. He sat back and folded his arms across his chest. "You left a message for me at the station."

She nodded and drew in a lungful of oxygen. "I went to see him today."

Surprise flooded his features. "At his house?"

Kate bit her lip and forced the ugly memories aside. "Yes. I went to ask him for my mother's laptop."

She challenged him with her eyes, daring him to object. "After you mentioned seeing it the other night, I had to get my hands on it. From what my mother said, Darryl never cared much for computers. It's possible she kept files on her computer about the two of them—you know, like a diary. Given his total lack of interest, she would have been confident Darryl wouldn't stumble across them."

Riley's gaze narrowed. "Did you find anything?"

"I haven't been brave enough to take a look, yet. I only collected it this afternoon. Then I called you."

Riley's lips compressed. "You're scared about what you might find."

Kate looked down at the table, fighting the familiar feeling of dread. "Not scared. Terrified."

Riley reached over and squeezed her hand. "We could go back and have a look now, if you're up to it."

Her gaze found his and she was comforted by the strength and understanding reflected there.

"Really? You'd do that?"

He nodded.

"Thank you. I'd really appreciate it."

Riley signaled for the bill and Kate finished the rest of her wine. He signed the credit card slip and then glanced over at her. "You ready?"

Nodding, she collected her handbag, drew in a deep breath and followed him out of The Bullet and into the cold, quiet night.

CHAPTER 17

Riley watched as Kate switched on the laptop with fingers that were far from steady. The motel room was comfortably warm, the central heating blitzing its battle with the icy air outside. He propped his hip against the counter, close to where she sat, and watched her fingers as they fluttered over the keyboard in the room's muted, golden light.

"So, how was Darryl? I take it he handed the laptop over without a fight?"

She glanced up at him. Shadows darkened her eyes. She touched her hair with a grimace. "Not exactly, but I got it anyway."

A desktop image came into view and Riley's gut instantly tightened. The wallpaper was a black and white photograph of a smiling Kate in a light-colored bikini, posing at the side of a swimming pool. Other children dressed in bathing costumes could be seen in the background. Kate looked about thirteen or fourteen, but even at that young age, her body revealed a promise of the womanly curves to come.

Kate's hands stilled. "That was taken during the summer before my fourteenth birthday." Her voice was soft and detached. "About six months before I left."

"Your mom took the photo?"

"Yes. She loved taking photos. It was one of the things she could do from her wheelchair."

Riley thought back to his conversation with Bill Cannington. "Did she get out much?"

Kate shook her head. "Not really. Not as much as she wanted to. Watervale didn't have a disabled taxi back when I was a kid. She was dependent upon Darryl to take her places and he always seemed too busy."

"I guess as the LAC, he had his hands full most of the time."

Anger flashed in Kate's eyes and Riley could have kicked himself for his lack of sensitivity.

"Yeah, right," she scoffed. "This is Watervale. The biggest thing to happen when I lived here was when old Mr Warwick wandered out of the nursing home in his pajamas and got struck by a motorbike."

"Was he hurt?"

"Only a few grazes and a dent to his pride, but it was the talk of the town for weeks."

Riley tried on a smile. "I can imagine."

Her face didn't soften. "Don't make excuses for Darryl. He's a selfish son of a bitch. Always was and always will be. And that's the least of his sins."

It was a throw-away line, muttered under her breath, but it snagged his attention. Before he had time to ponder what she meant, she turned back to the screen and began typing passwords.

Riley frowned. It seemed odd that Rosemary had protected her computer in that way, given that Darryl apparently didn't even know how to switch it on. It took Kate three attempts.

"What was it?" he asked, curious.

"My birth date. I tried hers and then Darryl's. Mine was lucky third." She tapped away at the keyboard and moved the mouse, opening windows and closing them. He watched as she opened her mother's email account and then frowned.

"What is it?" he asked.

"There's nothing here. Not a single message, new or old. Not even the ones I sent her when she stopped contacting me. At the very least, they should be here." Her lips tightened. She threw him a look. "Unless I was wrong."

"About what?"

"About Darryl. Perhaps he isn't as technophobic as he makes out. Maybe he said it to alleviate Mom's concerns he might access her files. I distinctly remember her saying Darryl couldn't stand computers."

She turned to face him, anger suffusing her cheeks. "What if it was just another one of his lies?"

Riley shrugged. "Who knows? Why don't you check the Deleted box? Some people don't realize an email deleted from the Inbox isn't gone forever. Even if Darryl had the capability to access your mother's emails, he may not have known about the deleted items or if he deleted them, he might not have emptied the Delete box afterwards."

"You're right," Kate murmured.

"If there are emails in the Deleted box dated after July tenth, we'll know someone else has accessed them," he added. "Given that the laptop has apparently remained in Darryl's custody, it won't be too hard to work out who it was."

"Why July tenth?"

"That's the day the cruise your mother had been booked on departed Sydney and, according to Darryl, the day he drove her there."

Kate's shoulders slumped. She turned back to the screen. Riley wished he could offer her better news.

"How many emails did you send her?"

"We used to email each other at least once a day. When I hadn't heard from her for a few days, I started emailing her asking her to contact me. I emailed her every day until the day I flew back from London."

Kate scrolled down to the Deleted items icon and gasped. There were more than two hundred and sixty-five messages. The most recent one had been sent only yesterday. All of them had been opened.

"Darryl went through them before he deleted them."

Riley nodded in agreement. "It looks that way."

Kate went through the emails that had been received after July tenth. Most were spam from various clothing stores, eBay reminders and a couple of online photography courses. But one name kept recurring: Daisyblu.

Riley moved closer, pointing to the most recent email. "Any idea who Daisyblu is?"

Kate shook her head and opened the email. Riley read silently over her shoulder. His gut clenched.

Rosie, where are you? We were supposed to meet nearly six weeks ago. I understand that you've changed your mind. That's okay. But please don't shut me out. Not after everything we've been through. I'm your friend. Let me help. Please.

Riley read it again. The timing fit pretty closely with what he already knew.

Closing the email, Kate scrolled through some of the other entries. There were nearly twenty-five others from Daisyblu that had been sent after July tenth. Most of them had been sent within a day or so of each other. The last two were a week apart. All of them enquired about Rosemary's change of plans.

The tone of the earlier emails suggested mild bafflement, but gradually changed to increasing concern. Daisyblu's final email was full of hurt and bewilderment.

"Let's see if there are any earlier than the tenth. It sounds like Daisyblu had an idea about what was going on," Riley said.

Kate scrolled down the list of old emails. Nearly two months earlier, in May, there was another email from Daisyblu.

Thank you for opening up to me today. I'm so glad you did. Have you thought about leaving him? I'm here for you, if you need help. Let me help you. Please.

Kate looked up at him, her face grim. "My mother was

planning to disappear—or at the very least, considering it."

Riley pursed his lips and nodded his agreement. "More than a month before she disappeared. Maybe it took her awhile to come around to it? And then, she would have needed to put a plan together. For some reason, she changed it."

Kate eyed him steadily. "Or someone changed it for her."

He grimaced. He may not have been willing to argue in Darryl's defence after discovering the man's penchant for dishonesty, but that didn't mean he was ready to concede the former commander was capable of murder.

"One thing we do know is that she didn't tell Daisyblu about any change in plans."

Kate sighed. Turning back to the computer screen, she scrolled through the messages again. Her mouse stopped on an email dated July ninth, a day before her mother had been scheduled to leave. It was another email from Daisyblu.

All good here. Are you ready?

Kate rolled the wheel on her mouse, cursing when her fingers couldn't make it move fast enough. With another click, she opened the Sent items and scrolled through them. She stopped when she reached an email dated the same date. She bit her lip and clicked on it.

I'm good to go. I'll see you tomorrow. Don't be late.

Kate turned to Riley, a haunted expression on her face. "I guess we now know she was alive until then."

Riley nodded. "It appears so."

"You're right. Now that we know Darryl is computer literate, we can't assume it was Mom who wrote it."

Riley compressed his lips and didn't answer. Kate turned back to the computer. With her jaw set at a determined angle, she returned to the Deleted box and once again, scrolled through the list of emails. She came to a halt on a message that had been received nearly two weeks earlier.

Riley's heart skipped a beat. The email was from Kate.

Kate opened the message and tensed, even though she must have known what it contained. Riley read it over her shoulder.

Mom, you still haven't responded to my emails. I've tried calling your cell, but you don't answer. Is everything all right? I'm worried about you. I'm coming over to visit—I'll book the next flight to Sydney and call you when I arrive.

Riley waited for her to lift her gaze to his. When she did, he almost winced at the bleakness in them.

"I'm not sure what was going on." Her voice was toneless. "Her emails had become very brief, her phone calls a lot less chatty. She always used to tell me about what she'd been doing—functions she'd attended, things like that. Darryl had retired, but there was still the odd invitation to a charity dinner or other similar events. He's a man much admired."

Her caustic tone as she spoke about Darryl was not lost on Riley and after meeting the arrogant son of a bitch, he could understand it.

"But something was different those last few weeks, before she stopped emailing altogether. I couldn't put my finger on it at the time, but looking back, and now knowing what we do about her connection to Daisyblu, I have to say, her emails started to sound like good-byes." Her voice cracked on the last word.

As her words sank in, Riley stared at her. Anger started a slow burn in his gut.

"I don't get it," he said, shaking his head. "Why the hell would you automatically think Darryl had done away with her? The very night you waltzed into town, you as much as demanded I arrest him for murder, yet before you'd even boarded the plane, you had suspicions that she was planning to leave him."

A dark-red stain spread across her cheeks. Her eyes shot daggers.

"It's not what you're thinking. There's *no* way she would have disappeared without telling me or contacting me right away. She, of all people, knew what it was like to be the one left behind. All the questions, the silent recriminations. Searching the eyes of every stranger she met. She told me about the agony she went through when I disappeared. She'd *never* have done that to me."

"Maybe she thought it was what you deserved?"

Kate stumbled away from the counter and paced the small confines of the room. Fury emanated from every pore. She rounded on him, her eyes flashing blue fire.

"My mother would *not* have done that. She didn't have a vindictive bone in her body. She loved me too much to put me through the hell she'd suffered."

"That didn't stop *you*." Riley braced himself as she came at him.

"You bastard," she spat. She raised her right hand and struck him hard across the face. His cheek stung. He seized her wrist before she could attempt a second blow.

"I was *fourteen*," she panted. "Little more than a child. I hated the thought of leaving my mother, but I hated the thought of staying even more. I gave no thought to the effect my leaving would have on her." She struggled to free herself from his hold, tears spilling down her cheeks. "All I wanted was to escape."

The helplessness in her eyes tore at his heart as fiercely as the sobs that shook her small frame.

"She wouldn't have left me like that. I just know it. I *know* it. I-I miss her. I miss her so *much*." Her voice hitched.

He pulled her against his chest and wrapped his arms around her, resting his chin on the top of her head. She cried and cried, tucked within the safe cocoon of his arms.

Gradually, she quieted and relaxed against him. He tried not to breathe in too deeply of the clean, sweet scent of her hair, or think too much about her soft curves that melted against him.

"We need to stop doing this," he murmured. "It could become habit forming."

She pulled away slightly and lifted her face. Her eyes were wide with sadness and vulnerability. She stared at him. Her lips parted on an intake of breath and his gut clenched in response.

He took her chin and tilted her face toward him. The tight rein he'd kept on his self-control snapped and he brought his lips down to hers. The touch of their mouths, whisper soft, left him yearning for more. Taking her silence for acquiescence, he did what he'd been longing to do from the moment she'd walked through the doorway of the police station.

Crushing her against him, his mouth claimed hers in a kiss fueled by long pent-up passion. Blood thundered in his ears, rushing through his arteries to center in his groin. His erection pushed against the softness of her belly and he struggled to contain himself when she stood on tiptoes, wrapped tentative arms around his neck and pressed even closer.

A groan rumbled deep in his throat and still he kissed her. The lips that had driven him to distraction were even softer than he'd imagined and enveloped him in sweetness and warmth. For all her outward sophistication, there was a shy innocence about her and he drank it in like a man dying of thirst.

With his heart hammering against his chest, he broke contact and lifted his head, breathing hard.

Kate looked equally affected. Her chest rose and fell rapidly. Her eyes had darkened to indigo and were filled with equal parts astonishment and fear.

Fear? That couldn't be right. What the hell was she fearful about?

But she'd already stepped away from him, hugging herself, her arms wrapped defensively around her slender waist.

He took a step toward her and she reared back. "Please, don't."

He frowned. "Kate—?"

"Riley, just go."

"I'm sorry. I thought—"

172

"I know. I know what you thought and I'm sorry. Please. I want you to leave."

He stood with his hands clenched at his sides—confused, bewildered.

Her breathing had slowed and she seemed to have recovered from their kiss. It was more than he could say for himself. Somehow, the fact that she seemed to have brushed off their shared passion with barely a second thought irritated the hell out of him.

His jaw tightened. "I guess I misread the signals. I apologize. It won't happen again."

He turned away and unlatched the door. Stepping through the opening, he walked out into the icy night and tried to ignore the cold despair that weighed down his soul.

Kate stared at her reflection in the mirror above the cracked Formica sink. She pushed back her hair with hands that trembled. Splashing cool water onto her hot cheeks, she tried to forget the look of abject confusion on Riley's face.

The quiet click of the door as it closed behind him had echoed through her heart. More tears stung the backs of her eyes, but she refused to allow them passage. She'd done all the crying she was going to do over the shitty hand she'd been dealt. It had ruined her chances of ever having a normal relationship. That was something it seemed she'd always known. Somehow, though, with Riley, she'd allowed herself the faintest glimmer of hope that this time, things might be different.

Then he'd kissed her. More than kissed her. He'd consumed her. His passion had exploded in her heart and had turned her molten with need. The yearning deep inside to hold him close and never let him go had been painful in its intensity and had almost overwhelmed her.

Then the fear had set in. The fear that her past would rise

up and contaminate anything they could ever have together. The terror that when it really came down to it, she'd never be able to let him touch her in the way she knew he'd want to.

So she'd pushed him away, like she'd pushed all of them away, even the most persuasive ones—the ones she'd thought would make her forget, only to discover they couldn't. No one could.

She couldn't keep doing the same thing, over and over. She had to deal with it. With a groan, she pressed her face into a soft, clean towel and scrubbed her skin dry. A decade ago, she'd walked away from the nightmare that was her life and had vowed not to look back. But now there was so much more at stake... She was damned if she'd let her past continue to dictate the terms of her future.

With renewed determination, she flicked off the bathroom light and walked back to the bed. The smell of Riley's aftershave lingered in the air, on her shirt. Her thoughts ricocheted back to him and the tightness in her chest returned tenfold. Regret, sharp and bitter filled her mouth.

If only...

If only things were different. If only she could stand to have him hold her, have him love her.

But it was too late for 'if onlys'. She'd seen the look in his eyes, right before the door had closed. At this point, she knew he wouldn't settle for anything less than a full explanation—and that was if he was ever willing to listen to anything she had to say again. She might have lost her chance.

She had to go to him. She had to make him see that the problem was *her*, not him. As lame and as trite as it sounded, it was the truth. And he deserved that, at the very least.

Throwing herself face down onto the coverlet, she buried her head into the soft mountain of pillows and recalled the feel of his arms as they'd held her close. The memory of his lips on hers made the longing deep inside her almost unbearable.

She thought of her mother and the choices she'd made. She thought of Darryl and wondered for the hundredth time if he'd taken her mother's life or arranged to do away with Rosemary another way. Or had she simply left, as Darryl claimed?

Kate had told Riley her mother would never leave without confiding in her, but what if she was *wrong*? What if her mother had been desperate enough to toss aside all of her concerns about how her daughter would react and simply packed up and left? What if she was wrong about Darryl, too?

Hot, swift denial twisted Kate's lips. She didn't believe for a moment he was innocent. He was evil to the core.

She recalled the way he'd spoken to her outside his house, the way his eyes had crawled over her skin, leaving her feeling dirty and ashamed. And she remembered the way he'd spoken about her mother. What had he said about the laptop?

'Your mother was never off it. Why she found it so interesting, I'll never understand'.

Kate's heart pounded. She lay very still. Her mind latched onto the words again and she tried to slow her thoughts.

Your mother was never off it... Why she found it so interesting...

And then she realized what had caught her attention: Darryl had referred to her mother in the past tense. *Why* would he do that? If he truly thought she was alive, he'd have phrased it differently. *Wouldn't* he?

Kate rolled over onto her back and hugged her knees tightly to her chest. Her breath still came fast and she did her best to steady it. She needed to keep her head clear so she could think.

She needed to call Riley.

CHAPTER 18

"**Y**ou'll have to try harder than that if you want to beat me, Munro."

Riley gritted his teeth and sent the squash ball slamming into the wall right above Chase's head, welcoming the discomfort in his muscles.

"So, you're taking body shots now?" Chase's grin faded at Riley's fierce, narrow-eyed look of determination. "You should have warned me about how seriously you take your squash."

"Hey, you're the one who agreed to the game." Riley smashed the ball, watching in satisfaction as it bounced off the front wall above the red line and onto the opposite side, completely bamboozling his opponent.

Chase frowned. "What's got you so riled up?"

Riley's jaw clenched. He wasn't about to tell him about Kate. He'd already spilled too much. He didn't need another round of gibing. Besides, *he* was still confused about what had happened.

The ball whizzed by his head and bounced off the wall beside him. His racquet came up instinctively but he missed it by a mile.

Chase yelped in surprise and pumped the air with his fist. "Score one for Barrington. Munro, you're going down."

Riley forced a smile. He pushed the thoughts away and buried them deep. He'd think about it later, when he was alone, when he was in a better frame of mind to deal with the complicated drama that was Kate Collins and the blows she'd dealt to his psyche.

With a well-practised flick of his wrist, his racquet connected once again with the small rubber ball and sent it flying toward the wall. There was nothing like hard physical activity to push other things from his mind.

"Hey, Munro? I think your phone's ringing."

Glancing to the back corner of the court where he'd left his things, Riley saw the screen of his cell light up. His stomach somersaulted with a mix of dread and anticipation. It was probably Kate. She'd left three messages already, one last night and two this morning. He wasn't ready to talk to her.

"Don't worry about it. We're on a day off. I don't know why I didn't switch it off," he replied, serving the ball up again.

"Yeah, might as well make the most of it." Chase grinned and lobbed the ball low on the wall. Riley didn't even bother to go after it.

"Another one to me, Munro. You'd better pick up your game before I whip your ass."

Riley's eyes gleamed. "Not in this lifetime, Barrington."

———————

Kate listened as Riley's phone once again went to voice mail.

"Hi, this is Detective Riley Munro. Please leave a message." The greeting was short and to the point and getting way too familiar.

She sighed and left another message. "Riley, I *really* need to talk to you. Please call me. Please."

Hitting the end button on her phone, she tossed it onto the counter next to the TV and dropped down onto the unmade bed. With her head in her hands, she fought off feelings of defeat.

He was avoiding her. Now, right when she'd made a

breakthrough, he didn't want to talk to her. And all because of her reaction to a stupid kiss. He thought her reaction was because of him. She'd seen it in his face. The hurt, the rejection. He'd thought she was rejecting *him*.

The truth was she liked him. *Really* liked him. And that scared her to death. The few times she'd allowed a man to get close, she'd panicked at the crucial moment. More than panicked—fought like a cornered animal was a more accurate description.

She still remembered making out with a young Italian guy a couple of years ago. He'd been good-looking enough to be a movie star. She'd even managed to get naked without the panic overwhelming her.

But then he'd started touching her and her mind and body had rebelled. It was like the jaws of death had tightened around her chest, squeezing the life out of her. She'd gone clammy and cold and had fought like an injured tiger to get out of his arms.

She'd felt sorry for him, but there had been nothing she could do about it—then, or now. She'd expected to feel the same way with Riley; had even braced herself for it. But it hadn't come. At least, not the way she thought it would.

Wariness had lurked beneath the surface, but the gut-wrenching, mind numbing full-blown panic attack hadn't eventuated. Perhaps she'd made progress, just like her four-hundred-dollar-an-hour English therapist had said she would. Or perhaps it was Riley.

Grabbing a pillow, Kate lay back on the bed and hugged it to her chest. Hot, silent tears seeped out from beneath her tightly closed lids. Oh, God, why couldn't she be normal? Like other girls? Like Sonia and all the other young women who had boyfriends and ex-boyfriends? Like the girls who knew how to laugh and tease and flirt, instead of tensing with fear the minute a man happened to shoot her a second glance?

There was no guessing why she was like that. Now, she had even more reason to despise Darryl.

It had taken awhile, but once she'd managed to

compose herself after Riley's departure, she'd returned to her mother's laptop and had checked Rosemary's email contacts. Daisyblu hadn't been listed. Of course, it was possible she was listed under some other name—her real name, for instance, but without that information, finding her out of the hundred or so contacts in her mother's address book was impossible.

Then she'd had an idea. She Googled Daisyblu and had found a Facebook page.

Daisyblu was on Facebook.

A single click later and Kate had sent a friend request. She was still waiting for a reply. Impatience grumbled low in her stomach...or maybe it was merely hunger?

She rolled over onto her back and tried not to think of Riley and the meal they'd shared the night before. Until the kiss, things had been going fine. More than fine. He'd been charming and funny, considerate and kind. He'd shared his deepest secret with her. At least, what he considered his deepest secret. It wasn't much when compared with hers.

She still couldn't imagine sharing her secret with anyone— not even a man with warm, brown eyes full of compassion, kindness and understanding.

———

Riley wiped the sweat off his face with his towel and draped it over his shoulder. Squatting beside his gym bag, he tugged out his phone and checked his messages. Another one from Kate. This time, she sounded desperate.

"What's with the grim look? You just beat me soundly." Chase sauntered closer, his curls hanging damp around his face.

Riley forced a grin. "Sorry, mate. It's nothing. Work stuff; you know how it is."

Chase cocked an eyebrow. "Thought you were on a day off? How's that MP case going, anyway? Kate Watson still in town?"

Riley's jaw tensed at the mention of her name. "Yep," he muttered. He tossed the towel into his gym bag and bent low to zip it up.

Chase whistled. "Like that, huh? You've got it bad, mate."

Heat crept up Riley's neck, but he refused to take the bait. Ever since that kiss, things had gotten way too complicated. He couldn't believe he'd been so stupid. She was an integral part of his investigation.

But she'd seemed to want it as much as he had. At least, until she hadn't. She'd been panting like she'd run a marathon when she'd torn herself away from him. He might have put it down to the fiery passion they'd shared, until he realized she was panting from fear.

With a heavy sigh, he hefted the gym bag over his shoulder and offered Chase a tight smile. "I'll catch you later, mate. Thanks for the game."

Curiosity gleamed in Chase's eyes, but he let it go. "Yeah, okay. I'll treat you to a beer at The Bullet tonight, if you're up to it. You probably have to go and soak those tired, old bones after the match I gave you. You might have won, but you had to work for every point."

Riley's lips twitched in response. "In your dreams, Barrington. In your dreams."

CHAPTER 19

Riley brought the unmarked squad car to a stop in the visitors' parking lot. Kate's rental car was right outside her door. He frowned. She really had no idea about taking basic precautions. How easy would it be for anyone to draw the same logical conclusion and discover her whereabouts without even trying? He shook his head and sighed.

He'd thought about phoning her, but after ignoring her messages all day, a face-to-face meeting was probably called for. He drew in a breath and wiped sweaty palms on his jeans. He didn't know what he had to be nervous about. It was only a kiss they'd shared, after all. People did that all the time.

Too bad it hadn't felt like just an ordinary kiss. And too bad she didn't seem to feel the same way. He gave a mental shrug. He'd get over it. It wasn't like he was in love with her.

Before he could change his mind, he climbed out of the car and approached the door of her room. He rapped on the wooden panel and, a few moments later, caught the twitch of the curtain as it was pulled aside. The door opened and Kate stood on the other side, looking anything but welcoming.

"I see you've finally decided I warrant a minute or so of your time. I hope I'm not keeping you from something more important—like cutting your toenails."

He grinned. He couldn't help it. She didn't even come up to his shoulder, yet she was spitting at him like a tigress. His casual shrug seemed to infuriate her further.

"Why didn't you return my calls? I've been phoning you since last night. Do you realize I may have made a break in your case? No, of course you don't because you haven't bothered to ring me."

Riley held up his hands.

"Whoa, there, sweetheart. Back up a minute. I've been off duty all day. As for last night..." He eyed her meaningfully. "Let's just say I wasn't in the mood for talking."

Satisfaction warmed his gut when she flushed and looked away. At least she wasn't totally immune. Surely that was a good sign? As good as he was going to get from the tight set of her mouth. She folded her arms across her chest.

"If you're off duty, what are you doing here?"

"I've been asking myself the same thing."

Her face darkened. Before she could say anything further, Riley lifted his hands in a placating gesture.

"Hey, Blondie, it's okay. Put your claws away. I'm here, all right? And I want to know what's got you so worked up you had to leave four messages for me to call."

Her shoulders slumped on a sigh and she drew her light cashmere cardigan tighter around her shoulders. Riley glanced around, becoming aware of the chill in the air, noticeable now the sun had almost completed its descent.

"How about you let me in and we can talk inside, where it's warmer? I can't have you catching a cold. I'd never hear the end of it."

She eyed him balefully, but opened the door wider and stepped back. He walked into the room and closed the door behind him. Immediately her scent wafted toward him. Memories of her soft lips crushed beneath his crowded his mind and he forced them aside with an impatient grimace.

Mistaking his discomfort, Kate spoke quickly. "I can turn the heat down. I've put the remote control here somewhere." Her gaze cast around the room, her arms flailing at her side. "It's just that I can't seem to get warm."

Riley reached out and stilled the movement of her arms. She tensed beneath his fingers.

"It's all right, Kate. Don't worry about it. The heat's fine. Tell me what you've discovered."

When he released her, she stepped away and came up hard against the bed. Flustered, she lowered herself onto the only chair in the room. The laptop was open on the counter in front of her, displaying a Facebook page.

Riley perched on the edge of the bed and looked at the computer screen. He quirked an eyebrow. "Facebook?"

"I've found Daisyblu."

Surprise jolted through him. He stood and leaned over her shoulder as she explained how she'd found Daisyblu on the popular social media website and had sent her a friend request. The woman had responded by accepting her request and now they were able to communicate on Facebook.

Riley knew very little about the social networking site— barely any more than his younger sisters had imparted. He'd never had the time or the inclination to be part of it and he wondered how so many other people did. But if something on Facebook meant they had a break in the case, then he was all for it.

He watched while Kate clicked open more pages. The photograph of a middle-aged woman with bright, smiling eyes emerged on the screen. Daisyblu. Also known as Daisy Bloomfield. He scanned the information in her profile. Married with two adult children, Daisy lived in Grafton with her husband...a retired police officer.

Surprise shafted through him again, but then he considered the logic. It made sense Rosemary would be friends with the wives of other policemen. After all, coppers tended to socialize with their own kind. He was no exception. It wasn't a conscious decision, but that's how it usually was.

He leaned over and tapped the screen. "Grafton's nearly two hours away. How do you think they met?"

Kate looked up at him and frowned. "I'm not sure. Mom

was never one to travel too far afield. Maybe they met at a police function? Now and again she'd mention a ball or some kind of charity event they'd attended, although not in the last few months."

Riley scanned Daisy's Facebook profile. "She doesn't have her address listed, but I guess it would be easy to find her, even in a town the size of Grafton. Someone would know where they live. I could even look on the internal phone directory at work. If her husband retired in the last few years, he'll probably still be on it."

"Do you think she'll be able to tell us what's happened to my mother?"

Riley heard the hope in her voice and saw the spark of excitement in her eyes. He hated to be the one to crush it.

"I don't think so. From the tone of her emails, she's as much in the dark about everything as we are."

The spark faded and Kate turned back to the computer. Her body slumped. "I guess you're right."

Riley winced at the defeat on her face, but he wasn't going to lie to her and if she took the time to reread the emails from Daisy, she'd know the woman was as clueless as they were. But they could at least go and talk to her. She could shed light on the events prior to Rosemary's disappearance. At this stage, anything could help.

"Hey, look at me." His voice was gentle but insistent. Even though she wasn't interested in him, he couldn't bear to see her so despondent. With obvious reluctance, she turned her head to face him.

"You did good, okay. Finding Daisy on Facebook, that's great. And I'm sorry I didn't call you earlier. It was rude and cowardly."

Her eyes widened. He held her gaze and the world narrowed to her perfect, heart-shaped face.

He shifted his head, making the tiniest whisper of movement. Her lips parted in response. Desire kicked him hard in the gut and then moved lower. All the reasons this was such a bad idea fought for airspace in his head, but he couldn't help it. He was on the road to heartbreak, but there was nothing he could do about it. He took hold of her chin and tilted her face up to his.

Her eyes darkened, an ocean of need beckoning him forward. His lips found hers and he moaned from the impact. They tasted of coffee and warm, soft woman. They tasted like Kate.

Her mouth opened under his and he deepened the kiss. His lips tasted her, drank in her essence. He couldn't get enough. He buried his hands in her hair and held her head still. A wave of blond hair tugged loose from the knot on top of her head and spilled over his fingers. He luxuriated in the silky feel of it.

A pulse beat a frantic tattoo just beneath her skin. He pressed his lips to the spot, exhilarating in the knowledge she was as affected as he.

Lifting his head, he dragged in a breath and tried to calm the pounding of his heart. His cock was rock hard. His arms trembled with the strain of holding back. Kate stood and moved into his arms, pressing herself tightly against him.

His stomach muscles contracted from the contact. He sucked in a breath. Her breathing sounded harsh in the silence. She held onto him like a survivor from the *Titanic*.

Slowly, he became aware of the desperation in the tautness of her limbs. A fine tremor shook her shoulders. Her arms tightened around his waist.

"Hey, sweetheart. It's all right. It's okay." He ran a tender hand over her head, stroking the silky strands of her hair. Something was wrong. She wouldn't be holding onto him as if her life depended upon it if she didn't want to be near him. *Would* she?

Gradually, she quieted and the pressure around his waist eased. She lifted her head and offered him a shaky smile.

"I'm sorry. I didn't mean to—"

He placed a finger across her lips. "*Shh*, it's fine. No need to explain."

Of course there was.

He kept the thought to himself. Confusion rallied in his head. He didn't know what the hell was going on, but he wasn't prepared to press her. She'd tell him when she was ready. *If* he still wanted to know. It was as simple as that.

Kate splashed cool water over her flushed cheeks and patted them dry with a clean towel. She could hear Riley in the next room, flicking through channels on the television. She couldn't believe she'd broken down like that, but it was progress. Much better than the bone-shattering, mind-freezing panic attacks she usually experienced when a man got too close.

Not that she could tell him about it. To tell him was to open a floodgate she'd vowed to barricade until the day she died. And even though a warm pair of understanding eyes caused a yearning in her so deep she didn't know if she could stand it, she'd managed to tighten the reins on her emotions and bury them deep inside her, where they had to stay. Feelings meant pain and she'd already suffered enough of that for two lifetimes.

"Are you all right in there?"

His voice drifted through the closed door of the bathroom, the concern in his gentle tone almost weakening her resolve. Resisting the lure of it, she drew in a breath and answered him.

"I'm fine. Sorry. I'll be out in a minute. It must be the heat. I was feeling a little lightheaded."

"Are you sure?" His voice sounded louder, as if he'd moved to stand right outside the door. Kate's chest tightened in alarm.

"Yes, yes, I'm sure," she hastened to reassure him, hoping he'd move away. She needed him to move away. So she could breathe.

"Okay."

The single word was less audible and she gulped in some much-needed air. She should never have kissed him. Not only was he a man, but he was a policeman. The worst kind of man.

And yet, for a few moments, as the heat of his mouth had consumed her, she'd managed to forget the fear, the loathing, the panic, the occupation. Because of Riley. He'd done that for her. Wiped her memories clean, even if it was for just a few moments.

Riley. Strong, kind, considerate, Riley. She owed him more than a view of the closed bathroom door. Squaring her shoulders, she stared at the wooden panel and prayed silently for courage. Then, she opened it.

Riley looked up from where he sat on the edge of the bed. Kate's skin was still pale, but she had a determined look in her eye that almost managed to distract him from the slight tremor of her lips.

Her lips. Full. Luscious. Sweet. He tried to erase the images, the feel of them against his. She crossed the room with cautious steps and resumed her seat in front of the laptop, keeping her gaze averted.

"Sorry about that," she said, staring with fierce concentration at the screen.

"Hey, don't give it another thought. *I'm* the one who's sorry. If I'd returned your call yesterday, we could have driven to Grafton today and found Daisy Bloomfield. We'd be that much closer to finding your mother."

Her eyes met his in the mirror above the counter, huge and dark in the dimness of the room. "You said *we*. Does that mean you don't think I'm a suspect anymore?"

Riley paused and realized that was true. He wasn't sure exactly when it had happened, but he *had* stopped thinking of her as a suspect. He still wasn't ready to put the cuffs on Darryl, but he knew in his gut Kate couldn't have harmed her mother. She cared too much. She couldn't possibly be that great an actress.

He frowned as he thought of the kisses they'd shared. Twice now she'd devoured him with a fervor that had matched his own, until she'd changed her mind. Like a switch had been flipped, the wanton ball of passion had become a trembling bundle of fear, pushing him away, retreating to the solitude and safety of her bathroom.

Was it all an act to keep him off balance? His gaze ran over her back and he noted the tension in her muscles, the stiffness of her arms. She watched him in the mirror, awaiting his response. There was something so sad and defenceless in her eyes. When he opened his mouth to reply, he knew he was about to step beyond the point of no return.

"Yes. I don't think you're involved in your mother's disappearance."

The relief on her face was almost palpable. Her shoulders drooped and her head hung low for a few moments, until she raised it again and met his gaze in the mirror.

"You don't know how much that means to me."

Her voice was low and husky. The weight of emotion in it clutched at his heart. He dragged his gaze away and ran a hand through his hair.

"You think Darryl's responsible, and who knows? Maybe he is. But we still don't even know if she's really missing, let alone dead. From the tone of her emails, she was planning to leave. How do we know she didn't simply do that, this time without Daisy's knowledge or involvement?"

Tears glistened in Kate's eyes and Riley steeled himself to remain objective. He had to ignore the plea in her watery gaze and focus on the facts. It was the only way they were going to solve this.

"I thought you were on a day off."

Her words cut into his thoughts. He offered her a slight smile.

"I am. What's left of it, anyway. But I won't rest while there's a fresh lead in your mother's disappearance. I want to find her as much as you do." He caught the quick denial on her lips and cut her off. "Okay, maybe not as much as you, but I take my work seriously, despite what you might think."

She looked away and a faint blush stole into her cheeks.

"I'm sorry," she murmured. "I was awfully rude to you that day."

He flashed a grin and brushed her apology away. "Hey, as you said, you were jetlagged. We can all get a bit stroppy after twenty-plus hours in the air."

Her eyes suddenly widened. She swung around in her chair until she was facing him. "Oh my goodness, I forgot to tell you! It's about something I remembered last night. That's why I called you the first time."

Riley felt a stab of guilt, even though he knew she wasn't having a go at him. He sat forward, her excitement contagious. "What is it?"

"It was something Darryl said when I saw him yesterday. We were talking about Mom's laptop. He said she was never off it and he'd never understand why she found it so interesting."

Riley frowned and sorted through her words in his head, trying to work out what had gotten her so worked up.

When he didn't respond, she stood and paced in front of the bed. "Don't you see? He used the past tense."

Understanding dawned. Could it really mean Darryl knew she was dead? Surely if he expected her to return he wouldn't have phrased it that way? Riley shook his head. He couldn't say. It was definitely odd and just one more thing stacked against the man.

"I talked to your old housekeeper. She told me your mom was going blind. Rosemary didn't want Darryl to know."

Shock spread across Kate's face. "Oh, my God, I had no *idea*. Mom never told me. Are you sure? Did Mrs Fitzgerald actually say Mom said that?"

Riley nodded. "I think Maggie was the only one who knew. Your mother made her promise not to tell Darryl. According to the housekeeper, they hadn't been getting on so good."

Folding her arms across her chest, Kate pressed her lips together. "I could have told you that. I picked it up from Mom's emails over the last few months before she stopped corresponding."

"Did she say anything specific?"

Her eyes flashed. "Don't you think I would have told you—?"

He reared back and held up his hands. "Whoa, I wasn't implying—"

"It was more what she didn't say," Kate interrupted him, the indignation fading from her face. "She knew I didn't like Darryl. She was always trying to make me see him in a better light, like she could change my mind about him. She'd share things they'd done together and tell me how lucky she was to have him."

Her voice drifted off. Riley watched a myriad of emotions chase each other across her face.

"Then, there was nothing," Kate continued quietly. "The last couple of months, she didn't mention him, apart from telling me she was cutting him out of her will. She didn't elaborate on her reasons, but it was obvious things between them weren't good. I was relieved she'd finally given up trying to convince me he was a saint." She sighed.

The anger and tension slowly released her from its grip. Her shoulders slumped. She sat down beside him.

"I've said this before, but he's responsible for whatever happened to Mom, Riley. I know he is."

Riley nodded and reached for her hand. She tried to pull away, but he tightened his grip.

"I found out yesterday Darryl's been involved in police corruption. At least, that's the way it looks."

She opened her mouth to speak, but he shook his head. "I can't tell you any more than that. I've handed it over to Internal Affairs. Of course, it doesn't make him a murderer, but it does say a lot for his character."

Kate's eyes grew huge as they absorbed the ramifications. "We need to find her."

Chapter 20

Kate glanced across at Riley's strong, sure hands where they gripped the steering wheel. He'd phoned her from the station after locating an address for Detective Sergeant Barry Bloomfield, now retired, and a half hour later he'd collected her outside her motel room.

The morning sun filtered through the windscreen and into her eyes. She'd forgotten her sunglasses and now pulled down the sun visor to shade her face. Her skin wasn't used to exposure to the harsh Australian sun anymore, even a milder winter sun. Riley shot her a look and noticed her hands were clenched in her lap.

"Hey," he coaxed. "Try and relax. I know it's easier said than done, but we have the best part of a couple of hours, yet. I hope you don't get carsick because some of this road twists and turns like a rollercoaster and it's pretty steep."

Kate managed a small smile. "Don't worry, Detective. I promise I won't ruin your immaculate squad car."

A grin tugged at his lips. She wished she could see his eyes behind the Ray Bans as his head tilted toward the detritus of takeaway food packets, chocolate bar wrappers and soda cans that littered the floor beneath her feet.

"Hey, I'm not the only one who uses this car," he protested. "The fingerprint guys will be able to tell you most of it belongs to Chase." He flashed her another grin. "I'll be exonerated and then you'll have to tell me how sorry you are for besmirching my character."

Kate grinned back, thankful for his attempt to distract her. Her gaze lingered on his crisp white shirt and navy-blue suit pants. A dark blue-and-gray striped tie was knotted around his neck. She'd noticed a navy suit jacket lying flat across the back seat when she'd climbed in. He'd obviously dressed for the occasion and she couldn't help but feel pleased he'd made the effort.

Apart from the good impression it was sure to make on Daisy Bloomfield, she got to drink in the sight of him in business attire—she'd always been partial to a well-cut suit. With his broad shoulders and narrow hips, his good looks were only intensified.

Heat stole into her cheeks and she turned her face away and stared out of the window before he caught sight of the tell-tale blush and started drawing his own conclusions.

She thought of their last kiss and her heart picked up its rhythm, but it was excitement, not fear that caused it. The feeling was so new to her, she wondered at the reality of its existence, but she couldn't deny it was there.

She wanted to kiss him again. She wanted to feel his lips on hers and his muscular arms drawing her in against his chest. He made her feel safe, protected, loved.

Loved? Was she out of her mind? He didn't love her and she sure as hell didn't love him. She barely knew him. Just because he was the first man who'd made her forget about her past for a while, that didn't mean the tumultuous feelings went any deeper than a fleeting physical attraction. And even if she yearned for things to be different, if he ever found out about her childhood, he'd never look at her with desire again.

With that thought firmly in the fore, she pushed the faint spark of hope that things could be different to the furthest recess of her heart and vowed to focus on what was really important: finding her mother. Talking to Daisy Bloomfield was at the top of the list.

Riley glanced at the navigation system mounted on the windscreen and made a left turn. According to the GPS, the Bloomfield house was right in front of them, at the end of a cul de sac lined with modern mansions and manicured lawns.

The Bloomfield residence was equally impressive. A two-story, cement-rendered structure painted mushroom gray, bordered by a high-walled fence in the same finish, stood tall and imposing at the end of the street. A pair of black wrought iron gates guarded the entrance and provided a glimpse of vast, winter-yellowed lawns and tidy garden beds. Parking the car at the curb, Riley glanced over at Kate.

"Looks like it pays to be a police officer—at least, a retired one. My pay packet sure as hell wouldn't buy this kind of lifestyle. Between this house and Darryl's, it's hard to tell which one of them is doing it tougher."

"So you think Bloomfield might have been involved in corruption, too?" Kate shook her head. "I can't believe my mother wouldn't be more discerning. She lived with Darryl for twenty years."

Riley grimaced. "Perhaps Darryl didn't let her anywhere near the finances. At least one person I spoke to told me Rosemary had no real money of her own. She relied upon Darryl for everything. It's not beyond the realms of possibility that he liked that power and didn't enlighten her about his earnings."

"I guess so. I was too young to remember how things worked when I lived with them, but I can remember Darryl would pay for things when we were out, like shopping and movies and stuff. If I needed money for school activities, it was always Darryl I would have to ask."

Riley ignored the bitterness that had seeped into her voice. The more he came to know her, the more he accepted she probably had good reason for her animosity. His own run-in with Darryl had been distasteful enough. He couldn't imagine living under the same roof as the prick—and being under his control.

Riley's mind shied away from other, more sinister, possibilities.

"We'd better go in." He pointed with his chin to the security camera fixed to a tall pole near the gate. "From the look of the security system, they probably already know we're here. No need to have them setting the dogs on us."

Kate nodded. Her lips tightened and her skin turned a shade paler.

"I'll do the talking, okay?" he told her. "After all, this is a police investigation."

"Okay." The word came out shaky, but there was steely resolve in her gaze.

Lowering the car window, he pressed the button on the security intercom. They didn't have to wait long before it was answered by the cultured voice of a woman.

"Yes?"

"It's Detective Munro from the Watervale Police. I'm here with Kate Collins. She's the—"

"I know who she is. Please, come in."

The gates slowly opened and Riley drove the squad car up the short graveled drive. The scent of orange blossoms wafted toward them from the direction of an early flowering Murraya tree that stood near the three-car garage, its branches laden with glossy, green foliage and thick white flowers.

The front door opened before they reached it and a real-life version of Daisy Bloomfield's Facebook photo stepped out onto the wide porch to greet them. Riley knew from her Facebook profile she was fifty-three. The age sat well on her face, despite the uncertainty that shadowed her pale blue eyes.

He reached for his jacket and climbed out. Kate alighted without his assistance. Together, they joined Daisy on the front steps. The older woman assessed Kate with frank curiosity before a small smile turned up her mouth.

"You look even prettier than in the photos Rosie showed me. The color of your hair—like wheatgrass dancing in sunlight—no photo could do justice to that."

Kate blushed. Daisy lifted tentative fingers to her auburn locks, carefully styled in a short layered cut that ended just above her shoulders. She shrugged a little self-consciously. "I used to be blond, but I would have no hair left if I'd kept up with the peroxide treatment my hairdresser told me was required to stay that way. I eventually decided on this." She touched her hair again and offered a wry grin.

The whisper of a smile graced Kate's face and then disappeared behind uncertainty. Riley knew how she felt. His gut had started churning the minute he turned onto the street. This woman could hold the key to understanding Rosemary's disappearance.

He cleared his throat, impatient to get on with it. "Do you mind if we come inside, Mrs Bloomfield? I have a few questions I'd like to ask."

"Yes, of course. And call me Daisy. Everybody else does."

After settling them onto an enormous burnt-orange leather sofa that looked like it cost more than a couple of months of Riley's wages, Daisy left them for a few moments to speak to the housekeeper about organizing coffee.

Riley glanced around the room—tasteful and elegant, yet simply furnished. The off-white walls housed a scattering of original paintings of Australian landscapes. An uncluttered cedar coffee table stood a comfortable distance from the sofa and a huge flat screen TV took up a fair portion of one wall.

Riley's gaze met Kate's and her raised eyebrow reflected his own. It was obvious there was plenty of money in retirement for this ex-police officer. Unless it had come from Daisy.

The woman in question fluttered in a short time later, the myriad of diamonds on her fingers catching the mid-morning sun as it filtered through the floor-to-ceiling windows, sending a shaft of refracted color across the walls.

"Nellie won't be long. She's just pulled a tea cake from the oven, so you're in for a treat." She smiled as she took a seat on the sofa not far from Kate, but the smile didn't reach her eyes.

Riley leaned forward. "Daisy, we know you're friends with Rosemary Watson."

"I-I guessed that's why you're here, Detective." Her gaze went between him and Kate. "How did you know?"

Kate cleared her throat and Riley let her answer.

"I've been through my mother's emails. The last one was from you. It was a simple matter to find you on Facebook."

Daisy sighed. "Facebook. Yes, of course." Her lips compressed. "If you've read her emails, then you must know she was planning to leave."

Riley nodded. "That's how it sounded, but we wanted to talk to you about it. Obviously you and Rosemary are close."

Another sigh escaped and Daisy slumped against the sofa, squeezing her hands together until her knuckles showed white. Her voice was strained when she spoke again.

"Yes, we are. From the moment we met, we clicked. You know... We have so much fun together. It's like we've been friends forever."

Riley eased his notebook and pen out of his shirt pocket. "Where did you and Rosemary meet?" he asked.

A fond smile tilted Daisy's lined lips. "We met at the Police Ball in Lismore a couple of years ago. I assume you know Barry's a policeman? Well, was," she added. "He retired last year."

Riley nodded.

"The Ball's held at the Country Club every year," Daisy continued. "You've probably even been to one yourself, Detective?"

He shook his head. "I'm afraid not, Daisy. I haven't been in town long."

"Oh, well, I'm sure you will. A good-looking boy like you will be in real demand on the dance floor."

Riley blushed and averted his eyes, not daring to give as much as a glance in Kate's direction. Clearing his throat, he steered the conversation back to safer ground.

"You met Rosemary at the Ball. Is that where your husband met Darryl?"

"Oh, heavens no. They've known each other for years. They were at the Academy together."

Riley digested the information. Of all the people for Rosemary Watson to befriend, it was the wife of a man who'd known her husband forever. "Did Rosemary know?" he asked.

Daisy shook her head. "Not at the time. I assumed Darryl had told her. It wasn't until I mentioned it in conversation a few months after we'd met that I realized she had no idea."

"How did she react?"

"Well, naturally, Detective, she was surprised. I was probably just as surprised she didn't know. Not that it made a difference to our friendship. Our husbands had both been in the service for many years. They know hundreds of fellow police officers."

They were interrupted by a woman in her mid-forties, bearing a tray laden with a silver service coffee pot, matching cups and a plate of freshly baked cake that smelled of cinnamon and sugar. The woman placed the tray on the coffee table and turned to Daisy.

"Will that be all, Mrs Bloomfield?"

"Yes, thank you Nellie. We'll serve ourselves."

The woman departed as silently as she'd come and Daisy leaned forward and picked up the silver pot.

"Coffee, anyone?"

"Yes, thanks," Riley replied and Kate murmured her assent. They'd been on the road most of the morning and it had been hours since he'd quaffed a short black at the station.

As soon as Daisy had dispensed cups of steaming black coffee and offered slices of tea cake, Riley got to the point.

"It's clear from your emails Rosemary confided in you about her desire to leave Darryl. Do you know why she wanted to leave?" He heard Kate's indrawn breath and knew she was as anxious for the answer as he was.

The older woman set her cup down on the coffee table with meticulous care and drew in a deep breath.

"It's a long story, Detective."

Riley's gaze didn't waver. "We have all day."

Daisy shot a hesitant glance in Kate's direction and then gave a brief nod. "Okay, but the longer I don't hear from her, the more worried I become. Once you listen to what I have to say, you'll understand what I mean."

Riley flipped over to a fresh page, his pen poised in anticipation. "Let's hear it."

Daisy straightened her spine and eyed both of them. "Rosie hated her wheelchair. Her multiple sclerosis had turned her limbs useless, but it had left her brain fully aware of her predicament." She turned to Riley. "Do you know she was already in the wheelchair when she met Darryl?"

Riley nodded and waited for her to continue.

"She's been a burden to Darryl their entire married life. At least, that's how she sees it. And from what she's told me, Darryl's made sure she knew that...with everything from what he termed the exorbitant cost of her many prescription medications to the physical burden of taking her anywhere. Though he appears to be the doting husband prepared to shoulder the burden with humility and grace, let me tell you, he's far from that when he's away from public scrutiny."

"When did Rosemary tell you this?" Riley asked.

"About six months ago." She grimaced and ran a hand through her perfectly coiffed hair. "I'd already begun to suspect all was not quite as rosy as it seemed."

"How do you mean?"

"Well, Detective, let's just say there were times Barry and I would have them over for dinner and during those occasions, cracks in Darryl's polished veneer would show through." She shrugged. "I don't know if he felt comfortable enough around us to drop the pretense or if he'd imbibed just enough alcohol not to care, but on more than one occasion I saw him treat Rosie abominably."

"Like how?" Riley shifted forward on the sofa, his eyes intent on Daisy's face. Kate sat motionless a short distance away.

"It's not what you're thinking. I never saw him hit her or

anything like that. It was more verbal and psychological abuse. Making fun of her disability or refusing to help her when it was obvious she needed it. Nothing so bad that we thought we should intervene, but it was definitely a different side of Darryl than the one he shows the world."

"How did my mother react?"

Riley swung around. Kate's voice was scratchy with emotion and her eyes glittered with unshed tears.

Daisy's attention also shifted to Kate. "Oh, honey, I'm sorry. I wish I could tell you she stood up to him, but she didn't—none of us did. When I expressed my concern to Barry later, he told me to stay out of it, that it wasn't any of our business."

Kate's jaw tensed. Riley's gut clenched when a single tear traced a slow and silent path down her cheek.

He reached out to her. "Kate—"

"No, I'm all right," she muttered, swiping at her face. She lifted her coffee to her mouth with a shaky hand and took a sip. Her eyes implored Daisy. "Please, go on. I want to hear the rest of it."

"It was after one such evening when I found the courage to ask her about it. We'd become really good friends by then and I hated to see her treated that way. A couple of months ago, she told me about their life and how far removed it was from the image of the loving couple they showed to the world. She told me even her housekeeper didn't know the full truth."

"Who raised the question of leaving?" Riley asked.

"I did. I couldn't bear to hear any more stories about how she was treated—or mistreated. I couldn't bear to see her so unhappy." Daisy drew in a deep breath. "So, I told her to leave him."

"What was Rosemary's reaction?"

"Well, Detective, the truth is, she wasn't at all keen. I guess I can understand it. She's in a wheelchair, barely able to do anything without help and then there was the cost of her medications. She didn't have much money of her own. She couldn't see how she'd survive without him."

Kate inched forward on the sofa, her gaze fixed on Daisy. "What changed her mind?"

Daisy clenched her hands together, mirroring the distress in her eyes. "The thing is, I don't know. She never told me. We went from having conversations about all the reasons why it was impossible for her to leave him, to all of a sudden, her quizzing me about how soon we could organize it."

Kate stiffened. "Did you ever ask her why? I mean, you must have found it a little odd, her sudden change of heart?"

Daisy nodded. "Yes, honey. I did find it odd and I asked her about it. All she'd tell me was that something had happened and it was imperative that she leave."

Riley's eyes narrowed. "Did you take it to mean she was leaving permanently, or was it more like—I can't take it anymore, I need to get away for a while?"

Kate stilled. Riley's hands tightened into fists.

"You know," Daisy responded slowly, "I think whatever it was that happened, it finally triggered the courage and motivation she needed to leave forever. I don't think she had any intention of coming back."

"When did this conversation take place?" he asked.

"July second."

"You sound very sure of that," Riley said.

Daisy smiled sadly. "I ought to be. It's my birthday. Rosie had invited me to her place for lunch. When I got there, she surprised me with a bouquet of my favorite flowers and a huge chocolate cake. She's always been thoughtful like that."

Riley flipped back through the pages of his notebook until he found the notes he'd made when he'd spoken to Darryl. Darryl had said he'd driven Rosemary down to Sydney on July tenth, a week after Daisy's visit with her.

He eyed Daisy again. "It appears from your emails, you and Rosemary had agreed on a leaving date. Is that correct?"

"Yes, although I said we needed more time to put everything in place, Rosie was insistent she had to go as soon as possible. She didn't even want to wait for an upcoming doctor's appointment, despite the fact she needed to have some of her prescriptions renewed."

"Do you remember what date you decided upon?"

"Of course, Detective. It was July tenth. Rosemary was anxious to be gone by then."

The date hit him like a physical blow. The coincidence was too obvious to ignore. He glanced over at Kate. Her gaze remained fixed on Daisy. He kept his thoughts to himself and asked another question.

"Where did you agree to meet for the final parting?"

"We were supposed to meet in the car park outside the medical center. She's caught a cab there on numerous occasions in the past. She felt it was a place where she could be seen without attracting suspicion and if Darryl phoned the cab company to ask where they'd taken her, it would seem like a legitimate journey."

"So, you were going to collect her from the car park and take her somewhere?" he said.

"Yes. She was supposed to go to the Grafton Airport. When we'd made plans earlier, she asked me if she could borrow the money for a plane ticket. Of course, I agreed. I wanted to do everything I could to help her. I-I made the reservation online. She was going to catch a plane to London."

Kate gasped. Riley turned to her. Her face had turned white and she held a trembling hand to her chest, as if trying to calm her heart.

So, this news was a surprise to her, too.

Determination surged through him and a sense of urgency flooded his veins. "I take it you printed the ticket to give to her?"

Daisy nodded. "Yes, but of course, I-I still have it."

He stared hard at the woman. "Why didn't Rosemary show, Daisy?"

She shook her head and her eyes closed tight. Despair deepened the wrinkles on her face and the grooves around her mouth. When she opened them, tears crowded her eyes.

"You already know from my emails that I don't know, Detective. Everything was in place; we were all set to go. I'd done everything she'd asked—new clothes, new shoes. She couldn't take anything from her home. She said Darryl would notice. Besides, she would have needed help retrieving a suitcase from where they were kept upstairs and she didn't want anyone else to know."

The tears spilled over. "She even asked me to buy her some black hair dye," she choked. "She couldn't do anything about the wheelchair, but at least from a distance, she was hoping to fool the casual observer."

Riley's voice gentled. "When did you last have contact with Rosemary?"

Daisy unfolded a small, lacy handkerchief and dabbed at the moisture in her eyes.

"She rang me on the fifth. She wanted to confirm everything was ready. She told me not to call her again in case Darryl was there. She didn't want to have to watch what she said. He'd discovered she'd been to a lawyer and had changed her will. He'd started to keep a closer eye on her and she was scared he might have realized what she was up to."

"What about emailing her?" Riley asked.

Daisy nodded. "I sent her a message the day before we were due to meet. She confirmed everything was ready and she would meet me as arranged. The email gave me no cause for concern. I left for Watervale early on the morning of the tenth, believing I would find her waiting for me outside the medical center."

"How did Barry feel about you being involved in all this?" It was a stab in the dark, but Riley took a punt.

Daisy's eyes widened. "He was a little upset," she admitted quietly. "He heard me speaking to Rosemary that night she called, a few days before she was due to leave. He said it wasn't any of our business and I shouldn't have stuck my nose in."

"How does he feel about Rosemary?"

Daisy shrugged. "He thinks she's okay, I guess. He's never

really expressed an opinion about her one way or the other. He was happy enough about our friendship, though. And of course, he always enjoyed Darryl's company." Her lips tightened. "Men seem to be able to overlook more than women can."

"Do you think he would have told Darryl about what Rosemary was planning?" Riley probed.

Daisy's jaw fell open. She shook her head vehemently. "*Never!* Barry is a good and decent man. He may not have been willing to get involved in the Watsons' personal affairs, but it didn't mean he agreed with the way Darryl treated Rosie. There's no way he would have told him she was leaving."

Riley remained silent, unwilling to speculate, despite what his gut was telling him. He didn't even know the man. It was Barry's friendship with Darryl that was clouding Riley's judgment. He couldn't imagine wanting to be anywhere near the prick if he didn't have to be.

Another thought occurred to him. "Have you spoken to Darryl since Rosemary failed to show? What has *he* said about her disappearance?"

Daisy looked away, uncertainty flooding her face. "H-he hasn't returned my calls. I've left a number of messages. When I asked Barry to call him, he became quite cross and told me to stay out of it. He told me I'd only end up getting caught in the middle."

She shifted her gaze back to Riley's. "Barry thinks Rosemary's changed her mind. That she's decided to stay with Darryl after all and she's too embarrassed to tell me. That's why she's ignoring me. At least, that's what Barry thinks."

Riley drew in a deep breath and shot a look at Kate. She sat still, her hands clenched in her lap, her mouth tight.

"I'm afraid Rosemary's not at home, Daisy," he said. "Whether she changed her mind about leaving when she said she would, we don't know, but she's definitely not at home. Darryl told us she's gone on a holiday."

Confusion clouded the pale blue eyes. "Really? That's so

strange. All those plans we made... When she made up her mind to do it, she seemed desperate to leave him." She shook her head. "I'm sorry. A *holiday?* I don't believe it."

Dread tightened Riley's gut. "I'm not sure if she is on a holiday, Daisy. Certainly not the one Darryl told us about. The truth is, we don't know where she is."

CHAPTER 21

Kate watched the blood drain from Daisy's face. The woman leaned forward, her head hung low. Her hands clutched at her perfectly coiffed hair.

"Oh, my God, he's done something to her! The minute I saw you in the security camera, I knew something was wrong."

Kate's heart stopped. The fear that lurked inside her sprang to life and hurtled through her chest, seizing her throat in a stranglehold. She tried to speak. The words came out choked. "Wh-why do you say that, Daisy?"

Riley's gaze shot to hers, the brown depths full of concern. It warmed her to know he cared, but even that couldn't infiltrate the icy dread that had turned her limbs to lead. It was one thing for *her* to think Darryl could be capable of making her mother disappear, but to hear it from somebody else—the reality of that was almost unbearable.

Daisy's hands dropped to her sides. Her face remained pale. She squeezed her eyes closed.

"I don't know. It's just a feeling I've had almost from the beginning—especially when I couldn't contact her. She wasn't answering her phone and she didn't return my emails. And then when Darryl didn't return my calls..."

She lifted her head, devastation plain on her face. "I'm sorry. I'm so sorry, honey. I should have called the police myself weeks ago, when she didn't show. But Barry said—"

She broke off abruptly and hiccupped on a sob. Tears coursed down her cheeks.

Kate's heart hammered. She didn't want to hear any more, but she didn't have a choice. If they were ever going to find her mother, she had to know. Leaning forward, she took hold of one of Daisy's plump, be-ringed hands.

"Please, Daisy. Finish what you were going to say. What did Barry say?"

A deep breath shuddered through the older woman's body and her fingers tightened around Kate's. Tears continued to spill over her cheeks, leaving damp trails through her foundation. Kate held her breath.

"I waited nearly three hours. When Rosie didn't show, I drove to her house. If Darryl answered, I was going to make up some excuse that I was in town and thought I'd surprise Rosie." Her breath hitched.

"I knocked on the door, but no one answered. There didn't seem much point waiting around, so I went home. I was so upset. I couldn't believe she'd changed her mind and not told me. I'd driven two hours to collect her and another two hours home again. It wasn't so much the inconvenience I was upset about, but that she hadn't told me she'd changed her mind."

Daisy swiped at her tears with a trembling hand and continued. "B-Barry was here when I arrived home. He asked me where I'd been and why I'd been crying. I-I told him what had happened."

Dread settled heavily in Kate's stomach. She glanced at Riley. His face was dark and sober as he watched Daisy fall apart.

"What did Barry say, Daisy?" he asked slowly.

She seemed to take courage from his implacable attitude and drew in a deep breath. She looked him squarely in the eyes when she replied, "He told me I was being silly. That I'd watched too many episodes of CSI. He told me Darryl would never do anything so stupid."

"And you believed him," Kate murmured, her fingers tightening on Daisy's.

Daisy nodded. "Yes, I believed him. I guess I wanted to believe him. The alternative was too awful to contemplate. Besides, he knows Darryl a lot better than I do."

"Yes, he does," Riley agreed, his face grim.

Kate gently disentangled her hand and found Riley's gaze. "What do we do now?"

"I'll check the cab company and see if they had a booking for Rosemary on the day she was supposed to meet Daisy. That will at least tell us if she was still alive and committed to leaving at that time. We'll also find out if she ever took the taxi ride. Who knows? Something may have happened between her house and the meeting point. Or she could have given the cab driver different directions. Either way, it's worth looking into. I'm also going to check with her doctor about her medications." His gaze swung to Daisy's. "You said she was taking a number of prescription drugs. You don't happen to know her doctor, do you?"

Daisy nodded. "Yes, it's Dr Ben Shepherd. He has rooms at the medical center on Booth Street. It was where we were supposed to meet."

"I want to check if she had those prescriptions renewed, after all. If she was flying to the UK as you say, it would have been logical for her to renew them. Right now, we need to know exactly when Rosemary was last seen alive."

Tendrils of ice encircled Kate's heart although the announcement didn't come as any real surprise. She stared at Riley with foreboding.

"You think she's dead, don't you?"

He stared back at her for what seemed like a lifetime. Then his eyelids lowered and blanketed his eyes from her gaze. He nodded, once.

The breath whooshed out of her. She fell forward and brought her hands up to her face. Emotion welled in her throat and burned behind her eyes, but she bit her lip and dug her fists into her eye sockets, forcing it back.

Now wasn't the time to fall apart, not here, with Daisy and Riley looking on. She'd already leaned on him more times than was wise. She needed to channel her anger and grief where it mattered most—finding her mother, dead or alive.

The lunch hour rush had thinned to a trickle when Riley pulled into the drive-through of Watervale's only fast food outlet. He'd offered to get Kate something, but she'd told him she didn't feel like eating. At her request, he'd left her outside her motel room, promising to contact her with any new information.

His mind couldn't let go of the near-certainty Darryl was involved in Rosemary's disappearance. She'd been set to leave him, had put everything in place. Then something had happened, and Rosemary hadn't left—at least, not the way she'd planned.

At his request, Daisy had given him the plane ticket she'd purchased in Rosemary's name and he'd called the airline. They'd confirmed Rosemary hadn't boarded the flight, lending further credence to Daisy's story.

Darryl had explained Rosemary's absence with a holiday, but she hadn't left that way, either. Riley had called the only cab company in town with a disabled taxi and had been told that Rosemary Watson had made a booking for a cab on the morning of July tenth but had failed to show.

Another call, this time to Rosemary's doctor, confirmed she'd phoned more than six weeks ago to cancel her scheduled appointment. She'd left a message with his receptionist saying she had run out of time.

Dr Shepherd hadn't heard from her since. He expressed concern that if she didn't get her prescriptions renewed, her medical condition would worsen, including the problems with her vision.

When Riley quizzed him on whether it would be possible for Rosemary to obtain her prescriptions elsewhere, even in London, he agreed it was, but if she'd attended a doctor in Australia, it would be normal for that doctor to call him as a matter of courtesy and check her medical history. He'd received no such call.

Another check on her bank records indicated nothing had changed since Riley had first investigated: There had been no activity, apart from the fortnightly direct deposits of her disability pension.

Daisy had confirmed she'd withdrawn two thousand dollars from her own account to give to Rosemary, but the money had been with the other things Daisy had purchased that Rosemary had never collected.

Riley sighed as he waited for his order. Rosemary Watson had no money and no medications, both vital to her wellbeing. The only person who claimed to have seen her on the date that she'd planned to leave was Darryl—a man Riley now knew was up to his neck in corruption. A man who just happened to be friendly with the husband of his wife's best friend, who had learned about her plans.

A fresh-faced young girl appeared in the drive-through window and handed him his lunch in a brown paper bag. Riley gave her the money and nodded his thanks. Her cheery farewell irritated him more than it should have. It wasn't her fault that no matter how he looked at it, the rest of his day would be anything but great.

With the bag on his lap, he headed for the station. Tugging out the hamburger, he unwrapped it and took a grateful bite. He had a feeling in his gut that his investigation was about to get messy. It was time he took a closer look at Darryl.

———————

With his three iron, Darryl lined up the hole which stood at least four hundred yards away. He was already well over par and they still had another three holes to go. His game had been off ever since his stepdaughter arrived back in town.

Even now, the thought of the smart-mouthed bitch had his gut churning. He pulled the roll of Tums out of his pocket and tapped a couple of them into his mouth. His indigestion was still giving him hell.

With another glance at the hole he was aiming for, he pulled his iron backward and struck it hard and clean. His satisfaction was short lived. The ball dropped well short and landed in the sand.

"Bad luck, boss," Hannaford sympathized.

Darryl grimaced and didn't bother to reply. Hannaford took his shot and landed on the green. Darryl's bad mood rose another notch.

"How's that stepdaughter of yours?" Hannaford asked, seemingly oblivious to Darryl's dark thoughts. "I hope Munro isn't still giving you trouble?"

"Nope, I haven't seen hide nor hair of him since I sent him packing more than a week ago. I take it you reminded him of the importance of sticking together?"

Hannaford smiled. "Oh, yes. We had that little conversation."

"Did you mention you'd been in contact with his former commander? I bet he nearly shit himself when he heard you'd spoken to Shattler."

Hannaford lowered his gaze. "I-I didn't see the need to mention it at this stage. No need in threatening him with that before we have to. Next time, he might find the balls to go to IA. We can all do without that."

"Yeah, I guess you're right. It just shits me this holier-than-thou attitude coming through from some of the younger coppers. Anyone would think the Wood Royal Commission was still running, the way they want to play by the rules all the time."

Darryl shook his head in disgust and continued his tirade. "It's fucked. No one can do what we do and play by the rules. Look at the crime statistics in Sydney. They've skyrocketed since fucking Commissioner Wood took away our advantage. It was the only thing we had over the fucking criminals. Now look where we are!"

Hannaford nodded his head in silent commiseration. "Who knows where it's all going to end up?"

Hannaford's comment triggered thoughts of Rosemary. Darryl grinned to himself. She'd had no idea how she was going to end up. The shock on her face when she'd realized he was onto her had been priceless.

When Barry Bloomfield had called him on that Tuesday night, he'd been surprised to be informed his wife was planning to leave. Barry had overheard his wife talking to Darryl's and had been only too happy to pass on the information. Barry knew all about the ties that bound them.

At first, Darryl had been ambivalent. He'd lost interest in Rosemary years ago. If she wanted to leave, he'd help her pack. The only reason he hadn't kicked her out was the damage it would do to his reputation. Throwing his handicapped wife out on the streets wasn't a good look for a man who aspired to be the next mayor of Watervale.

But later that night, he'd got to thinking and the more he thought about it, the more it seemed strange that after putting up with their marriage for more than two decades, his wife had decided to call it quits. What was more, she wasn't even planning to let him know.

That was definitely odd.

With another three scotches under his belt, his thoughts turned darker. Could there be more to her sudden departure than he thought? With a moment of clarity, he'd hauled himself off the couch and had gone to the cupboard where he stored his things. Fishing out the key from its hiding spot, he'd unlocked the door and stared in disbelief at what he found.

Where once there had been a neat collection of photos and DVDs, there was nothing but bare shelves. He bent lower and pulled out the box containing the videos. They too, were gone.

Realization had hit him hard. She'd found them. Not only had she found them, she'd *taken* them. He'd shaken his head in shock and disbelief.

Twenty years of marriage and she'd never once appeared curious about the things he kept in his cupboard. He'd kept them downstairs so that he could watch them on his big screen whenever he wanted.

Rosemary retired early most nights and left him to his own devices. Installing another expensive television in a room upstairs would have roused suspicion. Whilst they were no longer intimate, they continued to share a bed. There was no reason for him not to watch them on the one downstairs once she'd gone to sleep.

So he'd kept his collection handy and for more than a decade, they'd remained undetected.

But she'd not only found them but had removed them.

His first thought had been panicked. He didn't have the hold over Rosemary that he had on the others, no matter what he told himself and it would take more than a smile and a logical explanation to appease her.

If she hadn't found the videos of Kathryn, perhaps he could have bluffed his way through it—denied any knowledge of the girls in the photos and on the DVDs and blamed it on one of his colleagues—but bluffing was no longer an option. No matter which way he looked at it, there was no explanation for her daughter's images being among the collection.

It had taken him awhile and most of another bottle of scotch, but he'd eventually realized what he had to do. There was nothing for it: He had to get rid of her.

Once the decision had been made, the rest was easy. He'd gone to the travel agency the very next day and had enquired about holidays—something long and isolated from easy communication. It was a stroke of luck that a four-month round-the-world cruise was due to depart Sydney within a few days.

He hadn't killed her right away, of course. That would have been foolhardy. He knew about her friendship with Daisy and assumed his wife would be in contact with the woman prior to her departure. He couldn't afford to raise either woman's suspicions. Barry had told him Rosie was planning to leave on July tenth. It gave him plenty of time to put his plan into action.

He was careful to go through the motions, purchasing a

ticket and even going so far as to drive all the way to Sydney and back. It had been another stroke of luck that he'd thought to purchase the building supplies and hardware he'd required to bury her while on that trip to Sydney.

In the end, he'd done it quickly, with the minimum of fuss. A knife across her throat while she'd been fast asleep and it was all over for Rosemary. It had taken him most of the night to clean up the blood.

It had now been more than six weeks. Until the arrival of his stepdaughter, he'd been feeling quietly confident his plan would hold up. He'd already started comprising suitably sad responses when people sympathized with the fact that his wife would be placed in a nursing home when she arrived back from her cruise.

But now her bitch of a daughter had turned up and was threatening to derail everything. Throw in the dogmatic detective and Darryl's stress levels had reached fever pitch.

He yearned to do away with the slut, just like he had her mother, but he hadn't gotten to where he was in life by being stupid. He knew having another member of his family suddenly disappear wouldn't go unnoticed—especially now that prick of a detective was involved.

No, he wouldn't be able to kill her, as much as he might want to. But he could put the fear of God into her, threaten her, like he used to. It had worked in the past; there was a good chance it would work again.

He frowned when he thought of the defiance in her eyes the last time they'd met. She wasn't the terrified teenager anymore, that was for sure. But what else could he do to get her to drop this? It was definitely worth a try. In the meantime, he'd put more thought into discovering the whereabouts of his collection—the one stolen by his wife.

After he'd buried the bitch, he'd turned the house upside down looking for them, but had come up empty. The only person who could tell him where they were was dead. He'd had a moment of regret when he'd realized his predicament, but by then, it was far too late to do anything about it.

Not knowing the whereabouts of the thousands of photos, videos and DVDs that made up his collection was the one thing that kept him awake at night. He was determined to find them, if it was the last thing he did.

"It's your shot, boss."

Darryl shook his head to clear it of his thoughts and spied his ball buried in the sand. He was filled with another surge of disgust. He'd had enough of everything going to hell. It was time to set things right again.

He selected a sand wedge and chipped at the ball, unable to prevent the tiny glimmer of satisfaction when it landed on the green, not far from Hannaford's.

"Good shot, boss. You might just beat me yet."

CHAPTER 22

"**H**ey, look what the cat dragged in. Where have you been all morning?" Chase ribbed him as Riley appeared at the top of the stairs.

Ignoring him, Riley strode across the squad room and dumped the paper bag containing the remnants of his lunch on his desk. "I clocked on at six this morning. Check with Hannaford, if you like."

Chase snorted. "Yeah, right. Like Hannaford would be here this time of day. It's Wednesday afternoon. He'll be at least four holes down by now."

Riley grimaced. "Dammit, I forgot that. I need to talk to him."

"What about?"

Riley heaved a sigh and threw himself down in his chair. "Darryl Watson. I want to get a search warrant."

Chase let out a low whistle and shook his head. "You sure know how to win friends, Munro. Didn't anyone tell you if you want to get on in a small town, you have to stay on the right side of certain people? And the town's former LAC and his successor definitely fit into that category."

Riley shrugged, unperturbed. "I couldn't give a shit who I'm supposed to get on with. I think that son of a bitch has murdered his wife. I'm not going to sit by and let him get away with it because he just happens to be considered a pillar of the community."

Chase held up his hands. "Whoa, there. Don't take it out

on me, mate. I'm only telling you how it is. You're a newcomer and a city slicker to boot. There are a lot of people in this town aren't going to welcome you slinging mud on their old commander."

"Well, like it or not, that's exactly what I intend to do. Provided I can get Hannaford to sign off on it. He's made it clear how chummy he is with Darryl."

Riley thought of the recent corruption allegations he'd uncovered and a smile of feral anticipation curled his lips. "But luck's on my side. Hannaford hasn't been doing himself any favors lately, so he'd better not prove too difficult."

With an eyebrow lifted in question, Chase leaned a hip against Riley's desk. "Sounds intriguing. Care to share?"

Riley shook his head, mindful of the need for discretion now that IA had taken over.

"Sorry, mate, my lips are sealed, but let's just say Commander Hannaford might like to dot his I's and cross his T's for the next little while, which includes giving me the nod to apply for a search warrant when I can show I have just cause."

Chase's lips pursed. "So, what's happened to make you all fired up about Watson? Last time I checked, you weren't even convinced his wife hadn't left of her own accord."

"Yeah, but there have been a few developments. I managed to track down a friend of hers. She told me about the escape plan she and Rosemary had hatched. The only thing is, Rosemary didn't show at the appointed hour. Darryl told me he'd taken her to board a cruise ship on the very day she was meant to leave him forever."

"Funny that," Chase replied.

"That's exactly what I thought." Riley pulled out his chair and sat. "Now, shift your ass off my desk because I have a few calls to make."

———

Kate switched on her laptop and opened Skype. She had

a major exhibition opening in London in a little over a week and the way things were going, it was unlikely she'd be back in time. She needed to speak to her senior assistant with a view to rescheduling. It would be a nuisance and her clients wouldn't be happy, but there was nothing for it. Her mother deserved to be put first.

Within minutes, the call connected. Her assistant answered, looking bleary-eyed. It suddenly occurred to Kate it was about four in the morning in London.

"Hi, Mary, I'm sorry for waking you. I-I didn't even give the time difference a thought."

"It's fine, Ms Collins. It's good to hear from you. How are things? How's your mother?"

Kate swallowed. She'd kept the reasons for her trip home close to her chest, not wanting to give anyone an opportunity to ask questions. She'd been living in London close to three years, but had done no more than share the most basic of information with the people she'd come into contact with, including those who worked for her.

"I-I haven't caught up with her yet. She's—she's missing."

"Oh, Ms Collins! Do you mean missing as in...?"

Kate sighed, wishing she'd stayed silent. "It's okay, I'm sure she'll turn up. The thing is though, I-I'm not sure how much longer I'll be here and I think we need to reschedule the exhibition."

"Reschedule? But—"

"Please call all our clients and let them know. I'll give you another date as soon as I can."

"Yes, Ms Collins. I'll get onto it in the morning."

"Thank you, Mary. I appreciate it."

"Wh-what do you want me to tell them?"

"Tell them I have been unavoidably delayed overseas and unfortunately, the exhibition will not be opening next week. Tell them it will be rescheduled as soon as possible and that I promise it will be worth their while."

Mary had a notepad and pen in front of her. Kate could see her taking notes. After saying good-bye, Kate ended the call. She leaned back against her chair and sighed in relief. That was one less thing to worry about.

Knowing she couldn't put it off any longer, she closed her laptop and booted up the one belonging to her mother. She tried to tamp down the nervous tension that twisted her stomach. She'd missed lunch, but the lack of food wasn't what had her stomach in knots.

The news that her mother had been planning to fly to London had come as a shock. Things between her mother and Darryl must have been much worse than Kate had thought.

But, why hadn't her mother emailed her to let her know she was coming? Rosemary had never been a keen flyer. With the challenges she faced in her wheelchair, boarding an airplane had never appealed to her. In fact, Kate didn't have a single memory of her mother flying anywhere. She could only imagine what had driven her to want to fly to London.

She clicked open Rosemary's email account. When she'd looked through the messages with Riley, she'd given most of them only a cursory glance. There was so much junk mail, it was hard to decipher legitimate messages. Once they'd found Daisy's emails and had realized the significance of them, they'd concentrated on messages from her.

But now, she took the time to look closely at the mail that had been sent to and from her mother's account, paying particular attention to the dates. If what Daisy said was true, her mother had started planning her departure just prior to Daisy's July second birthday.

Kate opened the Sent box and moved the scroll bar downwards until she found messages sent around that time. One message caught her eye. It had been sent on June twenty-fifth—a week prior.

It had been sent to her. Memories emerged and then collided. Clicking it open, she scanned the familiar contents. She'd received it early one evening, at home in her apartment. It had been raining—a cold, miserable London night—and she'd gone to bed early with her laptop and a hot mug of cocoa.

Her mother had written to inform her about the changes she intended to make to her will. She'd given no explanation, apart from saying she was leaving everything to Kate.

Kate scrolled through another half dozen spam messages.

And then she found it. The last email she'd received from her mother. The one that posed more questions than it had answered. The one Kate hadn't told Riley about. The one that still woke her in the middle of the night with fear tight in her chest.

I'm sorry, Kate. I'm so, so sorry.

Kate's heart hammered, just as it had when she'd read the email the first time. It had been sent on July first, but she remembered she hadn't opened it until two days later. She'd been staying in a remote village in the south of Italy on a buying trip and had been without Internet access. She hadn't checked her emails until she'd arrived back in London.

She focused on the date again. July first. The day before Daisy's birthday. The day before her mother had told Daisy something had happened and she had to leave. *Right away.*

Cold dread settled deep inside her and stretched upwards, sliding icy fingers around her heart.

Something had happened.

Kate's increasingly panicked thoughts went back to her mother's final email.

I'm sorry.

When Kate had first read the email, she'd panicked that her mother had been apologizing for an impending suicide. Kate had spent a restless night tossing and turning ten thousand miles away, feeling as helpless and scared as she'd been as a child. The memories of her hellish years in the house on Baxter Road had set her therapy back an immeasurable distance, but when the sun broke out through the clouds the next morning, she was able to look at the situation a little less emotionally.

Over the next few days, she'd emailed her mother endlessly, begging her to contact her. She'd left messages on Rosemary's cell phone and had even risked having Darryl pick up when she called the house line.

And still, she'd heard nothing. It had been the longest week of her life. Every day, she'd scoured the Watervale newspapers online with her heart in her mouth, waiting to find the article that would tell her about her mother's death.

But there was nothing.

The week after was the same and the week after that. She began to wonder if she'd been wrong.

Being confined to a wheelchair had its limitations. Her mother wasn't able to drive; she mostly relied upon Darryl or taxis to get around. If she'd been serious about ending her life, it stood to reason she would do it in the safety and security of her own home. It was the only thing that made sense. And yet, that hadn't happened. It was inconceivable the wife of a prominent Watervale resident wouldn't have made front page news if she committed suicide.

There was only one conclusion Kate could draw: her mother was still alive but unable to reach her. It was then she'd known she would have to return to Watervale, the place of her nightmares.

She'd had plenty of time during the long flight to stoke her deep-seated anger against Darryl. By the time she'd arrived in Watervale, she was out for his blood. It was the reason why one of the first sentences out of her mouth upon her arrival was when she'd insisted to Riley that her stepfather had murdered her mother.

Despite her accusations, she'd clung to the hope she was wrong; she'd prayed her mother was alive and well and that when the time was right, she'd contact her. But while she'd listened to Daisy talk about her mother's desire to leave and the plans they'd formed to make it happen, her hope shriveled and died.

It was beyond nonsensical to accept that a wheelchair-bound woman who had set plans in motion to leave her husband and had confirmed those plans the night before they were to be set into motion, would change her mind and go elsewhere, alone, hours before her bid for freedom was realized.

Sorry...sorry...sorry...sorry...sorry...

The word reverberated around Kate's head. A loud buzzing sounded in her ears. Her vision narrowed to a pinprick of light.

Sorry for what?

She clamped a hand over her mouth to hold in her gasp of shock.

Of course. The videos.

After all these years, her mother must have found them. It was the only thing that made sense.

Shame burned in her belly and scorched her face. Nausea threatened. She pushed away from the counter and bent double, gasping for breath. A tiny part of her was relieved the secret had finally been exposed, but mostly she just felt sick.

She swiped at the perspiration on her forehead and struggled to regain control. If her mother had discovered the videos and confronted Darryl about them, he would have had more than enough motivation to kill her, particularly if she'd threatened to go to the police with them.

Kate had always known about the vile recordings. She'd managed to push their existence to the far recesses of her mind, in the dark place where she stored most of her childhood memories.

After more than a decade of silence about their reality, she could well-understand if Darryl had become complacent about the possibility of her exposing him. And he would have been secure in his skewed logic.

Kate had worked hard to forge a life away from him, away from Watervale with all its dirty secrets. The last thing she dreamed of was going public with her humiliation. Darryl knew it. It was exactly the kind of reluctance he'd counted on.

What he hadn't counted on was having his wife discover the evidence of his monstrous crimes. The more Kate thought about it, the more she was certain she was right.

If Rosemary had found them and threatened to go to the police, he'd have had genuine fears she would go through with it. His reputation would be destroyed and that was the least of it. He'd be jailed and forced to live with the criminals he'd helped put inside. His life would be over. That was strong motivation in anyone's book. Powerful enough to turn him into a murderer.

Kate didn't doubt it. There was nothing for it. She had to tell Riley. She stood and hunted around in her handbag for her phone. Riley had told her he was heading back to the station to chase up the new leads. She didn't expect to hear from him until this evening, or perhaps even the next day.

But this couldn't wait. This new possibility fit too well. Despite her agony at the thought of revealing her sordid childhood, she had no choice. For her mother's sake, she had to tell him.

Her fingers clenched around the phone as she listened to it dialing out. She bit her lip in abject disappointment when the call went through to voicemail. Leaving an urgent message for him to contact her, she ended the call and tossed the phone onto the bed. It bounced once and then slid off the far side of the quilt and onto the carpeted floor.

"Damn." She took a step toward it. As she did, a shadow moved across the window. She froze.

There was someone outside her door.

She'd not yet drawn the heavy damask curtains and she could see the indistinct outline of a man through the gauzy covering across the front window. A knock sounded on the door.

Kate's breath halted, then rushed out through her mouth. She snatched another and tried to still her thumping heart.

She was being silly. It was broad daylight—well, as good as. The afternoon shadows had lengthened outside the building, heralding the evening to come, but there was still enough light to deter someone with villainous intent. *Wasn't there?*

Her legs were concrete pylons, but she forced them forward and with a trembling finger, inched the curtain aside. Catching a glimpse of navy suit pants and shiny black boots, she collapsed with relief against the doorframe.

Riley.

Fumbling with the lock on the deadbolt, she unlatched it and swung open the door.

CHAPTER 23

"Hello, Kathryn."

Kate took a step backwards, confusion warring with fear. Commander Hannaford's smile was wide and welcoming—and reminded her of a snake waiting for its prey. She tried to hide her unease beneath a veneer of bravado.

"Commander Hannaford, what a surprise. What are you doing here?"

The smile remained in place, but the midnight-black eyes were full of menacing speculation.

"I was out playing a few rounds of golf with your stepfather a little while ago. We were talking about you. He misses you, you know." He stepped closer and his voice lowered. "I found myself in your neighborhood and thought I'd pay you a visit."

Kate's stomach dropped. She pressed her knees tighter together to stop their trembling and vowed not to reveal her fear. Hannaford and Darryl. Nothing about that image was comforting.

He lifted a hand to pat back an errant strand of graying hair. The dying sunlight glinted off an ornate gold ring on the middle finger of his right hand. Horror struck her like a physical blow.

Rearing backwards, she slammed the door in his face, her heart thumping. She twisted and turned, mindless with fear.

Oh God, it was him.

Memories bombarded her. The flash of gold. The distinctive stone. Fear and loathing tore at her insides. More than a decade ago, Hannaford had played a part in her pain and humiliation.

She raced to the bathroom and leaned over the toilet bowl, just as the nausea hit the back of her throat and spurted out in hot, acidic bursts. She'd had nothing to eat since the slice of tea cake Daisy had served that morning, but it didn't deter her rebellious stomach.

Kneeling on the cold tiles, Kate held her hair away from her face and gripped the toilet bowl with the other hand. Tears streamed down her face. The acrid taste of vomit burned her throat. She gulped and choked and howled and heaved as the memories overtook her.

She didn't know how long she lay on the floor, but the light in the room was dim when she found the strength to stand. Tearing off her clothes, she stood under the shower. With the water as hot as she could make it, she scrubbed every inch of her body, shampooed her hair and then started all over again.

Her arms ached when she finally pulled on her nightdress and crawled into bed. The hot water had stopped the shivering, but a frozen knot of dread and despair had lodged deep inside her and no amount of hot water was going to thaw that.

Tugging at the comforter, she pulled it over her shoulders and half of her face, barely leaving enough room for breathing. She forced images of Hannaford and his gold ring from her mind and tried to focus on Riley. She longed to have him beside her, offering comfort, keeping her safe.

She reached out and felt around for the phone that had fallen to the floor. Her fingers closed around it and she checked it for messages.

Nothing.

He was probably busy. Hopefully he'd discovered something that would lead them to her mother.

Fresh tears welled up in her eyes. The tiniest flicker of hope still remained that they would find Rosemary alive, hiding somewhere safe, but it was growing dimmer by the day. Kate was surer than ever that Darryl had murdered her. If they didn't catch a break soon, they might never find her or bring him to justice.

There was no way her stepfather would confess. He was as tough as the most hardened criminal and knew all the ways there were to outsmart the police. Unless they found evidence to take him to trial, he'd get away with her mother's murder, just like he'd gotten away with the things he'd done to Kate.

The coldness inside her expanded and the agony of it intensified. She doubled over under the covers, cradling her stomach in both hands. A moan of anguish escaped her lips and she rocked against the torture of it.

The press of hard, cold metal against her temple startled her. She froze.

"Don't move or I'll shoot you and you'll disappear just like your fucking mother did."

Fear pounded through her veins and turned her limbs leaden. She squinted through the dimness and made out Darryl's bulky shape. The dim light from the laptop glinted off the barrel of a sinister-looking handgun.

"Wh-what are you doing? H-how did you get in?" Kate hated the trembling in her voice, but was powerless to stop it.

Darryl sneered. "The door was unlocked, my dear Kathryn. You really should be more careful. The country's not as safe as it used to be. Watervale's been experiencing a veritable crime spree of late—haven't you heard?" His broad chest rumbled with laughter.

Terror scattered her thoughts. Had Darryl admitted he'd killed her mother? It had surely sounded like it. Unbearable pain coursed through her like fever. She was burning from the inside out and there was nothing she could do about it.

She groaned from the agony of it and tried to draw her legs up beneath her. Darryl's weight held the bedcovers tightly in place. He leaned closer.

"Shut the fuck up and listen to me." He pressed the gun harder against her temple.

Kate whimpered. "You *bastard*. You killed her! I knew all along it was you. There's no way she would have left without telling me."

Darryl's eyes glinted maliciously. "That's where you're wrong, you silly little slut. She was going to leave. Scamper off without a word. I heard about her crazy little plan. My mate Barry knows all about loyalty. A lot more than your mother."

Kate defied the gun still pressed against the side of her head and threw him a scornful look. "You think you're so smart. You think you'll get away with it. But you're not going to keep me quiet. Not anymore."

Guffaws of laughter rumbled out of his chest, but his gun hand remained steady. "You always were a feisty one. I loved that about you. I hate to disillusion you, but even if I do let you live and you tell the world, who do you think's going to believe you, you stupid little bitch? The police force you're so eager to run to with your tales is made up of my friends. Every one of them owes me a favor or three. All but that new black prick, and he's hardly going to stand against my mates. A quiet word in the right ear and he'll be transferred to the middle of nowhere—again. He won't even get a job cleaning toilets by the time I've finished with him."

His smug words ignited a white-hot anger deep inside her. The fact he was right made it even worse.

"You might think you'll get away with one murder, but there's no way your cronies will tolerate two."

His eyes gleamed and a smile that made her skin crawl turned up his lips. He caressed the side of her neck with the gun as his words slid over her.

"I guess I don't have to shoot you. I'm sure we could always negotiate a mutually satisfying arrangement." The gun slid lower, the tip of its barrel burying itself between her breasts, naked beneath her nightgown. "There are plenty of other ways to keep you quiet, don't you think?"

Sheer terror paralyzed her. She clamped her mouth shut

against a fresh bout of nausea. Her fingers hurt from their death grip on the bedclothes. She barely dared to breathe as he used the cold, steel barrel to slide the strap of her nightdress off her shoulder.

The satin fell down her arm. A tiny whimper escaped her tightly closed mouth and she hated herself for showing him her fear. She was fourteen all over again, powerless and afraid.

No, she wasn't.

She wasn't fourteen and she wasn't going to let him make her feel that way all over again. In some still-sane part of her mind, she guessed he'd have shot her already, if that had been his plan. And he must know she was right when she'd said two murders would look suspicious.

He wasn't going to kill her. Not right now, anyway. He was toying with her, screwing with her head, like he always had.

But it wasn't going to work. Not this time.

With a guttural growl, Kate hurled the bedclothes toward him, catching him off guard. Springing from the bed, she bounded across the room. Knowing the search for a weapon would be futile, she armed herself with venom.

"Get the fuck out, you filthy, murdering bastard." Spittle flew from her lips. Her eyes burned into his. "Go ahead, shoot me. I *dare* you."

Darryl raised his gun hand so she was in his line of sight. Kate's breath caught in her throat. The dull gleam of the barrel in the meager light looked even more menacing. Trying to ignore the fear that immobilized her, she lifted her chin and stared at Darryl, putting all the hatred she felt for him into a single deadly look.

"*Do it.*" Her voice was a hoarse whisper in the utter stillness.

Darryl stared at her, unmoving. For long moments, the only sound in the room was their harsh breathing. The hand holding the gun wavered and then lowered. Darryl's gaze fell away.

She swallowed the surge of relief that threatened to undo her and strode to the door. Flinging it open, she stepped well away as Darryl stalked toward her. His lower lip was thrust out and fury glittered in his eyes. He looked like a child who'd been bested in a game, but Kate didn't make the mistake of thinking she'd won. A wounded animal would be even more ferocious at the next encounter.

His sleeve brushed her bare arm and she shivered and tore it away. With a final deadly stare in her direction, he strode out of the room. She slammed the door behind him and this time made double-sure the deadlock and chain was secured. After drawing the curtains, she collapsed onto the bed and gave in to the shock that seized her.

Shivering violently, she tugged at the covers and rolled herself in them, rocking back and forth in an effort to get warm. She kept hearing Darryl's voice, whispering, tormenting. Over and over she saw the gun waving under her nose like an evil black flag.

Clamping her hands around her ears, she screwed her eyes tightly shut, trying to block the sounds and images that threatened to overwhelm her. A low moan started deep inside her and climbed up her throat. Burying her head in the pillows, she screamed and screamed and screamed.

CHAPTER 24

R iley pulled up outside Kate's motel room and cut the engine. It was barely seven, but not a hint of light escaped from the drawn curtains. He frowned in consternation. Maybe she'd gone out?

A quick survey of the car park showed her rental car two doors down. He quickly discounted the idea that she'd walked. The temperature had dropped rapidly with the coming night, hinting at snow. It wasn't an evening to be out in if you had a choice, even for a Londoner.

Climbing out of the car, he reached inside for his jacket and shrugged it on. With a last glance around the quiet car park, he strode to her door and knocked briskly on the wooden panel.

Silence greeted him. Moving across to the curtained window, he pressed his head against the glass and tried to see in, but the thick fabric was impenetrable. Stepping back to the door, he knocked again.

"Kate? It's Riley. Are you in there?"

More silence. A car door closed behind him and he whirled around to see an elderly woman adjusting her seatbelt in the passenger's side of a small sedan. An equally elderly man walked around to the driver's side. He offered Riley a brief wave. Riley acknowledged it with an even briefer nod.

Turning back, Riley tried the door again. She had to be in there. Where else would she be, on foot, on a night like this?

She'd told him it was urgent, but he'd been busy chasing up phone calls and a part of him hadn't wanted her to think he was at her beck and call. Childish, he knew, but he was still confused about her feelings for him and was wary of getting his heart involved.

So, he'd left it for as long as he could. He'd finished his shift a little after six and had spent time catching up with the general duties officers downstairs. When he'd finally left the station, he found himself turning toward her motel. And here he was, outside her room. Only, it appeared she wasn't in.

Pressing his ear against the door, he strained to hear something, anything, behind the closed panel.

"Kate? Please let me know if you're in there. Just let me know you're okay. If you don't want to talk to me, that's fine. I just want to know you're all right."

He was about to walk away when he heard it—the tiniest whimper of sound, a moan, a hiccup—he wasn't sure, but it was definitely a sound of distress. He pounded harder against the door.

"Kate, it's me. Riley. Open up. I know you're in there."

He waited interminable minutes. A light came on behind the curtains. Finally, he heard the click of the lock and the jingle of the chain.

The door cracked open. A lamp on the nightstand illuminated her from behind. He reared back in shock at the sight of her.

"Christ, Kate! What the fuck happened? Are you all right?"

She looked away self-consciously and covered her swollen eyes. Her hair hung messy and loose around her drooping shoulders. She looked lost and alone. She looked defeated.

A fierce protectiveness overwhelmed him. For so long, she'd remained strong, invincible, convinced from the outset her stepfather was responsible. And now, just as the evidence was beginning to prove her right, her confidence had deserted her and in its place he saw a vulnerability that touched him more than anything ever had.

Easing the door open, he stepped inside and closed it behind him. Flicking the deadlock, he turned to face her.

She'd turned away from him and now stared blindly at the blank television screen, her arms wound tightly around her waist. He tried not to focus on the pale pink nightgown that hung in soft, satiny folds on her body.

"Kate, please tell me what happened. Was it Darryl? Did you see him again?"

Her body looked taut enough to snap. She still refused to look at him. Riley moved closer and took hold of her elbow and gently turned her to face him.

Unshed tears glittered in her eyes and a brief nod was all she managed before her face crumpled and her shoulders heaved.

He stepped forward without thought or hesitation, knowing only that he needed to help her, hold her, offer her comfort. She collapsed against him and he folded her in his arms and drew her close. Unlike the previous times, her weeping was quiet, controlled, weary, as if she'd already spent countless hours crying—and from the look of her, she had.

He stroked her hair away from her face, his hand far from steady as it slid through the tangle of long, silky strands. The fall of Gwyneth Paltrow-blond across his fingers was as soft as a cascade of rose petals and smelled just as good.

Her sobs gentled and she pressed herself tighter against him. His breath caught. He cursed under his breath at his bulky jacket that created a barrier between them.

She seemed to understand his frustration. Easing out of his arms, she raised her hands to his chest and pushed at the offending garment. He aided her by shrugging the jacket off his shoulders and flinging it to the floor.

She came back up against him hard. Her arms went around his neck and she pulled his head down to hers. Unable to resist her unspoken invitation, Riley bent his head and kissed her.

The heat of it stole his breath. Her spicy scent of cinnamon and frangipani and freshly shampooed hair filled his senses and made his head spin. Her lips moved beneath his, warm and pliant and when his tongue pressed, seeking entry, he groaned aloud when her mouth opened.

She tasted of toothpaste and sweet, warm woman. His hands moved to cup her breasts through the thin silk of her nightdress. His fingers found her nipples and she shuddered. His thumbs stroked back and forth until they felt like little pebbles.

She moaned into his mouth. His cock pulsed with need. Christ, he was going to explode.

Pulling his mouth away from hers, he rested his forehead on the top of her head, gasping for breath as he fought for control. A pulse beat a frantic rhythm in the side of her neck. It pleased him to see her breathing was just as erratic as his.

Remembering the state he'd found her, he set her slightly away from him and caught her gaze. "Do you want to talk?"

She shook her head. Her gaze remained on his. She stepped back into the circle of his arms and once again reached for him.

"No talk," she murmured against his mouth, her lips opening under his. This time, it was her tongue that pressed insistently against his teeth until he gave in to the overwhelming desire to let her kiss him like she wanted to.

Fire raged in his groin. He groaned again when she pressed herself against his erection and ground her hips into his. Her intention was clear and he didn't need any further encouragement.

He bent and slipped an arm beneath her knees and lifted her. She was weightless in his arms. He took the few steps to the bed and gently lowered her onto it. Tugging impatiently at his tie, he loosened it with clumsy fingers and then went to work on the buttons of his shirt. He tossed his clothing to the floor and sat on the edge of the bed and pulled off his boots. His suit pants joined the growing pile of clothes. Within moments, he lay on his side facing her in just his boxers.

Her gaze traveled over him and paused at the bulge in

his underwear. He sucked in a breath. Her fingers scraped over his chest and across his navel before inching lower. He grabbed her wrist and held her hand to his mouth and captured her gaze with his.

"We don't have to do this. I didn't come here for this."

She stared back at him, her eyes luminous in the lamp's golden glow. "I want to. I've wanted to from the moment I saw you. Make love to me, Riley."

His body reacted to her plea, even as he frowned. "I think we should talk about—"

She pressed a finger to his lips. "*Shh.* We'll talk later. Right now, all I want to do is feel."

Kate slid her hand down the stubble-roughened side of Riley's face and then onto his bronzed chest. The well-defined muscles were bare of even the faintest sprinkling of chest hair and trembled under her feather-light touch. His nipples were small, dark nubs. She flicked at them with her fingernail, reveling in his sudden intake of breath.

She'd never touched a man so intimately before and the hard planes and valleys fascinated her. He was beautiful. Beautiful enough to make her forget, if only for a short time, the horror of her realization about Hannaford and the terror of Darryl's visit. Beautiful enough to allow her to push aside her fears and lose herself in the here and now, in her overwhelming yearning for mindless pleasure and release.

Her hand wandered lower, across his flat belly to trace the thin line of dark hair that trailed into his boxers. His erection strained against the silky fabric.

She wanted to touch it, but she was suddenly afraid. Her heart began a slow thud against her ribcage and her hand crept back upwards. She moved to align herself with his body and lifted her head up to meet his. Their lips met and melded. Desire arced through her, like an electric current, dissolving her fears.

She kissed him back with increasing desperation. Her fingers dug into his hair, holding his head in place while she ravished him with her lips. His heart hammered against her breasts and it pleased her to know he wanted her as much as she wanted him.

They were both gasping for breath when he pulled away. With his eyes on hers, he reached down to tug at the hem of her nightdress, his hands warm on her skin.

It slid up her thighs. She lifted her arms and the fabric slipped over her head and disappeared over the side of the bed. Naked to his gaze, she lay shyly before him.

"You're so beautiful." His voice was husky and low, his eyes wide with awe. He reached out a hand and traced the soft skin of her breast and she stilled at the sensations that ran through her.

Panic nipped at the edges of her consciousness, but she refused to acknowledge it. Riley leaned forward and claimed one of her nipples with his mouth. With single-minded determination, she focused on the feelings he invoked in her.

He suckled and laved the small, hard nub with his tongue and then rolled it gently between his teeth. She gasped aloud. Warmth spread from her belly to her core and she clenched her legs together to stem the flow of molten desire. She ached for him to touch her there, but didn't know how to ask.

Instead, she moved against him, pressing herself against the solid length of his erection, hoping he'd recognize her need.

"Not so fast, sweetheart," he murmured against the softness of her breast.

She grabbed his head between both of her hands and tried to make him see.

"Please. Please, Riley. I need it fast."

Something in her expression must have convinced him, because he shucked off his boxers and drew her up close against him. She gasped at the amazing feel of his nakedness flush against her bare skin and reached up to entwine her arms around his neck.

He lowered his head and kissed her. The strength of his passion overwhelmed her and the force of it brought her panic to the fore. The force of it...

Pulling away, she ducked her head and rested it against his chest, breathing hard while she battled to keep the fear at bay.

He tilted her chin up, his eyes full of concern. "Are you okay? We don't have to take this any farther if you don't want to."

She drew in another deep breath and held it, her gaze on his. The warmth of his skin and the strength of his arms around her pushed the panic away and her lips wobbled on an uncertain smile.

"I want to."

His eyes darkened and his head bent so that his mouth could claim her lips once again. "Oh, Christ, I want to, too."

He rolled her onto her back. Leaning over the side of the bed, he tugged out his wallet from the pocket of his suit pants. He pulled out a condom and quickly rolled it over his erection. With his weight braced on his arms, he hovered over her.

The dark shape of him loomed above her... Familiar, fearful images intruded. She squeezed her eyes tight and reached for him, dragging him down hard against her. Breathing in his unique scent of forest and earth, she concentrated fiercely on the feel of his hard chest against her breasts and the glide of his tongue in her mouth.

The tip of his erection nudged at her entrance and she caught her breath, clenching her hands into fists behind his back. With fierce concentration, she focused on the sensations he'd created and pushed the painful, humiliating memories aside. She fused her mouth to his and blocked out everything but Riley.

He entered her slowly. She groaned against his mouth and thrust her hips upwards. He hesitated.

"Please." It was a whisper of urgent need, before her courage failed her.

His body tensed. Scant seconds later, he plunged into her. She gasped from the impact, welcoming the hard length of him deep inside her. He moved slowly. She clung to him. Memories bombarded her, doing their best to sabotage her. She thrust them aside almost angrily and did her best to relax and surrender to the feelings building inside her.

Riley's movements grew more frantic. He leaned over her, his eyes glittering with desire and the strain of holding back.

"Let go, Riley. Just let go," she whispered.

He shook his head. "Not until you—"

She held his gaze, hoping he'd understand. "It's okay. I want you to."

Her words tipped him over the edge. He thrust into her again and again. Within moments, it was over. He collapsed on top of her with a groan.

Kate tightened her arms around him and listened while his breathing slowly returned to normal. She smiled, ecstatic, unable to believe she'd done it: She'd had sex with a man without running from the room screaming. And it had been more than just tolerating or allowing. She loved being close to this man she trusted.

Riley eased himself up and looked down at her. She could tell by the look on his face that he was embarrassed.

"Kate, I'm sorry—"

She pressed a finger against his lips and smiled again. "Don't be sorry. It was great. It was wonderful. More than I ever hoped for."

His brow knitted in confusion. "But, you didn't come. I didn't give you an orgasm."

She reached up and drew him back down against her. "You gave me so much more than that. You have no idea," she whispered against his neck. "Besides, I'm sure orgasms are way overrated."

Riley reared back. "What, you mean you haven't had one? Ever?"

She averted her gaze. The heat of embarrassment stole across her cheeks.

Warm fingers grasped her chin and gently turned her face to his. She had no choice but to meet his enquiring gaze.

"You've never had an orgasm?"

It was asked softly, gently, but all the same, she closed her eyes against her shame. He wasn't to know. He didn't know anything about her past. No one did. Except, Darryl and Hannaford. And now, maybe her mother.

"Kate, please talk to me. Don't shut me out. Not after what we've shared. *Please*."

His tender plea and the indefinable emotion that clouded his eyes tugged at her heart. Tears burned behind her eyes and she swallowed against the lump in her throat. Would it be such a disaster if she told him? Would it make him feel differently about her? Would he blame her?

A great weariness seeped into her bones. She was tired of carrying the weight of her secret. For over a decade, she'd borne it in silence, refusing to allow it to dominate her life. But it had always been *there*. How wonderful would it be to share the burden with someone?

Someone who might understand. Someone like Riley.

She stared at the tenderness in his eyes and fear clutched at her insides. But what if he didn't understand? What if she ruined the only chance she might have to live a normal life, in a normal relationship with a normal man? She might never find the courage to try again.

But would that be worth it? Building a relationship on lies? Sharing a life with someone who didn't know the deepest, darkest secret of her life? A secret that had slowly been devouring her, no matter how hard she'd tried to prevent it?

She had to tell him. She owed it to herself and she owed it to him. If he hated her for her past, so be it. Better to find out now, before too much of her heart became involved. If she didn't tell him, it would end up destroying them.

She squirmed a little underneath him until he shifted his weight. Turning, he lay on his side and pulled her in close against him. Reaching behind them, he tugged up the covers and draped them over both of them.

Kate snuggled her head against his chest. With her eyes

fixed on a point far beyond their tangled limbs, she braced herself for what she was about to tell him.

———————

Riley drew in a deep breath, unsure if he was ready for Kate's revelations. He'd asked her to talk to him, but now that the moment was upon him, dread weighed heavily in his gut. He wasn't certain what she was hiding, but her friend Cally had hinted at horrors he hadn't wanted to contemplate. Filled with a sense of foreboding, he tensed when she spoke.

"The day I turned ten was the day any chance I had for a normal life ended."

She said it matter-of-factly, as if she'd rehearsed the words over and over until they sounded almost normal. Riley tightened his arm around her, fearing what was to come.

"Darryl came upstairs after I'd gone to bed. It had been a nice day. Cally had come around and we'd had chocolate cake and ice cream. Mom had given me a new bike. I'd ridden around the yard on it all afternoon. She'd come outside in her wheelchair to watch me."

She paused, as if lost in her memories. Riley held his breath.

"I was nearly asleep when Darryl came into my room. He closed the door and told me he had a special present for me, one he didn't want Mom to know about." Her voice dropped lower. "That was the first night he raped me."

Fury detonated inside him, thick and molten-hot. It flooded his veins, his body, his skin. He was on fire with the heat of his anger. His jaw clenched. His arm tightened around her. Yet he said nothing. He didn't trust himself to speak.

She continued—her words subdued and distant. "It didn't happen every night, but often enough that each episode blurred into the next. Two years later, I got my first period. I'd never been so pleased. What the other girls feared and dreaded, I had longed for." Her lips twisted. "I stupidly thought it would make a difference. I thought it would make him stop."

Her voice broke on a harsh sob. Riley's heart cracked. He pulled her to him, pressing kisses against her hair, soothing her with nonsensical murmurings, all the while seething with indescribable fury at the man responsible for her pain. He could barely bring himself to lie beside her quietly and listen. All he wanted to do was haul himself out of there, find Darryl Watson and tear him to shreds.

The ferocity of Riley's anger frightened him, but he was powerless to control it. He eased a breath through his constricted lungs and spoke, his voice low.

"It didn't stop."

She shook her head against his chest and his hold tightened. He prayed for it to soon be over. He didn't know how long he could lie there and listen, pretending to be calm and unaffected. She needed him to be strong, in control. He prayed in desperation for the strength she needed from him.

"No, it didn't stop. He just got more careful. He began to use condoms. At one stage, he suggested I go to the doctor and ask for the pill, but I refused."

"What about your mom?" he asked quietly, careful to keep his voice neutral.

A tiny shrug. "She didn't know. My bedroom was upstairs. She lived on the ground floor. At first, Darryl told me she wouldn't believe me. Later, he threatened to throw both of us out on the street, back where we came from and then where would she get the money she needed for all of her costly medications?"

Her ragged sigh broke his heart. "I believed him. I was a child. Later, I knew he was right. No one would believe me."

"You didn't go to the police?"

She reared back, her eyes wide and accusatory. "He was the police."

Riley closed his eyes and nodded. "You're right. I can understand how that must have felt; you were ten years old." He pulled himself up until his back rested on the headboard and drew Kate up beside him. Capturing her face between his hands, he stared at her, trying to make her believe him.

"It wasn't your fault, Kate. Forget the way he made you feel when you were a child. Look at it from the eyes of the adult you are now. Strong, beautiful, free. You did that. You made you the person you are. Nothing Darryl did then or now can change that. It blows me away just how much courage and determination you needed to achieve it, but you have. You *have*. And you should be proud of who you are and what you've done with your life."

Tears gathered in her eyes. He brushed them away tenderly with the pads of his thumbs. His voice dropped to a whisper.

"He stole something very precious from you and he had no right to do that. His actions were evil and absolutely unforgivable and I'll celebrate every hour and every minute of every day when he's locked away. And despite everything, you haven't let him win. *You've beaten him*. You've found the courage to make something of your life, by believing in yourself, despite what he did."

Her tears fell in earnest now and he drew her down against his chest. She cried as if her heart would break and his broke right alongside hers. The burning anger congealed into an icy block of rage that sat coiled and deadly in his gut, waiting to strike.

Forcing his fists to relax, he stroked her hair, whispering assurances into its silky softness, giving her time to weep and to begin to heal.

It was a long time later when she lifted her head. She sniffed and offered him a shaky smile. "Do you mind passing me the tissues?"

He smiled softly and reached for the box that sat on the nightstand. Turning away, she blew her nose and wiped her eyes.

"Thank you," she murmured.

"No, thank *you*," he replied, his voice gruff. "Thank you for trusting me enough to tell me. You don't know how much your trust means to me."

Her eyes widened and another hesitant smile turned up her lips. The sight of it warmed his heart.

"Really? Do you really mean that?"

Emotions he refused to identify churned in his gut. He tried to speak, but his voice came out strangled. "Really."

She looked down at her hands where they rested on his chest. "I-I want to thank you for listening and for not freaking out. It feels so good to finally tell someone, like a weight's been lifted off my shoulders and even though I know it's probably too late to hope Darryl will ever be punished for it, at least I know he didn't best me."

Renewed anger surged through him. "What do you mean it's too late for him to be punished? Of course he'll be punished. There's no statute of limitations on rape. I meant it when I said I'll do everything in my power to see him behind bars, where he belongs. I only pray he gets some of his own treatment. I'm told even murderers don't abide rock spiders."

Kate's brow furrowed.

"Rock spiders. It's what they call pedophiles on the inside," he explained.

She drew in a deep breath. "Speaking of pedophiles, there's something else I haven't told you. It's about Commander Hannaford."

Chapter 25

Kate pulled out of Riley's arms and reached for her nightdress. Shrugging it on over her head, she stood and moved away from the bed. Riley watched her, concern and wariness warring on his face.

"What about Commander Hannaford?"

Crossing her arms over her chest, Kate hugged herself, struggling to find the courage to finish what she'd started. She'd come this far; it was only right she tell the whole story.

She drew in a deep breath. "Commander Hannaford called by this afternoon, just before Darryl."

Shock widened his features. "Hannaford and Watson were *here*? When? Why didn't you call me?"

"I did, remember? I tried to call you. I left you a message."

Her words, although not meant unkindly, rang with accusation. Riley's cheeks flushed with embarrassment and he looked away.

"That's why you were calling?"

Kate shook her head. "No, it was about something else, something about my mother. But then I had the...visitors and things spiraled out of control."

"What did Hannaford want?"

"I'm not sure. It's not important."

"It is to me," Riley objected, pulling on his boxer shorts and coming to stand beside her. "He's the one who's been blowing me off about this investigation. The more I dig, the more I'm convinced something has happened to your mother and that Darryl's responsible. Hannaford went out of his way to warn me away from Darryl. He also told me not to believe a word you said. There's no reason for him to have done that unless he already knows Darryl's guilty."

"Darryl is guilty. He as much as admitted it."

She said it quietly, but comprehension and shock flared immediately in Riley's face.

"Darryl *admitted* it? Are you *kidding?*"

Anger tightened her lips and she moved away from him, pacing in the small confines of the room. "Do I look like I'm kidding? I just told you. He came here and threatened me with a gun and told me if I didn't behave I'd disappear *just like my mother.*"

Riley's face paled. He stumbled back to the bed and hauled on his trousers, hopping from one foot to the other in his haste. His shirt was next, only half-buttoned as he searched the floor for his boots.

"Christ, you mean to tell me that son of a bitch drew a gun on you and threatened to kill you and you're only *now* telling me about it? What the hell were you *thinking?*"

She absorbed his anger in silence, knowing he was angry because he cared.

He cared. About her. It was a wonderful feeling.

"You want to know what I was thinking?" she said quietly, watching calmly as he tugged on his socks. "I was thinking about Commander Hannaford and how I'd just realized he was the man my stepfather brought into my bedroom the night before I ran away."

Riley's knees buckled. He sat down heavily on the bed.

Christ, how much more could he take? How much more could *Kate* take? He was stunned at her revelation, but he didn't doubt her for a second. The look on her face and the quiet sincerity in her words was enough. He didn't know how she could be so calm about it. He wanted to scream and rant to anyone who would listen about the horror and injustice of it. He strained to hear her over the blood that pounded in his ears.

"Up until that night, it had only been Darryl and his video camera. But the night before I ran away, right after my fourteenth birthday, he brought a friend."

She closed her eyes and her arms tightened around her middle. Riley wanted to go to her, to hold her, but he was paralyzed, his limbs leaden with the horror of it.

"I never knew who it was. Darryl never called him by name and he wasn't there very long. It was dark. All I remember was his ring. It was quite distinctive. Darryl told me I was to let him have sex with me, but I refused. I was getting older and wasn't the terrified ten-year-old I'd once been."

She smiled without humor. "Of course, Darryl was furious. We argued in front of the visitor and Darryl slapped me across the face. I think it frightened Hannaford off, because shortly afterwards, he told Darryl it probably wasn't such a good idea and he'd come back some other time. I decided then and there I wouldn't wait for that to happen."

She turned away and stared blankly at the curtained window. When she spoke again, her voice was devoid of emotion.

"Darryl raped me twice that night. After he'd finished with me, I packed a small bag and waited for the house to go quiet. I left in the early hours of the morning and never came back."

Riley's eyes filled with emotion he could no longer suppress. "Until now," he choked.

Kate smiled a small, sad smile. "Until now."

"Did Darryl say anything else about your mother?"

"No, only what I told you, but I know he's killed her. He sure as hell didn't deny it when I said as much."

"What do you think happened?" he asked softly.

Her shoulders slumped on a heavy sigh. "I don't know exactly, but I think she found the videos, or at least one of them."

"Darryl made movies?"

She nodded. "I was twelve or thirteen. One night, I noticed a tiny red light coming out of my wall. I went up to investigate and discovered the camera. I smashed it and told Darryl I would go to the police if he ever took pictures of me again." She shrugged. "He must have believed me because I never saw a camera after that."

She walked over to the bed and sat down beside him. "I don't know how long he'd been filming and I don't know what he did with the movies he'd made, but I went back over Mom's emails this afternoon. The last one I received from her was the day before she told Daisy something had happened and she had to leave. She told me in the email she was sorry."

Riley frowned in confusion. "Why didn't you tell me about her email before?"

Kate grimaced. "I was afraid you'd jump to the conclusion that she'd committed suicide—that the apology was meant to compensate for the fact she intended to take her own life."

She looked up at him. "When I first read the message, a couple of days after she'd sent it, that thought even occurred to me. I spent an excruciatingly anxious week in London scouring the *Watervale Daily* for news of her death. When there was no mention of it, and I still couldn't contact her, I knew I had to come back. I had to find out what was going on. It wasn't until I put everything together after speaking with Daisy that things started to fall into place."

She shrugged. "I still don't know for sure, but knowing what I do, the video possibility makes a lot of sense. She could have found one or more videos, confronted Darryl about them and made secret plans to leave. Maybe she threatened to expose him or maybe she didn't? Maybe he didn't want to take the risk that one day she might?"

"Either way, she had to go. When his good mate Barry Bloomfield told him about Mom's plan to leave, he knew he had to act fast."

Shock struck Riley like a physical blow. "Darryl *told* you that? About Barry warning him?"

Her lips twisted. "Oh, yes. With more than a bucketful of glee, I might add."

Riley shook his head. Daisy would be devastated.

Kate turned to face him. His gut clenched at the bleak desperation in her eyes.

"The only real question," she murmured, "is where the hell has he buried her?"

CHAPTER 26

K ate watched as Riley collected his jacket and slipped it on and then shoved his tie into his pocket. His face was closed, unreadable and she felt a sharp stab of uncertainty.

Had he changed his mind? Was he sorry he'd slept with her, now that he knew the whole sordid truth?

As if he could read her mind, he stopped in front of her and took hold of her hands. Bringing them up to his mouth, he pressed a soft kiss against each of her fingers.

"Even though I'm off duty, I need to call in to the station and talk to the officer in charge. Hannaford's now taken a couple of days off, so at least I won't have to worry that he's around. I phoned him earlier, before he left, and actually got the bastard to agree to let me apply for a search warrant of Darryl's house. Hannaford tried to stall me, but I'm going to the courthouse first thing in the morning. Now that I know he and Darryl are in this together, I'm going to ensure Darryl is arrested as soon as possible. The sexual assault charges should be enough to hold him for a little while—until I have enough evidence to charge him with murder."

Kate shuddered. "I'll have to testify, won't I?"

Riley grimaced. "Yes, sweetheart, you will." The hold on her hands tightened. "I know you're brave and strong enough to see this through and you know it's the only way. It's the only way you'll be completely free."

Her lips trembled. "You're right," she whispered.

Riley groaned and pulled her into his arms. "Christ, I wish I could stay with you. All I want to do is climb back in that bed and hold you all night, but I can't. I need to help get together an arrest team and pay Darryl and Hannaford a visit. Internal Affairs will need to be brought up to speed. We'll also need backup from Grafton...and all of that has to be organized tonight."

"I understand." She offered him a shaky smile. "Go. You need to go."

Leaning forward, he gave her a hard kiss on her lips and held her tight. Kate breathed in his strength. All too soon, he released her and quietly let himself out.

Riley's head whirled with a confusion of thoughts and emotions. He pulled out of the motel's parking lot and dialed the station. Off duty or not, it was imperative he report his findings.

The officer in charge of the station for the night shift was Detective Sergeant Brian Reynolds. Brian was a good officer. He'd transferred from the coast only a month ago and was unlikely to be tainted by Watson's influence. From what Riley had seen of Reynolds' character, he both liked him and felt he could trust him. He also knew Brian would act on the information right away. Darryl and Hannaford would be arrested. At the very least, charges of sexual assault would be laid against both of them and that was before they looked into the fraud and corruption charges.

The scent of Kate clung to his skin and he cursed aloud. In all the fantasies he'd had about making love to her, none of them had included him climaxing first. And even worse, that she wouldn't climax at all.

Heat scorched his cheeks again at the thought of it. Christ, that hadn't happened to him since he'd been a teenager, fumbling in the backseat with Harriet Dixon. The humiliation was about the same. The only difference was he cared more about how Kate felt about it. Much more.

He frowned, remembering. She seemed to have taken it okay, but it wasn't supposed to be like that. He'd wanted their first time to be perfect, mind blowing, unforgettable. He winced. He'd probably gotten the last part right.

His mind skittered around the secrets she'd shared. Anger still simmered beneath the surface, but the need to act on it immediately like he'd wanted to, had been replaced by the necessity of dealing with the facts concerning Darryl and Rosemary and Hannaford. He needed time to think the night's revelations through, one frame at a time—but minutes were scarce and right now, every one of them counted.

The call to the station connected and Riley was met with shocked silence when he relayed his information to the OIC. To Reynolds' credit, after a few short, sharp queries, he accepted the validity of Riley's story.

They made plans to hurriedly put together joint arrest teams. It was imperative the raids be conducted simultaneously to minimize the risk that one offender could tip off the other. Riley insisted he lead the team that would conduct the raid at No.16 Baxter Road.

In a little over two hours, it was done. Riley couldn't help his smile of satisfaction as he recalled Darryl's shock and outrage when the arresting officers had knocked on his door. The click of the handcuffs as they locked around Watson's wrists had been the sweetest sound Riley had heard for a long while and securing them just a little tighter than was necessary was the least that he could do.

With Kate's stepfather loudly protesting his innocence to anyone who cared to listen, Riley had marched him to the back of the squad car and driven him to the station.

Almost immediately, Watson lawyered up. Hannaford followed suit. Upon consultation with Reynolds, it was decided to let the pair of them stew over their situation until the morning, when Riley's team would also bring Barry Bloomfield in for questioning.

Knowing there was nothing more he could do until the

sun rose, Riley picked up his phone and dialed. It was answered on the second ring.

"Hi, Mom. How are you?"

———————

Riley climbed out of the heated car and shivered. Turning up the collar on his jacket, he made his way up the old stone steps. The night was black, but a sliver of moon and a lifetime of memories were enough to enable him to make it to the front door without incident. It was after midnight, but lights still showed through the curtains of the living room window. His parents had always been night owls.

Tugging off his boots, he dropped them on the wide porch, right outside the front door. With a brief knock on the freshly painted panel, he walked inside. His mother looked up in surprise and smiled, the knitting in her lap forgotten.

"Riley!" She stood and came toward him, her face wreathed in smiles. Flinging her arms out wide, she enveloped him in a warm hug.

"Where did you come from? I thought you were in Watervale?"

He hugged her back, taking comfort from her familiar form. The faint smell of citrus clung to her hair, like it always had.

He grinned a little sheepishly. "I was. At least, I was when I called you. Somewhere along the way, I decided to make a visit. It's so much better than a phone call, don't you think?"

Her brow furrowed with worry. "What's the matter, Riley?"

He averted his gaze. His innocent act hadn't fooled her for a minute. "Is Dad home?"

Throwing him another long look filled with concern, she let it go. "No, hon. He's doing a court circuit out west. He's in Bourke tonight."

Riley smiled. "He's catching up with all the relatives, no doubt. I bet he's loving it."

"Yes, I'm sure you're right. He was going to stay with Uncle

Gary and Aunt Susie. I think they were inviting a few of the others over for dinner."

Riley chuckled. "He'll be lucky to survive the night, wining and dining with that mob. I wouldn't like to be one of the defendants fronting up to his courtroom tomorrow."

Marguerite Munro smiled with fondness, shaking her head then offering to make coffee. He murmured his thanks and followed her into the newly renovated kitchen.

"This looks great, Mom. I love the color you chose for the walls."

His mother nodded as she set about making coffee. "Yes, they call it pea soup, which isn't at all inspiring, but it turned out all right."

"It looks good against all the white cabinets, and the black granite countertop really sets it off."

"I'm glad you like it, Riley, but enough about it. You didn't drive the better part of two hours, through a cold winter night to talk about the renovations. What's going on?"

He sighed heavily as he wandered over to the breakfast bar and pulled out a stool. With his elbows on the counter, he rested his chin on his steepled fingers and thought about where to start. So much had happened in two short weeks and it wasn't until he'd heard his mother's voice over the phone that he realized how much he needed to talk to someone about it—someone who'd understand.

With a deep breath, he began at the beginning. "There's this girl, Mom…"

She let him talk, uninterrupted. Two cups of black coffee later, he was finished. He sat in silence, feeling oddly lighter. His mother took another sip from her mug and set it carefully on the counter. "You really like this woman, don't you?"

He nodded, his gaze fixed on his empty cup.

"So what's the problem? Is her past the issue?"

"Of course not. I'm enraged at what she was subjected to and I hope I get a few minutes alone with Darryl Watson in a very small room before all this is over. As for it changing the way I feel about Kate, it only makes me admire her more. I mean, to become the smart, successful, self-assured woman she is after such a rough start—it's a credit to her and only goes to show the depth of her courage and tenacity."

Marguerite smiled tenderly. "It's been a long time since I saw you so worked up over a woman. In fact, I don't think I've ever seen you like this. Not even when you were with Iris."

Riley caught her gaze—her bright blue eyes, so different from his, were filled with love.

"You're right. I've never felt this way before, Mom, and...to tell you the truth, it scares me to death." As he made the admission, relief poured through him. It was the first time he'd said it aloud. Nerves thrummed under his skin as he waited for her response.

"Why, hon? Why does it scare you?"

All the old insecurities tumbled around in his head, filling his thoughts with noise and garbage. He squeezed his eyes shut and grimaced, waiting for them to dissipate.

Could he tell her? Could he tell his mother how he felt? If anyone was going to understand, it would be her. After all, she was a white woman who had married an aboriginal.

He drew a deep breath and released it on another heavy sigh. "I'm scared she won't feel the same way. I'm scared she'll be just like Iris and all the other girls I've dated—that when it comes down to it, she won't want to share her life with someone who's bi-racial."

He'd said it. The words were out there, hovering in the air between them. He snuck a glance at his mother. Her eyes were wide with shock.

"Riley! How could you think such a thing? You're a beautiful man, inside and out. What woman wouldn't want to be with you?"

He grimaced. "Plenty, believe me. Look at Iris. We lived together for more than three years. The day I started talking to her about something more permanent was the day she texted me to say it was over."

"Did she actually tell you it was because of your mixed heritage?"

"Not in so many words, but that was the gist of it."

Marguerite's eyes blazed with anger. "That shallow, little bitch. I always knew you were too good for her."

Now it was his turn to be shocked. "Mom, I've never heard you swear before! And when did you stop liking Iris? You two always got along so well."

"*Humph.* That's what you thought. I tried to get along with her because it meant so much to you. To tell you the truth, I was glad when she found someone else and ended it."

He was shocked for the second time. "Why didn't you say anything?"

She sighed and took another sip from her cup. "What could I say? You thought you were in love with her—you probably were in love with her. You weren't in a place where you were willing to listen to anyone on the subject. You even blew off Clayton at one point."

"Yeah, but he'd not long married Ellie and the whole world smelled like roses. Of course I resented it when he said he didn't think Iris was good enough for me. Who was he to judge who was good enough for me?"

"He only said it because he cared. We all do."

"Yeah, I know." Riley blew his breath out on a sigh. "The thing is, being bi-racial has seldom been an issue for me. I grew up in a home with two loving parents and a swag of brothers and sisters who were always there for me. We supported each other. The fact that we were part aboriginal... I couldn't be prouder of Dad and all that he's achieved."

His voice hitched. "Dad's been my inspiration," he continued quietly. Being of mixed race didn't define who I was when I was younger. It still doesn't. But that doesn't mean everyone sees it the same way."

"Listen to me, Riley. This Kate, if she's worthy of you, won't care about the color of your skin. She won't even *see* the color of your skin. If she loves you enough, if she loves you the way you deserve, it won't matter. *It simply won't matter.*"

Tears burned his eyes and he swallowed against the lump

in his throat. Hope and fear warred in his heart, choking him with their intensity. Could he really hope Kate would see the real him? That she would want him, love him, like his mother seemed to believe?

Clearing his throat, he swiped at the moisture in his eyes and offered her a shaky smile.

"Thanks, Mom. Thanks for everything. I didn't mean to unload on you like that."

Her eyes sparkled with emotion, but she offered a tremulous smile. "You can unload on me any time you want, son. Just remember that, okay?"

He nodded and bit his lip. "I appreciate that."

They sat in silence for a while, lost in their thoughts, the night still and quiet around them. Riley glanced at his watch and pushed away from his stool.

"It's late. I'd better get back. In a few hours, my day's going to start all over again and it's going to be another big one."

"You're right." Marguerite stood with him and stepped forward to give him a hug. "Are you sure you want to leave? The mountain will be foggy and they're talking snow. You could always stay here. There are plenty of spare beds."

Though it sounded tempting, he shook his head. "Thanks, but I'd rather get back. This thing with Hannaford and Watson—it's going to get nasty. We'll need every hand on deck."

"It's going to be very late when you get home."

"I probably won't be able to sleep anyway."

She nodded. "I understand." She hugged him again, a brief, fierce embrace. "You take care on those roads, okay? And let me know how you get on. Email me or call."

"I will. And thanks again." He put his arm around her and walked to the front door.

"I love you, Riley."

"I love you too, Mom."

Chapter 27

With a groan, Kate rolled over and squinted at the clock on the nightstand. It was nearly eight. Morning had arrived, although it hadn't yet announced itself through the thick motel curtains. Closing her eyes again, she savored the darkness.

She'd barely slept for most of the night. Thoughts of Darryl and Hannaford and her mother had chased themselves around in her head. And then there was Riley. Every time she closed her eyes, she felt him, the hard, warm length of him, the smell of his skin, the feel of him deep inside her.

She still couldn't believe she'd done it. She'd voluntarily, even willingly, had sex with a man. She'd almost given up on ever being normal enough to feel like that. And yet, with Riley, it had nearly been easy...natural.

There'd been a few moments when she'd had to breathe through her panic and focus on the man who held her, but she'd come through it, had even enjoyed it. She would have been on top of the world if Darryl and Hannaford—and what might happen with them—hadn't been foremost on her mind.

Her thoughts returned to Riley and she wondered how he'd fared fronting up to his colleagues and telling them about his suspicions. She could only hope he'd managed to convince them and that he'd received the support he needed.

With another groan, she threw off the bedcovers and

headed toward the shower. She needed to get herself presentable, just in case police officers arrived on her doorstep with questions.

Fear germinated in the pit of her belly at the thought of them executing the search warrant and what they might find in Darryl's house. Would they find the videos she was now almost certain her mother had? Could she bear the thought of the entire police department being witness to her degradation? On the other hand, if they didn't find them, could she bear the thought of Darryl going free?

That's what it came down to. She couldn't have it both ways. Either she remained silent and let the evidence of his pedophilia go unreported and unpunished, or she accepted that in order to see him punished, she had to expose him, and herself in the process?

She didn't have a choice. For ten years, she'd thought the best course of action, the one that would cause her the least amount of pain, was to bury her past in the darkest of places and pretend it had never happened. In return, she'd sacrificed the last decade with her mother. The ache of that loss would stay with her forever.

After returning to Watervale and meeting Riley, she realized she was stronger than she'd thought. Somewhere between the expensive therapy she'd received in London and the arrival back in her hometown, she'd empowered herself to face her demons head-on.

Seeing Darryl punished for his role was a vital part of the process. She realized she'd never truly heal and be able to put it all behind her until she'd acknowledged what he'd done, confronted it and seen the perpetrators brought to justice.

And then, maybe, just maybe, she could move on with her life—a life she hoped would include Riley.

She turned off the faucets in the shower and frowned. Was she being fanciful? Would a man like Riley really want to be part of her life? She'd bared her soul to him and he'd seemed to accept the nightmare of her past, but what if things were different in the cold, harsh light of day, when who she was and what had happened to her became real, something to be faced and dealt with—even at arm's length?

Reaching for a fluffy bath towel, she dried herself off. There was no point wondering and trying to second guess how Riley might or might not feel. She'd just have to see him, talk to him, ask him straight out if it mattered.

And she'd do that, just as soon as she found the courage.

Wandering into the other room, she dropped the towel onto the bed and opened the closet. Both pairs of her woolen pants were at the dry cleaners down the street. Her remaining clothes were limited to a couple of pairs of jeans and three long-sleeved blouses.

With no other choice, she tugged on a pair of jeans and teamed it with a white thermal undershirt and pale pink blouse. A dark-gray cashmere cardigan completed the ensemble.

She glanced at her reflection in the mirror and grimaced at the slight puffiness around her eyes. Her extended crying jag had left its mark and there was nothing she could do about it now.

Brushing her hair into a semblance of order, she pulled it back into a simple ponytail and swiped a generous amount of pink lip gloss across her lips. Not exactly high-end fashion, but it would have to do.

Her stomach growled and she was reminded of how long it had been since she'd eaten a decent meal. Not since the day before, when she'd eaten tea cake with Daisy. She glanced at the clock. Eight forty-five. The café on the corner might still be serving breakfast, or at least a decent cup of coffee.

Coming to a decision, she packed up her laptop and collected her handbag. She could always deter curious onlookers by immersing herself in her work. Besides, she hadn't checked her emails since yesterday afternoon. Collecting her jacket on the way out, she pulled the door closed behind her.

Kate glanced around the charming café with its clean white tablecloths and modern décor. Most of the dozen or so tables were occupied with other diners who chatted noisily among themselves.

Several paintings of local scenery adorned the walls. She moved closer to examine them with a critical eye and was excited by the knowledge they'd been painted by an artist with incredible aptitude. It would be worth making enquires. She was always on the lookout for new talent.

After jotting down the artist's name, she took a seat at an empty table and picked up the menu. A waiter approached her with a dubious look on his face and hesitantly took her order. She wondered at his curious reaction.

The noise and hum of conversation slowly faded. Kate glanced around her, wondering about the cause of the silence around her. The other diners averted their gazes.

Her eyes widened in sudden comprehension and her heart thudded. Maybe she'd been wrong about going out in public? She assumed Darryl and Hannaford had been arrested. The whole town was likely buzzing with it. It was probably what had been the topic of conversation before she'd entered the café.

Her appetite vanished and her shoulders slumped and with it, her courage. Did she really want to put herself under so much scrutiny this early in the proceedings?

Quickly collecting her handbag and laptop, she stood and headed for the door. It was cowardly, but at that moment, it was all she could manage.

Riley gathered the team of officers around him and explained the contents of the search warrant. His eyes stung from a lack of sleep and the bite in the frosty air, but he forged on, wanting nothing more than to put this day behind him.

With renewed determination, he put his shoulder to the front door of No.16 Baxter Road and shoved hard. The wooden boards creaked beneath his ear, but didn't give. When Riley and his men had attended the address the night before, Watson had met them on the front step. Riley had placed him under arrest and had cuffed him. It was now obvious Darryl had deadlocked the door on his way out. He sure as hell hadn't wanted to make this easy.

Two senior officers from IA had arrived from Sydney on the early Grafton plane and had taken over the investigation. Unsure who they could trust among the local police, they'd seconded four detectives from the nearby town of Lismore. Reynolds and Riley had brought them up to speed. The IA officers were keen to see the search warrant executed.

"Come on, Riley. Put your back into it."

He grimaced at Chase who stood behind him. With all his strength, he rammed the door again. The old wood groaned in protest and splintered around the lock.

"One more time, mate and I think you'll have it."

Riley threw him a dark look and Chase smiled with wide-eyed innocence. Taking a step backwards, Riley once again hit the door hard with his shoulder and took satisfaction from the sound of it tearing through. He halted inside the foyer and looked around.

The place was much as it had been on his first visit. The countertops were sparkling and the floor tiles were spotless. This time, though, the caustic smell of bleach permeated the air.

His lips compressed in anger.

Darryl had known they were coming.

His gut churned with anger and disgust, but there was nothing he could do about it. They'd never prove someone had tipped the former commander off. They'd just have to hope Darryl had forgotten something or had gotten sloppy in his haste.

"What are we looking for?" Chase asked, following Riley into the open-plan kitchen and living room.

"I'm not sure. Anything that looks out of place. Anything that might tell us what happened to Rosemary Watson." His gaze scanned the coffee table, which was still free from debris, except for the glossy magazines and holiday brochure.

His anger ratcheted up another notch. Darryl was laughing at him. He turned to Chase.

"I want you to look through everything, books, videos, DVDs, *everything*. And get one of those blokes from Lismore to go through the trash."

Chase grinned. "They're going to love that."

"Just do it. I'm going to take a look upstairs."

Riley took the stairs two at a time, his heart accelerating with every step that brought him closer to the top. Knowing Kate's old room was only a few feet away, increased the dread that weighed him down. The thought of what she'd endured in it sickened him and he wondered again how she'd managed to find her way into the light.

Donning a pair of gloves, he opened the first door he came to and found himself in a bathroom.

The tension in his gut eased and he drew in a breath. Dust and grime had collected in and around the basin and along the top of the toilet. Dead bugs littered the floor. An old tube of toothpaste sat dried and forgotten in a cup. A single pink toothbrush stood beside it.

His chest tightened. It must have been Kate's. He couldn't see Darryl using a pink toothbrush. Besides, the bathroom looked like it hadn't been used in years.

Swiping an old, faded shower curtain to one side, he peered into the cubicle. A rust-colored water stain tarnished the once-white ceramic. A piece of soap sat on a ledge, cracked and dry. He didn't know where Darryl showered, but it definitely wasn't in here.

Riley stepped out into the hall and moved to the next door. He turned the knob and walked inside. His pulse rate spiked.

Her room still had posters of almost-forgotten pop stars and movie idols littering the walls. The pale pink paint had faded a little, but the room looked like she'd been there yesterday.

The bed was neatly made, covered with a pink-and-white striped bedspread. The matching pillowcase was filled with a single pillow. An old white wicker chair stood in one corner, laden with a medley of soft toys. The innocence of the picture shredded his heart.

He walked over to the closet and opened a door. His heart clenched at the sight of the clothes still hanging there, as if time stood still and the teenaged Kate would reappear any minute.

She'd told him she'd packed a bag in the middle of the night and left. There would have been no room for a closet full of clothes, or a chair full of sentimentality. He ached for the little girl she'd once been. The one who had collected the rabbits, the teddy bears and the dolls. The one who had pored over the pages of *Popstar, Girls' Life* and *Teen Vogue* and had hung posters of movie stars on her walls.

He thought of Darryl and anger scorched his nerve endings. The bastard had stolen more than her innocence— he'd stolen a portion of her life.

"Find anything?"

Riley spun around. Chase strode into the room.

"No, but it doesn't look like anyone's been up here for a long time. How'd you do downstairs?"

"The usual junk in the ensuite. Toothbrushes, shaving cream. Nothing out of the ordinary."

Riley frowned. "Toothbrushes? As in, more than one?"

Chase nodded slowly. "Yeah, there are two, actually. A red and a blue. Both standing in the same cup on the vanity."

Excitement spread through him. "Bag them. We'll need to

check for DNA, but I'm betting one of them belongs to Rosemary."

"Surely he wouldn't be that stupid? One of the first things anyone packs is their toothbrush."

Riley thought of the solitary toothbrush in the bathroom next door. "Not necessarily. It can be overlooked, especially if there's a rush to leave. But it's worth checking out. If it is Rosemary's, it's another piece of evidence in our case against Darryl that suggests she never left here by choice."

"No worries. I'll get the boys onto it."

"You didn't happen to find a wheelchair? That would be kind of hard for anyone to forget, no matter what kind of rush they were in."

Chase winced and shook his head. "Sorry, mate. I can't help you there."

"Yeah. I guess it was too much to hope Darryl could be *that* stupid."

"So, what's next?"

Riley followed him out into the hall. "I'll go through the rest of the rooms up here. You and the others can check the backyard. How did things go with the trash cans?"

Chase shook his head. "No luck, I'm afraid. The ones in the house have fresh liners. The two outside were emptied this morning. They're still out on the street."

Frustration soared through him and he bit down on a curse. "So, apart from the toothbrush, we've got shit."

Chase threw him a look of silent understanding. Riley shouldered his way past him and continued down the hall.

Chapter 28

Kate's heart jumped at the sound of someone at the door. Her head told her it couldn't be Darryl or even Hannaford, but she was wary as she pulled back an inch of curtain and got a good look at her visitor.

Riley lifted his hand in a half-wave.

"Hey, there. Sorry to startle you. I should have called. It's been a shit of a day and it's not even lunchtime."

Kate struggled with the lock and chain and opened the door. Stepping aside, she let him into the room and closed it behind him.

Turning, she watched him pace the room, and recognized the disappointment etched into the taut lines of his face.

"I take it you didn't find anything?"

"No, nothing of much use. Darryl had cleaned the place out." His lips twisted. "He wasn't joking when he bragged about the friends he still had on the force."

"I guess I should be relieved you didn't find my mother." She said it quietly, barely maintaining her composure.

He was beside her in an instant. "Sweetheart, I'm so sorry. I should have thought. I didn't realize you thought her body might be there." He ran a hand through his hair, his frustration evident.

"There was nothing out of place. Nothing unusual. Nothing we could point to and say, something's wrong about this."

"So, what did you find? You said you found nothing of much use. I take it you found something?"

"Yeah, a toothbrush. Well, three, actually. Two were in the downstairs bathroom. One of them was upstairs. We're hoping one of them might be your mother's."

Hope leaped inside her. "Surely that proves she didn't leave? No one leaves without their toothbrush."

His gaze captured hers, dark and compelling. "You did."

She gasped, assailed by decade-old memories. "H-how did you know?"

"It's still there, in a cup on the sink in your bathroom."

Remembered fear and anger and hurt swirled inside her. The thought of her toothbrush—forgotten in her haste to leave because she'd been unwilling to switch on a light—standing as silent witness for more than ten years, tore something loose inside her.

"Oh, God... Oh, God." Her hand flew up to cover her mouth. She shook her head from side to side and tried to erase the painful memories.

Riley drew her into his arms and soothed her with murmured words against her hair. His hand, firm and warm, gave comfort as it stroked up and down her back.

She breathed deeply and tried to use her awareness of him to block out the harrowing recollections: Her fear of discovery as she'd crept through the house; the mind-numbing chill of the winter air as she'd eased open the back door; the certainty she would never be back—along with the uncertainty of the future that lay before her; the knowledge that she was forfeiting the presence of her mother in her life and accepting the guilt and the pain that came with that... And all of it as she jogged her way to freedom on sneakered feet

Her arms tightened around Riley's lean waist. He wore another suit, this one charcoal-gray, and the tailored cut fit him to perfection. The soft cotton of his freshly laundered shirt felt good against her cheek and she filled her nostrils with the scent of his maleness.

Heat from his chest warmed her through her blouse. She

moved against him and her nipples contracted with the friction. Her heart pounded, this time from anticipation as she lifted her head and captured his gaze.

He stared back at her, his eyes dark with need. His ragged breathing matched the rhythm of hers. She slid her palms up his chest, taking strength from the feel of his heartbeat beneath her fingers.

Standing on tip toe, she kissed him softly, tentatively, a feather-light caress of her lips. He stood still, the tension in his shoulders belying the flare of desire that ignited in the depths of his eyes.

He wanted her. Even after all she'd told him, he still wanted her. The realization weakened her knees and flooded her heart with joy. She clung to him, savoring the knowledge and the wonderment of it, hardly daring to believe it. And then, with a voice that was husky with emotion, he confirmed it.

"I want to make love to you, Kate."

She wound her arms around his neck and pressed herself against him. Unable to find the words, she used her lips and mouth and tongue and covered his face with kisses.

Heat centered in her core and she moved against him, needing to get closer. The clothes she'd been admiring only moments before were now a hindrance and she groaned her frustration against his mouth.

"Easy there, sweetheart. We don't have to rush it. This time, I'm going to make it perfect."

She didn't care about perfect. All she wanted was to feel his warm skin against hers, the comfort, the security, the strength he gave her just by being with her. But she pulled away as the rest of his words registered.

"What about your investigation? Won't they be wondering where you are?"

He shook his head. "They know how disappointed and frustrated I am. They're all feeling much the same way. They'll understand if I disappear for an hour or two." He grinned. "They'll think I've gone somewhere to blow off steam."

She looked away, suddenly assailed by doubts. "Is that what you're doing? Blowing off steam?"

He took hold of her chin and forced her to look at him. "No, sweetheart, that's not what I'm doing. God help me, I didn't come around here for this, but I can't help it. I can't think straight when I'm around you and I sure as hell can't keep my hands off you. I'm more worked up over you than I've ever been for an investigation and it scares the hell out of me because I—I've fallen in love with you and I don't have a clue how you feel."

He dropped his arms and stepped away. The uncertainty on his face tore at her heart. She'd never felt so safe, so wanted, so needed by a man—she loved how he made her feel.

From the moment they'd met, he'd felt right. Like an old friend who would always be there. Like a comfortable pair of shoes or her favorite fluffy house coat.

Oh, God, she couldn't believe she'd just likened the gorgeous man before her to her house coat, but the feelings he generated deep inside her were much the same: He felt like home. Like a real home, filled with love and laughter and acceptance.

And it was the truth. She'd fallen in love with him. Somewhere along the way, through the terror of confronting her past and the turmoil of finding her mother, she'd fallen in love with Riley.

She reached out to touch him, a shaky smile on her lips. His gaze roved over her face and her smile widened.

A tentative smile tugged at his lips, but uncertainty still clouded his eyes.

"Talk to me, Kate. Please, talk to me."

She stepped forward until she stood mere inches away from him. Reaching up, she pulled his head down to hers and kissed him.

It was slow and sweet and perfect. Every ounce of the love she felt for him found its way to his mouth. When at last she pulled away, both of them were breathing fast.

"I love you, Riley. With every fiber of my being. That's how I feel."

The smile erupted into a wide grin. He whooped and hollered and pulled her to him. His arms tightened around her, holding her like he'd never let her go.

Wriggling out of his grasp, she took his hand and tugged him toward the bed. He sat down on the edge, his gaze on hers. Shyness besieged her, but she was determined to show him how much she meant it. Lifting her arms, she stood before him and undid the buttons on her blouse, her gaze never straying from his.

Shrugging the shirt off her shoulders, she tossed it to the floor. Her white lace bra quickly followed suit before her courage waned. She stood proudly before him, pleased when his breath caught at the sight of her naked torso. Her nipples reacted to the heat in his gaze and puckered into small, hard nubs.

Leaning forward, she kissed him, her lips soft and teasing, his mouth warm and inviting beneath hers. His arms came up around her and pulled her close. She lost her balance and toppled onto him, relishing the feel of her bare skin against the cotton of his shirt. Seconds later, he rolled her onto her back and pressed her into the mattress.

He stared down at her, his eyelids heavy with desire. With quick movements, he pulled off his jacket, loosened his tie and undid the buttons of his shirt. Within minutes, his clothing had joined hers on the floor.

She stroked the well-defined muscles of his chest with her fingers. He gasped and sucked in his belly. A surge of pure feminine power flooded through her. She'd never felt in control of her responses or her actions and the thought that she could have such an effect on him was exhilarating.

Her hands strayed lower, slipping beneath the waistband of his pants to tangle in the soft hair below. With a grimace, he captured her hands in his and held them against his chest.

"This time, it's all about you, sweetheart. If you keep heading in that direction, I might end up disgracing myself.

Again." He bent low and brushed his lips across hers. "And I've sworn that's not going to happen."

She smiled and wondered again how she'd stumbled across this man and what she'd done to deserve him. Happiness spread through her. She threaded her arms around his neck and pulled him down hard against her. The feel of his bare skin on hers sent goose bumps along her nerve endings and she shivered with the need that burned deep down inside her.

Raising her head, she tasted the side of his neck with her tongue. He groaned and pulled gently away from her. He moved lower until he'd captured one of her rosy nipples between his lips.

She gasped at the sensation. His mouth, hot and moist, teased the sensitized peak. She pressed against him with wanton need, abandoning all pretense at control.

He turned his attention to her other breast and her heart pounded in response. She moved restlessly beneath him, her fingers clenched around his head, anchoring him against her and against the avalanche of feeling that threatened to swamp her.

"Easy, sweetheart," he murmured, lifting his head to peer into her eyes.

His mouth skipped over the soft skin of her belly and paused at the top of her waistband. Moments later, he slid open the button on her jeans and lowered the zipper. Her breath caught.

Lifting her bottom off the bed, she let him tug the garment down her hips, leaving her naked but for a scrap of white lace. Setting aside her shyness, she watched as he looked his fill.

"You're so beautiful," he breathed. His finger traced the outline of her panties, stopping to dip slightly beneath the elastic. Her stomach quivered from the strain and she yearned for his weight to be back on top of her.

His head lowered and his tongue replaced his finger, gliding across the lace. He buried his face between her legs. The feel of his warm breath on her flesh was unbearable.

Blood pounded in her veins and left her clit heavy and aching for more. As if sensing her need, his mouth opened over her sensitized flesh. She almost came off the bed in response.

Embarrassment burned through her. She tightened her legs together and pushed at his head. He looked up and his gaze found hers.

"Let me love you, Kate. I want to love you."

The love and sincerity in his eyes was what convinced her. The tension left her body and she relaxed against the softness of the mattress.

Riley tugged at her panties and slid them down her legs. With an effort, she fought against her instinctive urge to hide.

"Please, don't be scared, sweetheart. No one's going to hurt you, ever again."

His head lowered and his lips moved over her heated flesh, licking and sucking and sliding between the soft folds. She cried out at the exquisite sensations. With the palm of his hand, he pressed against her clit, stroking her with increasing pressure.

Kate's hands clenched into fists as sensations overwhelmed her. His fingers slipped inside her and she tensed. With sweet, tender strokes he moved in and out of her, the pressure of his hand never once relenting. Heat and desire blossomed. She pressed up against him, squirming under his touch.

The constant force of his mouth and his palm and his fingers continued and the pressure from deep inside became almost unbearable. She twisted and moaned, seeking relief. Riley lifted his head and looked at her, urging her on.

"That's it, sweetheart, you're nearly there. Relax and let it happen. Let yourself come. I want to see you come."

His words tipped her over the edge. She squeezed her eyes shut and cried out. Her inner muscles clenched and pulsed. Relief washed over her and she jerked against him.

Slowly, she opened her eyes and watched as Riley stood and pulled off his suit pants. His boxers quickly followed. Her gaze was drawn to the long, hard length of him that jutted proudly from his body. The tip of his cock glistened with excitement and she longed to taste him as he'd tasted her.

She half sat and reached out for him. He backed away with a smile.

"Oh, no you don't. Not this time. If you touch me, I'm going to explode and I want to be deep inside you with your tight warmth all around me when I do that."

Leaning down, he pulled out a condom from the pocket of his trousers and quickly sheathed himself. He took up a position between her legs. They fell open in welcome.

"I'm sorry, sweetheart, but this is going to be quick. I'm so hard for you, I can't stand it another minute." Plunging inside her, he shuddered and groaned and then began moving.

She reached up and pulled him down hard against her, lifting her hips to meet each fierce thrust. Tension built in his shoulders. His breath was harsh in her ear. She tightened her hold on him, loving the feel of him moving inside her.

He groaned again and his pace increased, faster and harder until he stiffened and stilled and then collapsed against her, his body spent.

Slowly, his breathing returned to normal. They lay face to face on their sides, touching and exploring with fingers gentled by awe and love. Long minutes passed.

Riley looked at the clock.

With a sigh, he rolled away and stood, collecting his underwear and trousers and pulling them on. "I have to go."

Kate nodded in understanding, even though she longed for him to stay. "I know. Things to do, places to go, people to see."

"Ladies to kiss." He swooped low and planted a kiss on her lips.

She smiled and watched him continue to dress. "You better not be kissing anyone but me. I don't think I'd like to share."

He growled low in his throat and pressed another hard kiss against her mouth. "That's good, because I *definitely* don't like to share."

She smiled again and tugged the sheet up higher, tucking it across her breasts. "Where are you going now?"

He grimaced. "Back to the station. Do a recap. See where we go from here."

"So you didn't find anything to suggest foul play at Darryl's house? No sign that anything was amiss?"

"Nope, everything looked completely normal, just like you'd expect it to look."

Kate frowned. "I wonder if *I'd* notice anything out of place? I mean, I haven't been there for ten years, but..."

Riley frowned and moved closer, sitting on the side of the bed and taking her hands in his. "Really? Do you really want to go back in there?"

"Do you think it could make a difference?"

He shrugged. "I don't know. But at this stage, I'm willing to try anything." He framed her face with his hands. "But only if you're up to it. I can't imagine what it would be like for you to go into his house again."

Kate stared at him drawing strength from the love in his eyes. "With you beside me, I'm willing to try."

Leaning forward, he kissed her softly, deeply, on the mouth. "Christ, I love you so much."

"I love you, too," she whispered.

CHAPTER 29

Kate looked across at Riley and drew courage from the warmth in his eyes and the encouragement in his smile. She looked through the window of the squad car to the house on Baxter Road. It appeared much as it had before. The only exception was that two marked police cars were parked in the driveway. A couple of uniformed officers stood in the garden and Chase Barrington waited for her and Riley near the front steps.

Riley glanced toward her. "Ready?"

Kate sucked in a deep breath, filling her lungs. The awareness of her breathing helped her focus her mind on the task in front of her. With gritted teeth and a lifetime of determination, she gave Riley a brief nod. He opened the car door.

Holding her elbow, he guided her up the path. His face was set in a grim line. His eyes were dark with concern.

He looked at her again. "You don't have to do this."

Kate offered him a tight smile. "I know. But it might be the difference between finding out what's really happened to my mother and not. If there's any chance the answer lies in this house, I have to take it."

His eyes filled with admiration and love. He bent and pressed a quick kiss on her lips and whispered, "You're the bravest woman I know."

She started in surprise. They were in full view of the other officers. Riley didn't seem to care. Warmth spread through her from her belly up into her chest and then it blossomed into her cheeks. But it was a happy kind of warmth and she squeezed his hand in gratitude.

Chase met them at the bottom of the steps that led to the front door, his face somber. "It's very good of you to do this, Kate. We really appreciate it."

She acknowledged him with a nod and swallowed against the rapid onslaught of nerves. She was right outside the front door, ready to enter for the first time in more than a decade. Her legs started to tremble and all of a sudden she felt sick.

Riley must have seen something in her face. He pulled her to the side, his brow furrowing with concern.

"Kate, are you all right? You're as white as a sheet. Maybe this isn't such a good idea?"

Drawing in a few quick, deep breaths, Kate made an effort to restore her equilibrium. She rested her forehead against the cool fabric of Riley's jacket and clung to his familiar scent. His arms came around her and drew her in close.

"It's okay, sweetheart, you don't have to do this. Let's forget about it. I'll take you back to your motel. We'll figure something out. Chase and I will just go back through the place again, see if there's anything we missed."

There was nothing Kate wanted more than to turn around and run away as fast as she could, back to the sanctuary of her motel room. But that wouldn't solve anything. Not the questions about her mother and certainly not her fierce determination to face her demons once and for all.

She lifted her head and offered him a weak smile. "Thanks. I really appreciate it. But I have to do this. Just give me a minute. I'll be fine. I have to do this."

She sounded like she was trying to convince herself as much as him, but it was the best she could do. The last thing she wanted was to step inside Darryl's house again, but she had to. There was no choice. It was as simple as that.

With another deep fortifying breath, she stepped out of the comfort of Riley's arms and marched back to the doorstep. Chase looked over her head to Riley who stood not far behind her and after a moment's hesitation, he slowly opened the door.

It was the smell of the place that hit her first. The unfamiliar, acrid burn of bleach in her nostrils distracted her enough to get her through the entryway and into the open-plan kitchen and living room.

She looked around her. The place was as spotless as she remembered. It was only the smell that was foreign. A decade ago, it had smelled of lemon and citrus and roses, not the caustic smell of cleaning fluid.

Her mother's desk was still against the wall beneath the big front window. Kate remembered when Rosemary would open the curtains wide and enjoy the view from her wheelchair. A writing pad and a couple of fountain pens littering the desk were all that remained on the desk. The will that Riley had said he'd seen there was nowhere in sight.

Steeling herself, she walked across the living room and stopped outside her mother's bedroom. The door was open and she could see the bed, neatly made up, in the corner.

Riley came up behind her and touched her elbow. She took comfort from his presence and, with another deep breath, she stepped across the threshold.

Like the kitchen and living room, the bedroom was spotless. Perfume bottles and tubes of hand cream were lined up neatly on her mother's dresser. A book sat on the nightstand. She moved closer and read the title: *My Reckless Surrender*. From the look of the picture on its cover, it was a romance novel, complete with a half-naked woman in a passionate clench with a man that looked too good to be true.

She flipped open the cover. It was stamped Watervale Public Library. There was nothing remarkable about it, except for the book's location. She turned to Riley.

"It's on the wrong side."

"What do you mean?"

"I mean, it's on the wrong side. My mother always slept on the other side of the bed, closest to the bathroom."

He caught on immediately. "I can't picture Darryl reading romance books."

"Exactly. He's placed it there because it's something you'd expect to see on a woman's nightstand. And it's a library book—more evidence to support his story that she hasn't gone for good." She shook her head. "The only thing I can't figure out is why he'd put it on the wrong side."

"Maybe he was in such a hurry, he didn't think? I mean, for him, going to that nightstand is probably as familiar as climbing in on his side of the bed."

Kate shrugged. "Maybe. Whatever the reason, it's definitely suspicious."

"Yeah, I agree." Riley turned to Chase, who hovered in the doorway. "Get onto Reynolds. Tell him we need someone down here with a camera. I want to photograph it *in situ* before we bag it. I also want to find out when it was checked out of the library."

"No worries." Chase pulled his phone out of his shirt pocket and backed out into the living room.

Kate wandered into the ensuite. White tiles and ceramic surfaces sparkled in the mid-afternoon light. The smell of bleach was fainter in here and she breathed a little easier.

"Better put these on," he said and he handed her some gloves, then pulled on his own pair.

Gloves on, she opened the top drawer of the bathroom vanity and pulled out two bottles of prescription drugs. The labels were from the local pharmacy and had been prescribed by Dr Shepherd. They were made out to Rosemary Watson.

"What have you got there?" Riley asked.

"Mom's medication. Some of it, anyway. From what Daisy said, she was on much more than this. It's odd she didn't take these with her. The bottles are nearly empty, but Daisy told us she didn't keep her appointment with her doctor. She wouldn't have had any more with her."

Riley came to stand beside her and took one of the bottles from her hand. He looked at the contents and checked the label. "Daisy was right. I called Doctor

Shepherd. He confirmed your mother hadn't renewed her prescriptions." He tugged a plastic evidence bag from his pocket and dropped the bottles in. Sealing it, he scribbled a time and date on the panel provided.

He looked up at her, his face grim. "I'm not sure why these were overlooked the first time, but we have them now and that's what matters."

Kate nodded and followed him out of the ensuite, into the bedroom and then out into the living room. She bit her lip and looked at him. "I guess that leaves upstairs."

Each step upwards took her closer to her room at the top of the stairs. Blood pounded in her ears. She was grateful for Riley's presence behind her, but even so, it was difficult to keep the panic at bay.

She held onto the wooden banister, her hands slick with sweat. She turned and stumbled and would have fallen if not for Riley's quick reflexes. Catching her against him, he held her tightly, allowing her to regain control.

"I'm okay," she said, her voice still shaky. "I'm okay."

"Are you sure?" The concern in his eyes was touching. It had been more than ten years since someone had looked at her like that, worried for her well-being. She owed it to him, she owed it to *both* of them to dig deep and find the courage to get through this.

Pulling gently out of his embrace, she continued to climb the stairs. Three more steps and she'd be in the hall. Her room was a tiny jump from there. A single, tiny jump.

She could do it.

With fierce concentration, she lifted one booted foot and then another. One more step.

She was there.

Her heart hammered and her chest felt tight, but she pushed forward, determined to get this over with. The door to her room was closed and she wished she could just turn away without going inside, but knowing Riley was right behind her, she turned the knob and stepped through the doorway.

Memories bombarded her from every angle, pummeling

her from all sides. The room was almost exactly as she'd left it, except the bed had been made and the soft toys she'd swept to the floor in helplessness and rage after Darryl and Hannaford left had been lined up neatly in their usual spot on the cane chair that stood by the window. Mrs Fitzgerald must have picked them up. She couldn't see Darryl taking the time to tidy—or to keep the room free of dust.

Her gaze drifted to the wall where the camera had been. She could still see evidence of the sizeable hole she'd smashed into the wall with her fist and then with a chair. It had been repaired with a new sheet of plasterboard, but it hadn't been repainted and the spot stood out a chalky gray against the pink of the rest of the wall.

She forced her legs to move, bringing her closer. Running her hand over the rough surface, she struggled to get a handle on her painful memories.

Riley stopped a few feet behind her. "Has anything changed since you were here?" His voice was low, unobtrusive and she was grateful for his understanding.

Her voice caught. "N-no."

His hand reached for hers, warm, strong, safe. "Let's get out of here."

She nodded and turned to leave. "Wait."

He halted. "What is it?"

"That wall. The one over there." She pointed to the wall opposite the bed. "It's different. It never used to be brick." Letting go of Riley's hand, she walked over to it and placed her palm against it. "Why would he have changed the wall?"

Riley shrugged and pursed his lips, a frown creasing his forehead. "It seems a rather strange thing to do. And brick for a bedroom doesn't make sense."

"You're right. It doesn't make sense. As far as I know, there was nothing wrong with this wall. The damage I did was to the one over there. You can see the new plaster work." She indicated the wall in question with her head. "Not that it's new now, but you can see it's never been painted."

"Yes, I see." Riley turned back to the brick wall. "What kind of wall used to be here?"

Kate shook her head, bemused. At least the surprise about the change in the wall had taken her mind off the horrors the room held for her. "It was the same as the others, plasterboard painted pink."

"I wonder why it was altered?" Riley mused, running his hand across the uneven surface. "It's a fairly rough job. Whoever did it wasn't much of a bricklayer, that's for sure. The mortar looks fresh." He bent and put his nose to it and inhaled. "I can still smell the lime. It can't have been put here too long ago. What's behind it?"

"Another bedroom. It was never used. At least, not while I lived here. Mom and Darryl slept downstairs."

Riley walked back through the doorway and into the adjoining room. Kate followed him, flicking on the light switch. The smell of dust and mildew was strong in the air. Boxes filled with old clothes, discarded furniture and three suitcases were piled haphazardly around the room. The only area clear of debris was a few feet of space beside another new brick wall.

Riley squatted and picked at a few specks of material strewn along the edge of the carpet. Pulling on another pair of latex gloves, he tugged an evidence bag out of his pocket and collected pieces of the chalky-colored particles.

Kate stepped closer. "What are they?"

"They look like pieces of mortar that have fallen off a trowel and then dried. They smell of fresh lime. They'll have to be examined by the lab to know for sure."

"Will they be able to tell how long they've been here?"

"I'm not sure, but they should be able to tell us how much dust is on them. If they've been here for a while, they should have at least some kind of coating like the other things in this room. "I'll collect a couple of the boxes over there and maybe a suitcase for comparison. Those things are thick with it."

Kate sighed, not sure what to make of it. "Why would

Darryl build two brick walls up here, of all places? It doesn't make sense."

Riley stood. Sealing the evidence bag, he dropped it into the pocket of his jacket and tugged off his gloves. "Why does anyone build a wall?"

"To keep something out, I guess. Or..."

"To keep something in," he finished.

The look in his eyes terrified her. She moved closer, concern flooding through her. "Riley, what is it?"

He shook his head, but the shock on his face didn't ease. "The wall..." he choked.

An awful thought took root in her mind. It was a horrible, sickening, terrifying thought and she didn't want to give it voice. She gulped. Her chest was suffocatingly tight. She gulped again, and emitted a harsh, strangling sob. Tears burned behind her eyes. "You think she's behind it?"

Riley stared at her. Slowly, he nodded.

Kate's body shook in time with the chattering of her teeth. She was suddenly freezing. She turned this way and that, rubbing her arms with hands that were icy as she tried to control the turmoil of her raging thoughts.

Riley dragged a hand through his hair and blew out his breath. Anger and helplessness darkened the depths of his eyes.

"We need to get some members of the Tactical Response Group in here to knock it down. They'll have to fly up from Sydney."

His words sent cold shards of pain through her heart. "Y-you think it's a possibility? You th-think my mother could be behind it?"

He stared at her and didn't reply, but his silence told her everything. She read the confirmation in his eyes. Turning away, she hugged her arms around her waist, willing the surge of nausea to remain at bay.

They didn't know for sure. Just because Darryl had built two walls in the house for no discernible purpose didn't mean he'd stored her mother's body behind them. There could be many reasons for its construction. Surely, as a former police commander, he wouldn't be so stupid. He would know of any number of places to hide a body. If she could just take a few minutes to think, she was sure she'd come up with some other explanation.

Then again, the fact that it seemed so obvious could be the very reason he'd been confident it would work. Who would be stupid enough to dispose of a body in their house? It was the last place the police would look.

A low, keening cry escaped her tightly compressed lips. It all made too much sense. She jammed her fist against her mouth, welcoming the discomfort against her teeth.

Riley's arms encircled her and drew her back against the solid safety of his chest.

"*Shh*, Kate. We don't know anything, yet. It might not be what you're thinking. I need you to stay strong. You can get through this. I know you can. You're the strongest, bravest, most heroic girl in the world. You can do this."

She turned in his arms and buried her face against the soft folds of his shirt. Tears ran down her cheeks. She sniffed and swiped at her nose. She riffled in her pocket for a tissue and was grateful when Riley handed her his handkerchief.

"I'm sorry, I'm really making a nuisance of myself. This must be the third time I've cried all over you."

Riley smiled down at her, his eyes filled with love. "Fourth, actually. But who's counting?" He pulled her back in against him and held her tight. "I'm here, sweetheart and I'm not going anywhere. I'm going to take care of you for the rest of my life. Nothing's going to hurt you ever again. I've told you that already, and I mean it." He pressed a soft kiss against her lips. "Whatever's behind that wall, we'll deal with it. Together."

Her eyes filled with fresh tears. "I love you."

"I love you, too."

They separated with reluctance, both acutely aware of the work that had to be done.

"I need to make some calls—"

"Yes," she interrupted him, pressing her lips tightly together.

"I'd better—"

"Go. Go and do your job. I'll be okay."

He frowned down at her, his face showing his struggle. He reached the only decision she knew he could.

His shoulders slumped on a sigh. "I'll drive you back to the motel."

"How long...?"

He grimaced. "I'm not sure. It depends when the TRG can get a flight. I'll tell Reynolds to put in a request that they get here ASAP, but it might not be until late this afternoon, or even tomorrow..." He shrugged. "Bureaucracy. It's not always easy."

"I take it Reynolds has taken over since Hannaford was arrested?"

"Yes. He's the acting LAC until they advertise the position properly."

"I guess whatever's behind there isn't going anywhere."

Closing the gap between them, he clasped her by the arms, his dark eyes intent on her face. "*If*, Kate. *If* there's something behind there. We don't know anything yet."

She forced a smile. "You're right. It could be just a stupid wall."

His answering smile didn't reach his eyes. "Exactly." He pulled her to him and kissed her hard. "Let's get out of here."

In the end, it was another two days before the TRG Unit arrived from Sydney and commenced hammering down the wall. Two long days where Riley watched Kate's face grow more pale and anxious by the hour. Two long nights where he held her in his arms and whispered words of love and comfort, knowing nothing he could say would take the sadness and uncertainty away.

He stood with Chase and a couple of uniformed officers, watching as the hole in the brick wall widened. With each blow, the gap became bigger and the cold dread in his gut weighed heavier. Concrete and brick crumbled and fell to the floor.

A huge halogen light had been set up in one corner. Directed toward the wall, it illuminated nearly half of the room. The heat of it burned across Riley's back.

He'd left Kate at her motel, knowing it was the best place for her to be. He didn't want her here. She didn't need to witness what might or might not lie behind the brick facade.

A shout from one of the men snagged his attention. "There's something over there."

Riley leaped forward and shouldered his way past the curious TRG officers. He looked through the opening to where the officer pointed. Riley's heart sank like a stone.

It was a trash bag—no, two. Dark green, heavy-duty plastic bags that could be purchased from any convenience store or supermarket. They were tied around the top with gray duct tape, sealing them off from the air. Only the faintest of foul odors reached his nostrils.

Nausea swirled in his gut. He didn't need to open them to know what was inside. Looking past them, he spied the mangled remains of a wheelchair, twisted and bent to fit into the narrow space.

Fury and anguish torched his veins—for the woman who'd been carved up and thrown into trash bags and left to rot behind a wall; for the woman who waited in her motel room for news; for him, the man who had to bring it to her.

Knowing he didn't have the liberty to lose control, he cleared his throat and began issuing orders.

"Barrington, make sure the scene's secure and close the house off from the road. I don't want any curious onlookers making their way across the garden."

He eyed the TRG officers, both of them pale and grim.

"Jones, I want you to call forensics. Tell them to get here ASAP. We need photos before we move anything. Davis, you can call the morgue."

The men scuttled to do his bidding. He pulled out his

phone and dialed Reynolds. After giving the acting Commander an update, he tugged on a pair of latex gloves and approached the first bag. Drawing in a deep breath, he steeled himself against what he expected to find.

CHAPTER 30

Kate paced the tight confines of her motel room for the umpteenth time and tried to concentrate on anything other than what could be happening at No.16 Baxter Road. With a groan, she threw herself down on the bed.

The waiting was doing her head in. The uncertainty, the not knowing. She clenched her teeth and made an effort to calm down. Riley would call her with any news. He'd told her he would.

When he'd kissed her good-bye outside her motel room earlier that morning, he still hadn't known what time the TRG Unit would arrive. It was now after three and her insides had twisted into knots.

It could go one of two ways—either they'd knock down the wall and find nothing, which meant the agonizing search for her mother would continue or, they would find something to indicate their search was over. Neither scenario gave her comfort.

Moving restlessly, she tried to block out the images that formed and shifted and chased one another through her mind. She groaned and pressed her hands against the sides of her head, shaking it in an effort to dislodge them.

Riley would call if there was news. He'd promised. He knew how she'd be feeling—waiting, wondering, not knowing. He hadn't called, so obviously there was no news. Maybe that was a good sign...

The sound of a motor vehicle idling outside her door suddenly registered. Leaping off the bed, she ran to the window and peered out. Riley climbed out of the unmarked squad car.

Her throat went dry. She fumbled with the lock on the door and opened it just as he lifted his hand to knock.

She knew before he said a word. He shook his head, his eyes dark with pain and regret. She backed into the room— hardly aware that he'd followed her—and stumbled into the chair.

With her head in her hands, she absorbed the news he hadn't even voiced.

The search was over.

"I'm sorry, Kate. I'm so sorry."

Tears burned behind her eyes, but she held them back. "You found her."

He nodded, his face grave. "Yes."

The stark confirmation was almost too much, but she took a few breaths and reined in her control. "What happened?"

Riley shook his head. "We don't know yet. Forensics will be there for a few more hours and she'll then be taken to the morgue. We won't know exactly how she died until we get the autopsy report."

Forensics. Morgue. Autopsy. Words she'd never dreamed she'd hear in a conversation about her mother. And yet, she'd known that was a possibility. Had even felt, deep down inside, that her mother wouldn't be coming home. That she'd never see her again... Ever.

She thought of the years she'd wasted, hiding ten thousand miles away. The saber-sharp stab of guilt and regret nearly bent her double. Gasping, she let the tears fall.

Riley carried her to the bed and gently laid her down. Not even stopping to pull off his boots, he gathered her in his arms and held her close.

She cried quietly though many of her tears were already spent. He pressed kisses against her hair, offering wordless comfort.

After long moments, she lifted her head and looked at him. "Can I see her?"

He squeezed his eyes shut and then opened them again. Slowly, he shook his head. "No, sweetheart. You don't want to see her. Best that you remember her the way she was, vibrant, happy, alive."

Kate bit back another sob and buried her face in his neck. "I don't know if she was ever happy," she choked, her voice muffled against his shirt.

"She was for a while—at least, according to Daisy," he murmured, his hand stroking her softly, rhythmically up and down her back. "Daisy said they had lots of fun together."

Kate sighed. "Yes, she did, didn't she? I only hope Mom didn't suffer. I hope it was quick."

Riley didn't answer. She could only imagine what he'd seen. He was right, she was better off not knowing. It wasn't going to change anything and it would forever destroy the good memories she did have of her mother. "What happens now?"

Riley sighed. "Darryl will be charged with her murder. We found a roll of duct tape in the kitchen drawer and trowel and a bucket in the shed out the back. For a man so much admired for his contribution as a police officer, he was a little sloppy."

"Or inordinately arrogant," Kate added. "Perhaps he didn't think anyone would dare enter his property or, if they did, that the items you found would raise suspicion. He wouldn't be the only man in town to have things like that around his house and he certainly wouldn't have counted on me returning. It was highly likely I was the only one who would know the walls were new. I can't imagine he invited too many of his friends upstairs."

Riley's arms tightened around her. "That's true. Maggie Fitzgerald may have noticed, but it would have taken someone else to even wonder about the brick wall. She had no cause to venture upstairs." He smiled grimly. "The good news is, the existence of the new all strengthens our case against Darryl. The odds that someone else did it are zero to none. It's going to be a little hard to explain to a jury how two brick walls were built in your house without your knowledge."

Kate shuddered. "Will I still have to testify?"

"I'm afraid so, unless he pleads guilty. And then, of course, there's Hannaford. Just remember, I'll be there beside you, every step of the way."

The promise in his eyes warmed her through and helped to dissolve a little of the chill that had plagued her since the discovery of the wall. She lifted her head and kissed him, communicating with her mouth the depth of her love and gratitude.

She pulled away gently and laid her head back on his chest. His hold around her tightened.

"I wish I could spare you the next few days, sweetheart, but you're strong and you're brave and you can get through this even if I can't be with you all the time. I know you can."

Kate blinked back tears. "I can't believe she's gone," she whispered. "I mean, I know in some part of me I'd accepted that Darryl must have murdered her, but there was another part of me that continued to hope. Now that hope's gone and I'm left with nothing."

"I wish I could take the pain away," he whispered. "I wish that more than anything."

"Thank you," she choked. A fat, silent tear slid down her cheek, unheeded. With tender fingers, he wiped it away.

They were silent for a few moments, each lost in their thoughts. Kate thought of her mother and prayed she'd finally found peace—from her debilitating illness and from her unhappy marriage.

"You need to go and see Ronald Westport," Riley murmured against her hair.

She frowned. "The lawyer?"

"Yes. The one who drew up your mother's new will. She gave him an envelope with your name on it and left instructions it was to be given to you in the event of her death."

Kate felt the blood drain from her face. Her voice came out hoarse when she spoke again. "Do you know what it's about?"

He shook his head. "Westport wouldn't say."

Kate closed her eyes and tried to come to terms with this latest shock. A second later, she gasped. "What if it's the videos?"

She felt the tension in his body, even before he cursed beneath his breath. His jaw clenched and then relaxed. It was obvious he was making an effort to remain calm.

"It still infuriates me every time I think about Darryl filming you. If it is a video, we'll deal with it. I promise you. He's not going to have another nanosecond of control or influence over your life."

He drew her in closer and kissed her forehead. "Don't worry about that right now, sweetheart. We don't have a clue what's in there. It could be anything."

Kate said nothing, but she wasn't convinced and she didn't think Riley was, either. The videos made sense. What else would her mother have taken to a lawyer's office, where she would be assured it was safe, and leave instructions for it to be opened in the event of her death?

The dread that had been her constant companion for more than a month once again found a place deep inside her.

"Will you come with me?" she whispered.

Riley tilted her chin up until she met his gaze. "Of course, I will. I've already told you I'm going to be there for you, no matter what." His eyes filled with love and sincerity. "I mean it, Kate. You'll never be on your own again."

Relief flooded through her. She lay her head back down and listened to the reassuring thud of Riley's heartbeat beneath her ear. With a determined effort, she pushed the weighty thoughts from her mind. The sleep that had eluded her for so long, beckoned. Slowly, gradually, she slipped away.

Kate looked around the waiting room of Cole & Westport; the nerves in her belly wound tight. The middle-aged receptionist who had announced their arrival via a discreet telephone call to Ronald Westport eyed her with a concerned smile.

"Are you sure I can't get you something? A cup of coffee? Tea?"

Kate shook her head and glanced at Riley who sat beside her. He gave her a reassuring look and tightened his hold on her hand. She took comfort from the pressure and breathed deeply.

Surely, she'd already been through the worst of it? Her stepfather had murdered her mother and buried her behind a brick wall in their house. Surely the contents of her mother's envelope couldn't be more shocking than that? She shivered and prayed that was true.

A door opened between the waiting room and what she presumed to be the inner offices. Her heart catapulted into her throat. She stood and grabbed blindly for Riley.

"It's okay, sweetheart. It's okay." His arm was a wall of confidence around her, supporting her, holding her upright. A tall, thin man with a mountain of thick white hair stepped forward and held out his hand.

"Miss Collins, I presume? I'm Ronald Westport."

She shook the proffered hand, although later, she wouldn't recall doing so. She vaguely registered Riley exchanging a greeting with the lawyer, but the words sounded like they were being spoken underwater. She followed the men through the outer door and along a short corridor.

Westport showed them into an office overcrowded with books and files and loose papers. He offered what she thought was an apology. She tried to dull the noise in her head so that she could hear him.

A large yellow envelope sat on his desk, in the middle of the mess of papers. A blue manila file lay next to it. Kate stared at the envelope, unable to look away.

"That's it, isn't it?" she croaked, her palms now slick with sweat.

The lawyer nodded briskly and took a seat behind the desk. Picking up the blue file, he opened it and withdrew a bound document.

"Please accept my condolences on your mother's passing. This is Rosemary's Last Will and Testament. She attended upon my office nearly two months ago and asked me to prepare it. Would you like me to read it?"

Kate shook her head. "My mother told me what was in it. I don't need to hear it again."

"Very well, then. As you are the executrix and sole beneficiary, I'll release the will to you. If you require assistance in its administration, I'll be more than willing to help."

Forcing a smile that felt more like a grimace, Kate took the document from him and laid it in her lap. "Thank you. I appreciate the work you did for my mother."

The elderly man shrugged, his eyes kind. "It was no trouble. I was happy to help out." He looked away and cleared his throat and then picked up the envelope.

Kate stilled. Fear erupted in gooseflesh along every pore of her skin. Riley flashed her a look full of concern and moved his chair closer.

"Your mother gave me this envelope the day she came in about her will. She asked me to lock it in our safe with instructions that it be handed to you in the event of her death."

Kate reached for the envelope with a hand that trembled. The paper was thin and weightless. Not a video, then. Relief surged through her. She felt lightheaded from the impact.

Riley's gaze captured hers, dark and impenetrable, but she knew he was thinking the same thing.

"If you'd like a few moments of privacy to open it, I can wait for you down the hall."

Kate nodded wordlessly, grateful for the man's thoughtfulness. When the door closed behind him, she unclenched her fingers from around the edges and drew in a shaky breath.

"You don't have to open it now if you don't want to." Riley's voice was gentle and she loved that he cared.

"No, I want to do it now. It's the final chapter. I want to have it over with. Besides, there may be things in here we can use as evidence against Darryl."

Riley didn't reply, but watched in silence as she tore open the envelope with unsteady fingers and pulled out a single sheet of notepaper. It was a letter in her mother's handwriting. At the very bottom was a small, silver key taped to the paper.

Taking courage from Riley's presence, she began to read.

My dearest Kate,

If you are reading this, then I am dead. Although I mourn the loss of my life, it is not entirely unexpected. I wouldn't have made these preparations if I was certain my life wasn't endangered...now that I know.

My plan is to get far enough away from him that I feel safe and then I'm going to the police. It's what I would have done ten years ago, if I'd only known.

You can't imagine my horror and guilt that it was me who brought this monster into your life. I was your mother. It was my job to protect you and keep you safe from harm and I totally and utterly failed you. I'll never forgive myself. The agony of it is unbearable.

The only thing that gets me through it is knowing he no longer has the power to hurt you. My brave, beautiful daughter. You found the courage to escape his evilness and make a life on your own. Now knowing what I do, I am beyond comprehending how you suffered it for so long.

You can't begin to imagine how proud I am of you and the strong, successful, tenacious woman you have become. Whilst I've longed to see you in person, to touch you, to hold you, I understood and accepted it wasn't going to happen—even when I didn't know why. My only regret is that I didn't find out sooner. I grieve so deeply for the years we lost.

I love you with everything that I am. My heart is shredded with the pain I have caused you. I can't ask for your forgiveness and I won't, but it tears me up inside to think that you might spend the rest of your life hating me. Not that I deserve your compassion.

With this letter, I have enclosed a key to the safety deposit box I have rented at the bank on Main Street. In it, is another key and directions to a secure storage facility where you will find all the evidence you need to ensure the monster who wronged you will be locked up for as long as possible. A lifetime, I hope, but I fear the law won't support me in this.

No one knows about the storage facility. I have left it to you to decide what to do...whatever you find easiest. No one need ever know. It is your decision.

Well, my dearest daughter, time is running out. I still have preparations to make if I'm going to get away from here alive. I long to see your dear, dear face again and tell you how sorry I am that I didn't see what was before my very eyes, but I'm dreadfully afraid the chance will be snatched away from me and I will take my guilt to the grave.

I only have one final wish, my beautiful daughter. I would hope you might find time to locate my dear friend, Daisy Bloomfield. You'll find her details in my address book in the top drawer of my desk.

Daisy brought light and laughter into my life at a time when I was in desperate need of it. She made it possible for me to keep going. She also made it possible for me to escape. We had a grand plan, a plan which should have worked. Alas, if you're reading this, it saddens me to realize it didn't.

I'd like you to pass on my love and eternal gratitude to Daisy. If our plan failed, it was only on me. Please reassure her it had nothing to do with her and that I will forever cherish our wonderful friendship.

After a brief farewell salutation, the letter ended with her mother's usual flamboyant signature. Kate fingered the key. She thought of the storage facility and her heart thudded. It had to be the videos, or something equally incriminating.

Riley reached out and touched her hand. "Are you okay?"

She looked up and met his concerned gaze, her heart tripping over at the worry on his face.

"I'm fine. She—she confirmed what we'd already guessed. Somehow, she found out about what Darryl did. She was making plans to leave." Her voice faded. Emotion tightened her throat and burned behind her eyes.

Riley's arms came around her, dragging her against him. Burying her face in his shirt, she cried big quiet tears.

"I-I thought I'd cried myself out, but look at me, sobbing all over you again."

His arm tightened around her. "You can cry on my shirt any day. Or night," he added.

A tiny smile tugged at her lips. She was grateful for his attempt at levity. The contents of her mother's letter clarified what they already knew, but to see it written in plain black and white made it somehow more real and more final.

She could only imagine what her mother had gone through after making the horrendous discovery. The shock, the anger, the pain, the self-reproach.

Kate didn't blame her in the slightest for what had happened. Her mother had lived downstairs. She'd never been off the ground floor the entire time she'd lived there. She couldn't possibly have known what had gone on above her head under the cover of darkness.

Kate shuddered. Riley bent his head and kissed her hair and she breathed a sigh of gratitude. She'd left that dark place behind her over a decade ago and would never let it define her again. With Riley by her side, she would continue to keep the blackness at bay.

Lifting her head, she offered him a shaky smile and swiped at the tears that lingered in her eyes. He pulled out a clean handkerchief and offered it to her.

"Thank you." She dabbed at her eyes and swiped at her nose. "I'm all right."

"I know you are. I've told you this before and I'll tell you whenever I think you've stopped believing it. You're the bravest, strongest woman I know. You've walked away from the hell you were dealt and turned your life into something anyone would be proud of." He stared into her eyes, his gaze bright with emotion. "*I'm* proud of you and you should be, too."

She tilted her head and waited with anticipation for his mouth to descend upon hers.

EPILOGUE

Six weeks later

Kate spied her husband across the other side of her crowded art gallery and her heart leaped with joy. Looking deliciously gorgeous in his black-on-black Armani suit, he moved with confidence and ease among the rich and famous clients who had come to pay homage to her exhibition. She'd delayed the opening by nearly two months, but the wait seemed to have only whetted the appetite of her buyers. Even the English weather had favored her.

She'd sold all but one piece—an exquisite sculpture in bronze and alloy. The figure of a woman cradling a baby in her arms. The curve of her body was both strong and feminine as she protected the child from the world. Kate had fallen in love with it the moment she'd seen it.

Making her way through the throng of people, she smiled when Riley looked up and saw her coming toward him. Out of the corner of her eye, she saw Mary glide over to the sculpture. Her assistant placed a "sold" sticker on its base. A pang of regret went through her and she brushed it away. She was an art dealer—she bought art and sold it. It was as simple as that.

She reached Riley and threaded her arm through his,

her heart taking flight at the look of love and devotion that glistened in his eyes.

"Have I told you how beautiful you look tonight?" he murmured, his lips close to her ear.

She shivered from the contact and laid her hand on his chest. She stroked the fabric of his expensive shirt, basking in the warmth and strength of him.

"I'm sure you have, but I never get tired of hearing it," she smiled.

He bent his head and kissed her. It was soft and lingering and sent fire through her veins.

"How long before we can get out of here?" he murmured against her lips.

"Um...I've finished with all the formalities and I think we just sold the last piece, so...anytime you like. The show's over."

His eyes flared with emotion. His arm drew her close. His erection pressed through the thin silk of her evening gown, hard and insistent, fueling the heat inside her. Desire surged low in her belly and centered in her core.

She gently disentangled herself and clapped her hands to draw the crowd's attention.

"Ladies and gentlemen, I'd like to thank you all for coming and supporting this event. I am truly grateful. The bad news is this is the last gallery show; I'm relocating with my husband back to Australia."

A murmur of disappointment went around the room. Kate smiled. "The good news is, I'll be leaving the gallery in the very capable hands of my senior assistant, Mary Costas and within the next few months, I hope to have opened a sister gallery in Australia."

A polite applause followed her announcement. "Before you get too carried away," she continued, "I have another announcement: Thanks to all of you, we've sold every last item on exhibition this evening. I'm delighted to say we've raised over one million dollars for Rosemary's Foundation for Women and Children."

The crowd erupted into loud, spontaneous applause.

Riley grinned and kissed her again.

"Congratulations, sweetheart. That's truly wonderful."

"Thank you. I couldn't have done it without your support and encouragement." Her voice hitched. "I-I hope Mom's proud."

"She's as proud as I am. I know she is."

Relief and happiness and overwhelming love surged through her. Mindless of the people around them, Kate threw her arms around him and kissed him thoroughly. They were both short of breath when she finally pulled away.

"Let's get out of here," Riley muttered, his voice husky with need.

"*Mm*... You read my mind."

Less than an hour later, with the clock just shy of midnight, Kate kicked off her four-inch heels in the bedroom of her tenth-floor apartment and sighed. Riley came up behind her and massaged the tired muscles in her shoulders.

"You worked hard tonight. And to think you raised a million dollars? You're amazing."

He bent his head and nuzzled her neck. She groaned and tilted her head to the side, to give him better access.

"*Mm*, that feels so good," she murmured. "It's been a hectic couple of weeks. I'm so grateful for Mary and Genevieve," she added, referring to her assistants. "They were the ones who were amazing. What with Mom and everything else that happened in Australia, I'd have never have managed to pull something like this together without their help."

Riley nibbled at the soft skin behind her ear. "You're right," he said. "Mary especially deserves the healthy pay packet you offered her."

Kate frowned a little, wondering why he'd singled the girl out. Mary was a godsend, but Genevieve had worked equally hard to make the night happen.

Without a word, he set Kate away from him and strode to his side of her super king bed. Bending low, he collected a package off the floor. "I had Mary wrap a little gift for you and arranged to have it delivered."

Kate stared curiously at the parcel in Riley's hands. The embossed forest-green and gold paper carried the logo of her gallery. He closed the distance between them and offered it to her.

"For you," he said simply. "With all my love."

Kate's heart thumped. Her fingers were less than steady when she untied the green ribbon that secured the wrapping paper. Smoothing it back, she revealed the bronze and alloy statue she'd admired earlier.

She gasped in surprise. Her gaze flew to his. "Oh, Riley, it's—it's beautiful. I-I don't know what to say." She swallowed the lump in her throat.

Riley smiled softly, his eyes full of love. "You've already said everything I need to hear. I love you, Mrs Munro, with all that I am."

Kate carefully set the package aside and threw her arms around him. With renewed hunger, she pressed her lips to his. Riley kissed her back, cradling her head and angling his lips to consume her with a passion that matched hers. His shirt and pants and Kate's Valentino dress were discarded in quick succession. Their underwear quickly followed.

Riley bent and picked her up and deposited her gently on the bed. Moments later, he joined her and Kate relished the feel of his hard, muscular body sliding against hers.

She threaded her arms around his neck and opened her mouth under his. His tongue glided across her lips, tasting, probing and finally thrusting inside. She groaned and moved against him, desire burning low in her belly.

He broke away and kissed his way down her neck, teasing the sensitive flesh beneath her ear until she shivered from the contact. He continued lower, his lips moving over the soft peaks of her breasts. She gasped when his mouth closed over her nipple, his tongue sweeping over the little nub until it stood hard.

Just when she thought she couldn't stand that another minute, he turned his attention to her other breast and she suffered the beautiful torment all over again.

Wanting to give as much pleasure as she was receiving, Kate slid out from underneath him and pushed him back against the mattress. Surprise and delight glittered in his eyes and a slow, sexy smile tugged at the corner of his mouth.

She sat back on her haunches and looked at him. *Really* looked at him. His skin was golden, smooth and exotic. She ran her fingers lightly over the strong planes of his chest, loving the feel of him.

She moved her hand lower and his stomach muscles contracted under her touch. She smiled, once again luxuriating in her power over him. His erection lay thick and hard against the cushion of his groin, beckoning her.

Giving into the temptation, she fitted her hand around his cock and stroked him. He groaned and the sound only fueled the flames of her desire.

"What you're doing..." he rasped. "It feels so good. Please, don't stop."

She flushed from pleasure, still getting used to the idea of being able to please him. With her hand around his shaft, she bent low and opened her mouth. He groaned again, his eyes closed, his head thrown back against the pillows. She used her tongue to lick the side of his shaft and swipe at the moisture beading the tip, all the while stroking him with her hand.

"You're driving me crazy," he muttered, clenching his hands at his side.

"I'm glad," she murmured, knowing it was true. She wanted to drive him crazy, to have him forget every woman he'd ever been with, to want no one but her. She sucked him into her mouth, harder and faster, in time with the rhythm of her hand.

"Christ, if you don't stop now, I'm going to come."

Satisfaction surged through her and she smiled. "Come, then."

"No." The word was wrenched from him on another

groan. Before she realized what was happening, he sat up and reached for her, flipping her over onto her back in one smooth movement.

"Riley!" she gasped as his lips found hers again.

"We're coming together."

Working his mouth over her nipples, he raised them once again into tight, little nubs. Satisfied, he moved lower, kissing his way down her stomach until his face was buried between her legs. Breathing in deeply, he flicked his tongue over her throbbing clit. When she gasped and grabbed for his hair he made a wholly masculine sound of satisfaction.

"Two can play at this game," he murmured, lifting his head to offer her a smile full of wickedness.

Not giving her time to respond, he licked his way into the core of her, moistening the way with his tongue. Heat burned between her legs and she gasped again when he slid a finger inside her. Moving it in and out in perfect imitation of her earlier rhythm, she clung to the bedclothes and prayed she could withstand the sensual onslaught.

He rose above her and pressed his cock against her. She welcomed the feel of it in silent relief. Lifting her hips, she met his thrust and groaned as he entered her, filling her, stretching her, fanning the flames of her need to a fever pitch.

"Christ, you feel so good." He moved inside her, his face taut with desire.

She matched his rhythm, her legs wrapped around his hips, urging him closer. Her climax was building, increasing with every urgent thrust of his hips. She clung to him, making mindless murmurs of need as she reached the pinnacle and toppled over the other side.

"*Ohhh!*" she gasped, her muscles clenching around him. At the same time, Riley's body tensed and he spent himself inside her. With a groan, he collapsed on top of her.

Long moments later, he propped himself up on his elbows and looked down at her. "I love you."

Her heart swelled. "I love you, too."

Their lips met in a kiss that was both sweet and

poignant and tender and offered a lifetime of promise.

Kate clung to the feeling and swallowed the lump that had lodged itself in her throat. Reaching up, she pulled his head down to hers and kissed him again. Digging deep for her courage, she asked him the question she'd been dreading.

"Does it matter? What Darryl did to me?" She held her breath, waiting for his answer.

"Of course it matters."

Her stomach dropped and she tried to pull out of his arms. He refused to let her go.

"But not in the way you think." His eyes burned into hers, dark and somber. "I don't think I'll ever get over the sheer anger that consumes me every time I think about what he did to you, but then I look at you and it doesn't matter, because you've won. You didn't let what he did defeat you. With your help, the police laid enough charges on him and Hannaford to keep them battling the court system for years to come. If they're found guilty, and with the evidence we have against them, there's no reason they won't, both of them will be spending many years at Her Majesty's pleasure."

His eyes filled with emotion and his voice cracked as he added, "I love you so much."

Tears pricked her eyes. Riley took her chin in his fingers and tilted her head upwards. "Don't cry, sweetheart. Please, don't cry. Just tell me you love me, too."

She hiccupped somewhere between a sob and a laugh and threw her arms around his neck. "Yes, oh, yes. I love you, too. I'll never get tired of saying it."

A grin turned up the corner of his lips. "Does that mean you're adjusting to the idea of leaving London and starting our life together as the wife of Watervale's newest Local Area Commander?"

Her eyes opened wide in surprise. "Y-you mean you got it? You got the job?"

Riley's grin widened. He nodded. "Yep, someone off the interview panel called this afternoon."

"Why didn't you tell me?" she exclaimed, joy and happiness spreading through her that her husband, the love her life, had found recognition at last.

"Tonight was all about you and your mom, sweetheart. I didn't want to spoil it."

His lips found hers, warm, loving, insistent. She opened her mouth to him, reveling in the sensations he stirred up deep inside her. There was no longer fear or disgust or panic or pain. There was no Darryl, no Hannaford, no past.

There was only Riley.

And their future.

Note to Readers

I do hope you have enjoyed reading Riley and Kate's story. The issue of racial prejudice affects all of us and I loved how Riley dealt with it, I also loved how Riley's mixed heritage didn't matter to Kate—that she loved him for who he was. It would be nice to think we could all embrace her attitude and make the world a nicer place to live.

In Book Three of the Munro Family Series, you will meet another Munro brother. **The Predator** is Brandon Munro's story and yes, he's every bit as gorgeous as his brothers. Here's a sneak peek:

Everything comes at a price…

*When Australian Federal Agent **Brandon Munro** walked out on his wife without a word of explanation, he had no idea the price would be so high.*

***Alex Cavanaugh's** world fell apart the night Brandon told her their marriage was over. Devastated over his refusal to tell her why and unwilling to keep him by her side out of a sense of duty, she conceals from him her pregnancy.*

Four years later, Alex has rebuilt her life and has found success as an Australian Federal Agent working in a High Tech Operations team hunting online predators. In conjunction with INTERPOL and the FBI, her team is in pursuit of a pedophile ring that has its origins in Belgium.

When Brandon transfers to her Unit, Alex's life is thrown into turmoil once again. Pitted together in a race to uncover a global ring of online pedophiles, Alex and Brandon are forced to confront each other…and their past.

As the pressure mounts, Brandon struggles to deal with his guilt and reconnect with the woman he still loves. Alex lives on tenterhooks that Brandon may discover he has a son. Despite her sound reasons for keeping the child a secret, she fears he will never forgive her once he discovers the extent of her treachery.

While both struggle with guilt and forgiveness and the resurgence of love, they are unaware of the predator who stalks close to home…

The Predator will be available in April, 2014. If you would like to subscribe to my newsletter to receive news on upcoming Munro Family stories, release dates, book launches and other snippets, please go to my website at www.christaylorauthor.com.au and follow the link. I love to hear from my readers. Please feel free to contact me at christaylor@antmail.com.au Let me know who your favorite Munro family member is.

The Munro Family Series

THE PROFILER
(Book One—Clayton and Ellie)

THE INVESTIGATOR
(Book Two—Riley and Kate)

THE PREDATOR
(Book Three—Brandon and Alex)

THE BETRAYAL
(Book Four—Declan and Chloe)

THE DECEPTION
(Book Five—Will and Savannah)

THE NEGOTIATOR
(Book Six—Andy and Cally)

THE RANSOM
(Book Seven—Lane and Zara)

THE DEFENDANT
(Book Eight—Chase and Josie)

THE SHOOTING
(Book Nine—Tom and Lily)

THE SCANDAL
(Book Ten—Bryce and Chanel

ABOUT THE AUTHOR

Chris Taylor grew up on a farm in north-west New South Wales, Australia. She always had a thirst for stories and recalls writing her first book at the ripe old age of eight. Always a lover of romance and happily-ever-afters, a career in criminal law sparked her interest in intrigue and suspense. For Chris to be able to combine romance with suspense in her books is a dream come true.

Chris is married to Linden and is the mother of five children. If not behind her computer, you can find her doing the school run, taxiing children to swimming lessons, football, ballet and cricket. In her spare time, Chris loves to read her favorite authors who include Richard North Patterson, Sandra Brown, Kathleen E Woodiwiss and Jude Devereaux.

Printed in Great Britain
by Amazon